BOOKS BY GEORGE GARRETT

FICTION

King of the Mountain
The Finished Man
In the Briar Patch
Which Ones Are the Enemy?
Cold Ground Was My Bed Last Night
Do, Lord, Remember Me
A Wreath for Garibaldi
Death of the Fox
The Magic Striptease
The Succession
An Evening Performance
Poison Pen
Entered from the Sun

POETRY

The Reverend Ghost
The Sleeping Gypsy
Abraham's Knife
For a Bitter Season
Welcome to the Medicine Show
Luck's Shining Child
The Collected Poems of George Garrett

PLAYS

Sir Slob and the Princess
Enchanted Ground

BIOGRAPHY

James Jones

CRITICAL

Understanding Mary Lee Settle

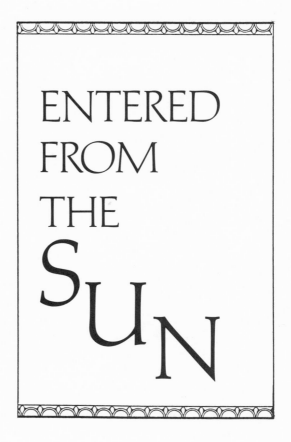

ENTERED
FROM
THE
SUN

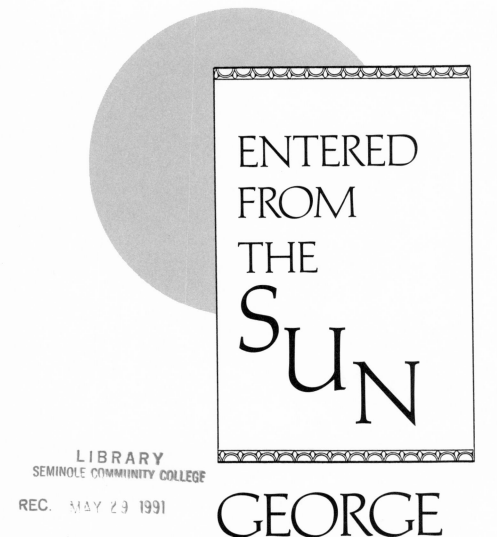

ENTERED
FROM
THE
SUN

GEORGE

GARRETT

DOUBLEDAY   NEW YORK · LONDON · TORONTO · SYDNEY · AUCKLAND

PUBLISHED BY DOUBLEDAY
a division of Bantam Doubleday Dell Publishing Group, Inc.
666 Fifth Avenue, New York, New York 10103

DOUBLEDAY and the portrayal of an anchor
with a dolphin are trademarks of Doubleday,
a division of Bantam Doubleday Dell
Publishing Group, Inc.

Library of Congress Cataloging-in-Publication Data

Garrett, George P., 1929–
    Entered from the sun / by George Garrett. — 1st ed.
        p.   cm.
    I. Title.
PS3557.A72E5   1990
813'.54—dc20   89-23473
                                                      CIP

ISBN 0-385-19095-6

FIRST EDITION IN THE UNITED STATES OF AMERICA
RRC

For Susan

With love and gratitude and admiration. Always.

Likewise with thanksgiving for the support of many, early and late, kinfolk and friends (living and dead) without whom nothing would have come to pass.

Doom is the House without the Door—
'Tis entered from the sun,
And then the ladder's thrown away
Because escape is done.

—Emily Dickinson

Our pleasance heir is all vane glory,
This fals world is but transitory.
The flesche is bruckle, the Fend is sle;
Timor mortis conturbat me.

—William Dunbar, "Lament for the Makaris"

Certainly there is no other account to be made of this
ridiculous world than to resolve that the change of fortune on
the great theatre is but as the change of garments on the
less. For when on the one and the other every man wears but
his own skin, the players are all alike.

—Sir Walter Ralegh, *History of the World*

AUTHOR'S GREETING

A few words of my own before I leave you in the hands of others. A few words, perhaps to reassure you or myself, before I step aside, step back to listen, as you do, to the voices of others, the noise of strangers.

A dark story we are sharing here. No doubt about it.

Into the hands of others.

Do not think of small hands, soft hands, jeweled fingers. Think, first of all, of fists. Clenched and hard-knuckled. Strong hands for gripping and clutching. For holding and hauling and hanging on for dear life. Crude and clever hands, bony or meaty.

Let them have life again. Look at your own hands and flex your fingers. Clench your fist and open your palm. Simple gestures. Immemorial signs for logic and eloquence.

In the books of rhetoric published in those days they printed, side by side, the symbols of the art—an open palm for eloquence and a clenched fist for grammar and logic.

Think of this as a story of clenched fists.

Here we meet with malcontents, with the disenchanted and disillusioned. Here are murderers and secret agents. Here are bitterly ambitious and lost souls.

So be it.

Not to forget, now or ever, the long-lost brightness and shine, the hope and glory of those times. But likewise to remember, keeping in mind, the other side of it. Stony discontent, cold despair, end-of-the-world indifference.

Bear with me, ghosts.

And bless us, one and all, your newfound, long-lost friends.

Speak to me.

Speak through me.

Speak to us.

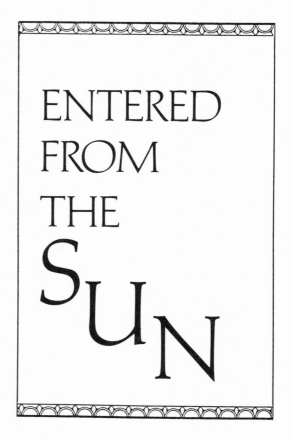

ENTERED FROM THE SUN

HOW IT BEGINS FOR JOSEPH HUNNYMAN

Laughing out loud, he turned away from laughing faces and the noise of voices, all of them talking again all at once, with one or two over in the chimney corner trying to join together to sing out the familiar melody of some old round or common country song, but from the first note so out of tune as to be beyond recognition and repair; in a few quick strides left behind him, as if tossed over his shoulder, the sweet and heavy, yeasty odors of beer and ale, these good things commingled with the undeniable and inimitable stink of a close crowd of freely sweating men and, too, the small white pungent clouds made by the smokers of pipes and the acrid grease-laden scents of the rushlights and the cheap tallow candles offering as much smoke as light; left behind, then, above all, the light and shadow, sway and dance of it, of the well-stacked, high-blazing fireplace.

Still smiling at the wit of his own jest and still relishing the loud response it instantly evoked, he opened the door and stepped out onto the carpet of light cast from behind him. And then in the next blinking of time the heavy door and the brightness it defended slammed to and shut. Leaving him alone in the chill and dark of the footpath. A shiver at the sudden splash of wet coldness and a very slight staggering (he had, after all, been drinking for some hours in the tavern, had consumed enough to put a lesser, weaker man down on all fours like a dog) and then, for a moment, the silence swallowed up everything except for a reassuring, clinking kind of music, a little consort of coins in his purse.

He called out loud and clear, "Links! Links!" Shouting for a boy with a torch to come now and walk him on his way. But there seemed to be none nearby to hear him. Strange . . . Perhaps the night had turned too damp and cold for lazy lads.

Next, then, as he would recall and reconstitute it later, came a shuffle or scuffle, a kind of whispering not of breath and words, more likely of soft shoes or of clothing, close by him from both sides. And he groped across his body, snatching to the left with his right hand, clutching for the hilt of his sword. Only to find there, with a flashing of pure cold and splashed across his whole body at one and the same instant, like the chills that dance hand in hand with fevers, another hand . . . Another hand, gloved but hard as horn and huge. Covering over and squeezing his own helpless hand, painfully clamped now and immobile on the hilt of his weapon. Another hand, fiercely strong and hurtful fingers, was gripping his arm. And before he could shout or speak out, truly before he could so much as draw and spend a breath, there came a point of steel beneath his chin, touching the softest part of his neck, with just enough force behind the thrust of it to break the skin; and he could feel a slight trickle of blood there. Could believe the very next moment could well be his last one, here and now or whenever that unseen hand aiming the short sharp point wished it to be so. Could not yet see anything, nor now hear, though he could surely smell a strong barny odor of beasts. As if whoever it might be (must be at least two of them, maybe more) shared a living and sleeping space with horses and dogs. Sheep perhaps. Pigs maybe . . .

Would have cried out and begged for life. Take my purse and jewels, he would have told them, all of it and anything else that may strike your fancy. But leave me, please! my worthless life!

Yet even as the shape of these words (and many others like a startled flight of whistling blackbirds) soared and fanned in his mind, he was discouraged by a soft voice, a voice softly whispering and as rough as the stiff brushy fur of a bear.

"First word you speak, I cut out your tongue."

He embraced complete silence as if that condition were a young virgin eager for his embracing. Very image of that, for one foolish and fanciful moment, sustained him. Aroused in him a sober wakefulness. As if, not weary and half-drunk and terrified, he, too, were young and tender and hopeful again. As if he had just now split himself into two beings, one of which (the soul?) being or becoming a young girl whose essential sweetness, whose cordial of sweet juices, seemed without question, then and there and forever after, more precious than all the substance of life in his flesh and bones.

Meantime, in simpler truth, his body, held tightly, was being half carried, half driven in a rush of walking which was like swimming and thrashing in rough water. Moving, quick and clumsy, with no more instruction where to go than some grunts and heavy breathing in reply to his own stifled, inadvertent groans. Stumbling and staggering through darkness, foot-dragging in mud, in a web of lanes and byways already lost beyond all possibility of finding where he might be or ever again remembering how he might have managed to come this way. And with no clear notion where it was that he and they, locked together like one single strange creature, a many-legged spiderlike insect, might be going.

Until of a sudden they stopped moving. He was still held as tight as if in knotted ropes. Sound of a heavy door being knocked upon. Pounding repeated. Then door swung open and he felt himself, still in the surprising dark, being swept forward, then plunged down, down a steep stairway, toward what would be a cellar chamber. Proved to be so, too, when yet another heavy door was knocked on and opened. Into a sudden extravagance of light. Blinding. Himself pushed forward and set free, blinking in the light of many candles, standing alone at last, sweat-drenched, heaving with deep breathing, seeing barrels and boxes, some large chests, piles of rushes and stacks of firewood. And seeing there, sitting on a three-legged stool, a handsome, smiling young man, splendidly and recently barbered and well dressed, spinning an elegant brimmed, high-crowned hat in his hands. Though his mouth maintained an easy smile and revealed his enviably excellent teeth, his eyes were as hard and unrevealing as a pair of dark, polished stones.

"Well now," he said, rising to stand tall, putting on his hat. "Will you drink some wine with me?"

Hunnyman, vain even in dire peril, is pleased to note that he, himself, looks as young, or younger, and just as handsome as this fellow.

"May I speak?" Hunnyman said. "Or is my tongue still at hazard?"

"Life perhaps, but your tongue is all your own for at least as long as you live."

"Why then, sir, I thank you most kindly." He was speaking slowly, carefully, without a trace of any feeling, lest his tone might somehow be construed as fear or arrogance or even, God save us, irony. Kept his eyes fixed on the fine-featured, cruel, smiling face of the young gentleman. "And, yes, I shall gladly accept your offer of a cup of wine."

Young man nodded and someone behind grunted in beast language. And there they stood, eye to eye, grinning like a pair of skulls freshly lifted out of the same grave, until the huge man appeared between them, a man who did, indeed, look to be as large and hairy as a Bankside bear and who truly and fully stunk of barnyard and doghouse. Fearsome fellow he was and all the more so in this bright light.

"Be thankful," the young man told him, "that I did not send these two, my fellows, out to find you in broad daylight."

To which he answered, more out of bad habit than good sense, "Ah, are they allowed to wander loose in the daytime?"

This bear gave each of them a full pewter cup and then vanished again, thanks be, out of view and beyond smelling distance.

It was dark, full-bodied sack, strong, toasted, and so sweetened that it set his teeth on edge. Nevertheless he swished it in his mouth, then drank it down, noting that the young man had no more than sipped at his. Cup empty, he began, in spite of best intentions and the common course of prudence, to speak. Knowing he should not do so. Knowing, with that part of his brain not already clouded over with fumes of this sweet and fiery sack, that it might truly cost him the price of his life here and now. But knowing, too, in his heart, which having fisted, clenching and unclenching, in a frenzy only scant moments earlier in the terrifying dark and now was being warmed back to life by wine and taking its pulse from the easy sway of candle flames and shadows, believing, then, for this once at least, that his life was not more precious to him than it could be to these his unknown enemies, a life not worth living, not worth a dog's turd if he did not now say whatever it pleased him to and in whatever insolent manner it pleased him to do so. Truth of it, what he was saying, was of no importance. Truth was not to be found in what he was saying but in what he was feeling. It was an inward and spiritual truth. And he felt it deeply and firmly and chose to honor it fully even if that choice, that arrogant gesture, should prove to be his last free act in this all-hating world.

How only a little while ago he, innocently about his business and pleasure, had been seized in the darkness and yanked and dragged away by these here two stinking, flea-bitten, lice-crawling, pox-ridden, mangy, and unworthy bears, disguised, and very poorly so in his opinion, as men, pretending to be creatures formed and made from the intercourses, lawful or unlawful, though most likely the latter, of man and woman, human beings, albeit clearly the poorest bad examples of their kind that could be found anywhere upon this island, instead of admitting themselves to be what they truly, indubitably are, namely and to wit, two scabby, crud-caked creatures vaguely in man shape, somewhat like scarecrows, taken up and assembled from the scum to be found at the bottom of a public privy by a diligent jakesman. And, oh, how fortunate these two cousins, close kinsmen to half of the slime-sucking toads of England, are that he had been unable to reach and draw his sword and to run the point of it through their worm-tormented bowels and to test thereby the proposition that neither of them possessed anything even faintly resembling an immortal soul to lose with his life and life's blood.

How, speaking as one gentleman to another, was altogether astounded that anyone of good birth and decent manners and any kind of learning at all—and never mind such virtues as courage or prudence or simple honor—could, by any means, conceivably employ such a disgusting pair of nightwalking rats, offspring of innumerable generations of whores and whoremongers, unless they should have happened to be, in sad and bitter truth, his very own kith and kin, unless he, too, were somehow or other the direct and lineal descendant of the same befouled bloodline, his ancestry going proudly backwards through time and history as far as some especial few among the most degenerate and unrepentant inhabitants of Sodom and Gomorrah!

And how . . .

Here lightly touching the hilt of his sword, come what may from the beasts behind him, and not taking his eyes, his unblinking gaze, off the widening eyes of the man standing in front of him; eyes locked in fury, as he took one, two, three small child's steps, slowly, toward the young man even as he was speaking.

How, sir, if you will now be so kind as to draw your own blade from the safety of its scabbard, I shall be pleased to teach you, without any charge, a lesson in the art and best use of the rapier in single combat, after which brief lesson I will proceed to spit you like a bird for roasting and shortly thereafter send off your foolish and careless soul to meet your Maker. Who is free to save you but almost certain, in my view, to assign you to the everlasting fires of hell!

Whereupon the young man drops his hat as if it were a hot plate, as if to free his right hand to reach for his sword and to protect himself. But instead, and instead of even so much as motioning for his hirsute minions to come forward and save his skin, he bends sharply at the waist as if he were bowing and fills this vaulted basement chamber with a huge whinny of irrepressible laughter.

In the face of which and in response to which poor Joseph Hunnyman feels his drawn shiny blade drooping. It might well be wilting. Melting away.

"I pray your pardon," the young fellow said when the last grasp of his laughter had dwindled away, spent itself in a little fit of coughing. "Pardon me for laughing in your face. I would most gladly accept your challenge. And then we could determine which of us is, in truth, the better swordsman. Though I must tell you, sir, that if by some ill chance you should prove to be half the fencing master you imagine yourself to be, if, by chance or mischance, you should happen to wound me or kill me dead, your troubles would be only beginning. For next thing you would have to kill my two bears who are still standing behind you. My poor, faithful bears, who, though their schooling was all too brief and, in any case, wholly inadequate, can nevertheless at least understand the gist of their own native tongue, the spoken English language, and are, sir, I would venture, already incensed at the many rude things you have said about them. And are eager to return the favor with payment in kind, with fists if not words. And would have done so, too, if I had not expressly forbidden it. They know next to nothing of the art and craft, the rules of fencing. But, count on it, they are not much intimidated by cold steel. And each of them is at least as skilled as any village butcher at the swift and expeditious separation of meat from bone.

"So put up your sword and let us get to the business at hand; though first I must tell you I am happy that my man did not cut out your tongue as he threatened to—and would have, too, if you had elected to test his resolve; for if he had done so, then I should have missed your extraordinary speech, the wild bravado of it, likes of which I cannot say I have heard in my lifetime. Except, perhaps, from some ranting player in an inn yard or at some village fair."

Joseph Hunnyman, who is a player himself, after all, though here disguised and playing a part as a country gentleman, winces and prays (in vain as it happens) that his face betrays nothing.

"Come now," the young man tells him, "let us not waste precious time on deceit or deception. You may have as many tricks as a lawyer or a dancing dog. I'll grant you that. But I know who you are. I know your name and condition and no doubt about it. And I do not for a moment mean any such person as this imaginary so-called William Ashborne come to the City from Wiltshire and, if report be true, a man with astonishing good luck when casting a pair of dice. No, sir! I know that you are not he or anybody else except a common player without present employment or any good prospects, one whose real name is Joseph Hunnyman and whose dice are as false as they are square."

"I believe you are seriously mistaken," Hunnyman says as firmly as possible, a picture of sincere puzzlement, though realizing, even so and even as he speaks, that he is speaking more out of form and good manners than any kind of hope or conviction, as he returns his sword, quietly, to its scabbard.

"Listen," the young man tells him. "I, myself, have seen you playing your part, and more than once, at the old Boar's Head in Whitechapel and at the Cross Keys in Gracious Street and at least once strutting the stage in some wholly unmemorable old play at that theater they call Newington Butts. And now that you are here and I can see you close up and by candlelight, I do believe that I must also have witnessed you, once upon a time and somewhat altered by costume and disguise to be sure, altered for the better if truth may be said, performing in public as an Italian fencing master newly arrived from Padua and going under the name of Guido Bassanio."

"That was at the playhouse called the Curtain," you say.

Pride now takes possession of you and takes precedence over good sense. Well, why not? This fortunate, spoiled young fellow knows you well enough. Too well. If it must be truth, well then, why not the whole truth?

"Why, sir, you could also have seen me rope-dancing as if I were a trueborn Dutchman when my sad fortunes reached their lowest ebb. I have some skills at these crude entertainments which have stood me in good stead from time to time. But in my time, also, I have likewise been on the boards and have earned my share of applause. At the Theatre. Often at the Inns of Court. And I will have you know, sir, that only this past Innocents Day I played a part, though it was but a brief, a modest role, before the Queen and her Court."

"I do not doubt it if you say so," the young man said, briskly motioning.

And here came one of the bear-men stinking forward with yet another full cup of sack to replace the empty one. In the absence of fireplace or stoves in this cellar, Hunnyman found it pleasantly warming.

Should you, therefore, be grateful for his kindly, good-mannered, arrogant indifference? How much you would enjoy to tell him your chronicle, your whole history of ill fortune and good fortune, an odd mixture (like sugar and sack, just so, bitter and sweet precisely) of both, from earliest childhood pains and memories up until this baffling and frightening scene in someone's cellar, with something or other, most likely, as the man has already allowed, my life, if not my tongue or nose and ears, at stake, myself in the hands of and at the mercy of strangers! And these strangers seeming to be, whatever else, completely merciless. Blessed be the merciless, for they shall see God's enormous shrug. But even worse to bear than that shrug, proclaiming an infinite and eternal indifference, would be the huge, lazy yawn that your life story, from beginning until now, would draw forth from this handsome and lucky fellow. Who, young as he is, would still take it for an old story. Nothing good or evil has happened to you, not yet and not likely to, to raise up one of the plucked and supercilious eyebrows on this man's face. It is one thing, perhaps the wisest, to learn to live with the tight fit and fashion of humility by birth and by station, to accept, with all possible cheerfulness, those things which are not so much earned as given, because with the gift of them no choice is also given to do anything else but, perhaps, to elect to deceive yourself by the folly of denial. Acceptance (*thy will be done*), then, of what you have been given, both the blessings and curses, being, you like to think, the source of the strength and wisdom of humility. But what if? What if your best strength and wisdom are in the eyes of others, in the view of this other, this trueborn gentleman who is not a player in a costume pretending, what if, as you sense it, you and your whole life, at best and worst, are equally contemptible?

"You have every right and reason to be perplexed, even enraged," the young man is telling you as if he could read your mind like a pamphlet. "And I would be doubtful and suspicious if you were not. I would have to conclude that you lack half wit."

"And what do you conclude?"

He allows himself a slight smile and even the dark eyes this time share some of the brightness of it.

"I conceive that you can be foolish, by habit more than purpose, and even to your own acute disadvantage. Yet I am inclined to take you for a man of adequate wit and of a certain kind of hard-earned wisdom.

"Listen to me," he continues, resorting now to proverb for emphasis. "I know your thoughts as well as if I were in your belly. And I do not, cannot, blame you for them. If there are many things about you that I am ignorant of, nevertheless I—and the persons I serve and speak for; let me say 'we'—we know much more about you than you might believe."

Next he is telling you your dead father's and your old mother's names. Tells the name, too, of the very Wiltshire village you were born in and from which you like to imagine and even now remember that you fled; though the truth, which you have managed to forget, but he has not, is that you were driven out and escaped the Law and a very different life.

"And your imaginary gent from that country, this Ashborne, whose name you are freely using now and have also done so, from time to time, on sundry occasions past, when it has pleased you to, may be no more than straw and air clad in some gentleman's pawned clothes, but you stand him upon the solid earth. For he shares your land and your memories. And a good thing too. For otherwise he would be too false to be believed and accepted by anyone, even yourself. And, ever and always the player, you have long since discovered that you must at least profess to yourself your belief in the truth of any role you take on in order that others may believe it. Is it not so?"

You can nod and you do so. What else?

Continues, then, without hesitation, to prove he is the master of the general outline of your life. Especially as it has been in these most recent years when, for one and another reason, your luck has run so thin and weak, your fortunes have so often been bleak. For instance, he knows how the company of players of which you were once a member, and as a full sharer and not a hired man, and whose prospects for good fortune looked bright enough only a few years ago, fell apart from rivalry and dissension first and then from disease. Sickness among the players. And sickness (including, the Lord save us all, the Plague again) in London and in the suburbs; troubles throughout the country and a very poor time for touring players. How in the end all of them, all those remaining, anyway, sharers and hired men and apprentices alike, fighting among themselves for what little money was left over. Like a wild pack of starving dogs snarling and fighting over a few poor bitter bones.

"And did you not, Joseph Hunnyman, in those days kill one of your fellow players with a sword . . . perhaps that selfsame sword you are now wearing?"

"It was my life or his, sir. A matter of self-defense. He attacked me—in the presence of many witnesses, mind you—with every intent to rob and to kill me."

"Which may be the truth. Who knows? For, as I take it, the

matter remains cloudy and unsettled because, somehow or other, it never went to the Law."

"No, sir, it did not, but I can explain."

"No doubt you could prove your case if it came to that. But it does not seem likely that you will have to, unless, of course, someone of a meddlesome nature and of a puritanical disposition, someone rigid of conscience and devoted to the strict letter of the Law, should reawaken the affair and call it to the attention of the courts. And, as you well know, having haunted the law courts at Westminster in all of their terms and sessions, as much as or more so than half the lawyers in England, as you well know, the discovery of murder has no limit in time and remains a heinous crime for as long as you live."

Not staying upon your assent or argument, but going on from there to some of your lesser crimes, committed in bad times. Such as, under one name and another, being a witness for a fee in more than one lawsuit. And, as if that were not enough to turn your hair white, this young man showed an even deeper knowledge of your debts and the kinds of felonies and other crimes you have been driven to.

"There is but one criminal practice, Hunnyman, which we have not yet found any evidence that you are guilty of. And that is the cutting and stealing of purses. You sure enough fill your own purse with the coins of others, taken by tricks and by a dozen and one clever and unlawful means. But we have not yet found anyone, friend or enemy, willing to swear under oath that you are a cutpurse. Still, by the same token, we have yet to find anyone who is willing to wager anything of value that you are not."

You can make no good case for yourself. Except to plead how many times Dame Fortune has turned her white ample backside in your direction and farted in your face like a trumpet.

He laughs at that and agrees that your luck has been shabby.

"Yet," says he, "a stranger, someone like myself, for example, might come to examine your life as if it were a piece of a play or some story from a book, and conclude that in one sense you can count yourself among the luckiest men alive."

"How can that be?"

Reminds you that you still have both of your ears and your forehead is unbranded. That your bare back does not bear scars of whipping. That even though you have slept in straw, the dirty straw of more than one prison, in your time, that time has never been long by any measure. Reminds you that you have not been required to spend even a modest portion of the time behind locks and heavy doors that you not only could have, but have fully deserved to.

"And yet none of this matters, Hunnyman, not a bit. Your great and amazing good fortune is that you have not yet been hanged. Surely in a better world, in a just world, you would have been hanged and forgotten long before now. You may, indeed you must, thank God, our heavenly Father, that the world in these its late days, perhaps its last days, is all in the hands of the Devil and all his servants. Otherwise you would have danced in thin air and bade us all farewell long ago. Left, perhaps for a better one and perhaps not."

From this which has left you grinning (like an ass chewing briers, what else?), if not openly laughing at yourself and your sad and foolish and hopeless, hopeful life as it has to be seen by others who can never know the whole truth of any of it without they went adancing for a while in your very own shoes, he next moves you, and in one instant, to the edge of tears. Which you must choke back and swallow to keep down.

For he then tells you of your worst wound. How in your best days when (briefly, briefly) this old world and your future in it looked as bright and strong as a full moon rising on a clear summer night, you found and took a good wife. How you loved and cherished this woman and by her had three children, two sons and a daughter, each and all as fat and strong and healthy as can be. Each and all becoming the very joy and meaning of your life. And then how, and not so long ago, in the first year of the return of the Plague, while you and your company were far away, out in the country performing your plays and interludes in guildhalls and great houses, at church ales and market fairs, the dread disease came and took off all of your family, wife and children together, in one great rush like a windy fire in a dry field. How you knew nothing of this until you returned. How you came back to the City to find your chambers empty of life. (And everything else of value, as well, had been stolen.) Your loved ones gone and even their bones and bodies lost forever in the heap of some common grave. And how then and there your life fell into ruin and soon went to rot. From which you have not yet fully recovered.

"And yet," he adds. "You have only lately, in this year, come to enjoy the company of the widow of a publisher and bookseller. She is a woman of good looks and good health and more than adequate means and has a place to sell her books and pamphlets and such in Paul's Churchyard."

How there does seem to be a kind of mutual affection there, tempered, but not lessened, by the practical awareness of the ways in which each of you may serve the ends and means of each other. This woman knows full well that you are and have been a common player by trade and does not find that makes you despicable. But Lord knows what she might think if she ever were to learn the full truth and story of you.

"Do I perceive a threat, sir? Or is that merely my oversensitive nature?"

"Take it as you will. More important to me, to us, is the answer to another question."

"And what would that be?"

And he, this handsome young gentleman, whom evidently Fortune has always favored and offered only her lips, her sweet breath, and her ample breasts, he possessing that one kind of happy innocence which is (as it seems to you) his only obvious weakness, heel of Achilles, resorted once more to the precedence of proverb:

"Hunnyman, if you will toil so hard for trash, what will you do for treasure?"

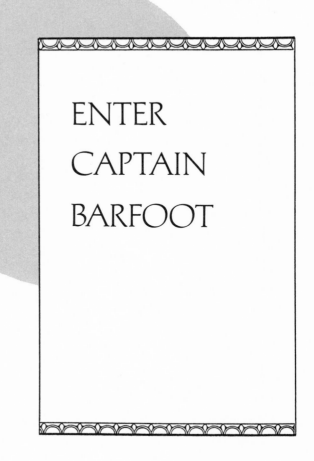

ENTER
CAPTAIN
BARFOOT

Seeing is believing. And if you could only see for yourself, you would be willing to believe almost anything said about him and, very likely, anything he said to you, face to face, his eyes as if lit from behind by some inner fire, his hard face a map of scars and trouble. Stout and sturdy as an oak stump he is. And clear enough he has been hurt so often and so much, hurt and healed, that his skin and bones are whole and held together is some kind of miracle of nature. Or maybe of art. There are some who are willing to venture that his skin and muscles, stretched tight over bones, many of which are bound to have been broken, some more than one time, yes, there are some who (never in his presence) guess that he puts on his body like a tent over his bones, dresses himself with flesh as you might put on doublet and hose, stretching, pulling, smoothing as best as can be, then holding in place, just so, with intricate laces and points, with hooks and eyes, with buttons large and small. Just as you cannot easily dress or undress yourself, so will Barfoot be in need of another pair of hands to put him together each day and to pour and dump into him the blood and humors and bodily fluids which give him life and character. And at night when he returns to wherever he keeps bed and chambers, why, there must be a great exercise of bleeding and draining and the pissing away of himself. Then the folding of skin and meat and inner organs and parts into a cedar chest. Hangs his bones, his anatomy, upon a hook and, nothing more left then a pure and invisible spiritual essence, lies him down upon a bed, no weight upon it, leaving its sheets unmessed and unmarked, proving his presence only by deep snores worthy of a mastiff.

It would take a woman to do all that, to take him apart, piece by piece, each night and to put him together, like some child's doll or a puzzle, each new day. A woman with deft, quick hands and an almost infinite patience. But the most terrifying thought of all is this: What kind of a woman could love him? Try to imagine her and you shall feel your heart turn cold as a stone.

Oh, to be sure, in the taverns and alehouses where he is known, not to mention brothels and bowling greens and the like, they exaggerate the terrifying aspects of Captain Barfoot. They will also, in his absence, call him a swaggering crow, the very figure, out of life and much literature, of the war-stained, bloody-minded, hardhearted, bitter-tongued veteran of many battles and (much the same) nightmares. But this is not true. There is next to no strut and swagger, no vulgar bravado about Barfoot. Truth is he walks his way as light- and soft-footed as a gentleman dancer waiting for the music to commence. His gestures are often as graceful and delicate as a girl's. But this is lost to the beholder for whom the battered and brutal solidity of Barfoot is as emphatic as the flame and smoke and deafening report of a cannon salute.

Like so many, great and small, virtuous and wicked, young or old, in this lost, late age of the century and the world (and, believe me, there are many thoughtful persons who in their wisdom profess to believe that this world will end with this selfsame century and with the reign of the old Queen), like many others, William Barfoot is not precisely what he seems to be. For one thing, it is his way to pretend to be something more and less than he is. And what he truly is, no man alive, probably not even the Captain himself, knows with certainty.

For example, he is in all probability a dangerous man, as fiercely so as a primed and loaded horse pistol, considering the size and shape, the look and the style of him. But who really knows for sure? Who's fool enough to wish to find out?

Meantime, among his tavern friends and acquaintances, he is taken and accepted as a creature of paradoxes and contradictions. Taken, too, to be a creature of habit, as dependable and predictable as a good German clock. Yet he cheerfully breaks his own habits and customs as often as not.

For instance. Barfoot is not known to be a man of much idle talk or many words. In the presence of facile and clever talkers, of the tellers of tall tales, he will glare. Will fist his face into a horrifying frown.

Captain Barfoot with a frown on his face has been known to silence a whole tavern.

And yet he has been also known, stepping into a silence he himself has created, as if he were someone stepping out of the dark into a puddle of lantern light, to begin to talk as if the only thing that stood between death and himself were the armor of his words.

Here is one of his digressions, this one on the subject of wisdom of wounds, the sapience of many scars:

"It is the folly of most healthy men to imagine that those others who have suffered, as I myself have, from long and dread sickness and those who have, as I surely have, earned a rich reward, a treasure of scars and scabs, if not much else, in this vain and hurtful world, are somehow to be counted as fortunate, as if they have been blessed with an acquired coating of hardness. Like a snail in his little castle or the turtle in his shell.

"It is the common belief that the maimed and wounded are somehow, by dint of their fearful losses, somewhat like saints. That time has taught them how, like the saints, to be careless of and indifferent to much that concerns others.

"Having lost so much to the depredations of time and tribulation, they have little left to lose now. And precious little to fret over or be

anxious about. Having tasted, to the dregs, all the worst that fever and
chills, cuts and bruises and broken bones can give a man, having
learned the lessons of that school, why, they are now imagined to be
fearless ever after. Having met the dark man, the world's schoolmaster,
and wrestled with him to the very edges of the pit of hell, wrestled and
then risen up again, not from the dead, true, but anyhow from
darkness into light, risen up again not hale and whole, either, but
touched and changed by the closeness of Death, just as Jacob was
touched and shriveled by his Angel, they are believed to be in
possession of a rare form of knowledge, if not wisdom, then at the least
a way of knowing and understanding which is only taught in the
school of hard experience.

"And it is this knowledge which, it is believed, leaves them
somehow or other less vulnerable to future wounds than those who
have been spared the same. That their knowledge allows them, after all
has been said and done, to be blithely ready and willing and able to
embrace every kind of pain and discomfort without any fear.

"It is believed that their knowledge leaves them on good terms at
least, if not friendly, with Death. Death who, having failed the first
time, will now be kind and mannerly enough, perhaps, to take them
away, bootless in their sleep, with no more noise or shuddering than
a cat's breath.

"It is all a pretty kind of fiction.

"Do not believe any, not a word, of it."

By now this scarred and battered man, who has enticed everyone
within earshot to try not to stare at his visible scars and lumps and hurt
places, will have awakened their envy for his condition.

"You want to hear the truth of it, friends? Truth is, I believe that
Death has spared me thus far and this long for the sake of something
truly terrible. I believe that those of us whose fate and fortune has been
to endure much and yet to be left alive are being saved and prepared
for something else, something far worse than any of us is able to
imagine.

"And what do I say to that? What can I say? What should I say?

"I say, good friends and true, let us fill our cups to the brim and
drink to this moment as if it were to be our last."

Now at this time and on this same evening, time long past curfew
and the hour of lawful closing, time when most folks are sound asleep

and dreaming, time when the Watch, if they should find you wandering in the streets, will stop you and question you concerning your identity and business, even now Captain Barfoot is wide awake and sitting on a stool as close to the fire and the hearth as he can set it. It is a smoky place and crowded, too, though not, as you might think, with roarers and roisterers and all the usual kinds of nightwalkers, but rather with mostly decent folk. It's an alehouse called the Cock, nearby the Church of St. Peter Cheap and to be found in Wood Street just to the north of Cheapside. It is, then, in the very heart of the City.

City he hates. Or, anyway, claims out loud to hate. Says so to anyone who will ask him his opinion.

To anyone who will ask him, and not many will choose or dare to, he will begin to define himself as a man of the country, not of this City or any other, a man who, weighing and considering all things, both good and ill—for it must be admitted that there are many good words to be said about London, just as there are many good and fair things to see and to enjoy there—hates this City in much the same way that we are enjoined in Holy Scripture to hate and to turn away from unholy Babylon, which may be taken, like London, to be the home port for the world, the flesh, and the Devil.

"I am a mere countryman and I am proud to say so," he will announce. "I do dearly love my village home. And I love to remember the long, slow turning of time and of the seasons there, time moving like clear water turning and turning a lazy mill wheel . . ."

Given some listeners, Barfoot will treat them to a serious and, at some moments, even an eloquent accounting, his North Country accent growing stronger and more pronounced as he talks, of the pleasures he takes in the country calendar, from Plough Monday in the bleak early days of January on through the times of the planting and sowing, the growing and gathering of crops, the raising and fattening of stock, of sheep and kine and swine, through the harvesttime and fall planting, November's bloody slaughtering and butchering, Christmastime at the parish church and the manor house.

And so, much like a mill wheel, turning round and round only to begin again.

They say he can rival the very finest among your city-bred pastoral poets. And if by any chance you happen to be unfamiliar with Mr.

Tusser's celebrated *Hundred Points of Husbandry*, why, he can astonish you with much lore, with many little mysteries of the craft of country life. Given any kind of encouragement, nods and smiles and a drink or two for his labors, Barfoot will soon be telling you how best to build a sturdy haystack or how to spin good rope from your harvested hemp. Will debate and argue until your eyes cross whether it is beech or lime wood which is best for a butter tub and whether ash or oak will serve you better for the handles of your tools and the spokes and shafts of your cart.

"Elm, you say? Would sooner have elm for your shafts. Well then, so be it. It is often done that way. And elm is strong against the power of dampness. When death comes at last to claim me (and, good Lord, may it please not happen here in London, but in my warm bed and in my dry snug house within easy hearing of the singing bells of my own parish church of St. Timothy), I shall be happiest to be laid out in a well-made coffin made out of elm. For elm will hold back the wet and the rot for as long a time as any kind of wood I know of."

And if you are still wide awake and listening and maybe someone has filled his cup again, Barfoot will describe the pleasures of a church ale as if he were talking of Bartholomew Fair. Why, he can and will recount the pleasures of a country market fair as if he were talking of the splendors of the Lord Mayor's Day here in London.

Can he be trusted in these matters? Is he sincere? Who knows? Is it all a kind of jest, his extravagant encomium of simple English country life? There is no certain answer to that either. Except perhaps in this sense, that since boyhood, his times at home have been few and far between. Truth is, he has spent more time in Venice than in his own village. He will have to admit that. And he has been in many other far places of this world. Lately he has spent more of his time and life here in London than anywhere else. He keeps chambers somewhere, though no one seems certain where that may be. Some say in Clerkenwell or Southwark on account of there are so many whores there. And, no question, Captain Barfoot does seem to know half of the whores of London by their Christian names. And, always shameless (perhaps he has no wife of his own; or does he?), he will greet them warmly in any kind of company. Others say he lives down in Blackfriars. Where at least he can claim and have the right of sanctuary, when and if he needs that, and in the meantime strut or stroll like a gentleman among others of his own kind and station if he wants to. He has been known to say that after too much time wasted in the company of such ill-mannered, lowborn and dissolute company, including yourself, too, if you are there among them when he tells you this, making no polite exceptions, he finds the company even of sour-faced Puritans, who also dwell in Blackfriars, among other places, to be both reassuring and salutary.

And there are others who argue that it is much more in keeping with his character that he make his home among the poor and disorderly folk of Shoreditch or Cripplegate where he can hide himself safely among them like a sly goat in a flock of sheep.

He will not say anything to the point. Except sometimes, once in a while, as if he knew the questions in their minds, he will bid farewell to his tavern companions and offer an invitation to come and visit his chambers at Cold Harbour, that sanctuary for vagrants and debtors. Or Bridewell, workplace for idle persons and for women of ill repute. Or maybe at Bethlehem Hospital, where the irremediably mad are kept.

Amid laughter, as if the laughter were a puff of smoke, he will turn away and disappear.

Some fools have tried to satisfy their curiosity and trail him home. A fox on the run is easier to follow.

For a man who claims to love and know the country best, he knows this City, its streets and lanes, byways and footpaths and hidden places, as if he had been born and raised here. And surely, whenever he finds the idle time for it—and what other sort of time does Captain Barfoot own and spend?—he will often be found among the crowds gathered for any kind of spectacle or ceremony or public show. Not surprising, then, to find him at Tyburn to bear witness to the efficacy of hanging, among other ways and means, as a reasonably swift method of ridding this world of some of its unlucky undesirables. Perhaps somewhat more surprising, he will dress himself in the elegant and expensive clothes of a gentleman courtier (more likely to be rented or borrowed than owned, wouldn't you say, though they always seem to fit him well enough, as well as if made and tailored for him alone) and pay the price for a seat at the Tiltyard on Accession Day. "Barfoot must have seen our Queen at first hand more than any other man in England saving only the late Earl of Leicester and our present Earl of Essex." Not at all surprising that his memorable face is often to be found at Bankside at the Bear Garden. Harder to credit, though there are enough reliable witnesses who say so, that he can be looked for and found, at least in these recent days since the Plague has diminished, at the performance of any new play, and many old ones, at playhouse or innyard.

Here's another paradox of the character of Captain Barfoot. If he sometimes puts others on the calm shores of sleep with his tales of the pleasures and pastimes of country living—which most of you, coming from the country also, do not wish to waken and encourage the memory of—he is just as likely to wax fluent on the wonders of the foreign places he has been to. For instance, he was overheard telling someone here tonight, to considerable doubting and scoffing, how in the ancient and wicked city of Venice they permit women players— yes, women!—to play the parts of women on the public stage. And he has claimed, despite a chorus of hoots and jeers, that the same practice will come to England one day, too. Soon enough. When the level of general wickedness rises a little like the flowing tide.

He can be silent among strangers. But among his old acquaintances he will talk freely on any number of subjects. Almost any subject. Except the subject he knows best—the business of warfare. He offers up next to nothing about the wars of past or present. To someone who does not know or honor his habit of silence on that subject, in response to a remark or question, he will either shrug or reply with stone-faced, glaring silence. With a look that could frighten a serpent.

Tonight, then, some acquaintances at the Cock on Wood Street are about to be surprised. In a few moments a man, a perfect stranger to them, will come inside out of the foggy night. He will greet Barfoot warmly. And Barfoot will jump up from his stool by the hearth and embrace the fellow, a man, as it looks, of roughly his same age and, judging by his appearance—sword and dagger; clean leather harness and leather jerkin; high boots and soft cap and good woolen cape— perhaps another old soldier like Barfoot.

"By God," Barfoot will announce in a herald's voice to one and all. "Here is a gentleman worthy of all your honor and respect. This man served by my side in good times and bad, in the Lowlands and on the coast of France. Bled and suffered pains for the sake of this kingdom and the comfort and safety of worthless leeches like yourselves. So that you could sit on your arses in London taverns, long after the lawful curfew, and make yourselves stupid and even more foolish with strong drink, he stood between you and terrible *tercios* of the Spanish infantry. Who would have buggered your wives like Gypsy boys and turned and roasted your children over slow fires, if they had ever been able to come here. Stood between them and you in more than one place and has the scars to prove it. Stood between you and your soft, worthless, wasted lives and the Spaniards and the Frogs, among others, and for food and sustenance had the pleasures of spoiled and maggot-ridden meat and biscuits hard enough to break teeth in two, and for his drink had ditch water if he was lucky."

"Ah, Barfoot," the fellow will interrupt in a loud, clear voice, "you have not changed at all in all these years. Your mouth is still as quick and agile as a hare running for his life. And you still make the life of a soldier of this Queen and country sound far better than it really is."

At that Barfoot laughs out loud. Throws his arm around the fellow's shoulders and orders quarts of ale for everyone in the place. And then again. Soon after that the tavern is half singing and half snoozing.

And Barfoot and his friend have gone out into the foggy darkness. And what you will never know then or forever (unless you should happen to read it here) is that that stout fellow whom Barfoot greeted and embraced and introduced all around the room while so much ale was poured and consumed was not any kind of soldier at all. Not exactly. Put it another way. He was, indeed, a soldier, but of another kind than you may have imagined and from another army than you would have guessed.

A priest is what he was. A Jesuit priest. Had been chased and harried and hunted over half of England. Stood in fear and trembling for his very life, his bowels and balls and his four quarters. And this same night, night of Hunnyman's abduction and night of Barfoot at the Cock in Wood Street, at risk of his own life, too, every step of the way, by devious ways, Barfoot will lead him to the River. And then by the River will take him to and hide him safely aboard a ship bound for France.

Captain Barfoot has many and various secrets that he keeps and might not reveal under the strictest interrogation and torture. And this is one, that he is of the Roman faith. Born so, baptized so, and still so, more or less, to this very day. Hopes and prays to be buried so.

Another. That this aid and comfort to others of the faith, like this Jesuit priest, is not by any means his occupation, as it is quite profitably, for some others, but an act of charity. For his own living, now that he is home from the wars, he acts as a factor, an agent, probably an intelligencer, for his own brother, a man of importance and high station in his native North.

For him he will perform any service, great or small, that may be required. Including, if need be and it comes to that, cutting your throat from ear to ear.

There are many little services, day to day, including the management of some properties in London, to be performed. But his chief problems at present include a lazy suit in Chancery Court, brought by one of his distant relatives, and some complex negotiations with a City wool merchant who may be able to increase his brother's profits while also increasing his own.

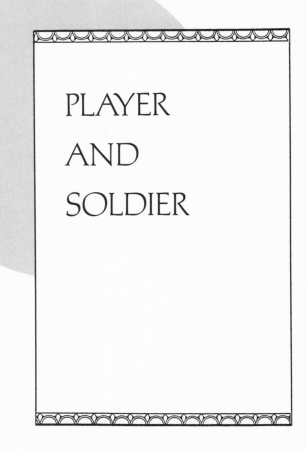

PLAYER
AND
SOLDIER

Now you know two of the chief actors of this story. Witnesses who will give testimony. And it will be, as you have seen and will see, mostly a matter of observing them and listening to them, separately and together, a consort of voices making their own kind of music. Whispers fading in and out of the darkness.

Ghosts, no more and no less, they cannot be clearly seen by daylight. Vague and brief as frosty breath on coldest days, they float through time.

No, say instead that we float on the surface of time as you might float on a lazy stream on a soft summer afternoon. That's an image which is true enough. Except that, for ourselves, the lost time of living and being, our brief time to suffer and to rejoice, is now and always an eternal February. It can be summer again only in your memory.

You will have noticed how I have suddenly said *we*, as if claiming a place for myself. For though I play no part in this tale, I am nevertheless ever present, a witness to it all, first to last.

The others must speak for themselves. Believe them as much as you care to, bearing in mind that even though there were saints living and dying then, in my time, as there may well be, no, surely must be, true saints alive even in yours, there are no saints to be found in this story. Coming from anyone less than a saint, or a truly innocent good heart (of which there are none mentioned here either), the truth, even if it accepts an invitation to be present, is likely to be somewhat tainted and confused. At the very least it will be twisted into strange shapes by whoever tells it.

Well now.

One of these is a common player. Need I say more? Truth is not very dear to his heart. Or, if I may put it to you somewhat more precisely: truth is dear to his heart mainly because it is so much of a stranger to him. Plain truth is such a stranger that he often might not recognize it, even though it should come, transformed into a large, barking watchdog, to snarl and snap at his running heels.

Something of a clown, then. You see what I am getting at. Pray remember, though, that like every other fool and clown since old Adam himself crouched down with Eve amongst the leaves and hoped, thereby, to be safely hidden from the burning eyes of God, he takes himself most seriously. His life's no comedy. His aches and pains hurt him as much as, perhaps more than, Hector's. His rages at Fortune's blessings and injustice are, in their own way, equal to those of proud Achilles. And he is like neither one of these. Not noble hero or kin to any, although—and give him this much with acknowledgment that it is much more than most of us will ever have the right to claim—he has played the parts of both of them and of many other great and proud men also. In his time, the best of his times, he has hushed unruly crowds to attentive silence and then aroused their enthusiastic applause. He has moved fellow sufferers to shed tears. Oh, to be sure, he has failed at it also. Has earned his full share of hoots and jeers and other rude noises. He has been pelted with orange rinds and nutshells and gnawed bones. He has run, fleeing from the stage—though that stage may have been no more than a piece of yard, of green grass at the edges of a church fair or, maybe, the far end of a smoky hall in some drafty castle or crumbling old mansion in far country—has left the stage in a hurry and with tears in his eyes. Well, tell me, how else can you learn and practice a mystery, a craft, except by the constant doing of it and sometimes doing it all wrong? If there have been plenty of bad times, there have also been moments of glory. Those times when he left the tiring room, surrounded by smiles and good wishes, his hand swelling from warm, firm handclasps, and himself secure in the certainty that the magical sound of applause which has sent him on his way like a ship running with a fair wind behind her has now at last and once and for all, as in some child's tale, transformed him into a very prince among our English players. Never again to be ignored or to be relegated to stand, rigid with envy, in the shabby shadows well beyond all the pools of brightness wherein his luckier betters do splash and dance in all the joy and shine of this world's good fortune.

I have to be first to tell you (as you may, in your worldly wisdom, already have guessed) that at just such a triumphant time, in triumphant and joyous mood, head held high, shoulders back, his best pair of shoes shining, he is liable to step down firmly into some fresh dog shit or the steaming droppings of a draft horse. As well as he knows and is sure of anything, he knows this will happen to him. It tends to take the keen edge off even his finest hours. He is most apprehensive when he should be most content.

You see what I am saying. Bad luck is his constant and dear old companion. Dame Fortune may perhaps love him well enough (who can tell?), but, love or not, she has chosen him to be her faithful fool in cap and bells.

So often so unlucky in life and in love, he possesses one great strength, one kind of magic. Whether it may be foolish or not, he chooses not (not yet anyway) to allow himself to surrender to despair. At least, he defers that. In his heart of hearts he knows that this world, with himself in it and of it, is beyond all possible redemption and so is well lost. Because he knows that, he knows also that to win the world would be, then, to come into possession of nothing worth having.

In his secret heart, he can see himself clearly, naked as God made him. And to see himself thus, a poor creature, pale and sad as a winter root, is to know beyond doubting that he is a fool. But, don't you see?, he still loves this tired world, worthless as it has been and may always be. And calling upon St. Paul and St. Augustine and any others he can think of, he tries to learn to love himself, too. Which is why he is busily seeking the love of others (especially the love and ministrations of fair women), as if he needed to confirm his own best aspirations.

Yet it is these lies, falsehoods, and very present frailties which give to his life, his sometimes desperate and always anxious life, its power and its energy. And it is from his deepest falsehoods that his finest moments as a player and performer, in life as much as on the boards, are slowly and surely drawn out of deep and dark and into light like the sweetest and coldest well water that can assuage the most burning thirst.

The other fellow is not much like him at all. A creature of fire and ice, blood and thunder, he is, as allowed, a rusty, much wounded soldier home from the wars. In one piece, to be sure. And thanks be to God for that, he'll be the first to tell you. For many of his best friends have left behind chunks and pieces, the best parts of themselves, in far, forlorn places. But he is bitterly scarred in both flesh and spirit.

Despair is the way that he walks in. He would not admit and confess that, even under brutal duress, and even to himself. He denies it. He simply allows that he is not and never will be a seriously (foolishly) hopeful man. He believes that he has lost much of his faith and, with that loss, has managed to shed the fear of hellfire. Thinking: "How could hell be any more terrible, any worse than so many things I have already seen and felt?"

It is the ineradicable fear of the fires of hell, together with the logical certainty that if there is a hell, then he has long since earned himself a place in it, which makes him seem to be utterly fearless, as careless as any saint, amid the dirty, daily business of this fallen world. Believe me, he would as soon kill you as look at your face. Yes. And yet by the same token, he would kiss you full on the lips if the spirit moved him to do so. By which I do not mean to suggest that he is one of those openhanded, open-faced, openhearted fellows, a bag full of the wind of gusty feelings and with no decent rectitude about him. He is not one of those savages of the latest generation who neither hold nor allow any reins upon themselves, but, instead, run away in whatever direction their thoughtless hungers and crippled fancies may lead them. Not one of those, by any means! Indeed, that crew and all others like them, men and women alike, baffle and disgust him. He thinks of them as wild beasts. For just as the player is, in large part, a creature of the experience of his craft and vocation, so this one, also, a soldier once upon a time and for perhaps too long, is shaped by and clings to the virtues and vices of his trade. Rigor is his closest friend. He long since learned to fix his face into a blank mask, ever the same in pain and pleasure, hope or fear. No one, not his proud betters, not his inferiors, not his lovers or his victims, will be given any signs or clues to what he may be truly thinking or feeling. In that one sense, then, his craft is much the same as the player's, though it is turned inside out.

He and the player have that much in common. With some differences. If it is the figure of thirst that can name and define the spiritual man—and does not Holy Scripture, in the Psalms and in many other places, summon up hunger and thirst as the aptest similitudes for the ineffable desires of our deepest selves?—then it can be said that this soldier satisfies himself inwardly just as he has so often done outwardly. Dirty, sweaty, panting like a dog, with perhaps blood, his own or someone else's, no matter which, flecked and clotted on leather and armor, he tosses his heavy helmet aside to kneel down next to some stagnant ditch and to plunge his hands through the coating of scum and slime and up to his elbows in muddy water. Lifts his cupped palms to his lips as careful and ceremonious as if he were an anointed Roman priest and as if this were the blessed chalice with the blood of Christ Jesus he were bearing. Then he drinks it down. Tongue lapping like a dog's. Eagerly in spite of the foul stink of it. Finished, he wipes the back of his hand across beard and lips and then looks up, as if to catch your eye, and winks, and laughs out loud. Laughs as if he were daring the dirty water to work on him, to sicken and kill him if it can.

Outwardly he has a face of stone.

These two, then, and myself.

Together with some others, greater and lesser.

Of them all, the strongest and strangest voice belongs to the poet Christopher Marlowe. Who died young enough and badly enough, as was, in the view of many, bound to happen. Died too young, badly and sadly, but who wrote words of such power and shining as to outlast all but those of a precious few, all but the finest wordsmiths of his (our) age and many others, before and after. He will say next to nothing here, having spoken for himself, once and for always, and being dead and gone even as this story begins. It is the murder of this man which becomes the reason and occasion for bringing together player and soldier and some others, lesser voices, though some were inestimably grander in life and light than they can or should be here.

Marlowe, who was first a scholar, then a poet and playmaker, and something of a spy in his time. It is not at all the kind of story he would have created. Yet I do believe, and we can safely guess, he would have seen through the masks and costumes of both the player and the soldier to the bare and common human nakedness they all three shared.

As for myself.

Why, that's nothing to concern yourself about. I am here present as a voice only, a voice from the dark. Hoping by the power of words and words alone (though they may sometimes cast real shadows like sudden wings) to permit you to see and to judge for yourself.

Otherwise think nothing of me. For this is in no way my story. I insist on that. Except, perhaps, this much. To know what I profess to have known and to believe what I claim to have believed, I must have lived out a watchful life, as awake and alert and as thoughtful as I could manage. You can say I watched and waited, bided my time until, as Holy Scripture promises and soon enough fulfills, death arrived and surprised me like a thief in the night.

If you insist on coherent figures of speech, then ask me if I was thirsty, too. And I will answer yes. But neither for cold well water nor for the dregs of any ditch. Wine was my weakness. Wine to warm my heart and my bowels and to brighten my disposition. Wine to shut down and lock up the forge of my mind. Wine to cancel out my debts of pain.

But that is altogether another story and has no rightful place here.

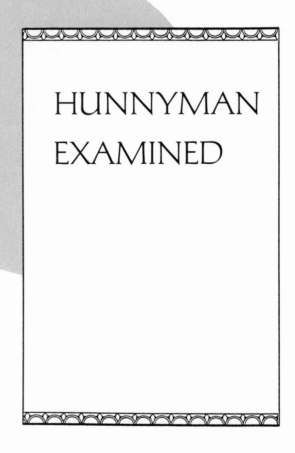

HUNNYMAN
EXAMINED

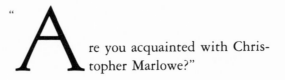

"Are you acquainted with Christopher Marlowe?"

"The poet?"

"The same."

"I am surprised you do not speak of him in the past tense. He has been dead for some while."

"Since May of '93."

"Well then," Hunnyman tells the young man in the cellar, "at that same time our company was performing in the North."

"On account of the Plague."

"That summer we went as far north as Carlisle."

"Plague did not kill Christopher Marlowe."

"So we heard."

"What news did you hear?"

"One thing and another. That, most likely, he was killed in a drunken brawl."

"Did that surprise you?"

"The man had a choleric quick temper and more than a full share of bad habits."

"True enough."

"Besides which, by then I had already arrived at an age when truly surprising things are few and far between."

"Do my questions surprise you?"

Hunnyman chooses to answer with some caution.

"I confess that I am troubled by some doubts. I cannot conceive what it is you want to hear from me."

"The truth. Only the truth."

Here Hunnyman allows himself the relief of a faint, brief smile and the slightest kind of a shrug.

"Why then, I am happy to oblige you," he says. "Even under these strange circumstances.

"If, as it seems, you are seeking to find someone who knew Kit Marlowe well, why, you have made a mistake. It is true that I am . . . or, more truthfully, that I have been from time to time a player. And I think it would be truly remarkable to find any player alive in England who is altogether ignorant of Marlowe's plays. Is there any company, large or small, celebrated or obscure, which has not, one way or another and in one version or another, performed his plays and earned both profit and general applause for their efforts? I doubt it. Is there a living poet in England who has not flattered Marlowe and honored his memory by trying to imitate the matter of his plays and the thunder and lightning, the drums and trumpets and gunpowder blasts of his words? Not to my knowledge. There was a time, believe me, sir, and it has not yet fully dissipated, either, when all that the managers wished to see and to consider for performance was something or other, anything really, which had at least the counterfeit sound and echo of Marlowe in the lines and some shadowy copy of the astonishing spectacle of his fables.

"I am telling you no news there.

"For a little time, no, for longer than that in this foolish age of fashion, when fashions in all things flare and blaze and poof! are gone forever, for a good time the poetry of Marlowe was the very model and fashion of excellence for most of us. Not many can or ever will equal that influence.

"And though it may seem to you, sir, as it does to many men, that there is a kind of army, or, better, a veritable armada of common players and suchlike, men without any honest craft or employment, in this weary kingdom, though it may well seem to you, sir, that we are as thick and noisy and as annoying and dangerous to the good, natural order of things as a cloud of locusts on the wind, the truth is (and you asked me for the truth, did you not?) that we are few enough in number and, despite many differences of degree and of good fortune, are joined together in a kind of shadowy commonwealth. We are brothers in our general disrepute if not always in adversity. And because we are few, we are much concerned, indeed fascinated to the edges of obsession, by all the bits and pieces of news of our little world. Rumor, bruit, and alewife's gossip, these are among our greatest pleasures.

"Sometimes, to the more notorious among us, this can be a special kind of tribulation. For I do believe, sir, that there is no man (no woman, either, for that matter) in all this kingdom, perhaps in all the wide world as well, who would not relish the prospect of good report, good repute, and good fame among his fellows. Perhaps—I do not exclude them—even your stinking hairy bears there, at least among others of their kind."

"You have played that tune more than enough."

"Anyway. Consider that we live in an age in which, shall we agree on it?, good fame seems to be desired by almost everyone, from turnspits to dancing masters, from jakesmen to great lords and even, God save us all, common stage players.

"But if it is good fame that we desire for ourselves, it is nevertheless the ill fame of others, our enemies and rivals, which gives us most pleasure. Just so good fortune is not half so sweet as it is when it can be, like the rose in its nest of thorns, surrounded by the misery and bad fortune of others."

"I think you may be wrong in that supposition. But never mind. Pray continue."

"I have reached the age—and I am not an old man yet by any

means—when I never feel quite so much alive as when I hear the news of the death of one enemy or another. Sometimes it even pleases me to contemplate the death of my friends."

"Marlowe?"

"In that case, believe me, neither my friend nor my enemy, but someone else, someone celebrated for the good fame of his words. But, why deny it, the old black trumpet of ill fame loudly saluted many of the things which he said and did."

"Are you thinking of the buggery of boys?"

Most cautious again. Who could tell what the habits and frailties of this handsome young man, his abductor and interrogator, might be?

"I am well aware, sir, that the practices you refer to, together with many others of the like, are known to be unnatural and, in the eyes of every kind of Christian church and sect, to be mortal sins. And in the Law are most grievous crimes and most grievously punished . . ."

"But?"

"Sir?"

"But what?"

"But, sir, I have lived long enough in the world to know that there are many creatures of God so swept and overcome by strange hungers and sinful appetites as to be undeterred from these practices by fear of any earthly or eternal punishment. It is a pity, but the truth."

"And was Marlowe one of these?"

"I have heard so, but have no evidence of the truth or falsehood of the rumor.

"It is undeniably true that he earned himself considerable ill fame on account of what he was supposed to have said and done. And we often talked of him in those days as if he were a kind of player playing a kind of role—himself. In our talk and minds he became one of those beings who so often seem to be appropriate emblems for our wicked age, these dying times. He was a stranger whom we came to imagine that we knew well.

"Having said all that, I have to say, also, sir, that I have indeed seen the man in flesh and blood, when he still had living flesh to wear around his bones. Perhaps a dozen times in a dozen different places. Taverns and playhouses usually. Yet only as a face among a crowd of faces, somehow oddly familiar because of his fame. In all my life I spoke to him, have spoken with him, only once or twice, exchanging maybe a dozen or two of inconsequential words. If he had outlived his last brawl (if brawling was truly the death of him) and if he were here instead of myself, I am certain he could not recall my name or my face. Not even if he were being tortured to encourage recollection.

"In long and short, then, sir, I find I knew a good deal, much of it indifferently true or false, with myself not caring ripe figs or farts to distinguish between the two, about Kit Marlowe. But no, sir, I did not truly know him, nor could I, in any serious sense, even claim him for an acquaintance."

"Were you surprised at how he died?"

"Well, sir, it did seem . . . how shall I say it? . . . a fitting ending for his story."

"And you felt neither sorrow nor regret?"

"Why should I?"

"Not an answer to what I asked you."

"Very well, then. I felt nothing at all at the time and have felt nothing since then. Other deaths—as you well know—have moved me and wounded me. When Marlowe died, I had no place in my heart to mourn the fate of strangers."

"And did you ever hear anything at all as to why Marlowe might have been murdered?"

"You are asking me to try and remember what was of no consequence to me at the time."

"What was it you heard?"

"Well, finally, after all the rumors and wild tales, only what the Coroner's jury found. That it was self-defense. That the man who killed him—his name escapes me now, if I ever even heard it or knew of it . . ."

"Frizer. A man called Ingram Frizer."

"If you say so."

"Does the name mean anything to you?"

"Nothing at all. I reasonably assumed, at the time, that this man (Frizer did you say?) was not likely to be a fellow of enviable good repute."

"Upon what grounds?"

"Kind of place he was. Kind of company he was keeping."

"Please continue."

"All that I ever heard was that a jury found that Frizer acted in self-defense when he killed Marlowe."

"Do you believe that?"

"I take it for what it is, the finding of a jury in a certain case. So be it."

"Do you care?"

"You keep prodding me in the matter of my caring or not caring. How can I make this clear and simple to you, sir?

"Look you. You—or, anyway, in your name and at your orders it has been done—had me seized off the street and dragged and carried away against my will, and in dire peril of my health and welfare, to this place, this cold bright cellar. Here you have told me more about myself than you have any right to know. Here you have threatened me in plain fact and by implication. Here you have kindly served me strong wine—and a very good sack it is, too—to loosen my tongue even as it clouds over the brightness of my mind. And you have examined me concerning my knowledge, and the lack of it, of a dead man, a dissolute poet, a man of great gifts and many serious vices. A man who may be sorely missed by someone or other, but not so by me.

"And now, sir, do you know what I have come to think?"

"Pray tell me."

"I have learned that your interest in me derives mainly from the matter of the life and death of Christopher Marlowe. And I know for certain and can cheerfully tell you that, between yourself and your bears, you have managed, by an easy enough error, to take the wrong man to serve your purposes as a witness. If only I could serve you, I would gladly do so, if only for the sake of my hide and hair. But since I know nothing beyond what I have already said, I can only plead with you, sir, to acknowledge your error and let me be. Let me go about my humble business. Please, sir, give me leave to depart this place and I do solemnly promise to forget that any of this happened."

"Are you finished speaking?"

"Is there anything left to be said?"

"Not by you, Joseph Hunnyman. And now it is my turn. To tell you that you have somewhat misjudged us and our intentions and have undervalued yourself. Everything that has been said here tonight confirms that you are the man we hoped that you would be. And so I deem that you are precisely the man to perform the task at hand."

"What is it you want me to do?"

"To find out how Marlowe was really killed. And why."

LET US TAKE AND CONSIDER THIS CAPTAIN BARFOOT

Barfoot is your true northern man, coming from a large and gentle (once honored) family in that hard country. A family strong in the Old Faith. "The True Faith," they will say steadfastly, if secretly. And in this age of ours, when all the world is on fire with change, they have paid a bitter price for the sake of their old beliefs. There were heavy fines and the loss of much land back in the time of the Pilgrimage of Grace. Some close and unlucky kin to Barfoot's family were hanged for their part in all that sad business. But worse and closer home were all the dangers and troubles which came down upon them, thirty-odd years later, in his own youth, after the uprising of the northern Earls in '69. After the failure of that, confirmed and finally settled at

Naworth in Cumberland on a bleak February day when the Queen's cousin, Lord Hundson, defeated the forces of Leonard Dacre ("a most wicked and pernicious traitor," as the Royal Proclamation of March 4, 1570, called him), though pardons were promised by the Queen, it was fire and sword and the hangman's hemp that, in fact, followed. Queen proved herself to be (in the view of the Northerners) as duplicitous and merciless as even her father, Great Harry, ever had been.

Death, prison, heavy fines and ransoms, confiscations. All things cracked and fell apart. Scavengers (as always) took up the broken pieces.

Barfoot's uncle and some cousins were hanged in their own villages. His father would surely have been hanged, too, if he had been taken. But fled the country. Went to live in exile. First with the frightened Earl of Westmorland in Flanders. Then, on his own, into Italy. Died there, a few years later, of the Roman fever.

Meanwhile Barfoot's mother, overthrown with grief and sorrow and fear and dismay, distracted beyond reason, wrapped herself in madness as if it were a warm and invisible cloak. And nothing—not prayer, not powerful opiates and medicines, not months alone in a dark room—would seem to cure her.

She, who had been to him all light and warmth and a soft musical voice, she who had been a garden of sweet odors and a pair of strong, dry, gentle hands, withered and shriveled like a dying leaf. Drifted into shadowy twilight, and was gone into her own inner darkness, like a forlorn ghost in a sorrowful, ancient place, long before the strictest treatment was tried.

Soon enough she was a ghost in fact.

Barfoot was a small child, a toddler at the beginning of the Rebellion, and can only vaguely recall these things. That lost woman has left him not many memories, though sometimes she reappears in a dream. And he cannot remember his father, either, with much clarity. Sometimes he, too, will come in a dream; though more often he is a presence on the edges of dreaming, that moment or two just before sleep takes command of body and soul. There will be a bearded, bright-eyed face, huge as the rising full moon, that seems to float over him. Sometimes moon face will speak with a thundering deep voice in a language he cannot understand. And aside from that, there is nothing more, in truth, except for whatever he has made up from a painted portrait of his father as a young man and from the words and fragmentary recollections of others. Though (as we all know well) these things, too, become true parts of memory and can be summoned up out of thin air and nowhere. Can be revised even as they are being reclaimed.

What he recollects from these sources is, first of all, a fall morning, November, frosty, the breath of men and horses frosty, as a crowd of mounted men have gathered together before the house. And then the noise of it—shouting voices, heavy boots within the house, barking of the leashed and tied dogs (who must have believed it was going to be a hunt without them), with one or two large dogs running free among the legs of the horses; bells from the parish church in the village ringing and ringing and ringing in a very strange way (rung backwards as a signal, he was later to learn). Women sobbing—no, that was to come later at year's end, when the whole plot unraveled and the men who had gone forth so proudly, with such noise and bravado and courage, came back home, if at all, by dark and as silently as thieves.

Back to that morning.

He can imagine, see himself in a high room of the old house, himself with all of his brothers, faces pressed out of shape against small panes of cold glass, looking down at the tall men on their horses, all of them armed for battle and clad in blue (like the old Crusaders), with a red cross on their chests. They are mostly mounted and ready to ride off when his young and handsome father comes out from the house, half running, clumsy in his high boots, buckling on his harness and sword. He wears a fine hat with bright feathers fixed on the brim of it.

Glass is cold and cloudy. Child wipes it clean with his sleeve. Presses his face hard against it as if to kiss his own reflection. Just in time to see his father, now mounted tall and straight in saddle, turn to ride away with the others through the open gate of the gatehouse and down the long, tree-lined lane to the high road. His own heart is beating fast and there is a kind of catch in his breathing that makes him wheeze. He is urgently afraid he may begin to weep in front of his older brothers and then they will laugh at him. His sudden sadness is that his father has turned to ride away (forever; somehow, with a child's lightning wisdom, he knows that it will be forever . . . however long forever may prove to be) without so much as one sign or gesture of farewell. His father has forgotten them.

But then . . . not so! At that same instant his father pulls up, turns his horse halfway around and likewise himself in the saddle. Waves one hand toward the house. Then, looking up toward their little faces pressed against the window, he fills that empty hand with his fine feathered hat. Waves hat back and forth, smiling widely. Turns again, hat still in his hand, kicks and spurs his horse to run down the lane following behind the others.

Forever and a day . . .

So Barfoot will be left with a memory (perhaps his own or just as well given to him whole by one of the others) of that handsome man, sitting on a good horse, smiling and waving his hat in farewell just before he rides off and out of their lives for good and all. Memory of it coming unexpectedly when he is most defenseless, cast up on the strange shores of sleeping and dreaming, can still shorten his breath and bring a few tears (no more than that few) to his hard eyes. And at that moment, whether the memory is true or not, he can truly feel the cold glass against his nose, his lips, his cheeks. Can see and feel and clearly remember the high window of the huge old house. House that will so soon after that be taken away from them. That high window and its cold small panes are the best and most he can now remember of that long-lost place.

Barfoot was raised, then, elsewhere. In reasonable good comfort, too, though beholden for it, by distant kinfolk. Brothers and sisters were scattered. But he was treated with loving-kindness by his kinspeople. And he was given the beginnings of an education.

There was a tutor for the children in that country village. A tall, thin, bent, weak-eyed, sour-faced man. Perhaps, as Barfoot thinks of it now, a Papist priest who had long since lost his sense of vocation with his office. If so, anyway, he would in due time marry a sturdy country girl, one whom he had probably got with child behind a haystack. He would take the Queen's oath and become another kind of priest in the Queen's own Church of England. Matter of great shame, it seemed, at the time. Barfoot, remembering these things, will laugh at the idea of that kind of shame. Like any other old soldier, he has come to believe that there is no great shame in any kind of betrayal except for the betrayal of comrades. And also in the act of dying badly, awkwardly, with obvious fear and trembling.

Yet, like any man long and sorely tested, he believes that, shame or no, things cannot always be well managed. Believes that a time and place and circumstance (unimagined though never unimaginable) can come together when even the proudest and most courageous and honorable man will gladly trade even the lives of others, and as many as need be and can be, in the probably vain hope of saving his own. He believes, too, that at the proper time and place, things unimagined, yet not unimaginable, can come together to bring out a cold sweat of pure cowardice from the most courageous man alive.

"That fellow, the priest who was my tutor," he will tell you, "was surely a fool to bedevil himself (if he ever did so) for the frailty of his flesh and for his failure to persevere in his old vocation. He left us, bedraggled, hangdog, sorrowful. True. But any shame for himself was nothing but an excess of baggage to carry with him. Still, I honor the memory of him for his folly. If you follow my argument. And—and I have seen it, the truth of it, so many times, times beyond counting— humility, true humility, whatever its cause or source or inception may be, is a power and a strength beyond all measuring. The greatest power of this world breaks and shatters to pieces, like teeth on hard rock, when it meets with true humility.

"Anyway, I would guess that the fellow must have become a better minister to others precisely on account of his own failings and his imaginary shame. I have heard, round about, that he did well enough for himself in the Queen's Church. And I would like to think it is the truth."

As a teacher the man had wakened in the boy a desire, a love of learning, and a hunger to know everything he could. He taught kindly and gently and seldom, if ever, by pure rote or by the rhythm of a birch rod across a bare backside. In another time and place, given a little more time and occasion to study with just such a teacher, who somehow was able to bring out the best from him, Barfoot might have gone on to study at one of the famous colleges of Cambridge or Oxford. Might even now be a scholar and not without honor. But he does not often allow himself to imagine that, to think on what might have happened and what he might or might not have been. It can be a well of bitterness.

"Well, now. Consider this. I could also, just as well, have become a one-legged beggar on a crutch, licensed to beg at town's end. Or a blind man led about by a hired boy. Or be dead and gone and long forgotten by now.

"There is never any good use or value to gain in dwelling upon what might have been. Nor, for that matter, I do believe, no use in planning much, above and beyond the most rudimentary of reasonable and prudent precautions, for what may yet be to come. A man can never be truly free and clear from all regrets. And I must openly confess that I do truly regret, and always will, that I was sent off to be a soldier (or to die trying to learn how to be one) at just the age when I could and should have been at some college or other at Oxford or Cambridge. No matter which. Both remain splendid and golden places to my imagination. Though, truth is, as the world knows, some colleges at Oxford have been and are still more hospitable to those of us who keep and cleave to the True Faith. Cambridge is strong for the reformers.

"But that could not be. And never was to be. And what was, and came to pass, could have been far worse than it has so far proved to be. I understand the truth of that and I am ever thankful for it.

"It has, however, somewhat hardened my heart against some of those more fortunate than myself who were privileged to be scholars and have squandered that privilege and have wasted away their intellectual lives."

Over the years Barfoot's brother, tallest and eldest of those children at the window, has slowly and patiently and shrewdly managed to recover and to restore some part of the family's wealth and lands and honor. To do so has required of him many things, not least of which was to marry, not out of love or lust, but out of a more practical need, the plain and sturdy daughter of a rich wool merchant. One of those newly risen men possessing lands and money but lacking a name and a history. The elder Barfoot could give him that in return for an excellent dowry.

"Well," he tells his younger brother these days, "the woman has proved to be a good breeder, solid as a sow or a Scots mare, and a good mother to my children. And over time I have developed an honest affection for her. She is a good companion for long winter nights in the country. And she has some of her father's skills at the managing of affairs. Without which I suspect our present prosperity would not be the half of what it is."

To turn things around, to regain and restore and to prosper, has also involved him (as it must these days) in some duplicity, certain kinds of equivocation and betrayal. He regularly attends the parish church of the Church of England and, at some peril to his immortal soul, many might say, keeps to his Catholic faith secretly. Sometimes more furtively than secretly. For at times, and at peril to his mortal skin and bones, priests in disguise come and go from his house. Hearing confession and saying Mass.

When they talked of these things, when Barfoot came (somehow) home at last from his wars and foreign adventures, crippled, but healing, and they would walk together in the long gallery of his brother's house, himself hobbling and twisted and lame at first, but (slowly, slowly, *slowly* it seemed to him at the time) then able to walk a little and then well enough and then as well as anyone and then to go forth riding with his brother to enjoy ancient, simple country pleasures of hawking and hunting. Or maybe merely to spend the idle hours of an afternoon in good-weather fishing . . . When they talked, in the gallery, at table, or sometimes side by side, resting on the leaning place of one of his brother's extravagant glass windows, his brother, who had remained these years at home and was, at least outwardly, unwounded, usually treated him with a kind of shy deference. As if the younger Barfoot were, by dint of hard experience alone, the elder and wiser of the two, the tutor. Teacher of world's wisdom, anyway.

"I suppose it is laughable," his brother told him, "a bright and resplendent irony (in your eyes), that I should risk my soul and hazard my everlasting life by the sin of pretending to be a faithful communicant of our Queen's heretical Church while, at the same time, professing inwardly to be Romish at my heart and, indeed, going to some lengths and standing in danger to prove it."

"I think you are not alone in this. There are many among us who do the same and must be quiet about it."

"How lonely they, too, must be in the midst of all their double dealing."

"What do the priests say?"

"Ah, well," he says, "it would take a philosopher to untangle all their sundry arguments. To some, the most precise men of our faith, I am a sinner, inescapable in perdition. For some—and I never know which they will be until they come calling here and hear my confession—I am beyond any redemption. Others, more flexible by nature or from experience, allow I am living in sin, but that it is a kind of a sacrifice, an offering up of myself for others and for the greater good. The greater good being, in most cases, I guess, offering them some solace and comfort and protection here in Babylon. Helping them to keep the straying flock together. Helping them to bring the sacraments to the scattered flock. These middlemen allow that what I am doing is sinful enough, but surely not beyond God's infinite power to forgive. And then there are a few—I confess my heart goes out most to them—who are just too weary and too busy and too fearful to concern themselves with fine and subtle points of theology. Leave all that to schoolmen, they say. Offer up all the good works that you can. Pray for strength and forgiveness and have faith in God's grace and charity."

"I like the last argument best. It's like a soldier's view of things. But what do you think?"

"William, my brother, my thoughts change from day to day, as much according to the weather and my digestion as anything else. Good weather and good bowels, and I am as happy with myself and God's world as a young calf at the teat. Comes a gray wet winter's day, my joints all needles and thorns and my bowels a shrunken knot calling for a clyster or a purge, and I can let myself imagine that God Himself, in much the same sort of mood, has shrugged and given up on us, His last few degenerate Catholic servants here in England, and has wandered off elsewhere leaving us to whatever fate Fortune decrees for us. But as to what I think . . ."

"Never mind, then. What are your best and most persuasive arguments when you are in session with yourself?"

"Well then, that, come what may, come what has been . . . and you know as well as I, though you have been spared years of the worst of it by being elsewhere . . ."

"True. I'll grant you that, brother. And will argue nothing. Except to remind you that I had precious few choices in my life, none that deeply appealed, and could not have done much differently than I have done even if I had known twice as much of the world and what it had to offer me."

"One of the Latin poets, I forget which one, said it wisely and well: 'No one gets to choose what yoke to wear.'"

"I might have known that tag myself (and even remembered the poet's name) if I had enjoyed your opportunity for schooling."

"William, William, William. You do envy me, don't you?"

"Sometimes."

"Consider that I envy you, as well. Here I stayed at home in the heart of the country, plotting and scheming like a moneylender, playing out my youth and life like a game of cards. And all the time I thought, with envy, of you. Yourself free of the burdens of obligation to family, free to be out in the world, to enjoy adventures . . ."

"Each and every one is indelibly marked on me. I am the book of my own life if anyone could read the language of scars."

"I have envied you every one of them. And envy you here and now at home, slowly healing. And with your health—I can feel it—comes the restless itch to move on again.

"And I must reconcile myself to dying old in my bed, if I am lucky. Do you envy me that?"

"Oh, I may have. Along with many other things. But my deepest envy has always been for your schooling. It has been a sore spot on a hard body. Get back to your argument."

"I can be brief and simple about it, believe me. It is much simplified and refined by now. That the fate of England and the fate of my much threatened Roman religion, *our* faith, William, are beyond any power I may have to influence in any important way. Time flows and goes as it will. And I cannot change that. But, God willing, I could hold this family together. Put it back together when it was all broken in pieces. And I have done that, thanks be to God. I can restore and have restored our family to proper standing and local influence. I have accumulated some wealth, besides my wife's, in my time, honorably, and not by shrewd or hard dealing. And I consider myself not the possessor of that wealth, but only the steward of it for others. For my kin and for my servants and my tenants, all of whom I am bound to serve."

"And to lead."

"That goes without saying.

"William, if I were not duplicitous, the Queen's fines would have made us all paupers in no time."

"True."

"Would it not be a sin to squander God's gifts on the pride of being virtuous?"

"You will get no argument from me."

"Good. Because, as soon as you are well, I have some plans for you."

"I thought that might be so."

And so there is a fine house now, towers and turrets and half glass in the latest fashion. And there are fertile lands. And there are children and grandchildren and those of the other brothers and sisters. All of whom can go to school. And some of whom, Barfoot thinks and hopes, may have the blessed good fortune to turn out to be scholars and suchlike if they will. The choice may well be mostly theirs. One day there may be priests again in the family. Who knows?

Meantime Captain Barfoot, wifeless and childless, so far as he knows, is home from the wars and living in the City.

Meantime the world is older and the Queen is suddenly very old. She is failing, they say. And there is every chance that, at the least, the True Faith will once again be allowed, tolerated, if not restored, with the coming of a Successor to the throne. Such a Successor may even be a Roman Catholic. But even if this is not to be so, surely the next Prince to rule in England will most urgently need the loyalty and goodwill and good service of all those English Catholics who, with the exception of their immutable faith and religious practice, have been, so far, steadfast and loyal against all enemies.

So, anyway, his brother believes. So also many of his fellows, loyal Englishmen of the Old Faith. Patience and caution and fortitude and shrewdness (together with the Queen's own patient and cautious and shrewd policy of asking for no more in religion than an outward and visible conformity), taken with a well-maintained distance from the Court and all of its sly doings and undoings, its plots and stratagems, have spared his brother, and some others like him, from the fate that has befallen some who looked for other remedies than time to cure their grievances.

What his brother believes and hopes seems to Barfoot both reasonable and possible.

Which is exactly why he cannot imagine that any of it will come to pass. You and I know Barfoot better than his brother does. We know how he sits so close to despair that he dangles his feet over the edge of it and sometimes looks down into the eternal fires of hell. But, out of the love and loyalty of family and out of a soldier's habit of obedience to lawful command, he is willing to serve his brother well, to honor and obey his brother's hopeful vision, even if all of his experience seems to deny the validity of it.

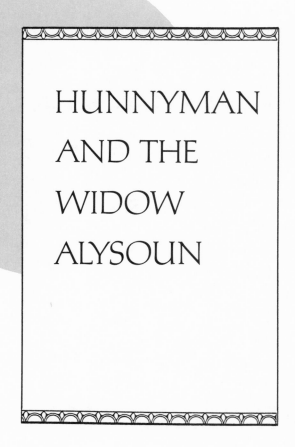

HUNNYMAN AND THE WIDOW ALYSOUN

—And so, by the time I was allowed to take leave of the
aforesaid young gentleman, I was so weary from the long night of
it—and, I must admit, fapped from drinking sack, cross-eyed and
thick-tongued—that I had all but forgotten how it was that I had
come to be there in the first place. At the end, with the last of the
candles melted or smoking farewell and the first sounds of the morning
stirring in the house above us, we had a show of good manners, he and
I. I took him to be a kind of a cousin or a dear old friend. We embraced
and I kissed him on both smooth rosy cheeks.

"Did you hug and kiss his two bears, too?"

—Please, woman, at least permit me to finish without more interruptions. May I?

"Pray continue."

—I could never in my lifetime be drunk enough from anything to choose freely to embrace those fellows. And I will venture that no one, man or woman, wife or poxy whore, has kissed either one of them since their mothers . . . no, let us say mother in the singular. For they must be brothers, if only as bastards. They are so much alike in their ugliness that they could only have been bred out of the same old sow. To believe that there could be two separate women capable of conceiving and giving birth to such creatures would be to allow that at last this late and degenerate age of the world has found the human form most worthy to stand as a figure for it.

"Lord, what are you saying?"

—That no one can have kissed either one of them since even their mother gave up the practice as a nasty habit while they were still cooing and farting in their cradles.

"Now that you have taken employment from their master, I imagine I shall see them sooner or later."

—Oh, I do hope not.

Her strong, long-fingered, sharp-nailed hand, jewels on thumb and fingers, drums lightly on his belly and plays idly wherever it will. And soon, sooner than he believes likely or possible, a limp spent fellow (the best part of him, she says) will waken from languor and rise up to stand straight and proud and tall like a, yes!, member of the Queen's own guard. This woman is a wonder, no question about that. But has she no shame or modesty at all?

—Yet . . .

He tries to continue as if they were still sitting at table for dinner in the company and presence of servants and companions, eating and drinking well, as always, and talking lightly of this and that.

—I left behind that strange and mysterious cellar chamber (perhaps the haunt of some necromancer or alchemist, another Faustus, who can say?).

—Led away by his beasts, blindfolded I was this time. And not much the wiser, maybe even less so, than when I had unwillingly arrived there. Nonetheless intact and somewhat richer than I had been before. And with the promise, at least, of more to come.

She smiles. Full wet lips and beautiful white teeth.

"And what will you promise me?"

A slant of pale afternoon light from the leaded window, where the hard rain lashed only a little while ago, gilds her smooth bare shoulders and her high firm breasts. Like a mermaid whose upper parts are made of gold.

An hour before now they were at table and enjoying an excellent dinner. Good food and good wine, as always at her house. Now they are enjoying the privacy of her best bed.

When he undressed her to reveal the remarkable white and gold, fine sugar and shine of her skin, as smoothly unblemished as a milkmaid's, only a brief while ago, and then, as the rain fell heavy outside, half danced and half pushed her to her bed, and both of them laughing like children, even before the two of them had begun the intricate business of untying and loosening all his points, setting free his neat little rows of buttons and hooks, he suddenly poured out the contents of his velvet purse, releasing a kind of spurt of bright coins which fell across the mound of her belly. She winced at the cold of those coins. (To which, out of simple pride and vanity, he had added his evening's earning from false dicing.) And then she laughed out loud. Not like a laughing child. More like a witch. If, in truth, witches laugh as they do when they are played by young fellows onstage. And when he knelt in the sweet surf of sheets beside her (. . . if he were a flea, then she would be acres of ripe grain in a light wind, freighted with the scent of flowers from somewhere) to begin his kissing with her navel, she gently rubbed a handful of gold and silver coins back and forth amid the blond hair between her legs.

"You are too trusting. You should be more doubtful and suspicious."

—I am doubtful and suspicious in all things. Careful as a hare.

"Do you doubt me, too? Am I much suspected?"

She is kneading now, smoothing and gripping and pinching as if he were fresh dough and soon to be baked bread. As if the best and brainless part of himself were her mute prisoner who must somehow learn to answer all her questions or else go directly to the gallows. This poor fellow will soon cry out everything he knows and ever has known.

—Nay, madame. Try as I will and must, I have never yet found any good reason to doubt and distrust you. But it comes to mind that, by the same token, I have no good cause to believe you either.

"Is this cause enough?"

He gasps out loud from her ferocious grip.

—I believe! Madame, I believe! Consider me your convert.

"Then we must celebrate your confirmation with due ceremony."

—How?

"Let us begin with the seal of a kiss."

Her soft lips, her sweet mouth. Her tongue touching, teasing his. Breasts cool against hairs of his chest. Hands smoothing and stroking the small of her back, the larger curving below. Guardsman now standing stiffly on duty. Wild with thirst. Thirst for honey like a bear. And then (now!) commences the most ancient of all dances, the sweet and sweaty country dance of Adam and Eve.

—Alysoun . . . Alysoun . . . My sweet . . . irresistible . . . Alysoun . . . !

He knows better, to be sure. But nevertheless he now listens while a serious voice, his own, asks him what could be better or more wonderful either in this world or the next?

For certain he knows that, even as this woman moves like a mermaid beneath him, she will be just as busy (and elsewhere) in her brain as a blacksmith at his anvil. While she transforms him, body and mind, from master (at least of himself) to her humble servant, dazzled by all of this flashing of white and gold, these thrilling and outrageous adventures of flesh and bones, poising, like a ship's boy atop the highest mast (his own mast), riding upon the pitching and rolling peak of the promise of unspeakable ecstasy, finer and keener than any fantasy had prepared him for, even as she deftly reduces and simplifies him from all manner of mystery, even unto himself, to become a common catalog of common hungers, she, herself, unlike so many others of her sex, being not the least indifferent to her own appetites and pleasures, nor troubling to pretend to be so, she, then, seeming no less eagerly, avidly engaged than he may be, and not seeking to disguise herself behind any of the veils, false or true, of womanly modesty, nevertheless managed always somehow to keep and defend some locked and secret place, a hidden chamber in and of herself, for herself alone. He pictures it as a kind of counting room wherein, like a wealthy city merchant (and is she not, truth be told, rich enough and avid to be richer, a kind of merchant, not merely of her corporeal self and priceless goods, but also merchant in fact as well?), she takes continual inventory of her treasure even as she makes plots and plans, schemes and strategies for survival and for ever greater gain.

Still young now, younger than he, and though his life may sometimes seem tediously long, he is still a young man, she was more than half a child when her mother and father were able to marry her off to the man who was at least double her age and probably more.

Is this some newfangled kind of story? Not in this age where, as the preachers will tell us if we trouble to listen, profit and loss, comfort and discontent, here and now and for a future not much further, at the furthest, than next Plow Monday, are the things that capture our hearts and souls above and beyond any hope of heaven or fear of hell. Here at the end of world, if prophets and soothsayers tell us truth (and who can imagine the world, old and sick and frail as it is, continuing very much longer with or without us?), we have become, as Scripture foretells, a corrupt and degenerate people, following, like wild dogs on the heels of prey, the devices and desires of our own hearts. No health in us. Which means we can be expected to say and do, indeed to think it as well, anything that serves the purpose of satisfying our boundless appetites and inestimable vanities. Limited only by the simple laws of Nature against which we everlastingly chafe and complain.

Who among us, if he could make and sprout wings and fly, would not shit upon all those beneath him?

There are no limits but Nature's own to our vanity, cunning, and depravity.

Is that not what the most radical of the Puritan preachers, in whatever dark corners or secret places they are driven to preach their Gospel, tell us? No matter, it is what Hunnyman, neither preacher nor scholar, has come to believe from the study of himself. That we are creatures, not of four humors as the learned doctors insist, but of every kind of animal appetite and cruelty. That we cover the naked animal, a monstrous creature, which is ourself in all the finery and fashions of vanity. That we are doomed.

No matter.

Return to this writhing and abandoned Alysoun. Who was once, he can believe it, a simple young village girl who had her youth and

good health and a remarkable bodily beauty to allow her to overcome
the burden of her station and the absence of any adequate dowry.

Comes then, at just the appropriate time, blushing time of her first
blooming, this widower, a printer and a traveling bookseller from the
City. Traveling far and deep into the kingdom in order to sell books
and pamphlets to country folk. And, yes, to try to forget grief and
disappointment. For when his wife died in childbirth, the child died,
too. He was a prosperous publisher, too, and very well esteemed
among the elders of the Stationers' Company. Not as wealthy as some,
yet possessing a steady and reliable income from the patents to print
various and sundry schoolbooks and texts, also books of helpful and
practical counseling for the common people far removed from the
polish and knowledge of the City. And, always profitable over time,
certain honorable gatherings of sermons and homilies by the best
preachers of the Church of England which thousands of country
families might read with spiritual profit and many a country preacher
might well find inspiring and useful, from theme down to the
placement of commas, for his own sermons. He would not hazard the
risk of publishing an occasional elegant and frivolous romance or even,
for that matter, poems and pamphlets which were safely dedicated to
the kind of noble patron who was able and willing to support such an
enterprise. Never a play in any form. For he was, as he ought to be,
a dedicated enemy to the vice-ridden stage. Still, since there were and
are only some fifty or so fully licensed printers in all of England, even
a man of indifferent ambition and cautious aspiration could make a
good living. Which he did. Secure, if unadventurous, and never
having to put much, if anything, in pawn or in hazard. Not even for
the sake and prospect of great gains. He was happy always with a
modest profit for his goods and labors. He gave secure employment to
others; was firm yet generous to his apprentices and journeymen. He
saved all that he could and was never, seriously, a debtor or creditor.
Oh, it was sometimes, in brief and bad times, necessary to go to a
goldsmith (though never a Dutchman or, Lord save us, a Jew) and
borrow under bond and for too much, indeed usurious, interest. But
as frugal and careful as he was fortunate, he was able to pay off these
debts promptly. And so he had come to own his own house,
tall-storied and solidly built, once a fine gentleman's place in days
gone by (they say), and by this printer very well maintained, kept

better than before. Here at his house, in Castle Baynard Ward on Knightrider Street, he had his printing presses on the ground floor, and he and his people lived in chambers of the upper stories. This place, is as you know, not far at all from the south side of Paul's Churchyard where, beneath the sign of a pair of running greyhounds, his bookstall was and is. And it is also only a brisk, short walk from Stationers' Hall.

Whatever they saw and believed in the village, here was a man of middle years and of earned good repute, more than reasonably well to do (rich as a lord by their measurement), possessing a future which seemed to promise him, barring always any unforeseen counterturnings of Fortune's wheel, a gradual accumulation of this world's good things. More than his share of worldly goods. So that at death he would pass on to his heirs—and how he longed to father a brood of healthy children!—enough for them to be much better off and more certain of themselves and their futures than anything he had known.

When he first saw the fair young girl, her fresh perfection as rare as any he had ever seen or imagined, her sturdy, healthy brothers and sisters, and caught the unmistakable glint of greed in her parents' eyes (how could they dissemble and conceal such a thing from a successful London printer and bookseller?), he knew that he would have her for himself, knowing that the only bargain to be struck would be the price; and perfectly willing, out of eagerness to possess her and not to waste precious time as well as money, he made them an offer, which must have seemed to these country folk who seldom have or handle more than pennies in all their lives, magically extravagant. A similar beneficence entrapped the parish priest. And, somewhat more expense in the long run, for the fellow had no serious intention of repayment, he won over the village landlord, a fat and impecunious old knight, with a much needed loan. Ostensibly for repairs on his crumbling manor house, the money was frittered away in no time at all upon lighthearted, merry times and strong drink.

"I cost the old man, my late lamented husband, about as much as a fine jewel. Which was how he took me, anyway, to be his jewel and pride," she has told Hunnyman. "Well, I gave him his pleasures, all he could manage at his time of life, as soon as I learned what his pleasures might be. But I learned other things, many other things, as well and quickly, too. And, even before I was a fully grown woman, he had changed from a pedagogical master to a doting old fool whom I could and did lead wherever I pleased like an ox with a nose ring."

—He would have been like so many others among those old men, Hunnyman has told her. All those old fellows of the age and generation of our Queen—long may she live and reign—if not even older.

—For these days many of them are living to be very old, too old to believe. Too many are living beyond a ripe old age, if you ask me. And too many of them are, alas, our betters. Are masters of us and rulers over us in everything.

Fatherless, himself, meaning not that he was a common haystack bastard, by any means, but that his father was dead and gone of a fever long before Hunnyman was old enough to have stored up any clear memories of him, he has always listened attentively to old men, studied them as a scholar pores over a text. And he believes now that he knows what they think and feel and what they will say and do before they do it. He has studied how they move about, how they carry their bodies as, day by day, the body becomes a peddler's sack, well stuffed with aches and pains. He has learned, and can mimic well, how they will set down that sack of old bones on a low joint stool in the chimney corner. Will sit and sigh a long sigh, as if they imagined they could breathe out and set free the imprisoned soul to fly away, free and light, to heaven. And he can imitate the ways in which they collect themselves, carefully, one stiff leg and then the other one, as if all their parts were strung together like those of a puppet. Groaning, as much from habit as pain or need, as the old body demands full allegiance again. He has lain wide awake and listened to their troubled phlegmy breathing as they sleep and dream. Heard the soft whimpering that follows after a deep breath, a sound like an old hound dog who is dreaming of coursing the hare again. All this study and looking and listening, Hunnyman had told himself, has been mainly for the purpose of making his performance in the roles of old men in stage plays appear more natural. In the latest English players' fashion; for they all will be natural in performance these days. And it may be that he has accomplished that much. What's for certain is that his close study of the ways of old men has left him somewhat fearful and confused. Like many a foolish, thoughtful man, Hunnyman wants to live forever without ever growing old.

—These old fellows, our fathers and grandfathers, came out of hard and bleak times, if we are to believe them. It was all a turbulent and topsy-turvy world when England was torn in two and even those two parts were split up and divided into many angry fractions.

—What they longed for, first and foremost, was peace and quiet. They prayed for calm weather. And those who have managed to survive, even to prosper, cannot ever shake off the memory of their lean years.

—Always they were and are exceedingly cautious in thought, word, and deed. Committed to prudence. Dedicated to the strict reining in of ambition and aspiration. Most especially determined to leash in any outward and visible signs of either or both of these things among all of those, meaning all of us, younger and inferior to themselves.

—They were pious, too. Exemplary models of civic piety. Whether they follow the old religion (most secretly on account of the penalties) or profess to believe in the newly discovered, or restored, versions of the faith, they are equally pharisaical. Be humble and strong in your humility, they tell us. Honor your elders and your betters—and your elders are all your betters. Be steadfast and modest in all things. Especially in all of the outward and visible things and especially by the appropriate dress and proper decorum for your station and vocation.

—And the truth is that these old hearts do honor the outward and visible far more than the inward and spiritual. They would have us act like grateful children to them for the most part of our lives. They would have us to be obedient dependents upon them and their goodwill.

—And, God's body wounds, I cannot abide the hypocritical old rogues!

—Picture it. Here am I and I must stand humble, my hat in my hand, before some fat, proud London merchant. Picture him seated in huge-arsed comfort upon a huge woolsack of money, busily counting and totting up the sums and totals of the rack rents owing to him from lands he has purchased with the orts of his extravagant profits. And given half a chance, he, exactly like any and all of the others, will sternly urge it upon me that I must ever be thoughtful and careful not to lay up for myself treasures upon this earth. Lest, thereby, I should lose my passport to heaven.

Alysoun's sharp, strong laughter when he says these things, and others in the same vein, much the same, never fails to reassure him.

Her predictable laughter at his habitual and extravagant dismissal of all that is old and gray and comfortable in the state of hypocrisy serves to assuage an inner pain also. For, if only out of ingrained lifetime habit, itself strictly enforced by Law and penalties, he is as much a child of the Church of England as of these times and enough of a true believer to fear, from time to time, for the future of his immortal soul. Likewise he fears that the fathers and grandfathers, despite all kinds of hypocrisy and double-dealing, may have been correct. Fears that the way of life they advertise may prove to be best after all. He is left wondering (deeply, secretly, to be sure) if all his ambitions and desires, his learned player's craft, the dozen and one quick-footed stratagems which he is required to plan and then to execute simply to stay alive, are all folly. Wondering next if his whole life might not be called a waste. Then wondering if his fortune can ever be good. Pondering sometimes, alone on the shores of sleeping and dreaming, if it is not already much too late to save himself. Or, as the case may be, to be saved.

In that sense, as you can see, her harsh and cynical laughter is merciful.

She is harder than he is. Surely she is more fearless and much less troubled by the many things that can cause him fear and pain. He has yet to hear her say one word concerning heaven or hell or the inhabitants thereof except in an oath or a jest. All these sermons and debates, fine points of divinity, are of no importance and have no meaning for her except as a proper and popular subject for her printing and bookselling.

"So long as they go on preaching their sermons and some people wish to read then and are willing to pay for their pleasure, you will find me publishing these things. But you and I both know I would gladly do the same thing for Turks and Jews, infidels and atheists, if there were any market for their wares."

—And if it were a safe enterprise under the Law.

"You trouble yourself about safety too much. It might be wise, prudent at least, if you held high office or were a great lord or some greedy courtier of the Queen. But for a man like yourself, a baseborn fellow with nothing to lose except your insatiable appetites and your unappeasable bad habits, it betokens nothing but weakness."

—And my greatest strength is that I have you close by always to remind me of my faults.

"And your greatest folly is that you too seldom listen to me."

—No, lady, it is not true. Whether you speak folly or wisdom, you can be sure that I hear and weigh your every word.

Yet she remains in many ways mysterious to him. He can only vaguely imagine, with no sense of certainty, whatever it is she believes in and lives for. Not her creed and catechism, that is for certain. True, she will dress herself, demure in expensive clothing, a picture of humility in the richest fabrics and only lightly bejeweled. And then you and all her neighbors can see her go out, this dutiful and prosperous widow. Accompanied by her little band of servants to the parish church of St. Mary Magdalen. She makes a show of worshipping there for more often than the Law requires. She is generous in charitable giving, well beyond the necessary tithing, and she is well respected for it. Honored for piety, too. And when some distinguished or celebrated preacher comes to preach a sermon to the crowd at Paul's Cross, especially if he happens to be such a one as she can well conceive will bring a good profit from the publishing and selling of his sermon, then, dressed every modest and expensive inch as a proper widow, she will arrive early to stand in clear view of the fellow in the great stone pulpit there; and she will straight-faced listen and nod, completely attentive for as long a time as the man can rant and ruff.

In one pretty ear and out the other.

He, if it is his misfortune to attend on her and be there too, will be even more attentive and wrinkle-browed with intensity of concentration. For it will fall his duty, as a player trained in the quick study and memorization of windy speeches, to learn the sermon by heart or, anyway, as close as can be. So that if there is no written text, there can be one promptly enough, whether the preacher—presuming he is not so powerful and influential as to be dangerous—may like it or not.

Truth is, Alysoun has never allowed her quick mind to be burdened with weighty and ponderous questions of religion. Not for her life and death debates on such implacable questions as the nature of transubstantiation, justification by faith or by good works, the exegesis of Scripture, or the power and glory of the Bishop of Rome.

Nor, for so much as one delicate wrinkle of her beautifully smooth brow, will she for one moment seriously consider such urgent questions, ones which can cost a living and sometimes a life, as what the proper rights and privileges of bishops should be. And whether one set of vestments is more ostentatious and papistical than another. And should there be kneeling or standing during prayer and at the Holy Communion. None of this is a matter of any concern to her except as a publisher.

"Do I not look as well whether kneeling or standing? What does it matter to me?"

She will always do whatever must be done. And her first thought is to render unto Caesar and be done with it.

—I think, madame, if you went to Rome, you would kneel down and kiss the Pope's ring and think nothing of it.

"I might even kiss the Pope's bare arse. But if you want to find out, you shall have to accompany me to Rome and see for yourself."

By which she means, pure and simple, that if he wants to know what she might do in Rome, or even at Paul's Head Tavern at the end of this street, why then, he must take her there first. By which she also means to remind him, as if he did not already know it every moment, waking or sleeping, that whatever she may seem to be at the dinner table or here and now in her high-posted feather bed may not be safely taken as any indication, sign, or clue as to who she might be and what she might do in another place and at another time.

Like the wondrous chameleon, she is whatever color light and air allow.

You may well ask, you are entitled to: Why hasn't her complete hypocrisy (in so many different things) offended him?

Well, he is hooked like a fish to the line she has cast, and he knows it. Knowing it well, he nevertheless sincerely believes that in some eccentric fashion, beyond any explication, she is no double-dealer. He believes that she is not faithful to anything under sun and moon and this side of the rainbow except for herself. But, ah!, in that simple and single faith she must be a saint.

Though she may be stronger and harder than he is—as he is the first to admit now that she has taught him so well what all of his weaknesses are and where they can be found—they nevertheless have much in common. Not only beauty of face and body. For he, himself, is uncommonly fair and handsome. Else it is hard to imagine what pleasure she would find in him. But also they have come here to London, the beating heart of this kingdom, from much the same kind of quiet and yawning village life. Parish church and manor house; guildhall and schoolroom; barn and bakehouse and brewhouse; dovecote and deer park; market fairs and church ales. World where both lives and events move mostly (barring sickness or catastrophe) at the stately, lazy rhythm of a haycart pulled home by an old horse. All things timed to that slow mill wheel turning of the seasons. World of almost ceaseless chores and hard labor. Small hopes, true, but smaller fears. A world where memory is more cherished and trusted than any red new sunrise.

—In all my youth, he has told her, there was only one marvelous thing that happened in my town.

He calls it a town and she never challenges him on that point; though they both know it was no more than a large village at a river's edge. Perhaps it had been truly a town once long ago when ships still could come up and down that slow, narrow river.

—It was the time when a great bolt of lightning, out of a fair and clear and unthreatening sky, struck and set afire and burned down to the very roots the oldest and largest oak tree in town, the one that stood nearest to our church.

"Once, when I was very small, it snowed again after May Day."

—Nay, you cannot say so! Truly?

"Would I lie to you?"

—I should hope not.

What happened to them both, what changed everything forever for them, was London. They came to the City at about the same time, give or take a year.

He came as an apprentice in a scruffy little company of players. Who had walked, slow and sure, behind their heavy-loaded, bright-painted, high-wheeled cart, crossing and crisscrossing England's length and breadth. Performing old and familiar plays in country innyards and markets, in the halls of manor houses, on village greens, in the guildhalls of country towns, and even, once in a while, in some places properly named and called cities.

A pretty boy he was, then, slight and skinny, though tough as old saddle leather and already able to mimic the swagger of a veteran soldier or the lazy, provocative stroll of sunburnt mariners home at last from improbable voyages and adventures. And meantime did he not know by heart all the words of more than a dozen stage plays? Could he not make people laugh when he willed to? Make them cry real tears when tears were called for? And, by God and thank you, Lord, he could summon up applause from an audience as if they had just witnessed, not some weary play, but the public working of a miracle.

And had he not, by then, seen the best and worst of England?

No, he had see neither one. For he had not yet come to London.

Hunnyman hopes and believes that he will always be able (at least until the light of memory, like a summer twilight, begins to fade irresistibly into everlasting dark) to reconstruct the time of summoning to the City. It was in late spring or the earliest part of the summer. He cannot recall for certain, only that Easter was past, behind them, and the days were warming then and each day a little longer.

—We had been wandering and working for a time in Norfolk, a flat place to be, for sure. We then performed successfully and earned some shillings in Ely, where there had been no companies of players for quite a while. Next we followed along the pathway of the River Ouse all the way to King's Lynn at the edge of the sea. Many fine buildings and houses there, good signs of prosperity. And suddenly we were possessed by high hopes; for we had somehow been able to arrange to begin with our first performance at the huge old Guildhall of St. George. High hopes and cheerful feelings we had. But something, and I have never know what it may have been, went wrong. Went badly wrong. Sweet turned sour. Looking back on it now, I think it may have been the play. Some old clownish farce. Some play which had always wakened mirth in the distant villages. But must have been too bumptious for the folk in a place like King's Lynn. Where half the merchants had been to the Continent to trade and more than once. Maybe it was simply our fashion of playing, the old-fashioned style, with much ranting and gesturing and strutting about, oh, far away from what is to be seen nowadays. Or perhaps it was our worn and tattered costumes, faded things which by that time in the tour looked more like the well-pawed and often fingered leftovers at the Houndsditch clothes market than anything you would expect to have to look at if you had paid a penny for the privilege.

—Well, now. I ask myself. What had they really expected to see?

The Lord Admiral's Company? The Chamberlain's Men and suchlike? We never made no claim to be anything more than what we were—a company of traveling players, with a patron of no special importance. We were a hardworking crew, doing our business better than many. Because we had to do so or starve. Surely we were better than many of the players they had seen in King's Lynn for a long time.

—Perhaps they had already suffered through too many clumsy performances by faulty or indifferent companies and were now waiting for the time to enjoy some revenge.

—Or it may be, I sometimes think now, that they were weary to the very edge of death, tired of each other and of everything else in that far corner of our kingdom. Or it may also be that the natives and inhabitants of King's Lynn are naturally ill tempered. I believe I might be in a choleric or melancholic humor if Providence had arranged it for me to spend my life in King's Lynn.

—Nevertheless, and no matter what the cause of it may have been, they were certainly primed and fully loaded to despise strangers on that day. And so we earned more orange peels and rotten eggs and nutshells, more hoots and jeers and hisses, than any kind of applause.

—In the end (which came early) the adlerman gave us only part of the money that was due us and hurried us out of the town and along the road toward Norwich with stern threats of whipping and even worse.

—It had commenced to rain (perhaps it is always just beginning to rain at King's Lynn), and we were trudging along, all as wet and disconsolate as could be. When, lo and behold, here came, riding hard, a post-horse, with the rider wearing the proud livery of some great lord, oh, greater by far than our down-at-the-heels patron. Pulled up sharply and saluted our master, white-haired Henry, and presented him with a letter to read. Henry, a vain man (like so many players) if a kind one and a good one, was forced to put on his spectacles, and then someone had to hold a cloak over his head to keep off the pelting rain while he read it.

—Now then. When our old master emerged from beneath his wet wool canopy, his smile could have lit those gray skies of Norfolk like a flash of lightning. Perhaps there was lightning at that moment. If not, there should have been. Henry stood there, smiling like a Bedlamite, and waving his arms like a windmill, calling out to us in words that might as well have been Turkish for all that we could either hear or comprehend them. He was dancing a stiff little jig there with his muddy boots in the muddy roadway, waving the paper from which ink was already running and melting in large black drops, but from which the proud, beribboned seal glowed like a large rose in candlelight and looked likely to last out this rain and every other kind of weather until the end of the world.

—We all run up to gather around him and his dance. And the tall postrider, proud in his badge and livery and smiling beneath his broad-brimmed hat, nodded and nodded. None of us noticed how the cart had gone on, disappearing around a deep-rutted curve. For, you see, William, who always drove the cart, was more than half-deaf, as was the old sag-bellied, swayback mare who pulled it. And so in the rain, dozing there with the reins loose and slack in his hands, William had seen and heard nothing of what had happened.

—And I was sent off running after him through the mud.

—Wait, William! Wait! I shouted. Pull up and wait. We are turning back now! We are going to perform in London!

Oddly, he has no recollection of the journey to the City. He might as well have been walking in his sleep. A kind of dream then, seeing nothing at hand, only a vision in his head, until he woke to the real world when he had already passed through Bishopsgate and into the walled City. Waking from dreaming to find himself in a place more dreamlike than any he had or could have imagined. A forest of towers and spires and tall buildings. A blinding dazzle of colors and brightness. Waves of rich strange odors. And the noise . . . The noise! All those street cries. Pounding of hooves, creaking of carts. And music. Music from here . . . from there. And voices and voices and voices. All of them speaking at once.

And then another voice, his own, spoke to him as if whispering in his ear. He heard himself solemnly swear that he would now make this place his home and himself, one way or the other, by hook or crook, the master of it.

Which was simply childish. And he knew it even then, already discarding childhood as he was losing his past. He knew in his heart he would never live to be master of much, if anything. That was foreordained. But something in the wild energy of the City challenged him beyond the limits of good sense. He swore his high oath of mastery as a kind of joyous tribute that must be paid. And the true meaning of it was his high hope of never being mastered.

—And, in God's good truth, though Fortune has often turned against all my hopes and wishes, I am still here, a free man and young enough to hope to find my home here.

For Alysoun, childish bride of the old printer, it must have been very much the same. Except that, unlike Hunnyman, who had traveled across the country, she had until then been no farther away from hearthside than the nearest market town. London, from her first sight of it from Watling Street, coming up from the south, besieged and attacked the five gates of her five senses which were ready to surrender and welcome the experience. She was conquered in a matter of minutes.

As for her husband . . .

"He was a decent and gentle old man, kind and mannerly to me. He took time to teach me all that I know of many things and much more, too, than he ever knew he was teaching me."

Came to live in her commodious house on Knightrider Street. Every story of which had twice the space and more than that than what her whole family had enjoyed.

"And no need to share any of it with pigs and cows, either."

A place where even her husband's apprentices were apt to be older than she was. And where his older servants and companions were skeptical, suspicious of her. She astonished them by taking command of the household and by managing and maintaining all things, from the larder and stillroom to the laundry and sewing, and by doing so as well as or better than any gentlewoman born and trained to the tasks.

—How on earth did you do that?

"Just as I always had. I listened closely; I learned; I copied. Even as a little child I had been able to teach myself never to feel foolish or ashamed of myself for any unavoidable ignorance and inexperience. I was ever ready to learn. And I believed then, as I believe now, that if an art or craft can be taught and learned, then I can master it. To learn is worth any kind of pain or shame. Even as a child I knew I could learn new things, and quickly too, if only I set myself to it.

"And so I was bound and determined to do well in all ways as his wife and to keep him content as could be for as long as he lived. Which seemed to me not such a long time. I knew I would be a widow soon enough and I hoped and prayed that it would not be too soon. I hoped and prayed he would live long enough for me to learn what he knew of his printer's craft and of the world.

"Now then, it seemed to me that if I were ever to learn how to manage his craft and affairs, I would first have to free myself by mastering the easier arts and crafts of being a good wife and by maintaining his house and his goods and his servants in such an exemplary way that he would be completely content with me and willing to trust me.

"You swore your secret oath and I swore mine. I was set on my course, from which I never turned back, from the moment I crossed the threshold of this house for the first time.

"Do you believe that?"

—It would never occur to me to question it.

As they lie, then, half-asleep, lapped in soft sheets (and those sheets lightly perfumed with sweet herbs and flowers), they can hear dimly from the ground floor below the sound of voices rising as the printers and their helpers are beginning to work again this afternoon. Soon she will have to rise up and dress herself and descend from her chamber to attend to many things.

What she had done, then, in all due time and yet in less time than even she can easily believe it now, was to become a master of the domestic arts and next, one quick, bold step after the other, to learn the mysteries of his craft. First how to sell books at the stall in Paul's Yard. And next, having proved to him how she could increase his earnings and profits, she undertook to learn everything that she could about his affairs. And she learned all that he was able to teach her; for the fellow was soon convinced that she was a prodigy who could quickly learn anything and everything she set her mind to.

By the time he died, quietly enough and in this selfsame bed where Hunnyman and Alysoun have more than once enjoyed some pleasant, sporting recreation, she was able to send him off into the next world with the full knowledge and confidence that the estate he would leave behind him on this temporal strand, this transitory world, assets and income, had never yet been so ample and would surely be well and faithfully maintained. To her old husband, as to most elders of the Stationers' Company, all but an impecunious and envious few, she had proved herself to be a credit to their ancient and honorable craft.

She won over the impecunious and envious few, to grudging admiration, anyway, with her generosity and with long-term loans at better rates of interest than any London goldsmith would offer.

And she did not hesitate or stint, either, in the quality of the monument she endowed for her dead husband at the parish church. Where if you wish to, as Hunnyman has, you can go and see his solemn and unremarkable face well carved in stone and can read some unmemorable pious verses carved underneath.

It is all too good to be true. Hunnyman is the first to admit that. The twists and turns of a player's life have taught him the habit of reasonable suspicion in and of all things and most especially in the case of those things which appear to be most attractive. This habit, arising from training and experience, however, is often upset by his other, deeper habit of rarely, if ever, acting on his suspicions. Who that you have ever heard of has ever allowed that in the life of a player wisdom could grow and flower from experience?

Hunnyman first met her some time ago when his company, one of a series of unsuccessful acting companies under the patronage of unimportant and equally unsuccessful noblemen, left London to travel and perform in the countryside. Not, as would be sadly true a few years later, on account of Plague or of troubles with the Queen's Council or the City fathers. But because it was painfully clear that they faced a slow death by starvation if they tried to remain much longer in London and the suburbs. They had only old plays and not enough money (nor the prospect of any), even that slight sum, to hire themselves a petty poet or two to make some new ones.

"It may well be," someone in the company said then, "that that crowd of fastidious folks we so outraged and offended long ago at King's Lynn has finally packed up and come to London for a visit."

"No," said another. "Much more likely that they have given up and abandoned that wet, windy, godforsaken place and come here to live in London, where they are welcome to scorn and revile everything to their hearts' content."

Joseph Hunnyman was full grown, if not much more than a boy, and already a hired man in the company. Old Henry and others of the old group, all but a couple who had been apprentices at the same time he was, had gone on to other things or were, God save their souls, dead and buried. With a word and a little scene he could have demanded it and have been made a full sharer of the company. But he was too shrewd for that. What else would he have had a share of besides a full cargo of debts and obligations? And by then he was married to the dark-haired Margaret, the daughter of a cobbler, whose modest dowry had been spent before the birth of their firstborn—a son who was called Joseph also. And Margaret was heavy and close to time with the second child.

They were living at an inn in Holborn and performing shows in the yard there. The innkeeper, out of nothing more than a sense of charitable pity (he said), announced to them that he was prepared to offer them the benefit of some wholesome, menial work in his service to pay for their keep and chambers. Earlier he had been content to contract for a part of their profits. But part of nothing is nothing, and the time had come to leave City for country. Where they could, sooner or later, always find some place where people might be pleased enough to pay money to see them.

Came, then, this handsome gentlewoman (it seemed) directly to the inn, together with one of her servingmen, to seek him out.

She had come, she told him, because as a woman who enjoyed a well-written and well-performed stage play as much as any other sort of vulgar entertainment, she had witnessed him in performance more than once. And she had much enjoyed his interpretation and playing of one role and another.

He was at once too handsome and young and too vain to be either astonished or doubtful. Or, for that matter, even much pleased. For it was not the first time that a woman, sometimes a respectable woman of good character, had sought him out to tell him how much she admired his art. He knew well enough what aliens and foreigners so often said: how there are no women anywhere in the world who are as independent, as free-spirited, and, of course and consequently, as unruly as the women of England. How they will go forth from their houses, with or without their husbands, and most likely with or without their husbands' permissions, to go wherever they please in London. Even to stage plays. Still, he had never yet met one of that tribe so elegant to behold and so obviously desirable (if only to the imagination) as this one. Like every other fond fool since Adam, he had fancied that such a time would come, that somewhere or other there was someone who was entirely worthy of him, able to recognize and to admire in an instant his virtues and charms, and who was waiting only for the proper time and the appropriate occasion to discover him.

From which discovery, be sure of it, anything and everything might come to pass.

Not wishing, at that moment, to be interrupted by Margaret and his toddling son, and not wishing to encounter the innkeeper, either, he suggested that they should repair to a nearby tavern for a glass or two of malmsey.

The truth is, the woman had a reasonable proposal to make. She was, she began, a printer's widow, etc., etc. Managing her late husband's affairs and his estate. And not without some success at it. Doing well in all things saving one. She had found, as yet, no expeditious way or means to sell her books and pamphlets in the country. As her husband, may he rest in peace, had done so well in years gone by. True, most London printers were busy enough—and she was among the busiest—to ignore that old-fashioned practice. Profits were too small for all the trouble. Too much effort and expense for too little gain. An old story. Ah, yes. Yet, on the other hand, who was she, a widow on her own, to spurn any kind of gain however small it might be? And she had been thinking often lately that, what with all of this schooling of young people (even the girls!) in England in this good Queen's reign, why, there might be many more people, of all kinds and conditions, than there used to be who would be glad to purchase useful books and pamphlets and suchlike. If only they were there to be bought . . .

Seemed to her, the more she considered it, that honest and lawful travelers—for instance, an acting company—moving hither and thither and passing through many places in a short time, might well be able to do her some good service by also dealing as booksellers. In return for which she was prepared to offer them a share of the profits. If any. True, they could not hold a lawful license for it. As she understood the Law. But that was no serious matter at all. Truth is, is it not, that they ran a far greater risk of the Law for being common players, even though licensed and wearing the livery of some patron.

And here her servingman produced an elegant parchment document, richly embellished with many legal terms in Latin and Law French, and decorated with fat wax seals and bright ribbons.

She could bond him as her very own agent.

Which piece of expensive parchment, without any valid or lawful authority as far as she knew or cared, ought nevertheless to suffice in any dealings with any country constable or justice of the peace that she had ever known.

"You might not guess it, on account of my City clothes and ways, but I was born and schooled and brought up in a far country village. A place you will never have heard of."

"Well, if it is in England," he bragged over the rim of his wineglass, "I have no doubt that, one time or another, I have performed on your very village green. It is all the more certain if your home place is sufficiently obscure."

She laughed. "Never in all my life did we see any entertainers there, as far as I can remember, except for a one-legged juggler and, to be sure, our very own clumsy, stiff-legged Morris dancers. And once we ourselves performed a play of Abraham and Isaac, partly in the church and partly on the green."

He smiled and, truly without thought or any serious intention, touched and patted her hand on the table, tentative and reassuring.

"As a native-born son of this great City," he said, "let me tell you that I took you to be born and raised here, too."

To his genuine surprise, then, she took his hand in hers, her warm and strong hand, with her pale blue eyes, long-lashed and unblinking, not seeming to be looking for or at anything else but his own.

For a while afterward Joseph Hunnyman would well remember that woman's hand. The smooth feel of it, the strength. Those pale eyes, their dangerous light. Even while poor Margaret was still living and acting altogether the part of his good wife, he would sometimes allow himself to imagine that warm, soft, strong, long-fingered, avaricious hand exploring his body's most secret places. Those bright eyes stripping away all his disguises. And he, too, being allowed to enjoy the treasure of her nakedness.

When he thought things like these, often even as he and Margaret were coupled together in their own bed, he would be ashamed of himself. But he could not help himself. Perhaps he was bewitched.

To sweeten her bookselling proposal, the woman produced from her purse and offered him a certain sum of money, here and now in advance. To be kept by him whether or not he was ever able to sell so much as one book or a pamphlet.

And so it was that sweet reason prevailed. Reason, together with the prospect of profit in the course of a long hard journey which might otherwise bring in very little. Yes, to be sure, he would cheerfully add one large chest of her books and pamphlets to the other baggage to be carried in their cart.

Agreement was sealed with a firm, manly handshake. And they stood up from the tavern table. While her servingman paid the reckoning, she stepped close to him, sharing briefly with him all the sweet and probably wicked promises of her perfume and that smile of perfect teeth. He suddenly longed to hold her body and to kiss her lips. Yet never imagined he would do so.

And now, in her bed, private in her bedchamber, she strikes him a blow in the ribs with the sharp point of her elbow.

"Wake up, Hunnyman! You are snoring out loud."

—I am awake, wide awake.

"Then time for us both to be up and be about our business."

Next moment they assist each other with the ordeal of dressing their bodies for the world.

—There is something I have never known, he begins.

"Now what on earth could that be?"

—Do you remember the first time we ever talked to each other? When you came to hire me to be your itinerant bookseller?

She nods, says nothing.

—Why did you choose me?

"I liked the look of you. I felt there was, or could be, a certain kinship of the spirit."

—And is that all?

"All that you will ever need to know," she says. "Someone I know told me that you could be . . . easily persuaded. I could not spare the time for anything but an easy persuasion."

Now he laughs.

—Marry me, woman, he says.

It is something he has said before.

And her reply is also familiar and consistent: "Not now. And perhaps not ever. Who knows? I may yet catch the eye and fancy of some rich man."

He will soon take his leave, crouching, by a low hidden door behind the bed and a narrow back ladderway that leads down to the garden. But now he follows behind her to the chamber door and there turns her around. Grips her tightly and kisses her mouth as if to make up for years of abstinence.

"I can help you," she says in a whisper.

—In what way?

"In this matter of the poet Marlowe. I believe you will need me before you are finished with it. Well . . . depend on it. Count on me."

Then she is gone and the door closed to, tight, and the lock turned from the outside.

Alone with his company of thoughts and, always, his larger crew of doubts and fears, he slips out the back way.

After a brief flash or rinse of sunlight, it is pouring rain again as Hunnyman comes out of the house and sneaks away through the back garden.

Why should he always have to sneak about so? Like a thief . . .

Everyone in this household, from the youngest apprentice to the old grandame in the kitchen, knows he has spent half of the afternoon, all of the time since dinnertime, alone with the widow, their mistress, in her bedchamber. And knows the time was not spent reading sermons or romances out loud or playing at cards, either. Indeed they all must and do know exactly where he is at this moment without even troubling to look up from their tasks as the widow comes into the shop to oversee the work of printing. No need to go to a back window and see him, since, time and again, he has been seen going out through the garden, leaving through the little picket gate, which allows for no returning, and thence along the narrow footpath beyond the low back wall. A wall low enough so that any witness could easily follow his progress along the path by the crown and feathers of his hat.

Why sneak about this way?

Perhaps because, as a player, he finds himself always engaged in acting some familiar role or other. Cannot help himself, try as he will. And so it is in this case that, leaving the widow's house and garden, he straightway becomes, from spangles of his shoelaces to sprigs of his feathers, the very spit and image of a sly and furtive lover. As if there were no ghost but a young, living husband to contend with, to hide from, to avoid, some poor fellow to whom he was awarding the ancient immemorial horns of cuckoldry.

But Hunnyman also acts in this foolish fashion because it is his given nature to do so. Ever since childhood, for as long a life as any memory allows him, he has been stricken by guilt and shame for his misdeeds. Large or small no matter. He is guilty equally for all. Since he is so guilt-ridden, he tends to act and to seem guilty except by the player's craft and by a huge exercise of the will. Strangely for a player, he seeks by every means he can to be no more noticed or noticeable than, say, a lone shadow in a crowd on a sunny day. He moves as if he believed that by the purity of stealth he will be able to come and go as he pleases, unseen and in safety.

Ah, well then, Hunnyman, where is it that you must go next?

What plans do you have for here and now beyond a quick change (in your own shabby chambers) of clothing, slip and skip into a good doublet and breeches, and then a meeting with some of your fellow players at the Mitre, that one nearby to Mercers' Hall and the Great Conduit of Cheapside?

An excellent and merry place to be, the Mitre.

Now. As per the clothing. On which you have spent more money that you ought to. And not to your shame or embarrassment.

Well, what is a man if he does not know how to wear his apparel according to the best and latest fashions? Whatever he may be, he is no gentlemen. That's for certain.

Are you called a gentleman? Are there many who take you to be one?

Time . . . Given a little more time and a little more money in my purse, and I tell you I shall be every bit as much a gentleman as anyone you will ever meet.

Meantime, however, you are busily and blatantly breaking the Law, both of many statutes and proclamations. Long-standing customs. You, with your velvets and silks and satins, your ruff, your lace and embroidery, you, with your sword and dagger, are an impostor.

Peace! It is only a most trivial infraction. And whoever heard, I ask you, of any of these foolish sumptuary laws being enforced, or seriously enforceable, here in the City? To be sure, some poor zany dawcock, some country clown in a far, poor country town, may one day affect too many of suchlike things and then shortly find himself punished for his folly. But here all men are players of one kind or another. Here in the City honor is the same thing, nothing more and nothing less, as reputation. In such a world how can anyone tell and separate the true from the false? If plain truth were ever permitted to rule in London, why, we would sooner be depopulated than by a long season of the Black Plague.

Now then. Pray consider this. That some of us must always serve as models and good examples. Surely you will have to agree that I look the very part of a gentleman far better than most of these new-risen and upstart knaves, though they may well qualify as gents because of their income and by owning enough land and being in lawful possession of an authentic coat of arms, etc. These types, sir, have no more right to honor and distinction than I do to claim a kinship with the Queen. Finally, sir, if all that I have said is true, if I do in truth look and act the part of a gentleman, a perfect gentleman, in every way, and if others take me for the same and then treat me with deference and due respect, even, may I say it, others among the gentry, then can I not make the claim to be (as we say in Law) *de facto* a gentleman?

The Law? As we say in the Law? Have you set yourself up now as attorney and judge?

Well, to be sure, I have served as a witness in many different cases at Law, far more than I can remember and count.

And you have done so under several different and false names and wearing sundry different disguises.

Look here, sir. We live in a litigious time. For most of us it may well be a brazen age. But surely for lawyers it is a golden one. And as for my witnessing, why, it is an ancient custom here. Half the cases heard in the courts at Westminster Hall would have to be very quickly settled or even dismissed without the good services of skilled witnesses.

You mean false witnesses.

Your words, your opinion, not mine.

They can hang you for it and will do so, too, if they ever catch you.

Sweet Jesus, there is no news to me in that. I know the danger well. I console myself that I have some friends in power and of high station.

Power or no, friends become as rare as unicorns when there is any prospect of a hanging.

I have risked the gallows and that galliard in thin air more than once. What is a poor man to do?

To make himself rich?

No, sir, to endure.

Why, be of blithe heart and cheerful countenance. Remember the saying, that all true greatness comes out of poor cradles.

I have often heard that said, especially among beggars. But I have yet to see any living examples of it.

Well then. Let us think and talk of more cheerful matters.

Gladly.

Consider your supper with players this evening at the Mitre. Will any good come from that?

Chances are nothing except indigestion.

Come now. Come now. You are not entitled to hang your lip and wear such a long sad face.

Very well, then. The men I am planning to dine with this evening are all members of the Lord Admiral's Company. Who are these days, when weather allows, performing their plays at the playhouse called the Rose over on Bankside. Rumor has reached me that lately there have been some changes, comings and goings, in that company. Quarrels and shifting about. Every man for himself.

And you have some notion that they may be looking for a new hired man.

I have some hope it may be so.

Always some hope, Hunnyman.

Well, it is my nature to be hopeful. Which leads me, like an old milk cow coming home to the barn, back to my original question of you.

Which is?

What do you truly want to happen? Where do you truly want to be? I do not mean supper at the Mitre. I mean from here and now onward into the future for as far as you and I can possibly imagine it.

I do not know . . . Forgive me, but I do not know.

Leave him there. Hunnyman playing an old familiar scene with and within himself. Wrapping his short and stylish cape, too fashionably short to do him much service outdoors in this raw, wet weather, tightly around himself. Wind now and steady pelting rain. Large fat raindrops staining and soaking the fine, delicate cloth of his doublet, his breeches and hose. See, already, how his bold, extravagant feathers, proud as a fighting cock's, begin to sag and droop and wilt.

Like the forlorn, neglected flowers in the widow's stricken garden. Stricken as all of this kingdom is, and has been for some years, from bad weathers, from too cold and too hot, too wet or too dry. Her little house garden being as sad, in its own way, as the wide grain fields and the pastures in the countryside.

Leave him, Hunnyman, for the time being, as wild rain dances to the gusting wind, and he begins to pick and choose his way, careful as a dancer, along the mud-slick, narrow footpath that leads away from the widow's house toward Carter Lane.

A MEETING AT THE ROSE

So many parts of a man's lifetime, especially the life of a man like yourself, Barfoot, someone rich beyond his years, richer than most other men alive and of any age, with the accumulated treasures of experience and memory and, yes, as well, your harvest of dreams—so many things are vague and timeless, outside of all accurate measurement and definition. Yet, soldier as you have been and agent (intelligencer) as you are being in these days, it is also a most important quality of your mind and character to insist upon exactitude, or precision whenever that is possible.

Thus it is not surprising, at least from your point of view, that you date your involvement in this matter, matter of the late Christopher

Marlowe, which is what chiefly concerns us here, from a particular time and place.

For you the time begins on the afternoon of October 11, in the year of our Lord 1597.

It is on this day that the staging of plays at the playhouses begins again for the first time since July. When it was, not Plague, but great offense taken on account of a satirical play called *The Isle of Dogs*, performed at the Swan, which caused the closing of playhouses, and sent some of the players and one of the poets, young Benjamin Johnson, to sleep on straw for several months at the Marshalsea prison.

And so it is that on this fine light-filled, breezy fall afternoon, you have enjoyed an excellent dinner and some good and merry company. You dined at the Duck and Drake just off the Strand in St. Clement's parish. It's an inn that you visit, from time to time, for the sake of the oysters when the season is right, and for the company of some of the Papist country gentlemen who favor the place. Some of whom have come from all corners of the kingdom to lodge there since the Michaelmas Term of the Law Courts is already under way and the new Parliament, to begin its sessions in a fortnight, is beginning to arrive and assemble in London and Westminster. Your Roman Catholic friends have business with the former, not the latter. And yet some of them, still, after all, loyal Englishmen, even if they cling to an ancient, outlawed faith and must pay dearly for the priviledge, feel the need to be somewhere nearby while new laws, perhaps concerning themselves, are being made.

After a pleasant dinner, you indulged yourself more. Taking a pipe of tobacco with old acquaintances and talking of the news of the world. Listening more than talking when you could. After a time, as you knew they would, they turned the talk to the subject of the wars, hoping that you might be able to tell them something more substantial than old news and recent rumors.

"Truth is," you told them, "I know less about the wars than any of you. If you want the true stories about many old and half-forgotten battles lost and won, I shall be glad to tell you everything I know and can remember. But as to today's share of blood and thunder, friends, all that I know is that the wars continue. They continue, as ever, with no ending in view."

Later, after a walk in the garden, you went off alone. Strolled down to a public water gate. Called out for oars. Hired a wherry to row you across the River to Bankside. The waterman looked to be sufficiently insolent and surly to be entertaining. But it was too fine a day to spoil with that kind of banter. And no doubt your face, your own hard, scarred, sunburnt ugly face, discouraged the fellow from his usual traffic of gossip and complaining and impertinence.

Landing, you joined in and followed the crowd. Most of them going to the Beargarden. But there was a fair-size throng pressing toward the Rose. Planning to witness (once again for yourself and probably not for the first time for many others) the latest version of an old and popular play, now, it was claimed, newly scoured and shined—*The Spanish Tragedy.*

Alone, you chose to pay a penny and to stand with the crowd on the ground to watch it. No expensive bench in the galleries. Above all, no three-footed stool set on the edge of the stage, which practice has become the fashion among swaggering gallants. No, at least when you are alone, you prefer the ease of standing close to the stage in the crowd. Where you can see everything that happens well enough and yet at the same time not, yourself, be conspicuous or, indeed, noticed except as one among the many. It is an old habit of yours. You feel no threat. No, that is not the truth. Put it another way. You have every reason to believe you would not have lived as long as you have, if you had not, and as a matter of thoughtless habit, always simply assumed that there is some threat. And why not? For all of us, rich and poor, cowardly or courageous, is it not true that we are indeed continually threatened creatures? Are we not, from our first attenuated gasps of air onward, always only one heartbeat and one breath or swallow away from Death's power and dominion?

Never mind. Put it another way. Barfoot, though you may stroll or swagger whenever you walk, easy and unhurried, though you may sit upon your bench or stool in some tavern or alehouse, heavy-lidded as if half-asleep, as relaxed and easy as a rag doll, loose-jointed as some idle puppet, though you may well appear to be one of those rare few whom not even thunder and lightning can move to raise an eyebrow, whom Gabriel's trumpet of doom and judgment will not turn to panic and frenzy, yet you are ever and always (secretly) bird-eyed. You trust your feelings and your five senses. Even sound asleep you are like a

large watchdog. A little puff of wind from a new direction and with a
different scent and your eyes are open wide.

Besides which, something on this afternoon, as you walked from
the water gate toward the Rose, made you mildly uneasy. Not
anything you can name. Perhaps a matter of indigestion and perhaps
not.

Here at the Rose, anyway, you enjoy the pleasures of a play you
know well. And you can enjoy this crowd of a couple of thousand
people who have come together. They have come with every kind of
face and form. From every sort of office and vocation, high and low,
that you can find in London and the suburbs. Except, of course, the
greatest and most dignified of the kingdom's elders, who can neither
spare nor tolerate three hours of idleness, and that not counting the
time and trouble of coming and going, from a weekday afternoon for
pleasure without practical purpose. Excepting, also, the most rigorously pious from among the puritanical folk, who, it seems, will not
tolerate this idleness and pleasure for any reason. Now with the Law
Courts in session in Westminster and with the Parliament soon to open
its sessions, too, there is every kind of face and every kind of accent
that can be seen or heard anywhere in this kingdom. And there are, as
always, plenty of strangers, foreigners, too. Not only the usual Dutch
and German and French and Italian and Portugese (including, usually,
a smattering of renegade Spaniards), but others more remote and
strange by far—Easterlings, for instance, of one kind and another,
most oddly clad and no doubt baffled from beginning to end by all the
rush of English words and bold English gestures from the stage. This
crowd, come together on a day of good weather and for the sake of a
play that is well known, admired, and popular, this crowd is like a
flowering garden planted from all over the world. There are pale faces,
bearded and clean-shaven, and dark faces, too. Even, and darkest of
all, there are two tall Blackamoors in long white robes.

So many scents and odors, too. True, there's the meaty odor of
sweating bodies and the stink of garlic breath, joined with the odor of
rotting mouths filled with bad teeth, which so many of the more
fastidious sort complain against. But truth is that these people of
London are more fastidious than anywhere else in the world. Partly out
of necessity because of so many crowds and crowded places. Partly, too,
because our Queen has made such a noise at Court—and all the noises

of the Court are broadcast elsewhere as if by brass trumpets—about the need for and her own pleasure in good and wholesome odors. So the women and men alike at the Rose tend to be well powdered and perfumed. And so are you, Barfoot, for your own reasons. So often wounded, you have been all too familiar with the terrible stinks of healing. Pus and itching, oozing scabs, the stink of yourself to yourself was sometimes harder to endure than the slow-burning fires of the pain. You have pleasured yourself ever since those days by buying some of the best and rarest perfumes. You have splashed your body, unashamed, with these expensive potions. Hard and cruel as you usually look, you can depend on it that no one will ever remark in your presence that you smell like a lady's nosegay or pomander. Chances are that no one will say anything about the sweet smell of you even behind your back. Lest by some terrible mischance the words should somehow reach your ears.

It pleases you, in an odd and understandable way, Barfoot, to smell so sweet, like a lady, and yet to know that no one nearby will risk so much as a sniff or a snort.

There is something arising from the excess of energy and the happy anticipation of a crowd at a stage play that can restore your flagging spirits. Partly it is a simple matter of appetite satisfied, the strong ale and the apples and nuts you enjoy while the players rant and rave, huff and whisper, strewing the stage with a veritable carpet of corpses, and spilling more blood than the Beargarden to the applauding delight and instruction of the multitude. Who shall never live long enough in this world to see true justice done or the execution of satisfactory revenge except in some stage play such as this one. Oh, it's a wild, loud, savage play of ghosts and madness and murders! One of these spectacles for which the players must summon up all their craft, muster all their skills, and push themselves to the sheer edge of magic, to make themselves and this curious bombastic fable, which they find themselves forced to inhabit, at least credible enough, for the time of the playing of it, no more and no less, to save them from earning from their labors showers of apple cores and nutshells. To save them from a concert of hissing, hoots, and jeers.

But when this play, like others of its kind, is done to a turn and served up as it should be, who is to say that the bloody cruelty and madness of it is not a true and just and lively limning of the cruelty and madness of the world?

And with the words of this wonderful company of players, all of them (Jones and Juby, Downton and Donstone, Singer and Bristow, and the Towne brothers, Thomas and John, not to mention the well-trained apprentice boys . . .) excellent players, and most especially Mr. Alleyn, that incomparable and consummate player, why, it is so quiet here among the groundlings that even the common noise of the cracking of nuts seems suddenly loud and rude. And is immediately shushed from all sides.

Once or twice you have the sense of being watched by someone. You glance around casually when you can do so, but you can catch no one looking at you. Nor do you see any face you recognize.

Leaving after the play is done and the last jigs are over with, you discover something new to you, something you have not seen before. Here is a little bookstall in the playhouse, selling a selection of books, plays mostly, and pamphlets. You stop and buy a new street ballad. Which in limping, but forceful verses sets out to celebrate the unhappy occasion of the hanging of some felon or other at Tyburn less than a fortnight ago.

"Ah, the poets," you say to the young man who sells it to you. "They can have the epitaph and elegy ready for the printer before the body has cooled and stiffened."

For a moment this handsome young man lets wrinkles take over his smoothly untroubled brow as he squints his eyes to look you over. It is as if he were weighing the odds against irony. But then the wrinkles disappear as he offers a smile showing off his enviable teeth.

"I believe it is a kind of trick, sir," he tells you. "They have their stock and inventory of elegies and epitaphs, for any and all occasions, already on hand, ever in readiness. Then they need only to write in the names when the time comes and hurry off to the printer."

"And when it is a poet who dies?"

This time the man pauses longer before replying. As if your question might have some secret meaning. But you smile and lean easy against his countertop and you keep your smile and your gaze unblinking. Finally he smiles, too.

"Why, sir, the death of a poet, so long as it is not a rival poet, is the saddest and most sorrowful event that other poets can imagine.

They save their finest words for just such occasions. They sweat to make their verses scan."

"Perhaps, then," you tell him, "if a man wants a ballad made for himself wherein the lines scan and the rhymes are just and true, he will be well advised to write and publish some poems of his own before he dies."

"I would as lief earn oblivion as a penny ballad."

"Well, perhaps a man can have both."

You tip your head in brisk, informal salute and turn away to leave, noting, as you do so, that this particular young man seems wonderfully well dressed for a lad whose occupation is to keep a little bookstall at a playhouse.

And then it comes to you all of a sudden and, just as abruptly, you turn back. To find him staring at you.

"I know your face," you tell him. "But from where?"

"I cannot say."

"Are you a player?"

"Well, sir, it is true that I have been on the boards . . . here and elsewhere."

"Then I have seen you acting. Indeed, now that I think of it, I believe you were of this same company this year or last."

"Briefly, briefly," he says. "Before the playhouses closed."

"I compliment you on your craft. Especially your voice. Only Mr. Alleyn is more sonorous and audible."

"I thank you."

"It's a pity you are not playing now."

Spoken with a self-deprecating grin: "Tell that to Mr. Henslowe."

"Well, perhaps I shall do that."

You walk outside into the clear light of the afternoon, moving along slow and easy with the rhythm of the rest of the crowd toward the River again. And then you feel a strong firm touch, grip really, on your left elbow. Before you can turn to look, you hear a voice that you may dimly remember from somewhere long ago.

"Barfoot," the voice says. "You may well be no more than a younger brother and a far way from your old home place. But there is no question that you live in the life of a courtier. You sleep late, dine early and well, and then you spend your afternoon at a public playhouse. What comes next?"

"Why, sir," you begin to answer, softly so that if he wishes to hear you, he will have to lean closer to you. Not recognizing the man's face, not yet, anyway. But grasping at sight the type and character by which he wishes to be seen and taken. One of your own kind. By his bearing, by his clothing, by the tilted fashion with which he wears his high-crowned, flat-brimmed hat, by the way he hangs his sword and dagger, for comfort and quick access and not for show or style, he is or was once a soldier himself. Stout fellow he is, large-boned and heavy of meat and muscle, neck like a tree stump. Tall, too, and topped off with a florid face and a full red beard. Slightly awkward in motion on account of a limp, an injury to his left hip or thigh or both. Otherwise, aside from the limp, he is no less than formidable.

Once upon a time a soldier . . . You may, then, have known him then. Was it in France? Lowlands? As long ago as Ireland? Most likely the latter, or you would remember him better. So much of your memory of Ireland, all but the weather of it (and the fear), has begun to fade away. To whatever place lost memories wander. Anyway, once a soldier and now, like yourself, a hireling, working for . . . whoever it is who needs this or that probably dangerous thing done and done promptly and as well as it can be done. And is willing to pay a decent, adequate price for the doing.

"The next step," you continue, "in such a life as you choose to attribute to me, is to seek out the blithe and dissolute companionship of others very much like myself. Come now and allow me the pleasure of buying you a quart of ale."

"Only if you will permit me to return the gift in kind."

"Lord, man, it will take us some time to drink quarts. Even a truly thirsty man, fresh from all that bloody business on the stage."

"Time, Captain Barfoot, as you know well, is the one commodity and treasure that a couple of old war-horses like ourselves, put out to pasture, possess in gracious plenty."

The two of you have stopped now and are standing, face to face, hat brim to hat brim, eye to eye, while the crowd flows around you on both sides.

"Are you familiar with a place near here called the Cardinal's Hat?"

He laughs out loud and claps you, lightly, on the back.

"My very thought, Barfoot. I regret to say that it has long been a favorite place of mine, almost my home on this side of the River."

Side by side, the two of you, he just a little taller when he stands up straight and maybe a little older, judging by the few white flecks here and there amid his red beard, though neither of you has yet managed to lose the last glints of your youth yet, are walking toward that celebrated old Southwark inn. And you still cannot begin to remember the fellow's name. If you ever knew it. Never mind, if it is there, with the other lost ghosts of memory, it will come forth again all in good time. A quart or two of ale will dispose of all but the truly serious secrets between you. And far more interesting and more important than the name of this fellow and his own history will be the name of the master he is serving.

And that seems likely to prove to be the most serious secret of all.

Whereas the Queen's majesty, for avoiding the great inconvenience that hath grown and daily doth increase within this her realm by the inordinate excess in apparel, hath in her princely wisdom and care for reformation thereof by sundry former proclamations straightly charged and commanded those in authority under her laws provided in that behalf duly executed.

Whereof notwithstanding, partly through their negligence and partly by the manifest contempt and disobedience of the parties offending, no reformation at all hath followed; her majesty, finding by experience that by clemency (whereunto she is most inclinable so long as there is any hope of redress) this increasing evil hath not been cured, hath thought fit to seek to remedy the same by correction and severity to be used against both these kinds of offenders in regard to the present difficulties of this time wherein the decay and lack of hospitality appear in the better sort in all countries, principally occasioned by the immeasurable charges and expenses which they are put to in superfluous appareling of their wives, children, and families; the confusion also of degrees in all places being great where the meanest are as richly appareled as their betters, and the pride that such inferior persons take in their garments driving many for their maintenance to robbing and stealing by the highway. And yet in her gracious disposition . . .

—Royal Proclamation from Greenwich, July 6, 1597

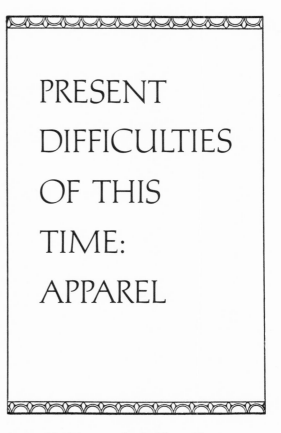

PRESENT DIFFICULTIES OF THIS TIME: APPAREL

I am an Englishman and naked I stand here
Musing in my mind what raiment I shall wear,
For now I will wear this, and now I will wear that;
Now I will wear I cannot tell what.

—Andrew Boorde, *First Book of the Introduction of Knowledge*

Dr. Dene made a sermon against the excessive pride and vanity of women in apparel etc., which vice he said was in their husbands' power to correct.

—*John Manningham's* Diary

It is impossible to know who is noble, who is worshipful, who is a gentleman, who is not, because all persons dress indiscriminately in silks, velvets, satins, damasks, taffetas, and such like notwithstanding that they be both base by birth, and servile by calling, and this I count a great confusion and a general disorder, God be merciful unto us.

—Philip Stubbes,
The Anatomy of Abuses

I have met with some of these trulls in London, so disguised that it has passed my skill to discern whether they were men or women.

Thus it is now come to pass that women are become men and men transformed into monsters.

**—William Harrison,
Description of England**

His doublet was of a strange cut; and to show the fury of his humor, the collar rose up so high and sharp as if it would have cut his throat by daylight. His wings, according to the fashion now, were as little and diminutive as a puritan's ruff, which showed that he ne'er meant to fly out of England, nor do any exploit beyond sea, but live and die about London; though he begged in Finsbury.

—*Thomas Middleton*,
Father Hubburd's Tales

An Englishman's suit is like a tailor's body that hath been hanged, drawn, and quartered, and is set up in several places. His codpiece is in Denmark. The color of his doublet and belly in France. The wing and narrow sleeve in Italy; his short waist hangs over a Dutch butcher's stall in Utrecht. His huge breeches speak Spanish. Polonia gives him the boots. The block for his head alters faster than the feltmaker can fit him, and thereupon we are called in scorn blockheads.

—Thomas Dekker,
The Seven Deadly Sins

England, the players' stage of gorgeous attire, the ape of all nations' superfluities, the continual masquer in outlandish habiliments, great plenty-scanting calamities art thou to await, for wanton disguising thyself against kind, and digressing from the plainness of thy ancestors. Scandalous and shameful is it, that not any in thee (fishermen and husbandmen set aside) but live above their ability and birth; that the outward habit (which in other countries is the only distinction of honor) should yield in thee no difference of persons; that all thy ancient nobility (almost), with this gorgeous prodigality, should be devoured and eaten up, and upstairs inhabit their stately palaces.

—Thomas Nashe, *Christ's Tears over Jerusalem*

Exceed not in the humor of rags and bravery, for these will soon wear out of fashion. But money in thy purse will ever be in fashion. And no man is esteemed for gay garments but by fools and women.

—*Sir Walter Ralegh*, Instructions to His Son

Be thou our clothing and apparel, to keep us warm from the cold of the world. For if thou be away, by and by all things do become numb, weak and stark dead; whereas if thou be present, then they be lively, sound, strong, and lusty. And therefore, like as I wrap my body in these clothes, so clothe thou me all over, but especially my soul, with thine own self. Amen.

—The Book of Common Prayer

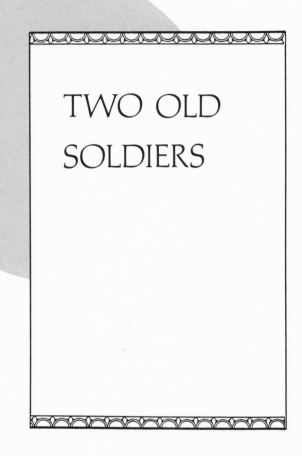

TWO OLD SOLDIERS

They began soon to play, as old soldiers are wont to do, as if with cards or with coins, with the names of places and of people. Barfoot had been far and wide in the world and was always hugely surprised to learn how small the world can be when it is measured by shared names and places.

What Barfoot wanted to know, first of all, was where and how this man would claim to have known him. To which he replied, to Barfoot's great relief (for no man, no matter how disillusioned, can enjoy the prospect of memory shrinking), that he had never known Barfoot directly, nor, indeed, talked to him, until now.

"Then how is it I know your voice?"

"I have been in your presence. I have spoken to others then. And my voice is easy enough to remember."

After which he allowed that he had served in some of the same places and at roughly the same times as Barfoot. So close in both times and places that it must seem to Barfoot remarkable that they had never met until now.

"In the beginning it was Ireland. Bloody Ireland. Bloody, treacherous, merciless, murderous, savage, sorrowful Ireland. A wound that will never be healed. Not, at least, until the Judgment Day."

"I was not much more than a child, an overgrown child, then," Barfoot told him.

"So were we one and all, no matter what age. So were we all, Barfoot, though not for long. Child or no, you served as an ensign under Sir William Stanley in those days. For a time. Time enough to make a man or a corpse of you. And it was almost a corpse you ended up becoming, too. For by the time you left in '85, when Stanley did, you were more dead than alive from wounds and fevers."

"Ah, sir, I may well have been half dead. And not for the last time either. But I was nonetheless glad and blithe as a man can be. To be somehow alive and breathing still. Blithe at heart at the prospect of soon being somewhere, anywhere else, and far from old Ireland."

"Now listen, Barfoot. And I shall name for you one time and place when we were together. Although we were as far apart in that fight that we might just as well have been on opposite sides of the ocean."

"Name the place. Name the fight."

"Glenmalure . . ."

"Glenmalure! Oh, my Lord God! Sweet suffering Jesus!"

Barfoot's first real fight. Stanley held command of the rearguard of Lord Grey's army during the march into the Wicklows. All fresh English troops that time, proud and foolish in their scarlet and blue, and only lightly trained, if at all, for warfare of the kind they would be facing. Half of them still clumsy with sea legs and arsie-versie stomachs from the rough voyage across to Ireland. Well, sir, off they marched to be cut to pieces in that glen and the steep, wooded hillsides. Ambushed, and they died by the hundreds on that day. Half of Barfoot's company was killed. Stanley would call it to be (later on) "the hottest piece of service for the time I ever saw in one place." A terribly bloody fight in the glen. Followed the next day by the terrible retreat to Dublin.

"And Lord Grey was always such a careful man."

"That one time he was sufficiently careless. At least with the lives of others."

"Do you have any recollection of the man who was our colonel?" Barfoot asked, as casually as he could. Matter of no importance.

"George Moore," he answered. "A very fat fellow. Very fat and very foolish on that day in Glenmalure."

"Well then," Barfoot said. "It does seem to be true that we must have been there together."

And so, then, cups freshly filled, they raised a brief toast to the dead and gone and long forgotten. Barfoot offered some bitter laughter and paused to repeat some popular verses from that time:

> "Ye curious carpet knights, that spend
> your time in sport and play,
> Abroad and see new sights, your
> country's cause calls you away!

"I do believe we could incite a riot if we were to go and cry out those words in the street today."

"Not so! Not so! All the duncified fools would surely join in and sing along with us. You have my word on it. They will be raising a new army for Ireland soon enough."

"Will you serve there again?"

"I hope and pray it will never come to that. But with my history of ill luck, who knows?"

He told Barfoot more about himself. How he was healed and well enough to join up again with Stanley in his newly formed regiment, mostly made up of Irishmen, to do some service under the Earl of Leicester in the Lowlands.

"There have been other places as well."

"I know some of them."

"More than you will mention."

"To be sure," he told Barfoot. "But let us continue with the Lowlands."

"If we must."

"You were at Zutphen."

"Where the famous Philip Sidney died."

"Together with too many others."

"Not really. It was a small affair, not much more than a skirmish."

He went on to remind Barfoot, as if he needed prodding to remember it, how he was with Stanley when he seized the town of Deventer in the middle of an October night.

"Not so mild a night as this one."

And how Barfoot continued in his service there until, just at the end of January of '87, Stanley suddenly gave the town to the Spaniards.

"It was a great act of treacherous double dealing."

Stanley surrendered the town to them, then next went over to their side.

"Before you go further, now's the time to mention," Barfoot said, "for you must know the truth of it if you know this much, how it was that some three hundred of us, and myself among them, were allowed by terms and agreement to keep our weapons and to remain faithful and true to our oaths to the Queen. And, by God, we fought the Spaniards for the sake of the Dutch just as we had done before."

"Yes, you did so. But you must admit that after Stanley's treachery, you and many others were never fully trusted as before."

"How can I blame them for that? Besides, there was the matter of religion, and that has rendered many of us suspect, though we have proved with our blood to be loyal Englishmen."

"By the celebrated summer of '88 you were home again in England to defend against Spain. And I know that in '91 you went along with Sir John Norris and his army to Paimpol."

"Aiming to drive all the Spaniards out of Brittany. And, ah, well . . . it was to be yet another lost and forlorn cause."

"We English are master craftsmen of lost causes."

"I fear it is the truth."

Told Barfoot next that nothing had surprised him more than to learn in this same year, this past June, when a great fleet with an army on board sailed out of Plymouth, Barfoot was not there among them.

"Listen," Barfoot said. "A trip across the River in a wherry on a windy day can make me seasick. How do you think I would fare on a long sea voyage?"

"It's a pity. There is much treasure to be taken from these adventures at sea."

"Perhaps. And I am a poor man, all in all, one who might be expected to risk much to seek to change that condition. For the world these days runs upon wheels, and the grease of those wheels is money. There is no honor in being poor and no shame for the rich no matter how they came by their riches."

"Amen."

"But, sir, on every single voyage I have ever made (and I have made a fair number), brief as it may have been, over to Ireland or to the Continent, I was so sick for the whole time of it that the only prize I longed for was death. Let other men sail the seven seas and live to come home rich, or poor as the case may be. Any surprising good fortune that comes to me from this time forward will have to come by land."

"You make a case," he said, laughing. "But I believe you do yourself an injustice."

"No, sir, I disguise the truth. It is true that I do hate to sail on the sea. For any reason. But it is not true that I fear it. If the right occasion came, I would not hesitate to go halfway around the world and back again."

"Then what is the truth?"

"That I am without the flame and heat for adventures anymore. I am a burnt-out candle. Not much arouses or excites my interest these days."

"I might even be willing to believe you if I did not know of at least two exceptions."

"Which are?"

"A pair of sturdy Dutchwomen who live in a house near Lambeth Marsh."

Barfoot laughed. "Oh my," he said. "You have certainly been a student of my comings and goings. No question. But what good will any of it do for you?"

"That remains to be seen."

By that hour of the evening they were at the Windmill, corner of Old Jewry and Lothbury, drinking sack and eating fruit pies. What could be more pleasant for a couple of old soldiers than sack and sugar and freshly made fruit pies? And maybe even a little sport between them.

"This may well be the last pair of honest dice in the City," the man told Barfoot.

Called himself Paul. Paul Cartwright. Might just as well have called himself Peter Trout or Cock Lorel. The name meant nothing, and Barfoot knew it. But was cheerfully willing to call the fellow whatever he wished to be called. For now.

A pair of honest dice, then. And all of a sudden, strangely perhaps, Barfoot's luck began to run with and for him. At least for a while. Long enough time to win back the pennies he had paid out for this day, to repay himself everything including the hire of the boat and the price at the playhouse and the printed ballad he bought at the bookstall.

"Pity your luck seems to have deserted you, Peter Cartwright."

"Paul."

"What?"

"The name is Paul."

"Then I ask your pardon, Paul. I reckon I have had too much to drink."

"Never!" the fellow says in a loud voice. Signals to the tapster. "What measure is too much for a couple of soldiers?"

"A couple of old soldiers who are soon likely to be known as a pair of old drunkards."

"No need for being known at all."

"There are no secrets in drunkenness, they say."

"Come now, Captain Barfoot." Looked away from Barfoot's eyes to pick up the loose dice again and rattle them together in his fist. "We both know better than that."

It seemed that the time had come at last for some serious talking. But the tapster put an end to that possibility. For he came to the table and reminded them, politely enough, that it was past the hour of lawful closing and past his own bedtime as well. Cartwright protested. Perhaps too much. There were only a few late drinkers at the Windmill. And only a few candles were lit and the fire had died down to no more than a poor bed of coals. Everything was shadowy and quiet. This fellow, Cartwright, his face was cut in half by shadow. Like the knave in a pack of cards.

It occurred to Barfoot that maybe he had signaled to the tapster not for more drink but to put an end to this evening.

They agreed, as they rose from the table, cloaking themselves for the night, that they would meet in the morning at Paul's Churchyard.

Outside, the soft, wet, chilly night air wakened them. They walked together, quiet as cats, for a short distance.

"Have you learned anything new tonight?" Barfoot asked.

To which this Peter or Paul, whoever he might be, snorted. Like a horse. Snorted and laughed and slapped Barfoot lightly on the back.

"Only this much," he said. "That neither one of us will ever live to be a schoolmaster or a clerk. And I think that neither of us can depend on dying in bed."

"Speak for yourself," Barfoot said. "For I plan to do exactly that."

But he was speaking softly to the man's broad back. He was already walking away into the foggy dark. Then abruptly turned back, reappeared like a swimmer bobbing up from deep water.

"Fine nights for vanishing," he said. "Did you hear the news?"

"What news would that be?"

"Why, sir, how only last week two Jesuit priests, on just such a foggy night as this one, managed to escape from the Tower. Tied rope to a cannon and came down to Tower Wharf. Where a boat was waiting to spirit them away."

"Well," Barfoot replied, as evenly as he was able to, "that would take some doing. But those Jesuits are said to be wonderfully ingenious. More tricks and shapes than Proteus himself."

"So they say."

Then he was truly gone. And Barfoot stood still and listening to his limping on the cobblestones until it was all out of hearing.

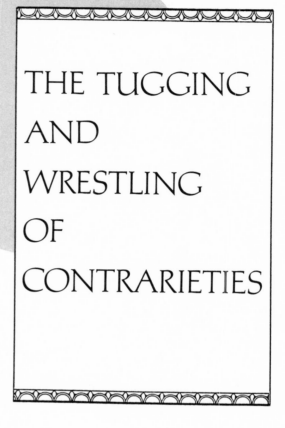

THE TUGGING AND WRESTLING OF CONTRARIETIES

There are those, wise men among them, who firmly believe that, saints and devils aside (and who can claim to have seen many of either kind lately?), the true, unfeigned character of every man and woman is formed, therefore to be found, in the tugging and wrestling of contrarieties. The opposites he or she embraces. Admitted or denied, no matter, it is the contradictions in and of himself that tell us—and himself as well, if he should happen to have the courage to examine himself without excessive flattery or contempt—who he truly is. Or, anyway, to reveal as much of truth, arising from inward voyaging and exploration, as any of us reasonably can bear.

Let us now talk a little more of this Joseph Hunnyman and of his true character.

You are already familiar with some of the paradoxes that mingle to make the essential character of Captain William Barfoot. How, for one example, he clings to the old Papist Faith. Hoping and praying for its eventual restoration in England. Even as he firmly doubts that any such thing can come to pass. Not in his lifetime. Not in any future he can imagine. How, nevertheless, at very real risk to himself and in defiance of the Queen's Law, he has performed acts and services for the sake of the Faith. How, while he is able to, he will probably continue to do such things and more.

Yet, at one and the same time, he has fought as a soldier against Spain, the Holy Roman Empire, and Catholic France. Somewhat to his own surprise, he has never even considered compromising his loyalty to England. He honors and obeys the Queen as best he can, hoping that he will never be forced into some final and irrevocable choice between obedience to her and her mortal enemy—the Pope in Rome. Does not know, himself, how he might choose then if he had to. So does not choose to ask himself that question. Bloody question, they call it, when they ask it of Roman priests. In the absence of any occasion requiring it, he mostly ignores the question. Though sometimes he thinks to himself that he would choose the Queen. Popes in Rome come and go. But he has known and served only one Queen of England all his life. He knows the lady is old and frail and must die soon. But he cannot imagine this kingdom without her presence. Surely, if only as a ghost, she will haunt this place forever and ever.

Barfoot is more of a mystery to himself than to others. Not much that he may do or not do will surprise you now. You are prepared for almost anything and everything from him.

(Still, wait and see, I think the fellow may have a surprise or two for you in his purse or up his sleeves.)

Joseph Hunnyman's case is somewhat different. To begin with, unlike Barfoot, he does not consider himself to be a creature of serious self-contradiction. He believes his works and deeds are a just demonstration of himself. Or so he says. He believes that as a player, gifted and well trained to his craft, he knows himself as well as anyone can. And without illusion and distortion. Concerning the outward and visible things of this world, he is convinced that he is a true believer,

not in what is or has been, but in what is yet to come. Hunnyman is
eager for the future to arrive. By which he does not mean Judgment
Day or heaven and hell like some of the preachers. For he does not, in
his own opinion, have a religious cast of mind. True, since childhood
he has listened to and even learned by heart the words of many sermons
and homilies and prayers. But the soul, the *sentence*, of none of them has
ever yet impinged upon his own soul. His eyes are fixed on God's green
earth. His view is toward the future.

Or so he believes.

Now.

This is a knotty problem from the beginning. For how can he
imagine himself ever to be at home in a landscape that is, by
definition, unknown and unimaginable?

To which he answers that if men had ever allowed themselves to be
shackled and hobbled by the petty limits of logic, why, then we should
all be like wild Irishmen or Red Indians, dancing around a fire, clad
in animal skins. Probable that we would not yet have troubled to cross
over the River to Southwark or followed the flow of it as far as Deptford
or the Isle of Dogs. Let alone, like heroic Drake on his *Golden Hind*,
sailed westward all the way round the great globe and home again.

Isn't he shameless?

Invoking the names and deeds of the voyagers and explorers who
followed the horizons, steering by the stars into the unknown. This
diversion is intended, in part, to protect him from having to admit
openly that for the sake of his own fortune he would as lief not have to
explore the world at any greater distance from the City than Holywell
in the north and Bankside to the south, Greenwich to the east,
Richmond and Windsor to the west. What he means to claim, and by
analogy only, is that he shares with the adventurers of his time a high
and aspiring mind. That, like them, he is eager to enjoy whatever the
new world will bring. In hope and confidence, he feels that the future
will be not only clearly and distinctly different from this present age,
different therefore from what everyone else, and most especially the
tedious and senile graybeards, who seem to believe that they alone are
capable of managing the affairs of the nation, can imagine. Different,
also, in that the future he hopes for will prove to be an improvement,
perhaps a wonderful amendment of the injustices of things as they are.
All things will be better.

It is precisely this undiminishing and inextinguishable sense of hope, in spite of all hard evidence to the contrary, hope like the first winds of March which seem freighted with a ghostly cargo of future flowers, foolish and even childish as it may be, which makes him such desirable company for others. He brings good cheer. Which is always welcome. Even when it is based on false premises and refutable assumptions.

Add another attractive quality, one that is close kin, but not exactly the same. In the face of many kinds and forms of disappointment, some of them surely bitter to taste and heavy to endure, Hunnyman seems to be somehow not very much disillusioned. Yet. Certainly he would not admit to it.

When it comes his turn to twang the strings and sing a song at the tavern, though everyone else may be mewing the saddest and most sorrowful songs the world knows, he is always for something blithe and bright.

Think of Hunnyman, striking clear chords on lute or cithern and eagerly singing "Tomorrow Will Be My Dancing Day."

Now.

In a world, and in the midst of an age whose chief diet for one and all, high and low, seems to be disappointment except for those very few upon whom Fortune seems to smile and wink, and even then only briefly, briefly . . . , there is something irresistibly charming about someone who seems unable to take notice of disappointment or to accept defeat. We enjoy the company of people like that because it is proof positive that there are bigger fools alive than we are.

Hunnyman will never describe his litany of defeats as anything but a procession of victories in disguise. A kind of alchemist of his own life story, he converts evident, undeniable losses into a golden chronicle of gain. To do so he ignores much. If Hunnyman were a merchant of the self, himself, though his creditors might be pounding on the door and though he could look down from a high window and see the accompanying constables standing by in leisurely attitudes, patiently waiting to arrest him for his debts and to hurry him away to enjoy the dirty straw at the Counter, still he would be calmly untroubled, convinced that, even now, there must be, therefore *there is* a richly laden ship being blown by favorable winds in his direction, carrying a cargo that will change his thin luck to fat, paying off every debt and obligation, raising him above the level of his usual friends and companions. Who happen to love him in large part because his luck is usually far worse than theirs.

A true friend to Joseph Hunnyman, if there is any such, might well be troubled with the notion that if Hunnyman's vision of a bright future should ever come to pass, most of his companions then proving to be foul-weather friends and no friends at all in good times, Hunnyman's astonished heart would break.

To which someone else might well remark that his heart was broken to pieces long before we ever met him. And there is truth in that, though very few, perhaps no one, not even the Widow Alysoun, who believes she can tease any secret out of Hunnyman, no one knows how in his own private chambers he still keeps a chest containing the clothing of his dead children. Keeps these things clean and folded and fresh-scented with sweet herbs. And once in a while, coming home half-drunk and weary to his very bones with the weight of the world and the flesh and the Devil, he has unlocked and opened up that chest and, one by one, unfolded the little clothes, holding them up to moonlight and starlight at the window. As if by holding these things high in the dim light he might somehow cause their emptiness to fill with life again.

As if, somehow, he might be able to dance them safely home from the cold and the dark.

Well, whatever he may hope and believe, dancing is what he does, then, light-footed, round and round his little room, clutching the soft, sweet clothes, feeling his body shudder and his shoulders shaking, crooning a little wordless lullaby until his throat fills up and he chokes on the salty taste of tears.

The Queen's majesty doth straightly for-
bid all manner of interludes to be played
either openly or privately, except the same
be notified beforehand and licensed within
any city or town corporate by the mayor or
other chief officers of the same, and within
any shire by such as shall be lieutenants of
the Queen's majesty in the same shire, or
by two of the justices of the peace inhabit-
ing within that part of the shire where any
shall be played.

And for instruction to every of the said
officers, her majesty doth likewise charge
every one of them as they will answer; that
they permit none to be played wherein
matters of religion or of governance of the
estate of the commonweal shall be handled
or treated, being no meet matters to be
written or treated upon but by men of
authority, learning and wisdom, nor to be
handled before any audience but of grave
and discreet persons . . .

—*Royal Proclamation, Westminster,*
May 16, 1559

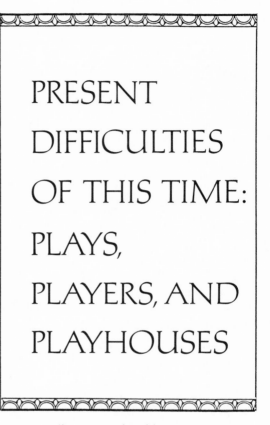

PRESENT DIFFICULTIES OF THIS TIME: PLAYS, PLAYERS, AND PLAYHOUSES

By his action he fortifies moral precepts with examples. For what we see him personate, we truly think done before us. A man of deep thought might apprehend the ghost of our ancient heroes walked again and take him (at several times) for many of them . . . The flight of hawks and chase of wild beasts, either of them are delights noble. But some think this sport of men the worthier despite all calumny. All men have been of his occupation; and, indeed, what he doth feignedly that do others essentially. This day one plays a monarch, the next a private person. Here one acts a tyrant, on the mor-row an exile; a parasite this man tonight, tomorrow a precisian.

—Sir Thomas Overbury,
"The Character of a Player"

Rich men give more to a player for a song
which he shall sing in one hour than to their
faithful servants for serving them a whole year.
I could wish that players would use themselves
nowadays as in ancient former times they have
done. Which was only to exercise their inter-
ludes in the time of Christmas, beginning to play
in the holidays and continuing until Twelfth
Tide or, at the furthest, Ash Wednesday.

—*Samuel Cox, letter to an*
unknown correspondent

Plays are the inventions of the Devil, the offerings of idolatry, the pomp of worldlings, the blossoms of vanity, the roots of apostasy, the food of iniquity, riot and adultery—detest them. Players are masters of vice, teachers of wantonness, spurs to impurity, the sons of idleness. So long as they live in this order, loathe them.

—Stephen Gosson,
Plays Confuted in Five Actions

Will not a filthy play, with the blast of a trumpet, sooner call thither a thousand than an hour's tolling of a bell to bring to a sermon a hundred? Nay, even here in the City, without it be at this place and some other certain audience, where will you find a reasonable company? Whereas, if you resort to the Theatre, the Curtain, and other places of plays in the City, you shall, on the Lord's day, have those places, with many other that I cannot reckon, so full as possible they can throng . . .

—*John Stockwood*,
A Sermon Preached at Paul's Cross

Whosoever shall visit the Chapel of Satan, I mean the Theatre, shall find there no want of young ruffians nor lack of harlots, utterly past all shame, who press to the forefront of the scaffolds to the end to show their impudency and to be as an object to all men's eyes.

—*Anthony Munday*,
A Second and Third Blast of Retreat from Plays and Theaters

One said merely that "interludes were the Devil's sermons and jesters the Devil's

confessors, these for the most part disgracing of virtue and those not a little gracing of vices." But, for my part, I commend not such sour censurers, but I think in stage plays may be much good, in well-penned comedies and specially tragedies. And I remember in Cambridge, howsoever the preciser sort have banished them, the wiser sort did, and still do, maintain them.

—*Sir John Harrington*,
"A Treatise on Plays"

All and every person and persons being whole and mighty in body and able to labor, having not land or master, nor using any lawful merchandise, craft or mystery whereby he or she might get his or her living, and can give no reckoning how he or she doth lawfully get his or her living; all fencers, bearwards, common players in interludes, and minstrelsy, not belonging to any baron of this realm or towards any other honorable personage of greater degree; all jugglers, pedlars, tinkers, and petty chapmen; which said fencers, bearwards, common players in interludes, minstrelsy, jugglers, pedlars, tinkers, and petty chapmen, shall wander abroad and have not license of two Justices of the Peace at least . . . when and in what shire they shall happen to wander, shall be taken, adjudged, and deemed rogues, vagabonds, and sturdy beggars.

—An Act for the Punishment of Vagabonds and for Relief of the Poor and Impotent

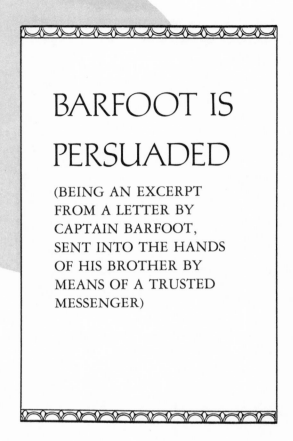

BARFOOT IS PERSUADED

(BEING AN EXCERPT
FROM A LETTER BY
CAPTAIN BARFOOT,
SENT INTO THE HANDS
OF HIS BROTHER BY
MEANS OF A TRUSTED
MESSENGER)

A . . . nd so, then, upon the following morning, as we had agreed, I kept my appointment. Met with the fellow in Paul's Churchyard.

Morning commenced with rain. So I looked for him, first, inside the Church along Duke Humphrey's Walk. But though there were, as always, plenty of rogues and villains there, some with familiar faces, he was not. Then the weather turned around. Old sun, too long absent, reappeared. And I took myself outside again.

Fine fall morning it was after all, the air now rinsed clean and clear. Not a sniff, yet, of stinking sea-coal smoke. The sky an even blue, as in a painting, and laced with thin clouds. All of the scents and odors of this ancient City seemed to partake of the blessings of the day, transformed, as if by an alchemical mystery in the breeze into the very essence of sweetness.

And, after all these years, I could not help myself from thinking of home at this season, this bright and gentle and too brief time to be grasped and cherished before the wet and cold of the long winter descends to send us to be as close as we can be to hearthsides.

I had come somewhat early and without any companion or servant. Wearing my best and bravest clothing so that I could be easily seen and swiftly recognized by this fellow. Or anyone else who might be looking for me. No trouble for me to find him, if and when he should come, with his red hair and beard and his lame leg.

Outside in the Yard I busied myself like a gent of the Court, the picture of studious idleness, browsing and grazing among the newly published books and pamphlets in the stalls.

There are some, I know, who out of all familiar scents love most the odor of new-baked wheaten bread or, perhaps, freshly brewed ale. But for myself, I must confess, sir, one of this world's most cheerful odors is that of a newborn book.

While I was wandering there, I encountered the same young man, the player, from whom I had purchased a penny ballad at the Rose on yesterday afternoon. It is not my way, as you know, to make too much of simple coincidence. Many a fearful fool has managed to lose himself on that bypath. Still and all, I would be an equal fool not to conclude that such an ubiquitous fellow deserves some thoughtful watching. Thus I stopped and engaged him in some lighthearted conversation. All the while allowing myself to consider if he might, in some way, be associated with the red-bearded man who calls himself Paul Cartwright and walks with a limp.

Who at that very moment, as if by some conjurer's trick, appeared at my elbow. I was sure he had been watching me for a little while. To determine, if he could, whether or not I was alone. He, of course, would not choose to be alone and was not. He had with him a long, lean fellow, lean as a greyhound and as rousy as a brown rat. Fellow with face as thin and hard as an ax blade. Whose duties, I surmised, would likely include chasing after me if, at any time and for any reason, I attempted to run away. This Cartwright with his stiffened left leg and clumsy limping looked to be unable to run even to save his own life. Come what might, he would have no other choice than to stand firm and hold his ground. A predicament that probably causes him to imagine that every hale and whole man in the world must depend upon movement, including a swift showing of heels, as a large part of any strategy of self-defense.

Plain truth was that I had no plan for any kind of trouble. I was anticipating none. When he arrived with his somewhat unsavory companion, I formed no plan beyond the most obvious one. If it should somehow come to pass—God forbid! But His will be done— that we should have to turn to blows or bare blades, why, then I would kill the greyhound first so as to deal with the cripple, Cartwright, at my leisure.

If he is, indeed, a cripple and not some other kind of actor.

"I was wrong," he told me. "I guessed you would be tardy and would keep me waiting this morning, if you came at all."

"That is another soldier's habit that I can somehow not yet forget or free myself of," I answered. "For no matter how late and well wasted the night before may have been, a new dawn finds me wide awake and fearful as a hare in high grass."

"What do you fear?"

"Truly, sir, nothing except for the fate of my immortal soul. Death of this weary and ugly body troubles me not at all."

"Perhaps that is why you are still alive," he said, laughing.

"As for my keeping our appointment. Why, sir, you managed to arouse my interest and curiosity so much yesterday that I would be here this morning to meet you even if I had received news that you were lying in ambush for me with a large band of your armed and dangerous friends."

We both smiled at that idea.

"But," I continued, "neither my punctuality nor natural curiosity will sustain me to stand here in your company for long. Unless you also have some serious plans for an early dinner."

"I do, indeed, and you must be my guest. But first there is something I must ask you here and now."

"Ask and I will answer if I am able."

"Captain Barfoot, what, if anything, do you know concerning the dead poet—Christopher Marlowe?"

I considered a moment. The answer was simple enough. But no good reason to advertise my own simplicity.

"Next to nothing," I said at last. "I know next to nothing about him, dead or alive. But since you are asking about him, you have come to a place as good as any, I think. For here, sir, this young man [*here I indicated the man, the player, selling books in the stall*], he has been a stage player here in the City. And I have no doubt that he has trod the boards and said the words in some of Marlowe's famous plays. Surely he must have met Marlowe on occasion. He may even have been very well acquainted."

Here this player astonished me. He turned as pale as the belly of a trout. Mopped at a surge of sweat on his brow. Swore a strong loud oath (which had to be a lie) that he knew next to nothing, either, about the life and times and death of any Christopher Marlowe. Nor did he care a rotten fig or a walnut shell!

Cartwright ignored him.

"It is you whom I am asking."

"I never knew the man!" the player shouted.

"I care even less than a nutshell what this fellow knows," Cartwright said, still not favoring the spluttering player with a look or any attention.

It was my part to say something calming and to the point.

"I must confess, sir, to being one of those who will go a good distance to see a stage play. Especially a new one which is said to be well written and well acted. And so I have witnessed a number of Marlowe's plays, all of them that I know of. I admit that and likewise admit that I always took great pleasure in his plots and fables, his wild and whirling words. I came to believe he was that rare being, a living poet worth listening to.

"But I also came to believe, from rumors which became his reputation, that he was someone to avoid in fact and flesh. If possible. At least for someone like myself. Having managed to live this long, I have come to prefer adventures and emotions which can be confined to the stage."

"I believe everything you have said so far," Cartwright said. "Except for that last."

"Meaning what?"

"Only this much and no more. That, all protestation aside, you do dearly and deeply miss the blood and thunder of your youth. That some of the things which can fill other men with fear and trembling, like leaves in the rain, can lift your spirits and warm your heart."

"There was a time when that might have been true. A time, yes, when I loved every kind of danger—excepting, of course, on the high seas. But, sir, that time has passed me by now. And peace and quiet are my most cherished companions."

"I trust you are not offended when I tell you I do not choose to believe that."

"Believe whatever you please."

"To be strictly honest, what pleases me most at this moment is the prospect of a good dinner. Shall we . . . ?"

I glanced at his companion.

"Will this fellow come, too, and spoil my appetite?"

Cartwright laughed and clapped me on the back.

"Believe me, he is harmless unless and until I bid him to be otherwise."

"I guessed as much," I said.

Cartwright tossed the fellow a coin.

"Meet me near here in an hour or so."

Fellow nodded his thin face. Turned on his heel and walked away.

The player had by now recovered himself and his craft. His face conveyed nothing.

I walked away with Cartwright to a nearby tavern.

He made his proposal, as I had thought he probably would, after we had enjoyed an excellent dinner and were at least mildly hazy from the wine.

Explanation and proposal as follows. That in this matter he is acting as the agent for some great man of the kingdom. Whose name will remain unspoken. All that I need to know is that his master is someone of considerable importance and distinction who, for good reasons of his own, has an interest in ascertaining the truth concerning the death of Christopher Marlowe. His master has, he told me, serious doubts that the whole truth of the matter has been established. Certainly not to his own satisfaction. He would, therefore, like to know as much as can be known, to learn whatever can be learned. For good reasons, which are none of my affair, neither he nor his servants can at this time openly reexamine the matter of Marlowe's death.

Believing, then, that I am not widely or well known either in the Court or City . . . except perhaps known at *sight*, for who could easily forget me? but, for that very same reason, something of an enigma, and, like many an old soldier and country gentleman whose luck has gone thin, I am very likely in need of some employment. His master was prepared to reward me generously if I were able to satisfy his curiosity concerning Marlowe's death.

I gave no sign of doubts. For all the good reasons. Not least of which is that it would seem somehow suspicious if I simply spurned his offer. For the size of the promised reward—of which I was and am, to be sure, more than mildly skeptical—was enough to catch the attention of any man. Moreover, as a token of goodwill and good faith, he gave me a purse of money, a sum which most of the men I am acquainted with here and must live among—who are, after all else is said and done, no more than knaves and rascals, the scum and orts of this nation—would kill one another to possess.

Since you have been keeping to the country, close to your own hearth, kith and kin, servants and animals—and wisely so, I would say, in envy, if you asked me, which you have not—you may find the world of Court and City, the large and shiny world where a signature and a seal upon a piece of parchment can make or break us one and all, since you are safe and sound and far from here, you may find it hard to believe how things go and are done these days. Truth is, you may not want to know too much of all this. And if you knew enough, you might not need me here as your eyes and ears in Babylon. I might have to find employment at the only craft I have ever learned well. And unless the Spaniard finally comes ashore with his *tercios*, then I would have to practice my trade elsewhere.

All of which is to say, in my own way, brother, that I am grateful for your patronage and willing to earn at least part of my keep by sparing you from much even as I pass along the necessary news, both good and ill.

I take it that every Court since the days of Saul and David and Solomon has been, by definition, a hive of factions. Much buzzing and stinging for whatever pot of honey there may be. And I take it as truth that faction has been a blessing, if a mixed one, for our Queen during her long life and reign. (And may she continue to live and reign over us for as long as God wills it.) But this our latest age has been witness to many changes, risings and fallings of fortune, shiftings of alliance and enmity. Who but some kind of mountebanks (or maybe Anthony Bacon, who is surely something of a wizard) could honestly claim to be a master of it? I sometimes think that the great men of the kingdom who are in the midst and thick of it, and in spite of all their servants and clerks and advisers and intelligencers—in some cases precisely *because* of their own crowd and crew—must be as confused as everyone else from one day to the next. Only an unlikely ignorance could keep the changing world in a state of any coherence.

Enough.

Let me be as brief as can be about these things. There are many factions in and around the Court and (somewhat separately) the City. Many great men, of Church and of State, all with their network of retainers.

(And almost all, as far as I can guess, with their spies and informers. If news and knowledge are the food and drink, nourishing the ambitions of great men, then you would have to say that all of us, the husbandmen of these abundant crops of rumor and report, are the true knights and squires of this time.)

If there are many factions, there are, it seems, only three that matter much. Here, sir, please note I am speaking only out of our native factions, not of foreigners, both allies and enemies, who are here in gracious plenty also, as you can well imagine. Likewise I say nothing here concerning the various Papist factions. Which, even though they lack lawful standing, are not without power and not to be ignored. Among the Queen's great men, there are this year three chief factions, those of Robert Cecil, the Secretary, of the Earl of Essex, and of Sir Walter Ralegh. Power (and glory) is split and divided among them, at least for as long as the Queen wishes it to be so. And it seems, to various trustworthy and wise men, that she needs each of these men and his faction for different purpose and as a check against the other. For the time being, then, each is secure, safe insofar as he resists the power of the other.

What this means is that no matter what gentleman is employing me to look into the matter of Marlowe, I am, however, distantly and indirectly, working for one faction or the other—for Cecil or Essex or Ralegh.

I have no notion (yet) what, if anything, they expect me to find out, whether they wish to affix blame or to cover guilt.

You must be surprised, as I would have been myself, even a year or so ago, that the murder of a poet and playmaker in a tavern several years ago could matter much. But nothing is surprising here. Except that the Lord God has not given up on all of us and all of our vicious little enterprises and misadventures.

And so it is, brother, that I allowed him to persuade me to look into this matter for his anonymous master. Be certain that I shall exercise the greatest caution and care. As ever, I do not plan to trust anyone beyond my own skull. I do not fully trust anything else. Not even my own shadow.

When I know more about this, you will hear from me.

Better burn this.

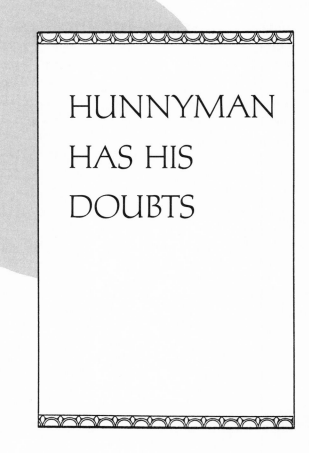

HUNNYMAN HAS HIS DOUBTS

"Good God, woman!" he exclaims, holding the pamphlet between thumb and forefinger, holding it high and away from himself as if he feared that, all on its own, it might explode or burst into flames. "You will place our very lives in hazard by printing this thing!"

"You are too fearful. It is your great weakness and the greatest difference between us."

"This thing is desperately unlawful. It may even be treason, if they should choose to look at it that way."

"Be reasonable."

Clothed in her ruthless innocence, she describes it, simply enough, as only an efficacious and sensible solution to a difficult problem. This pamphlet appears to be Papist in origin, probably coming from the English seminary of St. Alban's in Valladolid. It is without question treasonable. For it strongly argues (not for the first time, but Papist are relentless in this matter) that the old Queen is now, as she always has been, the unlawful and illegitimate ruler of this kingdom. The author concludes from that premise that therefore her subjects need not anymore trouble themselves to obey her or her government. The text then goes even beyond that into the forbidden topic of the Succession. Makes a case for the lawful right of the Infanta of Spain to succeed to the throne as soon as the Queen dies. Which happy event, the author boldly asserts, cannot come soon enough.

When Hunnyman first saw this piece of work, he broke out into a cold sweat before he had finished reading even the first page of it.

She is not so easily persuaded, not even by fear and common sense. To begin with, she argues, these poor, misguided English seminarians in Spain, and elsewhere, will surely continue to write and to publish their foolish arguments in any case, whether she helps them or not. All over the Continent, Englishmen in exile of one kind and another are busy writing tracts and pamphlets. Most of which, to say the least, completely ignore all the statutes and precedents of treason. They write and publish these things. Then they are with great risk and difficulty, and at great expense, smuggled into England. How much easier for them to have to smuggle in only one copy of the text. From which she can (secretly) set and print as many as they may need. Even allowing for her charges, including an extraordinary profit, it will still prove to be much cheaper and safer for her customers. Who otherwise must also, in addition to paying the high costs of printing and paper in other countries, give out large bribes and run grave risks, every step of the way, trying to bring in and distribute their books and pamphlets in England.

Moreover, she continues, before pointing an accusing finger at him, he, Hunnyman, should bear in mind that she intends to do much the same thing for other malcontents and exiles of different, indeed altogether contrary, persuasions. In short, since she is willing to print words for any sect or faction that is willing to pay the price, surely she cannot be held responsible for seeming to support any of their idle, foolish, and heretical views. For has she not likewise made a practice of publishing many of the sermons of the Church of England's best-known preachers?

"The Queen's judges will never accept any of that as a defense. Count on it."

"Judges! This is commerce. It has nothing to do with judges and lawyers. Anyway, how will they ever find us out?"

All too easily, he tells her. Never mind that there are paid spies and dark sentinels everywhere these days. Whose sole purpose is to find out the sources of forbidden writings. The danger is always closer to home. For example, one of her printers becomes discontented. Or, perhaps, an apprentice is disgruntled.

Those few who could know, those very few, would themselves be so much involved that they could not save their own skins by selling hers.

Yet, he reminds her, many have done just that. Sold their own lives cheaply, and simply for the sake of ruining the lives of their masters and betters.

"Well then, you will have to trust me in this matter. Consider that I am an excellent judge of the character of others. Bear in mind that I have other means of ensuring the loyalty of my own people."

"I will admit that I would prefer to face a public executioner than to endure the prospect of your stratagems of revenge, if you ever decided that in some way I had betrayed you."

She thanks him kindly for the compliment. Adding, however, that only a naturally fearful man could ever feel that way about her.

Then she offers another argument. Assuming the worst, he should please to remember that she has information that would be valuable to Queen and Council. Already she knows as much about these things as anyone in England. The truth is that she has precious knowledge to sell. Not only enough to save her own life, if that should prove necessary. But she must also consider that that day may well arrive when the possible gains from the betrayal of some or all of these rebellious subjects would not outweigh the profits from printing their unlawful, treasonous theses.

Meantime, she continues, all that she must do is to make sure that none of them, of any faction, knows her directly. That they should not know, for certain, which press it may be which publishes their documents. Because there will always be several people who stand between herself and her criminal clients.

"There!" he exclaims. "There is the weakest link in the chain. There is where the greatest danger lies."

Exactly. And that is the reason she has told him about these things. Now that he knows, he, too, will be accessory to everything, all of it, like it or not. Pray to remember that always. She needs someone she can trust.

"Alysoun," he says, "as I said, England is crawling with spies like fleas on an old dog. There is no household free of them. Soon, no doubt, there will be a new household rank for them in the domestic hierarchy, somewhere between the butler and the carver. Half the people in England are spying on the other half."

She laughs at him.

"You should know," she says, "being at least half a spy yourself."

Then she takes the dangerous pamphlet from him and tosses it in the fire. It burns to ash.

Lord, is she telling him any truth in these things? Or has she (most likely) made all of this up; only a fable, then, intended to tease and torment him?

Later in bed, locked in the sweaty thrust and wrestle of love, she suddenly finds some breath to continue the discussion.

"Well," she says, as if stumbling over the idea like a stone in the pathway, "it seems we shall have to find some other means to become rich. Something less dangerous."

"I would be more content to hear you suggest some ways and means more lawful. More respectable."

"I am certain you would be. But I cannot do that."

"Why?"

"Because, as far as I know, there are no lawful ways to arrive at good fortune. Everything worth having is already owned by old men."

"And their widows."

"Ha!"

"The old men are dying."

"Not soon enough," she says with an edge of bitterness. "Not soon enough."

BARFOOT BEGINS WITH PAPERWORK

"It is being said, and over and over again during these late restless days, said not only by old and old-fashioned soldiers, and by anyone who can lay claim to being a swordsman if nothing else, that this has become, not the brazen age foreseen and promised by prophets, but something new in the weary world. An age of ink and paper and hills of sand for the blotting thereof, of wax seals and bright ribbons, an age created for clerks and scriveners and notaries, men with nimble pens (and never mind their lack of nimble wits and witty tongues) whose purpose and design is to fill up all the shelves and coffers and chests, rolls and pigeonholes of the kingdom with paper and parchment! And, even before that is accomplished, to cover every piece of blank paper with words and numbers. Have you seen a good wicker beehive standing in some farmer's sallet garden or behind his barn? Well now, is that not what this world has become now, while the rest of us dozed and dreamed otherwise—a huge dung-daubed place of hay and wicker, humming night and day with the noise, the inconsequential plainsong of petty clerks? Proper heraldic beast for our time would not be lions and dragons, bears or stags, but something looking like a bee, a bee who can make no honey, proving on closest inspection to be a fat clerk with wings (a cupid of cupidity) whose sting is with the point of his pen. Who if stepped on or stabbed or drawn and quartered, sword-spitted or reduced somewhat in height by a chopping ax, will spurt no honest blood but instead ooze ink from every vein and wound and pore. Who can only, like the honeybee, be smoked away. But the smoke must be made of their own burning papers—bonds and writs, rolls and calendars, minutes and proceedings, apologies and confessions—to give these creatures any real distress!

"Harvests may be fat or lean, no matter. We may (as we have) endure drought or too much rain, fires and floods, or even come at last to the rich abundance which everyone must dutifully pray for. Yet, feast or famine, war or peace, there is no end to the harvest, the boundless crop of paperwork being created at Court and by the courts. And I hereby defy the Attorney General and the Lord Chief Justice, both honorable and learned gentlemen, I am sure, to name all the kinds and forms of law courts which have sprung up like sturdy weeds all over England; and I could declare one here and now—Barfoot's Court of Alehouse Complaint—and who knows but that with a couple of precedents and a writ or two in Law French or dog Latin, fair-copied and signed and sealed and delivered, it, too, might soon be studied by scholars at the Inns of Court? Not to mention the record keeping carried on by every great household, and every house with any pretension to greatness, which would have to include half the squatters' hovels that pester and clog Houndsditch, and every parish in the land, city and county, large and small and abandoned to the birds!

"It is no kind of irony to tell you, and especially any precise and theological types among you who may, in pluperfect innocence, mind you, have been cast ashore from the shipwreck of the world to find themselves here among us in a tavern, that God Himself has no need any longer to keep the golden books and ledgers of His own, not at least for his creatures in England, when everything we say or do—and no doubt, too, many things which we have never said and done—is dutifully memorized and reported by some informer, copied, recorded, and filed away, somewhere or other, by a clerk with a face like a playing card, to be guarded and preserved and finally used against us by the angels, assuming they read English or Law French or dog Latin, on Judgment Day!

"Meanwhile assuming that the latter day is somewhat delayed, comes not soon enough to clean up the dungheap we have made out of the world, well, there is still posterity to think about. We shall keep our records for posterity. Which may, after all, never find whatever it may one day be looking for amidst our alpine mountains and meadows of paper. And if our documents of every kind are of no use to posterity, consider they have many other good uses. May even be used to feed the insatiable appetites of worms. Or to kindle and feed the fires of many illiterate generations yet to come!

"And if there is any man here who is trying to keep up with my words, with a mind to inform against me, why, let him prove his manhood by raising his hand. And I will kindly direct him to one of those several places which love me least. Where, if he is in any luck, he may earn a penny and a pat on the head for informing against me.

"*What, nobody????*"

[*Well, here am I, a kind of a clerk and informer myself, filling some paper with some, not all, believe it or not, of Captain Barfoot's words. I was not there to raise my hand and spoil things.*]

For after a glare that would constipate a cow, he accepted applause like a player on stage. Ordered a round of pints for everyone in the tavern. At least some of whom, you can safely wager, will never be sober enough to be a clerk of any kind, and others, I regret to report, so drunk they cannot make their marks if they should happen to remember their own names.

What company Captain Barfoot keeps!

Sometimes. When he's not in a tavern.

Truth is, he has been much in the company of clerks these days. Searching for records concerning the late Christopher Marlowe.

Barfoot, as always, says what he means and means what he says. And yet, as he would be the first to concede in disputation, there is more to it than his tirade allows. Or put it another way. His tavern tantrum is no more and no less a rhetorical trope than, say, a sonnet or an eclogue. Each of which, as I take it, has its contentious heart and contains more than it seems to admit to. And that, surely, is how Barfoot's tavern companions take him. They are often drunk, but seldom fools. That is, without troubling their heads over his full meaning, they know what he means. Without troubling themselves by looking for any hidden sentence or clever contradictions, they take him for a player speaking lines. Sawing the air, as they say. Always half in jest at least. That half being the bitter half. Saves his sweetness for whores and horses and hunting dogs, they imagine, closer to truth than they know. They have seen him played on the stage at the playhouse—and if they have been there often enough, they have seen Barfoot in his person and in scarred flesh and bones squinting furiously to see someone very much like himself strutting and jetting on the boards. And which came first, chicken or egg?

Put it simply. He is a type they know, and he knows it. But more. He is a type they can enjoy, if not always be easy with. For who can tell for certain when one of these half-mad, bloody-minded fellows created out of the mud and blood of our all little wars will not, for once, begin to believe his own ranting and raving and, next thing you know, draw a rusty blade from shabby scabbard and commence with the art of carving new expressions on familiar faces?

Laugh as you want to, they will tell you. But have a care.

As for what can be found and seen Barfoot has this to say:

"If there is a clerk who makes or keeps records, I can find him and have a talk and reach an understanding. And why not? For I have never yet met the clerk, great or humble, who believes he is justly rewarded for his services. And truth is most of them are not well rewarded and depend on the interests and purposes of others, others like myself, to make their calling worthwhile. So I find the fellow and we have a talk, perhaps even a cup of wine together. And we reach an understanding, the end of which is he will let me have a peek at any piece of paper he possesses or has access to. And with time and familiarity I have come to know a clerk or two, at this place and that, and have come to be known, myself, here and there, for a generous disposition and a closed mouth. And, perhaps most important of all, for being no kind of a clerk myself. For I ask for no copies to be made of anything unless it be a copy of some harmless and commonplace writ or conveyance or suchlike and then only if it seems to me a means to make the copyist, who might otherwise be suspicious of my indifference to his documents, content. Nor do I ask to copy or take notes of any document myself. I bring no paper and leave with none. With a face as blank as a horse or a cow, I put on my spectacles—which do not improve my eyesight but seem to improve my appearance somewhat, at least in the eyes of clerks and others who earn their living indoors. I put on spectacles and put on the plain face of a card player. And I read as quickly as I can. Pondering nothing, at least nothing important. Pausing seldom to follow my finger and reread anything. And if I should ask any question, it will not be to learn anything but to reassure my clerk as to the boundless depths of my ignorance and inexperience."

He has taught himself to remember what he can and to ignore what is not needful, a habit of thinking made easier for him by his firm distrust of words on paper.

"These things," he would tell you, "have no more truth to them, indeed often less by far, than any sonnet. But, like a piece of Christmas cake, they have nuts and fruits which can be savored. Or put it another way. These documents and records are like charts and maps of the countryside. But you must walk the roads yourself."

Has something else to say on the subject of clerks and their papers. Though he might not ever say it out loud to any living soul. So call it his secret thinking and let it be. He thinks to himself, and true to himself and his old-fashioned views, that the older clerks, the generation who began the reign with the Queen and now, the few left alive, are old and feeble and (*pity for clerks!*) very forgetful and digressive, these old fellows had a certain kind of honor. Perhaps they believed God watched over their shoulders. And that God, a sort of Clerk Himself, can read a text or a true bill, any document or deposition, as easily as he can read the secrets of the heart. And that therefore no text was ever to be tampered with, altered, concealed beyond reasonable safety, or, perish the thought, lost. To do otherwise would make no more good sense than Adam and Eve did, hiding their private parts behind fig leaves out of original shame. These old fellows saw themselves as the guardians of the past for the future. Come hell or King Henry knocking at the door, and still they would not dishonor their obligation. At least not easily.

The newest generation of sly servants, studying the example of their cunning masters, has a regard for posterity also. The future is there to be seduced and mocked and deceived. If, in our words and records, we call ourselves virtuous (to do so we also must often assert that our vices are virtues), then the future will take us at our word.

There is a folly so great and so deep here, Barfoot believes, that it may well ensure that we shall have no future at all.

So be it.

First item he has seen and studied in his search is the finding of the Coroner's jury concerning the death of one Christopher Marlowe in the house of the widow Eleanor Bull in Deptford. Account of his death returned by William Danby, Coroner of the Household to the Queen, and a jury of sixteen good citizens and true. Story and scene of it simple enough, if riddled with questions. Well, he will remember it and ask questions later. For now he is diverted by the names of the three men who were with Marlowe in a chamber of the widow's house. One is Ingram Frizer, who killed Marlowe. In self-defense, as the jury returns it and the Law will rule when Frizer is granted, sooner than most in his shoes, a full pardon. The other two, witnesses only, are Nicholas Skeres and Robert Poley.

Barfoot is certain he knows Frizer by sight. Which means that Frizer will surely know him by sight as well, or else the fellow is desperately inattentive. Knows the other two by repute and perhaps, he will have to see for himself, by sight also.

He will know all three of them better when he follows their names in dusty records.

Frizer is still what he was and has been—a servant for Sir Thomas Walsingham. Walsingham, who only this very summer past, at his house at Scadbury, near Chiselhurst, Kent (and that only a few easy miles from Deptford), has been honored by a visit of the Queen and Court in her Progress. No doubt cost him aplenty, too; but may have been worth it, after all. For the Queen knighted him then and there.

Frizer handles his affairs of business. And must have done well, and well enough for himself, while doing so. For Frizer has been busy buying and selling property on his own. Was the owner of the Angel Inn in Basingstoke until recently, when he sold it for good profit. And he and this Skeres have been often joined together in various schemes and projections, often of shadowy value and dubious virtue and almost always at some trusting simpleton's acute expense and disadvantage. He finds that, like so many of this youngest generation of vipers, these clutchers and grabbers, they have often been embroiled and entangled in suits at the law courts. They are, he will discover easily enough, tricksters and moneylenders as well as adventurers. And even if large and complicated matters engage their attention, nothing, when it promises some gain, is too small for them. Nothing beneath them. Like the serpent on his belly in the dust. He will find that, clever foxes, and as merciless as hunting hawks or an owl with a ravenous hunger for mice, they have been well served by the Law. The Law which seems better designed for them and their purposes than for the protection of widows and orphans or for the long-suffering Poor. The Poor who, so long as Law endures, unchanged and unimproved, seem sure to be with us always, even until the end of the world.

Well, Barfoot knows that Parliament, even now in session, is seeking, among other things, to write a new statute on how to deal with the Poor. And, who can say, perhaps the new bill will be better. Can hardly be any worse or more impotent than the old one.

Nicholas Skeres, lawyer and son of a merchant tailor of the parish of Allhallows the Less, is said to be a servant to the Earl of Essex. Has been a spy and a messenger in his time and may be so yet. Meantime, with Frizer, has schemed a trick or two.

Both would know Marlowe, whose last patron was Thomas Walsingham. And who, in that spring of '93, had been living at Scadbury. All of these men have other friends in common as well.

The surprising odd face in the group is Robert Poley. Barfoot will know a good deal about Poley even without the benefit of records or without knowing him face to face. For Robert Poley was one among the conspirators, under Anthony Babington, who, it was said and is believed, aimed to kill the Queen and free the Queen of Scots and, with aid of Spain, set her on her rightful throne and restore England to the right religion. Much mischief there, more to the sorrow and disadvantage of the Catholic faith in England than anything else. Babington's crew paid for it with their lives and parts. All but this Poley. And Father Ballard was captured at Poley's house! Poley found himself for a time in the Tower, but not long after he became the servant of the old spymaster (and Sir Thomas's kinsman) Sir Francis Walsingham. Spy and messenger, then, for the Queen. And with old

Walsingham dead and gone, now, it would seem likely, like Nicholas Skeres, in the employment of Essex.

The young Catholic hotheads now claim, among themselves, yet not quietly, that the Babington Plot was, in large part, a trick, a trap prepared by Walsingham. And, in part at least, sprung by his double-dealing man Robert Poley.

Well, why not?

Poley, as Barfoot finds soon, was Walsingham's man, with some business dealings with young Thomas as well, years before the Babington Plot. Out of Clare College, Cambridge, but no degree and no kind of a university wit, Poley was a choir bird of several gaols long before he found himself in the Tower. In and out of prisons and so often in law courts, for this and for that, that he might as well have taken his lodgings there, he could have been seen for a kind of a clownish figure, if he were not so dangerous, so sinister, so devious, so rich. Owned nothing at all, not land or goods and chattels, so far as can be told. Yet always had handy large sums of money. And was, by record, careless and trusting concerning the security of his gold. Meaning one of two things and probably both. First, he had reason to believe there would always be more money forthcoming from some source or other. Second, that no one who knew of him would be likely to steal from him. And there is no record showing that anyone ever did so.

There is some evidence which Barfoot will find, together with an inference that he will arrive at, to show that this Robert Poley might sometimes have been sent into prisons, arriving as a prisoner himself, to dispose of others whom his master or masters wished to be rid of. Sometimes even servants of their own who might, as it sometimes happens, happen to know too much about this or that and whose mouths had better be stopped before the whole world also knew.

Poley could stop a mouth without leaving any kind of mark or trace. Why, it could happen even in sleep and leave the victim not any wiser though no less dead.

Barfoot will find that this Poley has a way with women. And one of them, Joan Yeomans, wife of one William, a cutler in London, gave him money and love and honored his trust; for he trusted her with money. Stood by him when the aggrieved husband sued him for alienation of affections—even while this business at Law was going on and Poley was lodged under lock and key at the Marshalsea, he managed to entertain Joan in his chamber there. Fellow was, in fact, married to some other woman at the time, but no matter.

And some few years later when a Mistress Browne, mother of the aforesaid Joan Yeomans, entered a chamber in her own house to discover Poley and Joan playing "Ride-a-cock horse" (this much a matter of lawful record also) "the sight thereof did so strike to her heart that she should never recover it." Since she had rented lodgings to Poley, she felt an awkward responsibility: "She prayed God to cut her off very quickly or else she feared she should be a bawd unto her own daughter." The Lord must have heard her prayer, for she was dead as a fish in the market in less than a week.

Do you suppose, Barfoot wonders, *the fellow was diddling the both of them?*

These three, then, shared the chamber and the last day of his life with Marlowe. One of them, Frizer—and why would he lie about something like that?—admits to killing the poet, but claims to have acted in defense of his own life. And the only witnesses, Skeres and Poley, a couple of gents under oath, solemnly support his story.

Well, even without looking deeper, there is this much to their story. None of these three would kill another man for sport. There would either have to be a reason, self-defense being one, or some gain. They would cut your throat for a shilling, though probably not Marlowe's. Or some grave loss if they did not *(stop his mouth!).* Or, as he takes it, they could all four have been so drunk that it was truly an accidental death. In which case the three survivors came to their senses and to the sense of one coherent story, shared by all three, very quickly indeed.

Of course, if it had all been planned in advance, they would have rehearsed their stories in advance.

But better not to think in those terms, or of anything else so simple and easy and attractive, yet. Not until he knows a good deal more than he does now.

What Barfoot already knows is that the missing pieces in this puzzle all have to do with Marlowe. What was he doing there and in such company?

BARFOOT TELLS A TALE

Awet rainy day is what it is, wind blowing and gusting now from one direction and now from the other. Streets and lanes muddy as can be. Taverns full up and shops almost empty except for a few bored apprentices. Nobody much abroad or outside, if they can help it, except for common laborers and those others whose errands and business must be tended to, like it or not, in any kind of weather.

It is a day to stay inside if you can and be as close to a fire as you are able to.

So you can safely wager that Barfoot will not be caught outside in the rain. Wherever he is, he will be warm and dry.

Most likely on a day like today he will be enjoying himself in the

company of a pair, a brace is what he calls them, of large and cheerful
young Dutch whores, the three of them in a commodious bed in a high
chamber in a large house across the River from Westminster and near
to Lambeth Marsh. Which will be rising slowly toward a flood on this
day.

His soldiering days have taught him many good lessons concerning
the various kinds and degrees of fear and discomfort and the pains a
man at war may have to feel and perhaps endure. Taught him, also,
more than a few words of several languages, though often the same
words in each. And he has also long since learned that there is genuine
solace and good comfort to be gained from keeping intimate company
with a large and healthy, and preferably untroubled, woman. Barfoot
believes there is even more of the same sort of pleasure to be enjoyed
with two women of that kind if they themselves are of an essentially
kind and generous disposition. Others, including most women of
every disposition, might not agree in general. And the truth is that
Barfoot's proposition is not derived from extensive experience, but
rather is descriptive of himself and these particular two Dutch whores,
the likes of which he might not find again from here to Cathay or
America. What is true is that here in London he has found these two
who can please him greatly and choose to do so. Most whores, abroad
as well as in England but especially the English whores, have failed to
lighten his heart. They are too tense and sour to offer much more than
the simple meat of themselves. But these, at least with him, are
different. And he deeply enjoys the pleasures offered up by these two
free and easy, undeniably simple, undemanding, milk-skinned young
women. Sturdy and hearty as can be, they are as warm and harmless as
cows in a barn. They are as wholesome as fresh sweet butter or soft
cheese on newly made wheat bread. These two are like twins, like
sisters anyway. Perhaps they are kin to each other. Heavy-breasted,
heavy-legged, broad-hipped, wide slow smilers with wide and smiling
blue eyes. And with a fine white acreage of smooth white skin which
is only very slightly, indifferently scarred here and there from what
must have been for them, like almost everyone else, a touch of the
smallpox sometime or other.

He is resting between them, as if they were the largest and softest
down pillows in the bed, a fire filling the space of the chamber with
its brightness and warmth and with the gentle swaying and dancing of

shadows (and sometimes spitting and smoky when wind and rain pour down the chimney) and the tiny leaded windowpanes lashed and splashed by the bursts of rain. Between them, for a moment spent and lax, Barfoot is sunburnt as cooked meat or a roasted nut. While he lies there, still and content, half a breath away from falling into a deep sleep, they begin to tease him by playing a kind of child's game and counting his body's commodity of large and small scars. All the nicks and slices and gouges, burned places, brute stitchery of barber surgeons. All his earnings from a lifetime of wounds and from every kind of sickness known to man. They giggle with a wordless joy that such a man, such an ugly and damaged one, could possess such power, like some kind of mountebank or necromancer, to waken within them and then satisfy a hunger felt deeply from the roots of their hair to the tips of their toenails. His earthy, animal color and undeniable, indeed assertive, ugliness serve to make them feel more than merely whole and healthy by contrast; but also, if only then and only briefly, beautiful to behold and as light of limb and flesh as young children. It is somehow as if his hurt body can take on and steal away all their sense of hurt and heaviness.

And there is something more, something like a puzzle to be solved. For even as they play at the game of cataloging his wealth of healed wounds, they are at the same moment, tempted to imagine him as he might possibly have been without them, unblemished and intact. There is no way they could find the words for it, even if English were their native language; but nonetheless what happens is that familiarity works its way. The more they study his ugliness, the more beautiful he seems to become, if only in the secret places of the mind's eye. But that is much, *much* . . . ! For, in love and in lust, the mind's eye is always the dancing master.

Now he smiles at them, laughs with them, though for a different reason. On the delicate, sheer edge of a sleep he will not, yet, be allowed to enjoy, he has to smile to imagine the next occasion when he finds a priest and a safe and appropriate time and place to make his confession. It will give a priest, especially a young and inexperienced one, fresh from seminary, too much to try not to think about.

—Father, try your best not to think about my two naked and delightful Dutch girls.

If you, a stranger to them all, were able to overcome the

predictably queasy objections of your stomach, its seasick condition being composed of equal parts of fascinated curiosity, controlled disgust, and the worldly-wise fear of creating any offense by looking too long and too closely at him, and were thus able to study the outward aspect and appearance of Barfoot at your leisure, there is much you could learn. You can seldom, if ever, have witnessed anyone else quite like him, not at least among those still walking about this world and busy with its ceaseless, quotidian business. As if by some miracle or magic, he possesses both arms and both legs, both hands and even each and every finger. Though the knuckles are somewhat scarred and swollen and one or two have turned vaguely black. He keeps both his eyes, too, if often mildly yellow and bloodshot and more and more, with years, squinting, brightly and in place, if nested among crow's-feet and little scars. His ears are somehow still whole and even decently shaped, neither clipped nor cut nor battered nor swollen. Lips are somewhat fat, to be sure, from too many brawls; and his nose is a wide and bumpy prominence. But all of it is there, and if it is not an object for envy or admiration, it is at least no worse to look at than many another. His teeth are as ragged as an old neglected hedge, and yet they are white enough (he is a careful man with toothpicks and tooth cloth) and solid and whole. He can and sometimes will smile and show his teeth like an old dog grinning to guard a buried bone.

Taken as a whole, then, his face and form are altogether better to look at than those of many a maimed and crippled beggar whom you might encounter at any street corner or churchyard or gatehouse. He can run and dance well enough, as well as many young fellows, sits a horse with pride in his posture and with a delicate balance. And he walks about the City with an easy, insinuating military strut. Just as if his joints and thews and sinews are youthful and supple enough to do whatever he wills.

Truth is, though, and you know it at sight and without a second thought, Barfoot has known every kind of pain. Pains that others can only imagine and therefore must fear. If every kind of inflicted wound has marked him with its indelible signature, then likewise every known, and several unknown, sickness and disease seems to have made an inn of his body and rested there for a time. He has shared himself with fevers and chills, fluxes and poxes, rashes and itches. And he has somehow endured. He has come through the sweating sickness. Not renewed or improved by it, to be sure, but not noticeably the worse for wear, either.

But that thing which astonishes all others most—for the people of England are justly and terribly fearful of it—is that he has suffered the Plague, taken sick with it, and endured the worst it can do this side of death. And he can, sometimes, when properly encouraged and in just the right circumstances, tell the tale of how that was for him.

These sweet Dutch whores, for whom the summer Plague seasons of London are always a most fearful time, love to hear him tell it. How the Plague came and how he survived it. It is as if his story, on its own, might serve them to drive away the danger like a necklace of garlic. But there is more to it than that. It is also true—let it be here and now admitted—that as whores, therefore unlikely to be wives and never to be ladies, they especially and profoundly enjoy all tales of magical transformation. Tales where dirty straw can be spun into fine gold and warty pigskin turned into silk and, who knows, even a whore from another country may suddenly believe herself, if only in fantasy, to be an English lady.

And also being of a more practical cast of mind, they like to take this as an emblematic tale of death and resurrection, a Christian homily.

And they are probably thinking that, by the time he will finish telling them his story, the best and finest part of him, perhaps the only part of him never yet wounded or scarred, though often taught humility through intensive hard labor, will have reawakened and proudly, handsomely risen up, eager once again to dance the oldest dance of this world.

• • •

. . . We were in France, he begins, during one of the bloody little wars there. Were in garrison, defending a town. Place of no importance. One which you will never have heard of even if I could remember the name of it now. I cannot. And most likely could not find the place again if my life depended on it.

Goes on. How there were four of them, all Englishmen, living in the house of a baker with his family. How all things were well and went well for a time. No enemy to fight and no serious threat of any.

The baker's wife and several daughters were as friendly and entertaining to them as anyone could be. Taught them to speak some of their language.

. . . And whenever the poor fellow, that baker, was gone out elsewhere, in the town or the countryside, about his business, which was often enough, those women taught us other French and froggy things. Things which were beyond the power of any words I knew then, even in my native tongue.

The sickness came on them and the town slowly at first, so slowly that they did not choose to notice or believe it. Denied it until the men in their own companies began to sicken and die of it. It was the Black Plague, the swelling kind, that swept into that town, and soon all around it, like an invisible fire. Burning them to death.

. . . Came first the ugly and painful blue and black swellings all over our bodies. And worst in most private places. One by one we one and all sickened until soon no one in that baker's house was left standing. Crawled and sprawled, we did, burning with fevers, shaking with chills, puking and beshitting ourselves.

Tells how they were by Law locked in the house. Fed by charity like prisoners. Until there was none left standing. None alive, as far as he could tell, but himself. And soon he was doubtful of himself because he could no longer make sounds to speak. If there had been anyone left to speak to. Could not smell the rot of the dead ones. Could not close his eyes to sleep or die. But soon could only see the ceiling of his chamber. At the last even the pain which had proclaimed he was alive was gone and he was only stiff and numb. Could feel himself cooling, stiffening.

. . . Somehow I heard, not without meaning but with the utter indifference of a ghost, the doors axed and smashed open and thieves came in to loot. To steal the coins in our purses, the jewels off our fingers (thank God my rings hung loose; for when a ring was tight they cut off the finger to take it), and the clothes off our backs. I felt myself lifted and turned like a log of wood as they stripped me naked and dropped me again to the floor. And I remember how I saw the blue-black swellings on these thieves themselves. Would have grinned then, if I could have. For here they were, dead men already, risking much for what little they could steal from us.

To what purpose? To buy a little more comfort before the Plague claimed them also?

. . . Who knows? Not I. I have seen men risk their lives, nay, *lose* their lives by lingering on a battlefield to pick corpses clean.

. . . If there is no limit to the cruelty of men in this world (and I know there is none), there is none, either, to the stupidity of greed.

. . . I lay on the floor, benumbed, next to my dead and rotting comrades, thinking, like a child slowly falling into a deep sleep: *We brought nothing into the world, neither may we carry anything out of the world. The Lord giveth and the Lord taketh away.*

He woke from death or dreaming, whichever it was, in a heap of bodies, flesh and bones of others, many others, heavy on him. Could not move a limb or open his eyes. But could feel himself sweating. And feel, too, other kinds of human juices, not his own, dripping on him, crawling on his flesh. Could hear again, and what he was hearing was a creaking and groaning, not human but of wood. Could smell a nauseous rot all around him. Though he had no energy to puke and nothing to puke anyway. Only a bitter drooling at the edge of his lips. Heard, faintly, human voices. Living voices. Would have cried out, then, if he could have. Yet could not manage to make a sound.

. . . Bit by bit and piece by piece, as if it were a kind of problem and myself, my life, only one part of it, I found myself thinking. Came to know that I was in a two-wheeled cart piled high with bodies, my own among them, and the cart groaning from the weight of its load of dead meat. And then as soon as I was able to imagine where I was, I began, slowly, to feel pain begin to reclaim first the suburbs, then the whole city of myself. In a while, I thought, I will have to move, somehow bestir myself, to ease this pain. And when I do that, they will see me and know I am alive.

No such good fortune. Cart stopped and some men began to unload it, heaving the bodies into a deep hole in the ground where other rotting bodies already lay in piles. He could feel their gloved hands as they gripped him, wrists and ankles, and, heave-ho!, hurled him arse over head, and a flashing view of blue sky and clouds before he fell among the dead bodies. Now pain was great and universal. Now his senses were as keen as ever. All but speech. Could neither speak nor groan. Could not form any sound. So formed words in his mind. Words of prayers. Prayed to Jesus and the Holy Virgin for his soul as he heard the cart rattle away and the voices of the men fade, too. He felt warm and sleepy, at peace, and dozed.

. . . Next thing—it must have been hours later, for it was full dark when I opened my eyes—I felt a sharp and sudden pain and cried out. I heard myself! Then heard a gasp nearby and sensed a face close to mine. Smelled it, the stinking breath breathing in mine. And thinking—I would have laughed if I had remembered how—how strange it was that this living breath was more stinking and foul by far than the ripe-rotten stink of my fellow corpses.

Next he knew, again in bits and pieces, he was pulled, groaning, from the nest of dead bodies, his bed of flesh and bones. Pulled slowly out of the hole and across bare earth, with much heavy breathing and frequent resting by his savior (if he were truly being saved) by his ankles. Dragged he was, but how long and how far he had no idea.

Later he was within some kind of rude shelter, some light from the dying coals of a small fire, and his head cradled in the lap of an old, old woman, wizened, ugly beyond imagining or telling. And she was spooning a bitter broth, wooden spoonful by spoonful, slowly, and crooning a tune that may have been a lullaby.

. . . Broth was bitter and foul to taste. God knows what mixture it was. But I did not gag. Swallowed it down like nectar and could feel, with each taste and swallow, warmth and life returning to my fingers and toes. To my limbs. Soon I could hear myself sobbing. Surely I was weeping for joy.

She stopped feeding him. Turned away to heap up the fire with fresh wood until it was blazing and filling the space of this shelter, hut, or hovel, with smoke. Pulled him, gently, closer to the fire. As close as could be without cooking. Covered him with a rough blanket. He lay there looking into the heart of the fire, hearing rain on the roof. Watching the raindrops fall flatly through the smoke hole of the roof, suddenly brightened, like clear jewels, by the firelight as they fell and spat and sizzled in the flames. And so, his head full of light, his body hot and sweating freely, he fell into a deep sleep.

. . . When did I awaken? Best to ask when was I truly awake again. For I would wake often, briefly, between deep sleeping. And the old woman, saint or witch I shall never know, cleaned me and fed me the bitter broth of life and hummed and crooned songs that followed me into my dreams.

. . . Much time passed, I am sure, before I could sit and stand on my own, then walk. Much time before I could walk outside, one tentative leg at a time like a man walking on stilts. It was spring and then summer and then the leaves were turning.

They could not talk to each other. For the language she spoke to him was not French or any tongue he had ever heard of. Perhaps she was a Gypsy. He learned to speak a few words from her, and to sing some others, but no one, not even Gypsies, seemed able to understand him later when he used her words. Perhaps she was mad.

. . . No matter there. A mad old woman in a mad old world. She was mad enough to give me back my life, to share that much of her madness with me. To feed me and clean me and, better than any physician I ever encountered, to keep me alive and allow me to heal. To find some plain clothes for me. Never mind where she may have found them or from whom they were taken. They were cleaned and brushed and aired, and I did not want to know. Even to find, somehow, a rusty old sword and the harness for it. So that, all in all, I looked to be what I truly was—a soldier.

. . . And then at last to send me on my way.

. . . It was a full year or more before I was free and able to come back to that part of the country again. I came back with money and with gifts. But could find no sign or trace of her. Nothing. Not any sign of the hut in the forest where we had lived together. Nor any indication of the great pit where they had heaped the bodies and bones of the townspeople.

The town was still there, to be sure, though much of it, including the baker's house, roofless, fallen down, half-burned, picked clean. And only a few people remaining. Some old folks, shy and wild-eyed, shadows of themselves. Shrill wild children who ran in packs like dogs. Not anyone who remembered him or knew anything to answer his questions.

. . . I began to believe that I could have dreamed it all. And in my degenerate sickness I could have dreamed such things. It is common enough. Except that I knew it was no dream. For it has been my fortune, for better and worse, always to know when I am dreaming. From my childhood until now I have known when I was dreaming. Which knowledge does not spare me from my full share of nightmares. But it can make the terrors of deep dreaming somewhat easier to bear. And besides . . .

Here he shows his Dutch whores some few coin-sized, bruise-colored places on his body, scars almost lost among the worse ones clamoring for attention, hidden in his armpits and crotch and partly concealed by his thin hair, just behind his right ear.

. . . Here's the proof. Proof that I have come back from the dead. Proof that I have endured the Black Plague and returned to tell you about it.

Laughs then, surprising them.

. . . Well, the truth is, he continues, that there must be many who, with a little luck, survive the Plague. I believe a man might be safer with the Plague than on many a battlefield. Somehow or other I have so far survived them both. I have walked in the shadow of the valley of Death. To what purpose? So that I can spend this rainy day with you.

Now they laugh.

He props himself on an elbow and with his free hand gently touches and teases the nipple of one remarkable breast.

. . . Dreams, he says. Something more about dreams. Sometimes, like it or not, I dream I am sick with the Plague and living in that smoky little hut with the old woman.

. . . And in my dream I find that I am very doubtful, untrusting. I fear she may be a witch. She will not give me my life-giving bitter broth unless and until I promise to love her forever and to seal my promise with a kiss full on her mouth.

. . . She is so ugly—uglier by far in my dream than in life or memory—that I fear she is the emblem or servant of Death and the Devil. Her breath has the stinking essence of every dead thing in the world.

. . . I must make a free choice. It is not simply life or no life. For even though the broth may give me life and strength, her kiss may be a powerful poison like a toad's. And will kill me dead. But I must make my choice. And I do so. I pucker up my lips and close my eyes tight and lean toward that face all full of warts and wrinkles and wild gray hairs and rich with the overwhelming stink of her breath.

And then?

. . . Why, then the dream always ends. And I find that I am wide awake and will never know what might have happened next.

What do you think might have happened?

. . . When I finally kiss her, there is a great puff of colored smoke. And then she reappears, utterly transformed. I discover she has turned into you two.

And then?

. . . See for yourself what happens next.

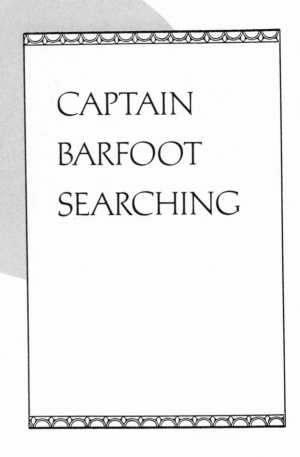

CAPTAIN
BARFOOT
SEARCHING

By now he has already been there and seen for himself. Seen what can be seen.

He has been downriver to Deptford Strand and visited the commodious old house owned by the widow, Eleanor Bull. It is neither precisely a tavern nor an inn, but, rather, a private house with some of the customs of both. For you can take a sleeping chamber there. And you can order food and drink to be served. It costs a little more than either tavern or inn, but offers what neither of those places can: true privacy. No doubt, though, that Eleanor Bull's house is as busy and lively as any inn whenever the Court has come to settle nearby at Greenwich.

Barfoot decided to take along with him one of his Dutch whores, the more presentable one of the two, well scrubbed and well dressed, looking better than many of the whores you might see, though not to be confused, either, with any man's good wife. The two of them looking as if they were stealing away from the City for a quiet, illicit day. As if they had come down here to see the ships and the docks and maybe even Sir Francis Drake's *Golden Hind*, now slowly rotting at its last dock in Deptford.

Barfoot's thinking was that a man who appears to be nervously dedicated to seduction, not, he guessed, a type unfamiliar to Eleanor Bull, is not likely to be taken as much of a menace. Is less to be feared than to be pitied.

They arrived early and ate dinner close by the fireplace. For it was beginning to be blustery cold on the River. Drank some of her strong double-brewed beer. "Drake's Surprise," she calls it.

It proved to be a clean, pleasant place, warm and well lit. Not many others to share the dinner with them. A few who looked to be serious voyagers, awaiting passage to the Continent. Some local folk, especially from among the shipwrights and mariners and such. Decent people in a decent place.

Finally, with the table more or less cleared and himself puffing his pipe, Barfoot asked for some cakes and three cups of sweet wine. One for their hostess. Who was a large woman, cheerful and outspoken, with a face as plain as a fruit pie. She accepted Barfoot's compliments for dinner and the pleasures of her own wine. He talked a little of this and that before he asked her anything about the day in May four years ago when there had been a bloody murder in this place. Spoke gently, hesitantly at first, lest he should frighten or offend her. But soon it seemed clear that the woman was not at all frightened by the subject. Was ashamed of nothing and, indeed, seemed to enjoy rehearsing her story. Clear, too, that, because she must have told it often as the time passed, all of the pieces of her story had come by now to fit together as smoothly in place as if cut and fashioned by a master joiner. Time and familiarity can do that to the wildest and most wonderfully confused tale. By now rigors of torture could not have restored the ragged edges of truth to her version.

And so his stance changed ever so slightly, from quietly gentle to simply casual. Her accounting meant more to him than a wide yawn and a shrug. But (like a player, yes) he seemed to be making himself, out of good manners, maintain an appropriate and apparent interest.

He was much more interested in what she might show him.

Later, to clear their heads and freshen themselves, the three of them went outside to walk the paths of her garden while she showed them how, in friendlier seasons, it must bloom and thrive. Inside once more, standing close to the fire, happy to be out of the cold wet wind, they drank more wine. And when he suggested that it would be worth her while, Eleanor Bull was willing to lead them upstairs and to show them the chamber where the killing had happened.

It was somewhat larger than he had guessed it would be. There were a pair of long windows looking north through bare autumnal trees toward splashes of the River and pieces of docksides. At the eastern end of the chamber another smaller window allowed a view of some of the towers and high places of the palace at Greenwich. There was a solid and simple bed, built more for warmth and privacy and comfort than for luxury. A clothespress and a single chest large enough to serve for a sea voyage. Perhaps it was, truly, a sea chest. Bench and table. Couple of joint stools. Embroidered cushions. On the blank south wall hung an old-fashioned painted cloth, large and fading, depicting the story of Abraham and Isaac.

"Such a clean, spare, pleasant place," he told her. "I cannot picture anything terrible happening here."

"Well, it happened here, all right. No question about that," Eleanor Bull said. "And I'll tell you it took some cleaning and scrubbing, too, to set it back in order."

"Bloodstains . . ."

"They always splash and splatter here and there where you least look for them. And what with all the wrestling and thrashing about, these men managed to break up two of my best stools and to rip up a cushion also. They paid me for all of it, to be sure, and a good deal more than it was worth. But nevertheless it took time and trouble to set it right again."

"Was everything much the same as we find it now?"

"It is furnished and equipped as it was then. People seem to prefer it."

"What people?"

"Oh, you know well enough. Folks—and there are always some of them, and there is no explaining of it beyond the truth that it is the inherited contagion of Adam and Eve—they come here especially to spend some time (an hour, an afternoon, sometimes a night) in the same chamber where a famous man was murdered."

"Was he famous, then?"

"Kit Marlowe?"

"Who else?"

"I think so. I think he must have been well known. Though, for the life of me, I do not know what for. I knew him, for he often came here with his friends. And he was pleasant and cheerful enough and usually polite as a choirboy. Except when he had been drinking too much. Sometimes when he was drunk he could be insolent and arrogant. He would speak harshly to my servants and to me, as well. But he was no great respecter of persons; for he could be, would be, indeed, as rude-spoken to his own friends as to anyone else."

"So it seems. And it seems to have led him into trouble."

"Next day, if he had been particularly obstreperous, he would come by, on the way to or from Scadbury, and bring me some presents, some herbs or some flowers, a fine bottle of the best sack, the sweet kind I have always favored."

"Perhaps if he had lived through this occasion he would have given you a fine jewel. Or even married you on the spot."

"Shame on you, sir!" With a laugh that showed that sack and sugar, among other things, had left her with teeth like the toppled and crumbled crenellations of an old castle. "I do not believe Kit Marlowe was likely to be a husband."

"Pity . . . for him."

"It pains me to speak ill of the dead."

"To be sure."

"But I have a suspicion that he favored men and boys for his intimate comparisons."

"Do you know that to be true, Mistress Bull?"

"As I said," (she primly now), "it is only a suspicion. And as I said, there are other strange people who like to spend some time in the room where he died. And they will pay for it. And it pleases them to be told that the room is almost exactly the same as it was on that day. Does that astonish you?"

He laughed now, softly and politely.

"Have a look at my face in the light, good woman, and then try to imagine what in the world—from bloody birth to bloody murder— might still astonish me."

"Faces tell as many lies as tongues."

"True, true. And I thank you kindly for reminding me of it," he said. "But what a pity. Would it not be ever so much better for all of us if the books of the world were easy reading. If things were no more and no less than they seem to be."

"Amen to that," she said. "Though I must confess that I am not often a reader of books."

"Did you suspect nothing, no danger, from the faces of the other men who came with Marlowe and hired the chamber from you on that day?"

"They came separately and met here."

"Ah . . ."

"Kit and Mr. Frizer came out together by a hired boat from the city. The other two, as I remember, had horses. But, you see, I knew them all already, from one time and another. And they were decent folk, gentlemen. Or so it seemed. I would not have allowed them into my house otherwise."

"Certainly not."

"I may be a widow and somewhat poor, but I have my pride."

"I can see that and I honor you for it."

"Only there was this much, sir, now that you ask . . . and it is a strange thing, but I had not thought of it, really, or remembered it until now. I did allow myself that morning to feel some vague suspicions concerning poor Kit Marlowe. It seemed to me . . . I had a feeling that he was likely to be drunk and cause trouble. Nothing to do with anything he said. Nothing to do with the look of him, either. True, as I told the Coroner and the jury, he did look somewhat troubled and distracted; but, then, he always did. No, it was a womanly thing, what they call . . ."

"An intuition."

"Exactly. He had an uneasy restless humor that day and it showed itself to me in his eyes and the look on his face. But he was kind and courteous. He was a gentleman at heart, at least when he was sober."

"And the other three?"

"I cannot speak for their hearts, not then or now or ever. If you follow my meaning."

"You are telling me they are close with truth and with the secrets of themselves."

"Tight as a clenched fist, sir. I had known them all three as long or longer than I had known Marlowe. And yet I knew them not at all. And I can swear to you, as I did then, that I would never have dreamed in my worst nightmare that Kit Marlowe would die here in my house. All bloody on the floor . . . !"

"And this, mistress?"

Barfoot lifted the edge of the painted cloth of Abraham and Isaac to show and point to a rust-colored smudge the size, perhaps, of a small child's hand.

"Could this be a little splash of Christopher Marlowe?"

At that the woman laughed out loud and her large breasts shook beneath her gown before she answered him.

"Lord save and forgive me, sir. But I must confess to you that it is no more than a bit of blood from a chicken or a calf. From time to time, I rub a little blood there, myself, to please the desires of curious folk who like to discover such things."

"Does it please them?"

"As far as I know, sir, you are the first one ever to notice it."

"That is because I am far worse and far more curious than any of them."

"Not more curious than one, I will tell you."

"Who would that be?"

"A handsome young fellow, a player, I believe . . . no, I know it, for I saw him once or twice upon the stage and he is handsome enough to remember."

"Do you frequent playhouses?"

"Oh no. Not ever these days. But when my husband was still alive and well (and that was not so long ago), we sometimes took ourselves to the Rose. And once or twice west over to Shoreditch. It was a merry time, and I did not know then what a wicked place it was."

Captain Barfoot fished in his purse and gave her something

adequate (more than adequate, his whore thought) for all her kindness and trouble.

"Pay no attention to the preachers and such," he told her. "Take my word for it. Stage plays are a harmless diversion with much to teach us even as they please. You must go again and see for yourself."

"Ah, but who would ever take a fat old widow to see a play?"

"I would for one. And, by God's wounds, I will, too, if you let me. Count on it."

"All of you men are the same."

"How is that?"

"You make promises and then you break them like piecrusts."

"Wait and see," he told her. Then: "This handsome young player, did he promise you anything?"

"No, sir, but he was very generous."

Giving her more money (despite the Dutch whore's hard look, as if it were her money he was giving away), he thanked her for remembering the generous player and urged her to forget everything about himself, even his own handsome face, except for his promise to come one day and take her to see a stage play.

A final cup of wine together downstairs. And he bade the widow farewell.

Next he and his whore walked down to the River, where they found a pair of idle boatmen with a wherry, blest with cushioned seats and a blanket and a little canopy against the chilly weather of the fading day, to carry them back to the City on the rising tide.

"So, then," said the young woman, lying in his arms for warmth and pleasure, she who had been all smiling with large good teeth and good manners, and likewise as quiet as a country mouse, all day long, "did you discover whatever it is you are looking for?"

He stroked her rich, thick blond hair. Ahead of them the towers and steeples of London and Southwark glistened in late weak light. Gulls circled and cried out like hurt children. The anchored ships were beginning to hang out their lanterns, and he silently offered a small prayer of thanksgiving that he was not boarding any one of them for a voyage to anywhere. Already he was mildly queasy from the ripples and light waves of the River.

"No," he said. "I did not find exactly what I went for. But I found out something else. Something I had not expected to, though God knows I should have . . ."

He might have talked on and told her much more than he ought to, but she was weary and, as well, a little dizzy from the wine she had drunk. Warmed against the cold twilight by the woolen blanket and his arms, she was already half-asleep and in a moment or two would be cheerfully snoring like a well-fed dog at fireside.

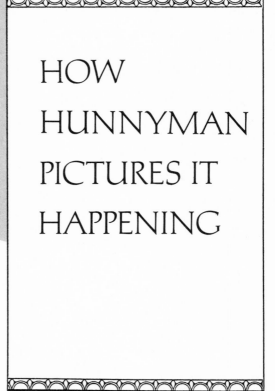

HOW HUNNYMAN PICTURES IT HAPPENING

Four men in the room. Three of them, playing cards at a table, he does not know by sight and still only vaguely by repute. They are: Nicholas Skeres and Robert Poley and Ingram Frizer. Frizer is—or claims to be and who is Hunnyman to question this?—a gentleman. As do they all three insist. For certain Frizer is an agent, a trusted servant of Sir Thomas Walsingham of Scadbury. Is still now what he was then. The other two were, maybe still are, also, agents, perhaps trusted or perhaps not, anyway messengers for the Court. And in all likelihood servants of and for some great men of the Court. He does not know or guess (yet) whom they may serve. Poley he knows by name, along with half the population of London, as a spy for the late Sir

Francis Walsingham, one of those who turned and betrayed the Babington Plot against the Queen.

But Hunnyman does not need to know them or their faces to know the type. Gentlemen or no, and no matter, they are not civil and gentle men. Are rough and ready, hard-bitten, hardhearted fellows. Gamblers with their own lives, they are not notably cruel with others except as a wild beast might be cruel. That is, they are sometimes suddenly cruel, without thought or premeditation. But here, on this evening he pictures them, out of a time not so long past, they are only gambling, not seriously, for money. All three are somewhat drunk. Well, they have been drinking since ten o'clock in the morning or thereabouts. And it is now well past suppertime.

Fourth is drunkest of all. Never a graceful drinker, he is now sprawled on the bed, half in the shadows of the chamber. Sprawled, loose-limbed like a child's neglected doll, he groans softly.

Hunnyman knows him and his face. A small man with a soft pale boyish face. Trim little mustache that seems an afterthought, a boy's disguise. Large dark wet eyes. Soft hurt weak look about him that could deceive you if you could not guess beyond first impressions. For truth is he has a fiery violence about him and the fuse of a quick choler. In some ways, of all these four, he is by far the most dangerous. Even his innocence is dangerous. And if you did not know him or know of him you might make the mistake of taking him to be as weak as he looks.

He is Marlowe, the poet and playmaker, who has found himself on this particular day not among other poets or among the players of stage plays. But, instead, among some ruthless hired men from the world's bloody stage. Where all bloody wounds are real and the dead do not rise up and dance jigs and take bows.

It has been boisterous much of the day. Now the three laugh and drink and continue to play at cards. Poet, pain in his gut, is half dozing but cannot sleep. On account of the noise of them, he thinks. Props head on hand, himself on his elbow, and glares at them. Says something aloud.

Whatever it is he has said evokes a sharp reply from Frizer. Who does not even trouble to look back over his shoulder when he speaks contemptuously to the man on the bed.

Marlowe replies in kind.

What?

May be that Frizer's luck is bad, running thinly, and Marlowe mocks him for this. A moment later, anyway, they are speaking of money and the reckoning for their long idle day—a chamber, much drinking and eating in the house of Eleanor Bull of Deptford. No doubt a sufficiently extravagant reckoning.

And then Frizer tells Marlowe that while he was asleep or trying to sleep, the three of them have reached an agreement that Marlowe should pay the reckoning for all.

Are they merely jesting, teasing him? No matter if they are or are not. The very idea of it outrages the poet. Who now curses them from the safety of his shadowy place. Then, becoming even more the victim of his own rage when they laugh at him and pay him no more mind, staggers to his feet. Stands and moves toward them. Sees, then snatches for and grabs Frizer's expensive knife from its scabbard. Frizer tries to stand up and turn away, but the poet seizes and holds him, wrestling him and slashing with the knife. Twice he cuts Frizer in the scalp. Not dangerous wounds, but with much blood.

Frizer grapples to regain the knife. It is then and there (as all will swear in testimony) in that desperate grappling and wrestling, both men gripping the hilt of the knife, that the poet is stabbed. Point and blade into the dark wet jelly of his eyeball and some inches of thrust before it sticks in brain or bone and the poet goes suddenly and completely limp. Crumples in a spreading stain and puddle of lifeblood. He falls limp without a sound even as Frizer, with a strong yank, pulls free the knife and holds it high. There, see, clotted on the point, like a piece of soft cheese or mincemeat, is a gray wet gob of Christopher Marlowe's brains.

Three men bend over him, looking down at him as if he were a fallen beast. The only sound in the room is Frizer's heavy breathing.

Hunnyman thinks he can hear that breathing in his own chamber, in his own bed, alone in the dark where he is not sleeping and dreaming and yet not fully awake either. He is playing along the edges of sleep, like a child at the waterside, when he pictures these things happening. No! When these things happen and he cannot help seeing.

In a moment the heaving of his chest and the fierce beating of his heart will tell him that he cannot be hearing any sounds from the room in Deptford. He is making the sounds himself. All of them. Even the gasp and the sharp cry of the poet. Who was killed so clean and quick that he cannot have uttered any cry at all. He was stone dead before he fell to the floor.

Hunnyman cries out for him.

Sitting up in his bed in the darkness, Hunnyman hears his own voice pleading for the poet's life, then mourning for the loss of it. As if it were his own. As if he might have saved that life. As if he had somehow failed to do so. As if it were somehow his fault.

Feels himself shaking and weeping. And swears out loud, between gasps of weeping, that he will never tell anyone else about this. Will never admit to another living soul in this cruel world that he has experienced this childish, weak, and womanly thing. This fear and weeping. This sorrow, these tears for a dead man who was almost a perfect stranger.

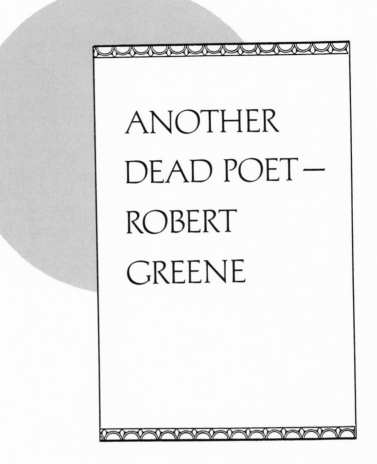

ANOTHER DEAD POET— ROBERT GREENE

A poet is a waste-good and an unthrift, that he is born to make taverns rich and himself a beggar. If he have forty pound in his purse together, he puts it not to usury, neither buys land nor merchandise with it, but a month's commodity of wenches and capons.

—*Robert Greene,* A Quip for an Upstart Courtier

I was altogether unacquainted with the man and never once saluted him by name. But who in London has not heard of his dissolute and licentious living? his fond disguising of a Master of Art with ruffianly hair, unseemly apparel, and more unseemly company? his vainglorious and thrasonical braving? his extemporizing and Tarletonizing? his apish counterfeiting of every ridiculous and absurd toy? his fine cozening of jugglers and finer juggling of cozeners? his villainous cogging and foisting? his monstrous swearing and horrible forswearing? his impious profaning of sacred texts? his other scandalous and blasphemous raving? . . . his infamous resorting to the Bankside, Shoreditch, Southwark, and other filthy haunts? his obscure lurking in basest corners? his pawning of his sword, cloak and what not when money came short?

—*Gabriel Harvey,* Four letters and Certain Sonnets, Especially Touching Robert Greene

I was somewhat acquainted with him. He was red-haired, fair-skinned, and much freckled. With his long (and celebrated and remembered), tangled, sharply pointed red beard. Slight of size, though blessed and cursed with the appetites for rich food and strong drink, for laughter and loose women, for aimless tavern talk and for sweaty, desperate gaming, of a giant twice his size and girth. Greedy for the means to satisfy the mutinous army of his hungers, he was nevertheless generous to a fault. And, ah yes, greatly gifted in the art and craft of words. Onstage, on the page in both prose and verse.

Of his skills his friend and fellow university wit Thomas Nashe once wrote: *In a night and a day he would have yarked up a pamphlet as well as in seven year. And glad was that printer might be so blessed to pay him dear for the dregs of his wit.*

Even though he would lie about it sometimes, later on, he was born and grew up in the old walled city of Norwich, county of Norfolk—that wide, reedy place of large, cloud-browsing skies and slow, ale-colored rivers. One of which, the Wensum, having swallowed up the Yare whole, and then looping and turning there, north and east and then northward again, edges the city.

City with a castle on a little hill, on whose walls the rebel Robert Kett from Wymondham was hanged in '49. City of the Cathedral Church of Holy Trinity, cloister and close. Bell-haunted city of more than half a hundred parish churches, most of them made from cut flintstones, glistening and black, as if polished, in any rain.

Father was a saddler there where Englishmen worked leather and Dutch and French exiles came, bringing their pet canaries and their strangers' ways, to live and to prosper at the weaver's trade. Great wool merchants lived grandly and more quietly over the river in Colgate.

There was a ferryman named Sandling would take you across in those days . . .

But quiet was not his pleasure in youth. Bells rang in the air rich with peat smoke and there were many fires in the thatched roofs (before they were finally forbidden) to bring a schoolboy running hard to see.

And if you happened to walk up Guildhall Hill and down the other side, you came directly to the marketplace near the church of St. Peter Mancroft. Market where every kind of spice scented the air and there were stalls with all kinds of fine things not only from England but from all over the world.

Fine things there to be had and owned by anyone with money to buy them.

He would have some money now and then, by one means and another. Defending him from the posthumous charges of Gabriel Harvey, Nashe said: *In one year he pissed as much against the walls as thou and thy brother made in three.*

Never enough and never for long.

He, himself, would write in satire and in the bitterness of worldly wisdom, but half meaning it, too. It was, after all, the wisdom of our age: *Multiply in wealth, my son, by any means thou may . . . Thou shouldst not stand on conscience in causes of profit, but heap treasure upon treasure, for the time of need . . . Seest thou not that many perish in the streets and fall to theft for need whom small succor would relieve? Then where is conscience and why art thou bound to use it more than other men? Seest thou not daily forgeries, perjuries, oppressions, rackings of the poor, raising of rents, enhancing of duties, even by them that should be all conscience if they meant as they speak?*

But that kind of hardheaded, hardhearted, satirical wisdom would come along later. Then and there, for a quick-witted schoolboy, the world was wide and bright and accessible through an open door.

In late, cold, damp November of '75 he crossed the Fens to St. John's College, Cambridge. Marlowe would come there five years later, not to populous St. John's but to St. Bene't's. Marlowe was a lucky scholarship man. Greene was a sizar, required to work hard to pay his way. Rose at four o'clock; chapel at five; study till dinner time at ten; supper at five; and study until ten, when all lights must be put out. *And those being without fires are fain to walk or run up and down for half an hour to get a heat on their feet before they go to bed . . .*

And yet, for all his hard labor and his studying, he spent some of his time at other things in nearby places, at the White Horse and the Black Bear and the Rose and Crown. He claims and confesses it: *For being at the University of Cambridge, I light among wags as lewd as myself with whom I consumed the flower of my youth.*

He graduated in '78 as a bachelor of arts.

• • •

Middle of August in '78 and the Queen and her Court, in Progress, came to Norwich. Met at St. Stephen's Gate by Sir Robert Wood, Mayor, and sixty young men of the city, all dressed in black and yellow, to begin six days of pomp and show and ceremony. Surely he was there among them:

> *Great is the joy that Norwich feels this day:*
> *If well we weighed the greatness of your mind.*
> *Few words would serve, we had but small to say.*
> *But knowing that your goodness takes things well*
> *That well are meant, we badly do proceed.*
> *And so good Queen, both welcome and farewell,*
> *Thine own we are in heart, in word, and deed.*

Soon after he and some of his friends crossed over to the Continent to see some of the world, including Italy and Spain . . . *in which places I saw and practiced such villainy as is abominable to declare . . . At my return into England I ruffled out my silks, in the habit of Malcontent and seemed so discontent that no place would please me to abide in nor no vocation cause me to stay myself in.*

Returned first to study once again at Cambridge, this time at Clare Hall, close by King's College Chapel and Trinity Hall, and took his degree as master of arts in '83.

I left the university and away to London where (after I had continued some short time and driven myself out of credit with sundry of my friends) I became an author of plays and a penner of love pamphlets. So that I soon grew famous in that quality . . . Young yet in years, though old in wickedness, I began to resolve that there was nothing bad that was profitable . . . I was drowned

*in pride, whoredom was my daily exercise, and gluttony and drunkenness were
my only delight.*

• • •

Came a brief repentance and recovery. Prodigal son was the parable
he turned to most often for the spine and spirit for his own work; so
no surprise he was so often so eager to repent in public.

Returned to Norwich and there heard a sermon of great power and
zeal preached at St. Andrew's Church. Vowed then and there to reform
himself. And did so, too. For a time. Married "a gentleman's daughter
of good account" and had a child by her. But soon: *I cast her off, having
spent up the marriage money I obtained by her.*

And back to London where: *I fell again with the dog to my old vomit
and put my wicked life in practice and that so thoroughly as ever before.*

• • •

In the City his friends and enemies, allies and rivals, came from
among those other university wits who earned their ways by the
writing of poems and pamphlets and romances and plays. Those
whom, at the end, he would call: *those gentlemen, his quondam
acquaintance, that spend their wits in making plays.* He was one among
them and merry company on the best days. A quick and ready and
careless wit. And unafraid of labor; though now, as a gentleman
scholar, himself, he had learned better than ever to be seen at work,
laboring over a line or sweating about scansion. I do believe, though
he never showed it then, he envied Kit Marlowe and any others who
had been luckier and enjoyed an easier time at college. Maybe, as I
think of it, he had to envy Marlowe most. For Marlowe, the
shoemaker's son from Canterbury, had been recognized and rewarded
early, first at King's School and next at St. Bene't's where he was an
Archbishop Parker scholar, meaning he was better off by far than
anyone else except the truly rich, the children of the nobility. And
then, also, even though Marlowe properly earned his master of arts
degree, they bent the rules somewhat for him to take it. And that
would have nettled Greene also. Who was so acutely sensitive to such
things as many envious and ambitious souls are bound to be.

Still and all, he and Marlowe were friends almost to the end. Marlowe honored him (and was taught and influenced by him) for his gifts, his art and craft. And from the first, Greene, for all his faults, was too wise and just not to have seen that Marlowe had the seeds of greatness.

Greene lived in the liberty of Norton Folgate, in Shoreditch, out north beyond the gates and walls of the City, close by the Theatre and the Curtain. Lived with a woman, whom Gabriel Harvey called "a sorry ragged queen," by whom he had a son (unluckily) named Fortunatus. Her brother was the well-known felon called Cutting Ball who was later hanged for his crimes at Tyburn. Greene's friends and acquaintances came more and more to be rogues and rascals, baseborn, low-life, masterless, scuts and skroyles, whom he admitted to be (at the least): *odd madcaps I have been mate to, not as companion, but as a spy to have an insight into their knaveries.*

And who, then or now, cares to believe that?

Wrote and published pamphlets about them and their crafts and arts, secrets and secret words, as if they were the pride of England.

In all those countries where I have travelled I have not seen more excess of vanity than we Englishmen practice through vainglory. For as our wits be as ripe as any, so our wills are more ready than they all to put into effect any of their licentious abuses.

On the third of September of '92, living in a room he had rented from a shoemaker near Dowgate, Greene died after a month-long illness. Died desperately poor and all alone except for his child and his mistress. Who pawned and sold whatever she could to pay for his burial.

Before he died he sent a letter on behalf of the shoemaker to his cast-off wife:

Doll, I charge thee by the love of our youth and by my soul's rest that thou wilt see this man paid. For if he and his wife had not succored me, I had died in the streets.

I think, even as those who knew him were sorrowful over what had become of him, the first of that bright company to go, were struck as much with fear as with sorrow. Greene had seemed, for his time, so . . . *indestructible.* So bright with promise. There would be time. Time to prosper. A time to laugh and (please, Lord, later) even a time to repent. They were golden lads, touched by Midas and made invulnerable.

When Greene died and died badly, I believe Marlowe felt it first and to the quick. Knew, somehow, that the game, their time, brief as it was, was almost over and done with.

• • •

Greene was not fully cold and stiff before his friends and enemies began to quarrel over him.

Harvey was piously savage:

I rather hope of the dead as I might wish to the living, that grace might finally abound where wickedness did overflow; and that Christ in his divine goodness should miraculously forgive the man that in his devilish badness blasphemously reviled God. The dead bite not; and I am none of those that bite the dead . . .

To which our Thomas Nashe replied . . .

(Nashe had clashed with Harvey more than once in print. Lord knows we fought each other, dueled with words and without mercy.

(Here are a few, only a few, mind you, of the names Nashe had already imposed on Harvey: His Gabrielship, Braggadocio Glorioso, Gabriel Huffe Snuffe, Gamaliel Hobgoblin, Brother Hoddy Doddy, Doctor Hum, etc.)

Nashe answered Harvey simply enough, saying, irrefutably (among other things): *Debt and deadly sin, who is not subject to? With any notorious crime I never knew him tainted.*

• • •

Like every poet since Adam himself named the beasts, since Cain and Abel offered up their gifts for God's inspection and pleasure, since the poetry of Job was silenced by the voice in the whirlwind, Robert Greene had lessons to learn and teach. In death as well as life. In his last work, written in his illness, he had many sharp and satirical words for some of his friends and fellows—Marlowe, Nashe, and Peele and Kyd. And, almost in passing, in an aside, and as much for the sake of pun and allusion, he mentions a player who was already earning a popular reputation as a playwright as well: *Yet trust them not, for there is an upstart crow, beautified with our feathers that, with his tiger's heart wrapped in a player's hide, supposes he is as well able to bombast out a blank verse as the best of you; and being an absolute Johannes Factotum, is in his own conceit the only Shake-scene in a country.*

Thus Greene, who, like every poet since Adam on naming day and despite all his protestations otherwise, yearned most for a measure of immortality, has earned that exactly. Being now known to your age chiefly on account of his malicious mention of William Shakespeare in London in 1592.

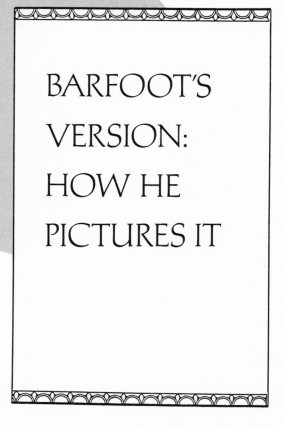

BARFOOT'S VERSION: HOW HE PICTURES IT

We know the place where Marlowe died.

We know when his death took place.

And we know the place (nearby parish church of St. Nicholas) where his body was hastily buried.

How it all happened is less certain.

Why it happened remains (so far) a mystery.

The findings of William Danby, Coroner of the Queen's Household, and of his jury of good men and true, while sufficient in Law to have saved the skin and bones of Ingram Frizer and with all the alacrity the Law can allow, are not wholly satisfactory. This version of events is somewhat difficult to believe, at least without asking some more questions.

For the present, let us begin with what we can be reasonably sure of. All of the rest of it, if only bit by bit and piece by piece, will have to follow after.

Four men. Men who know each other and have some things in common. They spend most of an idle spring day together at Eleanor Bull's house in Deptford. Time together begins around ten o'clock in the morning when Marlowe is returning from Westminster. They meet. They drink together. They eat dinner. After which they repair to the garden. Where they pass some hours walking and talking.

Talking about what?

Eleanor Bull will not venture a guess. Nor will any of her servants who came outside, from time to time, to serve them. The four men are served regularly all afternoon, drink freely. All that the servants noticed and will allow is that the conversation among these men is close, cautious, serious. All in whispers and soft voices. Drinking or not, they manage to maintain their habits of caution. Drunk or not, they are not at any time truly idle in that garden. They are all engaged in some kind of business, something calling not for jests and laughter. Not calling, either, for signs of strong disagreement, for argument and loud voices. It must be something about which their assumptions can be presumed to be much the same.

Then comes time for supper. And they ask for the use of a private chamber and that their supper be served there. Perhaps they have by then arrived at a settlement or conclusion to the business that concerned them all afternoon. For now they are merry and cheerful. They eat well. They drink more and they remain in the room.

After a while Marlowe dozes on the bed. The others (with their backs to him, it is said) are playing at backgammon at the table. Though there are some stools with cushions, the three are sitting on a bench by the table, cheek to cheek, to play the game.

At some point a quarrel begins. Quarrel over the matter of the reckoning. Marlowe, whose rashness and intemperance, whose sudden rages and fits of violence, are a matter of lawful record (and, more to the point, are surely familiar to these three) loses his temper. Leaps up from bed. Snatches Frizer's knife. Frizer is unable to move to defend himself. Important point of Law, he is unable to move and to put himself out of harm's way. If he could still flee for his life, then it would not be a matter of self-defense.

Marlowe cuts Frizer twice. Deep and long, but not dangerously. Wounds him in the scalp. Then there is blood enough for those who take pleasure in the spilling of it. Blood enough and plenty to spatter walls and floor and even the painted cloth of Abraham and Isaac.

Then.

Thus.

Blood flowing, pouring off his head, half blinding him, Frizer fights for his life. Finds some way to grasp for and grip the hilt of his knife. Thrusts with it even as Marlowe (somehow, perhaps in clumsy drunkenness, perhaps slipping in the blood of Frizer) falls upon it. Thrust and fall. Blade goes in easy through eyeball directly into Marlowe's brain.

And down he goes. Dead as any gutted fish. One of the other two—Poley? Skeres? Who truly remembers?—rushes out of the chamber calling for help. The other, seeing that Marlowe is already beyond any aid or comfort, turns and tries to staunch the wounds of Ingram Frizer.

Now.

Because the Queen and her Court are in residence at Greenwich, banners of St. George announcing it from every pole, and because Eleanor Bull's house is well within the limits of the verge of Court, it falls the lawful duty of Mr. Danby to deal with this matter. First thing next morning the Coroner brings his jury of sixteen men, mostly from Deptford, to view the place, to look at Marlowe's body where it lies, and to hear testimony. Chiefly the testimony of the three witnesses. Thereupon Marlowe's corpse is carried away to St. Nicholas's church and immediately buried.

Frizer is held, for Law requires it, but briefly. On the strength of William Danby's findings Frizer's actions are declared to be a just and lawful defense of himself.

In defensione ac salvacione vita sua . . .

Matter is thereupon closed. Like a slammed and locked chest lid. Matter is so tightly closed, in spite of all the usual gossip and bruit and speculation, that many people believe Marlowe died of the Plague. In that terrible season of it. Good Lord deliver us.

Others pass around a tale that he was killed, stabbed to death, by a common servant in a quarrel over a whore.

Either way, many more precise and religious souls see it as a clear warning from God.

Some of our better poets are not at all displeased by Christopher Marlowe's permanent absence from the scene. It is an excellent occasion for heartfelt elegies by his friends. For satirical thrusts by his enemies.

If there are again these days, and just as the public interest seemed to be diminishing, just as it seemed that the fashions of playmaking were changing, large crowds coming together for the performances of his stage plays and (again) large profits for the playhouses and their companies, why, sir, that is the way of the fickle crowds of this foolish world. And who but his worst enemy would begrudge the dead poet this renewed attention, this brief posthumous fame? With his body rotting down to slick bones in an unmarked pauper's grave at St. Nicholas's, with his poor ghost now long gone to wherever it may please God, there is no part of him left to enjoy his latest eminence.

Here is yet another proof of a just (and justly ironic) Providence.

Don't you agree?

All well and good. And so be it.

Except that there remain questions and doubts.

Back to the murder.

Let us, for the time being, choose to assume that the witnesses described the events honestly and accurately.

Still.

When Marlowe jumped up from bed to attack Frizer from behind, why was it that the other two, seated on the bench, close on either side of Frizer, continued to sit there? They do not seem to have moved at all until Marlowe had snatched Frizer's knife and was slashing at his head.

For that matter, why did Marlowe use Frizer's knife and not his own?

Did the other two at any time draw their knives also?

Did they try to flee from the chamber?

Did they try to come to the aid of Frizer and to disarm Marlowe?

Frizer's wounds.

Inflicted from above and behind. Except for much bleeding (and all scalp wounds bleed freely) Frizer's cuts proved to be scarcely serious enough to call for the attentions of a barber surgeon.

Were those wounds accidental? That is, did Marlowe really mean no more harm than to threaten and frighten Frizer? Was it a clumsy accident when he slashed Frizer with the point of the knife?

Was it with the point? Or did Marlowe not slash at all, but strike a blow with the hilt of the knife? If so, though it is clearly an act of rage, is it the action of a man, even of a drunken and angry man, whose purpose is to kill another?

If it is murder, then this is a clumsy beginning to it.

More pertinent. Crouched below Marlowe, half-standing, wrestling awkwardly, grappling for possession of the knife, there is Frizer. And how did he manage to thrust the knife so deep into Marlowe's brain? Thrusting upward from below, it would require enormous strength and force. More than the strength of any one man I know of.

But.

Thrusting downward, full weight and strength behind the blade— it could have happened that way. But only if Marlowe's head were still. Otherwise, with the head moving and twisting and turning, hands locked on the hilt of the knife, the chances of finding the eyeball with the point are poor. Most likely the cheeks would be cut and slashed. Even if the poet somehow slipped and fell onto the blade, it would still require an extraordinarily great force for the wound to kill him. Oh, easy enough for the point to snag and rip the jelly of his eye. And many the eye that has been lost, trickling bloody down the cheek, that way.

But there was, evidently, only that one great wound.

It's a story, then, so flawed, so full of doubts and of questions without good answers, that Barfoot thinks it may well be true. Truth being so often shapeless and ill fitting. More a matter of rags and ragged edges than tailored seams.

And the faults of the story may be taken, too, as evidence that these three witnesses were not lying to the Coroner and his jury. No one, except a wiser man than any of those three, would ever contrive a tale made up of such unlikely parts.

And who would take it as given and accept it as true? A Coroner's jury.

And why?

Barfoot is not yet prepared to answer any of his own questions or to dispense with his doubts. He is willing, as he must be, to continue to consider Marlowe's murder from all sides. Skeptical in his considerations of all things under the sun and moon, and especially of the actions and motives of men (himself included), he is usually able, like a juggler at a market fair, to hold and to keep a number of contrarieties in mind simultaneously. And equally. Of equal weight, he is far away from any conclusions.

Yet (another kind of contrary) he nevertheless has his own vision of what came to pass in Deptford on that evening. He can see something happening.

What he sees is this:

Marlowe sprawled on the bed. The other three, backs to him, bent over the table playing at their game. It is quiet in the chamber. Until Marlowe begins the deep breathing, perhaps snoring, of sleep. After a moment or two, they exchange a look. Frizer nods. They ease themselves to their feet. Tiptoe to the edge of the bed. Skeres and Poley bend close to the sleeping Marlowe, on each side. Frizer draws his knife. With his left hand he reaches suddenly to clap his palm across the poet's mouth. The other two seize him, arms and legs, and yank him off the bed. Staggers, slips, is forced onto his knees. Frizer holds the point of the knife, bright in candlelight, to the point of Marlowe's soft round chin. Gripped too tightly to speak or open his jaws to bite, Marlowe can taste the sour sweaty palm of Ingram Frizer.

Does Frizer tease him with the point of the knife? Likely. Does Frizer speak to him, in rough whispers, breathing hard? Most likely. There would be various and sundry things, hateful and surprising, to be said. Irresistible when the victim cannot answer back. Can only groan softly. Can try to shake his head. Until one of the other two grips head with his arm so that it is fixed and cannot move. Frizer with a tight hard grin. Grins like a dog, as they say. And then the sudden full downthrust of blade into the wide eye of Marlowe. Lips against Frizer's palm go tight, go soft and slack and wet as Frizer jerks free the bloody knife blade and, released by all three, the dead Marlowe slides to the floor as if he were boneless.

Frizer, still speaking in a half whisper, still with that tight grin: "Quick now! Cut me! Cut me here!"

They draw knives and lightly slash at his scalp. His grin turns to a grit of teeth now. Bleeding, he turns to kick over the bench to sweep some of the clutter of supper and backgammon off the table.

Looks quickly around the chamber. One of the two—Skeres?

Poley?—has turned away to vomit. Frizer shakes his bloody head with a dry mirthless laughter. Says to the other:

"Go now. Call for help."

Stands looking down upon the corpse of Christopher Marlowe and hears his companions shouting bloody murder.

Heavy footsteps on the stairs. Shouts!

Says something, then, so softly Barfoot cannot hear the words. Barfoot being as deaf as the dead Marlowe to Frizer's moving lips. Says something private and silent. Barfoot knows what it is, though. It is a simple epitaph. Something oddly without malice. But also not even touched or tinged with the least hint of regret.

NOW HUNNYMAN'S DOUBTS BREED AND INCREASE AND BEGIN TO SWARM LIKE GNATS

Now her sweet and smooth milk-white flesh is neither a solace nor an inspiration. Far from it. Her handsome, unblemished skin and bones (his as well, more so) seem to be pitiably vulnerable. Better to have been plain and poor. Better to have been for all his life, as well he might have been if Dame Fortune had been playing with other dice when his time came around, a swineherd or a turnspit, some village lad, all sweat and dirt and common, ragged weariness, thirst and hunger. Better to have been gap-toothed, pox-pitted, richly gifted only with the blessings of short memory and half wit. Better to have been ignorant of the world five miles beyond his parish. Better to have had no more ambition than to have a full belly at feast time. Better to live like a beggar in the bush than this.

This fear.

This present danger.

"You fail to grasp it. You do not understand my predicament," he tells her, pillow to pillow, in whispers, faces close enough to share a single breath. "There were three of them. Rough and ready fellows all. Ugly as wild dogs. Came straightway to the bookstall and then mocked and threatened me face to face."

"Who do you think they can be?"

"Exactly what I ask myself."

"Not sent by your new masters?"

"Masters? My masters. What new masters? What are you saying? Good Lord, woman! I do not yet even know the true and proper names of these people for whom I have done . . . done what? Some simple service. I have asked here and there a few discreet questions. And that is all."

"And are they satisfied with your efforts?"

"How can I tell that? At least they have not made any complaint to me. Not thus far."

"Then I would take it that these men, this other three, are from another crew. They must serve another master with some other purpose."

"I believe so. But how can I be sure?"

"Perhaps they were sent to warn you. Or to frighten you."

"If that is so, they have succeeded admirably."

EVERY BITTER THING IS SWEET

Be careful now.

Be wary from now on.

For this is an age . . . *these are ages,* yours and mine, given to, if not wholly given over yet, rogues and roaring boys, to cranks and cozeners, magicians and mountebanks, fortune tellers and fortune hunters. High tide and the best time for every kind of nightwalking false knaves. For every kind and shape of crafty player on the stage of the world.

And if you know and trust Holy Scripture (as do precious few) you will have to agree with me that we must be near to the end of it all. Time for the demons and dragons, wild beasts and false prophets. Time when our inconclusive and inconsequential little play, neither comic nor tragic but something of them both, must stumble to a sudden ending. And then comes the final jig of Judgment we will all dance like ants in a hot pan. And the music for dancing will be a medley composed of the groans of the damned.

Easy enough to believe, as many do, that true piety has fled from this earth with eyes averted.

Am I too melancholy for you? Well, I am too sorrowful and melancholy even to suit myself. Truth is, I have always been, always was, anyway, at the time of this tale I am telling, a cheerful kind of man, sanguine, often merry as can be, even when the fashion was all for melancholy, for long faces, hard looks, and general malcontent. When heavy lids, as if falling asleep, and a heavy pout of the lip, as if every pleasure in the world were tedious and old, were all the fashion, I still found myself often smiling like a small child at a large fair.

But lately I have been thinking back, as I am wont to do too often, of all the waste and folly of my own life as it came to pass. In such a mood I am not good company for myself or anyone.

Confession, they say, lightens the burden of the soul. Let me make a modest confession to you. It will do you no harm at all and may even do me some good.

I confess I have played you false. Have withheld some little truth out of a certain acquired habit of slyness and for the sake of my fragile esteem of myself. I admitted, did I not?, and directly at the inception and outset of this telling, that I was something of a drunkard and that the habit was, in a sense, my undoing. I put it politely, as I recall, allowing that wine was my . . . *weakness*. Surely I made the point; and it was easily and unambiguously received, I hope. Yet it was nevertheless intended to deceive and to divert you. To turn your attention elsewhere before you saw me for what I was and would become—on my hands and knees, puking my guts empty and wishing not only that I could vomit up and out of my nose and throat the gray mess of my brains, but also that I could empty and scour my hollow skull of its whole hoard of memories and sorrows. Then you would see my skull grin! Like any other unknown anatomy shoveled up from a common boneyard.

Enough! Nothing is more wearisome and unworthy than the pity and sorrow squandered by any man upon himself. It makes a fool of anyone.

And you will not be allowed to see me play that part, an antic fool, clad in rags and tatters, wild-eyed and drunk when not sick to the edge of death. Or of deep sleep, snoring like an old dog, and dreaming things, terrible things that might make the Devil himself repent and amend his ways. A wild-eyed, wild-haired, toothless, snot-crusted creature, wearing his livery of stinking foul and beshitted rags like some Abraham man who has run away from his home in Bethlehem Hospital to beg in the streets. Begging and conning and cadging for food and drink. But seeking nothing so much as an early death. And finding death to be the one thing that was denied me. Not drink, not Plague or pox or any other sickness, not surfeit of feasting, nor shrink and pinch of famine, not flood or fire or war or the public hangman were predestined to be the end of me.

No, God's ironic will be done, I lived long and badly to die quietly of old age.

But all of that story comes long after this one ends. In this one I am and remain, mostly, what I from the first have admitted myself to be—a voice, albeit a hoarse one, often speaking in whispers behind my palm so as not to be overheard by the others. And all that I will come to carry on and over from this to that, from our tale to the other which is all my own, is the horrid scar I earn in this one. (Patience. All in due time and in its proper place.) Should have killed me dead then and there. Was certainly intended to. But did not. Lived and healed, instead, and carried away, as if a lover's token or a gift from Death himself, a memorial to his visit to my body, a raw and ragged scar from one ear all the way round, below my chin, to the other.

Never mind that. For now it is enough to confess that, for one reason and another, I have been false with you in several ways.

For instance, I did not choose to mention, for whatever it may be worth, that I was, quite separately and, indeed, unbeknownst by one or the other, somewhat acquainted with both Hunnyman and Barfoot. Likely you will have guessed that much even before now. Nevertheless I feel somewhat better for saying it out loud.

Captain Barfoot I knew first and long ago when I served some time as a soldier. Hunnyman I came to know later and better in London— my city, where I was born and raised and schooled. Never a player myself, I am proud to say, I nevertheless was, at one time and another, in the employ of Mr. Henslowe. And sometimes, I regret to say—he died poor but, rich and poor, he never paid me half of what he owed me—Mr. Langley also. Hired to work with and among the group of poets he used to put together new plays in the shortest order and briefest time possible. Of course, our new plays were, as they had to be, made and copied from the old, especially last year's best and most profitable ones. Henslowe cared not a rotten fig where our plays came from so long as large crowds came and paid to see them. And it was not for any of us, in those days, much of a craft or mystery. The others were mostly university men, scholars who had come here from Cambridge and Oxford with their earned degrees and their unfounded high hopes for everything, anything else, if truth is to be said and known, except for the ecclesiastical ministry which their schooling had prepared them for and their degrees had promised them.

Not for me the degrees and the promises and the problem of choosing my life's work. I was not, as they often reminded me, most often by simply ignoring me, one of those university wits (all but Greene, who did not choose his friends so precisely and who could not so easily have ignored me, since we looked alike as first cousins, if not brothers), a scholar out of Oxford or Cambridge. True enough, but I had my Latin and Greek from Mr. William Camden himself, at Westminster School, where I was, by God, a Queen's scholar, too! And could have gone to a university, too, if I had not gone as a soldier to Ireland and come home a kind of cripple before I was twenty. Besides which, I was that rare being of this age, a native of this City, born and raised here. They came from the country and country towns. And they had to learn, first of all, to keep from gaping and gawking at all the sights. Had to learn to find their way in the City I knew by heart. I hated them freely and fiercely. But never mind me. You have already been told what was to become of me.

But tell me, can you imagine Robert Greene, say, or even Kit Marlowe, living out their days as country priests? Nothing less than a bishop's staff and miter would have pleased Greene. Marlowe would not have considered any office or station in any church, except, perhaps, the Pope in Rome. Pity the parishioners who must learn catechism and commandments from the likes of them, who must be christened and buried and take the bread and wine of the Lord's Holy Communion from their hands.

Or suppose either one of them, still Greene and Marlowe, for example, had been fortunate to find a good place as a tutor or schoolmaster. Can you not imagine what kinds of things the serious pupils of Christopher Marlowe would learn?

Perhaps you will have already surmised that I, too, fancied myself a poet. It is common enough for poets to hate each other. More a matter of comedy than anything else. Unless you happen to be a poet yourself. But it is true, I aspired to be a poet for a time. Dutifully wrote my sonnets and songs, my pastorals, as well as plays for the stage. All these things are lost forever and no great loss there, believe me.

More to the point is this: that except for one thing and another, except for a piece of bad luck here and a bit of bad judgment there, except for some small injustice from one great man and the death of another, who seemed truly to admire my art and who might well have become my patron and protector, except for these things, the sum of which was so much more than all its parts, and except for the ease with which I surrendered myself to discouragement, why, I, too, might have been a name to be remembered in a book. Not like Marlowe and Greene and some of the others, those favored few, his equals and his betters. But, anyway, as one more honorable and worthy member of the tribe.

What can I say? That for many reasons and causes this did not happen to me.

And does it matter?

Once terribly much.

Once it mattered more than I would care to admit.

What a small, ridiculous ambition!

The undeniable condition of my failure in this one thing, something I believed, with reason, that I did well enough, and perhaps the one vocation that I loved most, ate me alive. Swallowed and consumed me. Destroyed my gifts. Or so I believed at the time. Crippled me as much as any wounded soldier. In many senses made me a beggar to lesser men. Above all, my life and times helped to make me as inwardly bitter as brown myrrh.

So even I speak, you should always bear in mind that old alewives' wisdom: *Who has gall in his mouth cannot spit honey.*

There are strange times (and maybe this is one of them) when the dead are knaves and the living are their foolish and vulnerable fair game. Which is to say, at the very least, that the dead are not to be trusted any more than the living. Maybe less so. The dead may be defamed or defiled, examined and studied, but not teased or tortured into truth. They may well suffer unimaginable torments. That you will have to find out for yourself. But you, the living, cannot inflict any pain on the dead.

Besides which—as anyone who has ever been haunted by a ghost will tell you—the dead, though weak, weaker than a sigh, nevertheless retain some powers. And one of these is the simple, irrevocable capacity, once challenged or insulted, to cease their whispering and to withdraw into a dark silence.

Remember that you are permitted to weigh and sift, value or scorn, only the evidence which they, by accident or by design, have left behind them.

You have heard the old story of Alexander the Great. How, at the last, when his warriors began to withdraw from the farthest places they had come to and conquered, they created huge objects and artifacts— enormous chairs, swords as tall as Kentish hop poles, heavier than plows, shoes the size of small boats, buttons as big as plates and hats, and so forth and so on—to leave behind them for others to find. So that the memory of these Greeks would become, on the strength of the evidence at hand, the recollection of a race of giants.

That kind of folly seems to be universal in this world, during all its times and ages, from Eden until now. It can be safely asserted that no reasonable person wishes to leave behind any memory of himself that is less than admirable. And when it happens otherwise, as it so often does, it is hardly ever intended. How much of our brief time of living here in this world is not spent in preparation for death and for eternity—death being the one sure fortune that we all will share equally—but, instead, is squandered upon deceit, wasted first upon the fabrication of good reputation and then on the hope of an honored memory? This labor is enormous and ingenious, no matter how far from the truth, how false, both repute and memory may be.

Surely you have to agree with me, drawing upon your own experience, that the great and greatly honored, those who, like the rich, have most to lose whenever Death arrives (whether pounding with bony fists on gate and door, demanding to be admitted, or else on subtle tiptoes like the proverbial thief in the night) and proceeds with ruthless indifference to strip away all of our glorious disguises, ripping to shreds our most cherished illusions, peeling off all things except for the essential, our naked and humbled humanity—they are those who are most deeply, sorely tempted to try to escape this common fate by creating vain memories, proud monuments to themselves. And not only will this prove to be in honor of whatever kind of power and glory, whatever station and high offices they may have achieved and held (which station and offices can never have shone half so brightly with excess of spangle and glitter as they are now remembered), but also they are concerned with qualities of character. Who does not seek to make some kind of posthumous claim to piety and courage and fidelity? Above all, who does not wish to be recalled as someone steadfast in the pursuit of honor and virtue and unflagging in abhorrence of the vices?

If we were to judge by the living reputations of our honored dead, we should have to conclude that goodness and virtue are to be found everywhere like grass. Then how can we explain all that weight of wickedness and sorrow and tribulation we found waiting for us in the world when we were born into it? Even as a little experience teaches us that there are no imaginable limits to human cruelty and human malice and folly, so, paradoxically, there seem to be no inhibitions able to restrain our insatiable desire for good report. Hunger for which extends equally to all aspects of reputation and accomplishment, no matter how trivial. For instance, I have never heard of anyone, no matter how ill informed, unlearned, and slow of wit, who has not attempted to establish, and then to leave behind for posterity, the reputation of a quick, sharp mind, even of some earned wisdom. And no matter at all that neither kin nor closest friends can think of any one ready example thereof.

This propensity to transform truth into something else, something which, if not always wholly false, is certainly new and strange, is to be observed in everything about ourselves. Even in such manifestly undeniable facts as physical welfare and appearance. I have never yet met anyone, be he or she ever so diseased or deformed, ugly and misshapen, who did not believe in the possibility of correcting this condition in *memory* if not in living flesh. If only by a false and flattering portrait on the wall.

I conclude that it is one of the deepest wishes of mankind to deceive the living after death. Especially to deceive the unborn.

Strangely, this simple truth is one which I have never heard any of our preachers, even the most austerely Puritanical among them, to make a sermon upon. They are masters at the detection and exposure of all forms of human vanity and hypocrisy. Yet even they do not seem able to conceive that the vanity of humankind is so infinitely great, so remarkably deep beyond all measurement, so overwhelming in all its force, that it will outlive the death, decay, and degeneration of the body that once housed it, happy as a songbird in a cage. They do not seem to understand how vanity lives on, invisible as a smile in darkness, long after the poor lost soul has departed for its final pilgrimage.

Try, if you dare to, to imagine the sum of the living and enduring vanity of the dead. Imagine the weight of it. All the world itself, with all its seas and mountains, cities and plains, cannot weigh half as much.

Only the poor are spared by their condition from the worst pains and fondest delusions that accompany this universal folly. The one undeniable reward of the truly poor is the power to be able to let go of themselves and of this world with no more effort or labor than a long sigh.

Not that I showed the good sense to envy the truly poor for their one great gift or to emulate them in hope of attaining to it. Not so. All my considerable envy was squandered elsewhere. Spent freely on whatever the world, the flesh, and the Devil conspired to teach me to be worthy of my envy and desire.

Even so, I reckon I may be the best one to be telling this tale, after all.

A bitter tale of and for a bitter age. And why not? No man, except a fool or a knave, can rest content in this bitter world, these bitter seasons. Must this make cowards or cripples of us all? I mean those of us who have, at least, seen our own faces clearly, without too much flattery or distortion, caught and reflected in a clean steel glass. Have seen that face, unflinching, and then turned away to look at the wide world in the same unsparing light.

I am thinking of those of us (may I include yourself?) who once upon a time eagerly swallowed the sweet wine of the world. And have lived to taste the dregs of it, bitter at the bottom of the cup.

I am thinking of those who, following the admonition of St. Paul, do not turn and straightway forget the face we greeted in its own reflection.

Look at the three of us. We are all bound together in bitterness and high ambition. The two great ills of our times. No, not the three of us. Call us four. For who was ever more ambitious and more bitter than Marlowe?

Well, he had the fortune, good or ill, of knowing his worst surmises prove to be truth.

Barfoot has seen more of this tired world than most men in a full lifetime. I shudder to think of what he may discover if he lives to a ripe old age.

Hunnyman, for all his clownage, has seen much more than he will admit. To himself or to anyone else. He denies and suppresses most of that knowledge. Of all of the four of us, still more or less strangers to each other, dark children of the times, he alone refuses to try to live on without hope or ambition. Which means, as a matter of fact, he is in danger of being the most bitterly disappointed of us all. But which also means he likewise can believe that any new morning may prove to be his dancing day.

His strength is this: that you can love him even as you are laughing at him and his folly. Indeed, you will at times find yourself wishing that half of his foolishness and idle hopes were true.

As for myself . . .

Wait. Someone will have noticed that I have neglected one among us who is every bit as important as any of the rest. I mean the Widow Alysoun. Because she is a woman, and one blessed with beauty, she is, in some ways, more mysterious to me than the others, changing in the light, a chameleon of many colors feeding richly on thin air. Yet (and you will see it is so) she is as much a part of this story as any of the others. Cannot be ignored. Will not be. Besides which . . . Lord, I hate to admit it, but how much more harm can it do me? I knew the widow Alysoun better than I have allowed until now. Knew her in fact and flesh as a printer. As—may I say it?—my publisher. It was she who published a little book of my sonnets and pastorals (and in the end it cost me a pretty price, more than money), dedicated to a great man (may he remain as unknown and anonymous as I from now until the ending of the world!) in hopes of patronage. It seemed a sound investment at the time. I would have been better off sailing to the New World in search of gold.

Knew the woman, then, in a business way. And even, for a time, as a friend. Knew her also in fancy. Without knowledge or permission she danced in my waking dreams. I would venture that, following the example of the venerable Onan, I broadcast enough seed, in her name and on her behalf, to repopulate the City of London after the Plague.

Which is only to claim I knew her far better than she knew me.

As for myself, then.

Well, I warned you never to trust the dead. Yet even as I say so, I doubt you will find a better witness. Better or more bitter.

And as for the latter. Do not let it trouble you too much.

Consider that in this age of ours, this late age when the best days of the world have long since blazed and gone up in smoke and left us with the heat and glow of dying coals, consider that, here and now, as we live in a duplicitous time, appearances, all alone and all too often, have far more weight and substance, thus *value*, than any naked truth. Consider that when the truth is too shabby, too shoddy, unflattering and umpromising, nothing more or less than a heavy cross to bear, we turn away from it as if it were part of our human nature to do so. As if it were created in us, our given and proper condition, to love the intricate pleasures of our idle fantasies (which are, after all, our own creation) more than the unavoidable wounds and sorrows of the world as it truly is.

Listen, we are each half-mad. And all that can be said for certain is that we live in a poor time for simple souls. But what a golden age for fantasticks!

Show me a simple soul, if one is left anywhere in England; and I shall kneel down in honor and offer up all that I have and all that I am.

Until then, though, be wary. Trust me no more than I trust you. And from the honor of that agreement all shall be well between us.

Even our bitterness is, finally, paradoxical. For it can sometimes lead to joy.

Remember what it says in Scripture, in Proverbs: *The person that is full despiseth an honeycomb, but unto the hungry soul every bitter thing is sweet.*

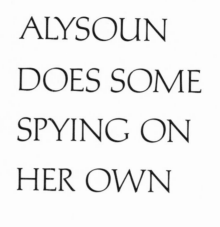

ALYSOUN DOES SOME SPYING ON HER OWN

W hat Hunnyman does not know (and may never know) about the young widow Alysoun—and how could he, being so dazzled by the beauty of her, blinded by his hopes and dreams for their future, chief among which is that she will soon see the wise necessity of marrying him?—is how sometimes, when she is truly troubled, she will inwardly shrink from her well-poised self, her well-learned and well-played part as a prosperous City lady, and become once more the innocent and ignorant village girl she had been and was likely to remain ever after until the aging printer and bookseller came and saw her and took her for his own like a prince in a children's story. And even if Hunnyman understood this about her, he is not well equipped to know, or even to sense, when she is troubled or not. First, because her sense of fear, anxiety, and unease does not usually arise from any particular threats or events. That is, she may be steadfast and untroubled in fire or storm. Indeed, she is often at her best when the world is at its worst. But she may be all but undone by an accidental stain on her clothing or the fate of a small bird in her garden.

Even so, like many another man, Hunnyman is at once so cloaked by his own private concerns and, oddly, so confident of his understanding of her, that if he had the ability to read her moods and intuitions like a book, he would be incapable of exercising that power. In short, she is and always will be in many ways a stranger to him.

Tonight when he comes to her house, as arranged, and tiptoes to her dark chamber, she tells him her news. Which surprises him both in general and in detail. So much so that he wishes he could light a candle and look into her eyes, overcoming a curious feeling that, despite the undeniable warmth of her wonderful body next to his, her voice is as disembodied as if she had been summoned up by a necromancer from the spirit world and were speaking out of the chilly darkness.

Image of necromancy has a certain aptness as the days draw close to All Hallows. And all the more so since today she has been over the water to Lambeth Marsh to seek out the notorious Dr. Simon Forman.

"Lord, why would you waste your time and money on the likes of him?" Hunnyman says. "All the world knows that he is not truly a doctor. He learned his skills under a hedge."

"So other jealous doctors say. But you must be quiet now and hear me out and not interrupt me with questions and arguments until I am done. I have some things to tell you. Can you do that?"

"I can try."

"I need your promise."

"I promise to try."

She laughed and then told him her tale.

How early this morning she and her maid dressed in their newest and best as if they were going to church.

Walked down to the River and hired a boat to carry them upstream, then over to Lambeth Stairs.

"Someday, believe me," she interrupts herself, "I intend to have my own boat to carry me where I please and when it pleases me on the

River. And my own coach, too, to carry me all about the City and from here to the Water Gate. For the City is becoming, day by day, so pestered with crowds of people, it might as well be a perpetual fair. And it seems to take a full hour to go from here to anywhere, no matter how near or far. How can that be?"

"If I may interrupt," he says. "Pray continue with your tale."

"I will. But before I do, I must ask you if you agree with me that I shall soon have need of a coach of my own."

"There are too many coaches in London already," he says. "They crowd the streets so that no one can easily pass and they splash mud and water in all directions with their great wheels. And they wear out the roadways. They are a damned nuisance and I am certain they will be forbidden before long."

"Do you think so?"

"I have it on the best authority. Pray continue."

How they went upriver and crossed. River windy and choppy. Boatmen rude and lewd (in speech and manner) at one and the same time. And she paid them no more than the least they were worth when they came to Lambeth. Left them cursing. Paid them no mind. And walked directly to a tavern, the Bull, in Lambeth Marsh. Where this fellow, Forman, is to be found.

She had made arrangements to receive some distilled, mixed medicines, of one kind and another, from him.

"Small, sturdy fellow he is, with heavy brows and a thick beard and very large bright eyes," she said. "And very fastidious in his appearance and with himself. They say he has a barber come often to his chambers, not merely to trim his beard and hair, but to wash and dry his body and all its parts."

She said Dr. Forman has urged her, from the first time he saw her, which was while her husband was still alive, to commission him to cast her horoscope and tell her the future.

"This morning, after we had drunk a little wine to warm ourselves from the River, the randy old goat said he would cast my future for me free and for nothing if I would only get up and go with him, then and there, to his chambers and show myself to him stark naked. I confess I was somewhat tempted, if only to see his chambers for myself. But I swore I would not and I offered him all the pleasures of Martha instead. In return for telling the future for both of us. And Martha, to my surprise, I suppose it was the wine, laughed out loud and seemed perfectly willing to go and do whatever he pleased.

"He seemed somewhat aroused, then, and willing, half in jest and half in earnest, to strike a bargain with us. And I was beginning to wonder if he might not have slipped a drop or two of one of his potions into our wine, when there came to the table two large, well-dressed Dutchwomen, as alike as twins, who seemed to know him well enough not to stand on ceremony or to wait for invitation. But simply sat down and joined us to drink wine and exchange some idle tavern talk. One of the two wanted to know if Forman had any potions which will forestall the French pox, and the other was asking him if it is true, as she had heard, that he had invented a salve which will allow a man to last the night long without firing off his cannon and going soft . . ."

"Woman, I fail to see how any of this, your day's adventure, has anything to do with me," he said, hoping that not a note of irritation entered his tone of voice and gave him away. For this matter lately of a quick-firing cannon does concern him and is a subject he would prefer not to discuss. Especially in bed.

"Wait a moment and see," she said.

Saving her the trouble, it was Forman who had laughed and asked the obvious question as to why it might be that a whore would want any man to last all night with her. Dutchwoman not so much as blinked or raised her eyebrows. Perhaps to be a whore is something wonderful in their country. Who knows? Instead she simply allowed it was not for a client or customer she would want such a medicine. But rather for a man she loved truly and well.

"And in a moment or two, as these things go, prompted by questions, she was telling us all about her man (except the other whore broke in to claim he loved them both and equally). How he was a famous soldier in the wars and is now the secret agent of some great man. How he will investigate and solve mysteries and can answer difficult questions.

"'Ha!' says Forman, misinterpreting her, thinking she meant her lover was a man of white magic like himself. 'And what great mysteries of body and soul has he lately solved?'"

How the Dutchwoman ignored his irony—perhaps she was too ignorant of English to perceive it—and told Forman that her man seems to be expert in the art of ascertaining guilt and innocence in baffling crimes.

"Does he summon up spirits to find murderers and such?" Forman asked.

How the Dutchwoman brushed this aside, saying he was more dark sentinel than magician. How only a few days before she had accompanied him to a house in Deptford where they spent the day studying and examining the very place where a famous poet, whose name now escapes her memory, had been cruelly murdered after supper.

"What?"

And how the Dutchwoman was sure that he had already solved that mystery for his master.

"Who? Who is this fellow?"

"I knew I would be able to waken your interest," she tells the distracted Hunnyman.

"Lord, I cannot begin to understand any of this!" he says. "First, poor Kit Marlowe is killed and buried and then all but forgotten except for the performing of his plays at the playhouses. And now, years later, it seems that suddenly half of this City . . . Forman guessed right . . . is busy digging up graves and summoning spirits."

"And you have forgotten the worst of it," she says, as calm as you please.

"What? What would that be?"

"They are digging fresh graves, too. For the likes of you, Joseph Hunnyman."

He groans into a feather pillow.

"But, sweet fellow, have no fear. I have a good answer to all this."

"I must give them back their money and get free of it," he says. "It seemed so easy and so simple at first."

"No need to be so hasty. I thought much the same at first, that you must quickly be free of this enterprise. But I think that would be a mistake. I can help you now."

"God's name, how?"

"It gives you something to report to your masters in this matter. You can tell them that you and they are not alone in this matter. That others, too, have doubts about Marlowe's death."

"How will that news help anything?"

"It may help them to see that they will have to pay you more money than they planned to."

He groans again. So she continues.

"Listen, Hunnyman. It should be worth money to know that there are others involved and to learn who they may be."

"Names. I would have to have some names."

"I have a name for you. I have the true name of the Dutch whore's soldier."

Hunnyman sat bolt upright in the bed.

"His name is William Barfoot, Captain William Barfoot. And, here's luck for you, Hunnyman, he has to be the one, the same ugly one who came to the stall at the Rose and to the shop in Paul's Yard. Nobody else. I have his name and his description. It's the same man."

"Sweet Jesus," he says. Then, doubtful again, "How did you come by this news? Did the whore tell you everything?"

"Not the whore, Hunnyman. I gleaned the news from good Dr. Forman in his chambers. And I can tell you it can be taken to be as true and sure as if I had had the fellow sweating and groaning on the rack."

"You had the fellow sweating and groaning, I am sure, but not on any rack."

"No need to be a spoilsport. I did it all for you. And that's not all."

"Is there more?"

She takes his hand and places something smooth and round, a little jar perhaps, into it.

"The salve, the magic salve!" she tells him. "Try a little. It will burn somewhat, Dr. Forman says. But it will keep you stiff as a Christmas candle until sunrise."

We beseech thee also to save and defend all Christian kings, princes, and governors, and specially thy servant Elizabeth our Queen, that under her we may be godly and quietly governed: And grant unto her whole Council, and all that be put in authority under her, that they may truly and indifferently minister justice, to the punishment of wickedness and vice and to the maintenance of God's true religion and virtue.

—The Book of Common Prayer
(1559)

*And be it further enacted by the Authority aforesaid, That all Laws, Statutes and Ordinances,
wherein or whereby any other Service, Administration of Sacraments or Common Prayer is
limited, established or set forth to be used within this Realm, or any other the Queen's Dominions Or countries, shall from henceforth be
utterly void and of none Effect.*

—An Act for the Uniformity
of Common Prayer

First, you see now your doings, so wicked, cannot be hid; your cruelty is come to light, your murders be evident, your pretty practices, your subtle sleights, your secret conspiracies, your filthy lives are seen and stink before the face both of God and man. Yea, what have you ever done so in secret and in corners but the Lord hath found it out and brought it to light? . . . Think your blood will not require blood again? Did you ever see any murder which came not out and was at length repaid? . . .

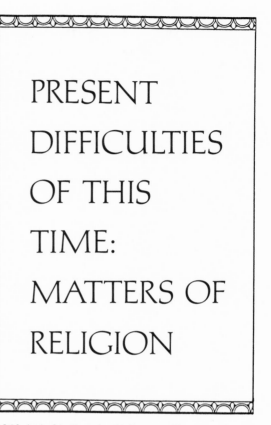

PRESENT DIFFICULTIES OF THIS TIME: MATTERS OF RELIGION

If Christ in his Gospel, which cannot lie, doth threaten a millstone to such as do but hurt the least of his believers, in what a dangerous case stand you which have smoked and fired so many of his worthy preachers and learned ministers! And what if the Lord should render to you double again for that which ye have done to them!

—John Foxe,
*"To the Persecutors of God's Truth,
Commonly Called Papists"*

Being therefore supported with His authority whose pleasure it was to place Us (though unable for so great a burden) in this Supreme Throne of

Justice, we do out of the fullness our Apostolic Power declare the aforesaid Elizabeth as being an heretic and a favorer of heretics, and her adherents in matters aforesaid, to have incurred the Sentence of Excommunication, and to be cut off from the Unity of the Body of Christ. And moreover we do declare her to be deprived of her pretended title to the Kingdom aforesaid, and of all dominion, dignity and privilege whatsoever; and also the Nobility, subjects, and people of the said Kingdom, and all others who have in any sort sworn unto her, to be forever absolved from any such oath, and all manner of duty of dominion, allegiance and obedience. And we also do by authority of these presents absolve them and do deprive the said Elizabeth of her pretended title to the Kingdom and all other things above named. And we do command and charge every the Noblemen, subjects, people, and others aforesaid that they presume not to obey her or her orders, mandates and laws. And those which shall do the contrary, we do include them in the like sentence of anathema.

—Pius V, *Regnans in Excelsis*

Look after this you your patrons and, lo, some are selling their benefices, some farming them, some keep them for their children, some give them to boys, some to serving men. A very few seek after learned pastors. And yet you shall see more abominations than these. Look upon your ministry, and there are some of one occupation, some of another. Some shake bucklers, some ruffians, some hawkers and hunters, some dicers and carders, some blind guides and cannot see, some dumb dogs and will not bark . . . And you, at whose hands God will require it, you sit still and are careless, let men do as they list. It toucheth not your commonwealth, and therefore you are well contented to let all alone.

—Edward Dering,
"Sermon Preached Before
the Queen"

For as to the wayfaring pilgrim, wandering in the dark and misty night, every light, though never so little, is comfortable: and to the stranger that travelleth in a land of divers language, any that can (though it be but brokenly) speak his country tongue, doth not a little rejoice him: So peradventure in this foggy night of heresy, and the confusion of tongues, which it hath here in our island procured, this dim light, which I shall set forth before you, and these my Catholic, though broken speeches, which I shall use unto you, will not be altogether unpleasant. And though I may say with Tertullian, that as the sickest are most willing to talk of health, not for that they enjoy it, but because they desire it, so I exhort you to patience, rather as one that would have it than as one that possesseth it, yet because sometimes a diseased physician may prescribe healthsome physick, and a deformed engraver carve a fair image, I hope no man will blame me if, for my own good and your comfort, I have taken upon me to address unto you this short treatise. Wherein I will enlarge myself but in a few points which seem unto me the principal causes of consolation to those that suffer in God's quarrel.

—Robert Southwell,
"An Epistle of Comfort"

For treason will not be hid; treason will out at the length. God will have the most detestable vice both opened and punished; for that it is so directly against his ordinance and against his high principal judge and anointed in earth. The violence and injury that is committed against authority is committed against God, the Commonweal, and the whole realm, which God will have known and worthily punished, one way or the other. For it is notably written of the wise man in Scripture, in the book called Ecclesiastes: wish the king no evil in thy thought, nor speak hurt of him in thy privy chamber; for a bird of the air shall betray thy voice, and with her feathers shall betray thy words.

—"The Third Part of the Sermon of Obedience"

On Maundy Thursday, the Pope cometh into his gallery over St. Peter's, sitting in the chair wherewith he is carried on men's shoulders. And there he hath a great painted holy candle in his hand burning; whereas a cardinal on each side of him, the one in Latin, the other in Italian, singeth the Pope's general malediction.

There he curseth the Turk and Her Majesty, our most gracious princess and governess, affirming her to be far worse than the Turk or the cruellest tyrant that is. He curseth likewise all Calvinians, Lutherans, Zwinglians, and all that are not according to his disposition. When he hath cursed all he can, saying amen, he letteth the candle fall; whereupon the people will scramble for it, and everyone catch a piece if they can, yea, our Englishmen will be as busy as the best.

—Anthony Munday, The English Roman Life

And furthermore, because it is certainly known and proved by common experience, upon the apprehension of sundry of the said traitorous persons sent into the realm, that they do come unto the same by secret creeks and landing places, disguised both in their names and persons; some in apparel as soldiers, mariners, or merchants, pretending that they have heretofore been taken prisoners and put in galleys and delivered. Some come in as gentlemen with contrary tales in comely apparel as though they had travelled into foreign countries for knowledge. And generally all, or the best part, as soon as they are crept in are clothed like gentlemen in apparel, and many as gallants, yea, in all colors and rich feathers and suchlike disguising themselves; and many of them in their behavior as ruffians, far off to be thought or suspected to be friars, priests, Jesuits, or popish scholars.

—Royal Proclamation Establishing Commissions Against Seminary Priests and Jesuits

It was not our death that ever we feared. But we knew that we were not lords of our own lives, and therefore for want of answer would not be guilty of our deaths. The only thing that we have now to say is that if our religion do make us traitors we are worthy to be condemned; but otherwise are, and have been, as good subjects as ever the Queen had. In condemning us you condemn all your own ancestors—all the ancient priests, bishops and kings—all that was once the glory of England, the island of saints, and the most devoted child of the See of Peter. For what have we taught, however you may qualify it with the odious name of treason, that they did not uniformly teach? To be condemned with these lights—not of England only, but of the world—by their degenerate descendants, is both gladness and glory to us.

—Edmund Campion,
Speech to the Lord Chief Justice

TRACKING
AND
TRACING
THE DEAD

Well, says Hunnyman, I myself had played the part of
devils, every kind of shag-haired devil you ever heard of. And so it was
completely appropriate that I should be given a little devil's part in
Faustus. Not a word to say, mind you, but much rushing back and
forth jabbing the air with my fork and wagging my tail like a dog at
the door wanting to come in.

You may remember (he continues), and perhaps they do the same
thing even now—I haven't witnessed a performance of *Faustus* since I
played in it, though they say it will still attract large crowds . . .

"Oh yes," says the player. "They love to see that damned old
professor dragged off to hell."

Well, you no doubt remember how we devils, in the absence of any words by the poet for us to say, had to carry some sparkling fireworks in our mouths. So that we seemed to spit little stars and comets as we ran about. God knows whose limp-brained scheme that was. Damn near poached my tongue like a trout. Blistered my lips and blackened my teeth. I thought they had died on me, every one, and that I was doomed to eat milk toast for the rest of my life. Singed my beard and burned my nostril hairs. But we did it, and it was a sight to behold.

Towne. You remember Jack Towne?

"Not so easy to forget as he ought to be."

Be fair. He could make you laugh till you wept.

"And he still can do so. But he owes me money."

Did you bond him for it, signed and sealed, at the Court of Arches?

"It seemed . . . *unnecessary.*"

Kiss your money goodbye.

Anyway, there was Jack leaping and jumping about the stage, like a clown with fleas in his crotch. He was bound and determined to be the most memorable devil of the lot of us. When all of a sudden he tripped over something, or was tripped by someone. And down he went, flat on his face, to the great delight of the crowd, who believed, I reckon, that it was a planned fall. Down he went and swallowed his mouthful of fireworks.

God's wounds! You should have seen the horror in his eyes. Poor fellow smoked at the nose and ears and farted fireworks for a fortnight.

"Well, that's an apt emblem for Marlowe's plays—farting fireworks in a five-beat line."

Ah, but the words are wonderful.

"To be sure. But much has changed since then. Takes more than bombast to keep crowds happy these days."

You talk as if a lifetime or two had passed.

"It seems that way," he says. "Strange, it has been only a few short years."

Did you ever know the man?

"Marlowe? As much and as well as I wanted to. Which is to say, never very well. A rash and intemperate fellow, don't you agree?"

Some people say so. For myself, I have to say I never witnessed that quality in him. I took him to be a quiet and scholarly man.

"Come now. I can speak with some authority. I was present there, a witness, and not much farther from him than we are from the fireplace, when he had his fight to the death with the fellow in Hog Lane."

Truly you were there?

"I was an apprentice for Mr. Burbage then. Was on my way to do some errand when I heard some shouting voices . . . ."

• • •

Barfoot will find the same story in various records as, patiently, office by office, clerk by clerk, back and forth across the City and Westminster, he traces and tracks his man. He will uncover, with no great difficulty, the legal documents giving account, in execrable and abbreviated law-court Latin, how in the early afternoon of the eighteenth of September, on Hog Lane, parish of St. Giles Cripplegate, one Christopher Marlowe and one William Bradley were fighting with swords. Along came another poet and playmaker, and a friend to Marlowe, one Thomas Watson. Who, as witnesses would swear and a coroner's jury take to be true, drew his sword and came between the two men, trying to keep them apart.

Whereupon this Bradley spoke to Watson, loud and clear enough to be heard by everyone.

"Art thou now come?" Bradley said. "Then I will have a bout with thee."

Marlowe has broken off and backed away. Now it is between Watson and Bradley. And now it is doubly dangerous; for they draw their daggers, also, to fight sword in right hand, dagger in the left. Watson defends himself, is lightly wounded and backs away from Bradley until he has been forced to the sheer edge of a deep ditch. From which he attacks and kills said Bradley with a stab of some six inches into the chest. Bradley is dead, and Watson and Marlowe together remain beside the body until they are arrested by the constable, one Stephen Wyld. Who marches them off to the appropriate Justice—one Sir Owen Hopton, Lieutenant of the Tower. He does what the Law requires and sends them off, across the City, to the prison at Newgate where they are kept, *pro Suspicione Murdri*.

Coroner's jury on September 19 finds Watson acted in self-defense.

Marlowe is freed on bail by October 1 and freed from charges at the Gaol Delivery session of December 3. Watson is finally granted a royal pardon and set free from Newgate on February 12.

Simple enough. And might, indeed, be taken mainly as an example of Marlowe's hot temper, taken together with some other documents which Barfoot is likely to find on his own without much clerical aid and comfort. One of these is a peace bond imposed in May of '92 by the same Sir Owen Hopton on Christopher Marlowe, gentleman, to keep the Queen's peace toward Allen Nichols, Constable, and Nicholas Helliot, Under Constable. Which could mean something. Though most likely nothing much. And nothing came of it.

Otherwise Barfoot will find no more papers to prove unlawful behavior, imprisonment, fines, and bonds. Cannot even—and this is rare in this, our litigious age—find records of debts undertaken or suits at law, for or against Marlowe, in matters of money.

Which means, to Barfoot, only that Marlowe seems to have had, during his London days, money enough to live and to do what he pleased. And it did not please him to live much like others.

For a moment Barfoot may wonder how a young man with plenty of money came by it. Above and beyond his earnings as a maker of plays. Which were not inconsiderable, but scarcely enough—look at his friends and his fellow poets—to live without other means.

Watson wrote poems and many plays, but also had to serve as a tutor in a Gentleman's household. And yet he had his money troubles. And it seems the true quarrel between himself and William Bradley (for theirs was the quarrel, not Marlowe's) was over some complicated matter of real or imagined debt. Rendered moot by Watson's six inches of steel blade in Bradley's heart.

Law was satisfied. Something in Barfoot is not. Something teases the edges of his mind. Altogether indefinite, yet not to be discarded.

Those two, Marlowe and his friend Watson, behaved circumspectly, indeed most calmly and soberly for a couple of gentlemen attacked in the streets by a man in high rage. Watson appears, in plenty of time to spare Marlowe any wounds. Steps between them. Confident, at least, that Marlowe will not attack him. Would he hazard his life as a peacemaker in a quarrel if his friend Marlowe were truly rash and intemperate, likely to do anything in a fit of his rage?

Bradley instantly recognizes Watson. Even as Marlowe steps back and away. *Art thou now come?* Bradley must have been looking for Watson in the first place. Expected to find him earlier and did not. What led Bradley to think he would meet with Watson at that time and on that day? An appointment, perhaps? To settle the business of the debt or to settle it once and for all in Finsbury Fields nearby.

So Bradley comes to Hog Lane looking for Watson with, let us say, good reason to expect to find him there. Finds, instead, Christopher Marlowe. Who, perhaps, so enrages and outrages him that Bradley loses the reins of himself and draws his sword to attack Marlowe. Yet no one made any claim that Marlowe was simply defending himself. And Marlowe's the man of the three known for his choleric temper. Ergo, Barfoot thinks, it is most likely that Marlowe drew blade on Bradley and made him fight in the street in the presence of many witnesses. Would Marlowe attack a stranger?

Suppose, for the sake of it, the whole affair was a scheme put together by Marlowe and Watson to dispose of Bradley. And to do so within the limits of the Law. Suppose Marlowe either challenges or provokes Bradley. Or simply attacks him, giving him no choice but to fight in defense of his life. Then here, surprise!, comes Thomas Watson.

Art thou now come? Then I will have a bout with thee.

Bradley goes after Watson and now shoe's on the other foot. Marlowe, the instigator, sheathes his blade and steps aside. Watson defends himself and backs away. This is his neighborhood and Marlowe's. They know it best. Nevertheless Watson retreats in such a way that soon his back is to a ditch. He has no place to go. According to the records, he has even been wounded, though his wound or wounds cannot have been so serious as to keep him from defending himself.

Nevertheless, bleeding a little and his back to the ditch, Watson is at least legally entitled to despair of his life. At which point, precisely, he shows a considerable swordsman's skill, not evidenced in the bout between them until now. One clean thrust and this Bradley is a dead man.

Then calmly Watson and Marlowe, as if certain of their lawful innocence, await the arrival of Constable Wyld.

What William Barfoot thinks is this: If he had it in mind to rid himself of some pest, a creditor, for instance, here in the City, it would be hard to think of a more expeditious way than what these poets managed.

And if they were not poets and gentlemen, but, say, fellows like himself—soldiers and intelligencers—why, it would be his very first thought to imagine the thing was more likely a scheme than accidental.

•   •   •

"Damned fellow had and held to every kind of atheistical and outlandish opinion. Do you know what he used to say? Said it to the great amusement of his fellows. All of whom, in my opinion, were very much cut of the same cloth as this Marlowe, if you take my meaning. Do you know what he would say?"

No, sir, I do not, Hunnyman tells the old fellow whose face is flushed red with the anger of old memory. Or maybe from the sack and sugar he's been drinking for half an hour. No, sir, I have no idea.

"He would look you dead in the face, eye to eye, with never so much as a wink or the hint of a smile to warn you he was jesting, and he would say: 'All they who do not love tobacco and boys are fools!'"

No.

"Oh yes, indeed. And sometimes he would mix his sodomitical opinions with horrid blasphemy. Right here in the Mermaid. Can you believe that?"

Well, sir, better here, among players and poets, than preaching from the pulpit at Paul's Cross.

"Better he never even thought such things, let alone spoke them out loud and in the presence of good Christian souls. I heard him say once—and I do tremble to repeat it—that St. John the Evangelist was the bedfellow of Jesus Christ, leaned always on his bosom, and they used each other in the manner of the sinners of Sodom."

No!

"Yes, indeed. And there were others besides myself that heard some of these things from his lips. And I have heard that some others put it in writing, too."

Hunnyman signals the tapster to come and fill the old man's cup again. Nothing new here. Except, perhaps, the matter of putting Marlowe's opinions into writing.

Tell me, sir, he says. You have been a player for so many years and a fine one, too, if I may say so, in the good old days. I remember I first saw you on the boards. This will take you back. For I was only a young apprentice then. In Henry Faircloth's little company.

"Old Henry, what a fine man! Here's to his memory."

Rest in peace.

Well, sir, now see if this rings a bell for you. It was in Maidstone, on the Medway, at the time of the Garlic Fair. You and your people were there to perform a play at the Star Inn. And we were passing through on our way elsewhere. Henry sent us boys over to see your play. For he knew we could learn a thing or two.

"Damned Walloons were half the audience or more, as I recall. Dutch folk who knew about as much English as a cat of a dog or a talking bird. Laughed loud and long, but at all the wrong times. It was a sorrowful tragedy we were playing, as I remember."

Yes, sir, it was that, though what the title was I don't recall.

"Nor I, and no matter. What you saw, my boy, was great players performing in great adversity."

Not for the first time.

"Likely not for the last time, either."

I think there ought to be an English town somewhere, a place called Adversity.

"Greater and lesser," the old man says, taking a puff of this wind in his sails. "Some horrid little dying market town in the West Country on a river that's silting and drying up day by day, a town full of pirates and fishermen, Puritans and soldiers pressed into service for Ireland. And all the rest are Walloons and Froggies, weavers and lacemakers and the like. And none of whom, natives or strangers alike, have enough language in them to fill up a hornbook."

And we all have to go to Adversity, sir, in the hope that they will pay us something *not* to play there. There were places like that and old Henry knew them all. But in Adversity they expect you to play for a full three hours and they'll pay you in apple cores and chunks of ragstone.

"Try playing the part of a King in Adversity and keeping your crown from being knocked off your head," the old player says. Then blows his nose in a rag and raises his glass in a toast to ghosts beyond counting.

"A hard life and a troubled world it was in those days," he says. "But oh, my boy, how I wish I could live it all again, the bitter and the sweet!"

Well, so would I, Hunnyman thinks, if I were no better off than this mangy old fox. Stiffened at the joints, bent with the ague and whatnot, stuffed with aches and pains from gray hair to gnarled toes. With precious little to show for your lifetime's labor but a peddler's sack of old stories you can bring out and dust off in return for something to drink.

Lord, let me live and die with some modest honor and more comfort, Hunnyman thinks. Like a merchant or a moneylender.

"You were asking about Marlowe," the old fellow says, proving at least that he's not sound asleep yet.

Yes, sir.

"Well now, I have seen his plays in the playhouses here in the City, seen them all, I reckon. And I have to say he knows how to play on the mood of the crowd like a pipe organ. So many wicked men, so many wicked thoughts, so much wickedness. The people love it."

I count religion but a childish toy, and hold there is no sin but ignorance.

"Exactly. That's old Machiavel in prologue to the *Jew*. I confess, I would gladly have swallowed my pride to play his Barabas."

So would we all.

"But, my boy, Marlowe *believed* all that wicked nonsense. He was, as I told you, a great atheist and eager to argue others to agree with him, too. He caused much trouble before they stopped his mouth."

What trouble, sir?

"Why, you remember what happened to poor Kyd, don't you? Taken off to Bridewell and racked till they broke him, body and spirit, and all on Marlowe's account."

I heard something of that, a rumor or two. But I have never heard Kyd's troubles came because of Marlowe.

"Why, boy, it was Marlowe's own atheistical papers they found, in the search, among Kyd's things. And Kyd was blamed for it and racked for it, too."

• • •

It's a young clerk of the Privy Council who will find a way to take Barfoot aside. To take a turn around a courtyard with him. Or maybe to meet with him at dinnertime at some busy Westminster cookhouse or ordinary frequented by clerks and the crew from the lawcourts.

No matter where, they will meet and talk.

"Captain Barfoot," this young man will say, "I know you by your good name and reputation. Because—it's no deep secret, sir, and not, in and of itself, a crime, not yet—we share the same form of the Christian religion. I have heard of your works of charity for our common prisoners. And I have heard nothing at all which speaks ill of your character or humor."

Barfoot (with a shrug): "It's easy to earn a modest repute, and for very little, if you happen to look the part of a rough and ready cutthroat. Any act of good manners becomes, considering its source, an act of kindness. Any simple kindness is taken to be a gesture of love and charity. But, by the same token, any sign of mild bad temper can be construed as murderous intent."

Clerk politely smiles, but presses on.

"In this matter of Christopher Marlowe . . ."

Does everyone in London and Westminster know that, too? Barfoot, that discreet and sly fellow, that marvelously clever intelligencer, has every tapster from here to St. George's Fields discussing his private business. Some wish him well and some are wagering that he will end his days on the gallows tree, if not sooner, then later.

"Sir," the clerk continues, seeing that Barfoot has stopped eating and drinking and placed both hands, half fists, lightly on the table and is squinting to study him carefully now, "I believe I might be able to help you somewhat. It so happens I myself have seen some kinds of papers concerning the late Marlowe which may be useful to you.

"Now, sir, it may prove difficult to see these things for yourself. But I have seen them and can give you some sense of the contents. And I think, if I may be so bold, sir, some of this may even surprise you."

Barfoot's hands on the table twitch, clench, and unclench, the little rings on his fingers giving off sparks of brightness. Then he clutches his cup and takes a large swallow of wine. Wipes his lips with the back of his other hand and laughs aloud.

"You can bear witness, in days to come, to the first miracle of St. William Barfoot. A triumphant transcendance of spirit over flesh. A moment or two ago, and I was my poor self, a well-bruised body and somewhat shriveled soul, blessed with no more than a hearty appetite for dinner and thinking of no future beyond a belch and the reckoning. When—it's a world full of wonders!—at a few words from you, perhaps a magic spell, I am almost completely transformed. All that you have before you now is no part of the old incorrigible Barfoot but one. All that is left of him is his battered, hairy ears. For better or worse, sir, I am all ears. Pray continue, if you please."

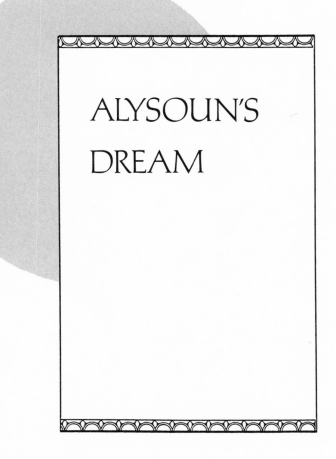

ALYSOUN'S DREAM

For as long as she can remember, she has been troubled by dreams and nightmares. An old witchwoman of her village, the same woman who turned Alysoun's head once and for all and fired her father's and mother's hopes and greed at the same instant and with the same revelation, staring into dying coals and announcing that she could see in that bed of brightness a vision of a great lady, grandly dressed and richly bejeweled, beautiful to behold, smiling, surrounded by creatures like herself, and all of these circling like glittering stars around another figure, half in shadow, who sat crowned upon a throne; that same witchwoman knew about her dreaming and would try to explicate the meaning of the dreams, though she mostly lacked the key to them.

Even though her dreams sometimes frightened Alysoun, sometimes woke her screaming out of sleep, it pleased her to have this mystery which was all her own and which nobody else could seem to decipher or fully understand.

The old woman allowed that Alysoun was, like herself, touched with something inexplicable, a power beyond the common powers of body and mind and spirit. The old woman, half-mad, but no matter so long as she never strayed farther from her village than a nearby market fair, which caution might well be applied to half the folk in the village, bitterly allowed that in every other example she knew of where a woman had been gifted with second seeing or with some uncommon, curse or blessing, intuition, the gift had come, as to herself, with age and decrepitude, with the frailty that allows for wisdom. Or the gift, curse or blessing as it may be, and sometimes in days gone by it brought them to the death by fire, came, if at all, to a young woman as a kind of compensation. Gift descending like the dove of the Holy Ghost or the fires that lit up the tongues of the first preachers upon the day of Pentecost, upon the ugly, the crippled, the sorrowful, and the poor of spirit. Old woman made signs in the dirt with a pointed stick and reported that she had never in all her life heard anyone tell of someone already so singled out with the bounteous blessings of truly extraordinary beauty being also gifted with the mysterious wisdom of heart and soul.

"I fear for you, child," old woman said. "These gifts cost a pretty price. And I think you may have to pay for them later.

"Although"—with a faint and broken-toothed smile—"it may be that these dreams which trouble your sleep are torment enough. Truly, I have never yet heard the like of them."

More fearful of being discovered and exposed, perhaps to ridicule—and Alysoun will go to great trouble to spare herself any sense of herself as ridiculous, as foolish—Alysoun has ever since childhood kept her dreams to herself. She is a kind of book of dreams. For she remembers them well and more vividly than many things, pains and pleasures, fears and joys, that have happened to her wide awake. There are times, especially those drifting, floating half-times, twilight between waking and sleeping, brief as they may be, blink of eyelids, no more, when she can believe that the only true world she has ever known, though it is a world without meaning, is the world of her dreams and that all of the rest of it, most especially the beauty of form and flesh that carries her sailing through her days like a fair and steady wind, all of it has no meaning. Sometimes, just before sleeping or waking, she has a vision of her body as if it were, somehow, separate from her, a clean and well-made cloak, perhaps, something that can be brushed and sponged, well cared for, kept hanging on a hook or perhaps folded in a chest.

In one sense it is a comforting vision, for it proves that men who desire her body are fools. She would as lief give it, all of it, to the fools to hang on a hook or fold in a cedar chest to fondle and tease or torment at their leisure and in her absence.

No man, not even Hunnyman, who, she imagines, must know her as well as any man can ever know any woman, knows anything whatsoever about her dreams, the power and the glory of them.

No man except one. And that man has been told, so far, only memories. He is the doctor of dreams, that curious fellow Simon Forman.

It is true, then, as Hunnyman surmises, that she has bound herself to him in some fashion. But it is not, as he thinks, an apothecary matter. If she wanted poisons or love potions or even, Lord spare us, something to empty her womb of an unwanted creature, she need not go so far and across the river. There are old women, witches if that is your judgment, close by, here in the City, who can furnish those things and more. She would not go to Dr. Forman or any man for those things. Though, no denying it, she has bought some of this and that from the man—including that fiery salve which had poor Hunnyman hopping about like a hare in high grass and fanning his groin with her best feather fan, till it cooled and so numbed his best parts (where, she thinks, his brains are) that he had no sense of himself and felt nothing at all for a couple of hours. She has, indeed, bought some medicines and potions, and one costly perfume, from the fellow. But only as a means to come to know him. And perhaps, if he seems, all in all, to be trustworthy, to talk to him somewhat about her dreams. For she knows he keeps a dream book and she has heard that Forman knows more about dreams than anyone in England.

So she went to him, at first for some of his medicines to disguise her true purpose. And in part, she would admit also, because she has heard rumor that great ladies of the Court come to him. And it pleases her to think that in this odd and intimate way she can share something with them—in this case a bearded, bandy-legged, wide-eyed little man with a large head, which is as full of lust and mischief as it is of magic and wisdom and science. It pleases her to know that ladies from the Court, and the like, come to Forman, most often in secret and in disguise, for whatever cures they may need.

At first, then, she shared with him only some old memories of dreams, well known and rehearsed, though told to him as if they were as new as last night. Nothing strange enough to trouble him deeply and, she hoped, nothing to frighten him. Merely some commonplace dreams of falling and flying, burning and freezing, of dwarfs and giants and huge boneless monsters, slowly moving like fat in a warm pan. Enough to widen his eyes and raise his brows in a satisfactory response. Enough to capture his attention and interest. Pleased and certain that no Court lady had ever told him anything like these dreams of hers; because, with all of their other fortunate blessings, they had never yet known of such things.

But she has not been visiting Forman to cure herself of dreaming. Far from it. She wants something else from him. Now that she has carefully used the memory of some of her old dreams to interest and arouse his intellectual faculties. It goes without saying she has long since aroused what's animal in the fellow and done so with next to no effort or subterfuge; for, she has learned, men who live mostly by and in the mind are easiest of all to arouse and to satisfy; you need only to pour some promises into their minds, like sweetening in stale water; and then their fancy will carry them away on wings; she knows the ancient story of the woman, never mind the name of her, who could turn men into pigs with a wand or a magic spell, some such; and that is a true and exemplary tale for as far as it goes; her own version, Alysoun's, is that the woman of Old Greece, or wherever—send me to school if you want me to be able to remember these things precisely— merely showed men the inward and spiritual truth of themselves; ergo all men are pigs; but what of these men like Forman, men of mind, inward to begin with and outwardly, at least in their own estimation, pigs already?; how can they be humbled and managed?; she is uncertain and, far as she knows, there is no good counsel from ancient

Greece or anywhere else; except perhaps in Holy Scripture; *the heart is deceitful above all things, and desperately wicked . . .*

These things are the burden on her mind as she and her servant, Mary, and an apprentice lad, brought along like a lady's page, are rowed upriver and then across toward Lambeth Stairs.

A blustery day, the river choppy and wind-wrinkled, speckled with sudden gusts of raindrops. Smoke of the chimneys of Westminster and Lambeth not rising, but pouring, hanging low in the mist. No swan in sight, though gulls circle and cry out something shrill, a music two parts warning and one part rage.

The two women are cloaked, hooded, covered. The apprentice lad, best-looking of those she employs, is all in correct blue with the proper blue wool statute cap also. But clothing tailored, against regulation, but at her command, to fit snug and smooth as a good glove.

She knows what will happen.

After some amenities and a cup or two, though he will likely produce his best Venetian glasses, of strong drink to take the edge off the damp and chill, the boy and Mary will be sent to the kitchen for warmth and refreshment while she and the doctor climb the stairs to the privacy of his chambers. Candles already lit and fire on the hearth. And all the clutter of his books and instruments and vials and jars. And there, after some kind of solemn abracadabra (likely they will lie down side by side without touching), she will tell him about this new figure in her dreams. Never until now encountered. Man with a terribly wounded face, bloody and beyond easy recognition, if indeed she has ever seen him or known him before. Which she is almost certain she has not. Terribly wounded stranger, then, who appears to be as real in her room as herself. First time she dreamed him she woke and then studied the floor and the carpet, on all fours, holding a candle, sure she would find fresh drops of blood to prove he had been there and not in a dream.

Man with a terribly wounded face appears in her room and tries to speak to her, to tell her something. But speaks in gurgles and pitiful moans, in groans like a ghost. Holds out his hands as if to take her in his arms and embrace her. Lifts his face toward hers as if to kiss her, as if she could kiss his face, as mother with child, and make it whole and well again. In her dream she determines to do that, though it sickens her even in her dream; in dreams she might vomit and, waking, sometimes fears she has done so. And so leans forward, closes her eyes, and purses her lips to kiss. And then and thus the dream ends.

What will the doctor of dreams tell her? She has no notion. And that's no matter. She thinks that telling it to Forman, and whatever meaning he gives it and remedy he may suggest (no matter), will be the end of it. It's a shy ghost who will vanish when she tells his secret. Shy ghost, she knows, and she thinks he was carried away to the spirit world suddenly and unshriven. That he is seeking a body to inhabit at least until he can make a peace with God or the Devil.

That he's the ghost of a man whose body sheltered all his life the spirit of a woman.

That he needs a woman's body for a home.

That he will take hers for himself unless she can find the means to prevent it.

That telling Forman will be the end of it.

That out of deference to the ghost—who, after all, cannot help himself and has not harmed her yet—she will not tell Forman how certain she is that this wounded creature is the ghost of Christopher Marlowe.

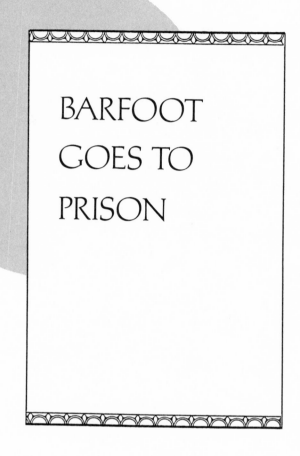

BARFOOT GOES TO PRISON

I t has indeed been the custom of Captain Barfoot, ever since he came to live in the City, to visit prisons from time to time, bringing some charitable relief to his fellow Catholics who are (for one reason and another) imprisoned there. With a horse cart and a hired man, he brings food and drink, medicine and clothing, blankets and bedclothes, pen and ink and paper. Most of these things are intended for the poorest of the prisoners, the truly destitute who cannot live without charity. More useful, however, to all kinds of prisoners is the money he brings. To pay their many and various fees—fees of commitment, for their lodging, for exemption from fetters, for liberty of the prison, for lights and fuel, and for food and the cooking thereof. And always, to be sure, for what they call the *garnish*, the gift of drink money for the underkeepers and for other prisoners. And usually he brings some gift or other, money or something worth some money, to the Keeper. Whose purpose is, after all, to turn a profit by his service to the Queen. In return for which gift the Keeper can expedite matters for the visitor and sometimes even bend a rule or two. For instance, allowing him some private access to close prisoners who are usually kept in isolation from their fellows.

Barfoot knows by sight and name the Keepers of all eighteen of London's principal prisons and of the five places in Southwark. But mostly he visits those places where the faithful, priests and laymen alike, are held for the practice of their faith. The Fleet in the City. Marshalsea and the Clink across the River in Southwark.

Has spent this gray November day doing his bounden duty. Came to the Fleet in the morning and ate his dinner there. Crossed over the Bridge, with cart and driver, to Marshalsea in the early afternoon. And now, as the last dull light of afternoon begins to fade, he walks in the garden with a priest who has been recently taken and is being held a close prisoner.

"Fellow's a gentleman, to be sure," the Keeper told him. "And no doubt but that something for his sake and comfort will soon be arranged. He has, as I understand it, taken his oath to the Queen and will soon be released from close confinement. But meantime I must obey the proper regulations."

"Certainly, Mr. Keeper," says Barfoot, playing with a pair of silver coins, rattling and revealing them as if they were dice in his palm. "I know you for an honorable man and ever obedient."

"And I know you to be the same, sir."

Barfoot smiles. "Here we are, then, Mr. Keeper, two of the Queen's honorable and obedient servants. Not her richest and most rewarded servants, to be sure, but ever honorable."

"Indeed, it is so."

"So much so that we can trust each other."

"Completely."

Two silver coins given in the discreet form of a quick handshake. Why, when there is no one else present in the Keeper's chamber to witness the exchange? Because the Keeper, an old soldier himself, prefers it that way. To pay him openly without exercising the good manners of subterfuge would be exceedingly insulting. They could come to blows over it. Maybe even to sword points. As it is, Barfoot soon has the prisoner out of his cell, indeed, arranges for the man to be moved to another one (another coin called for); for this one is only a small dark place that stinks more than most from being set next to a common privy. And now they are walking in the chill air of the Keeper's garden. Barfoot snorts at the stink of sea coal from the chimneys of Southwark.

"Stinking stuff will blacken the sky!"

"I had been told of you and your generosity," the priest tells him.

"That news does not cheer me."

"Why not? If it is true."

"True or false, I would prefer not to be the subject of idle conversation. One fine day I may well find myself a lodger here also. And I am not at all sure that I will be able to bear the loss of liberty half so well as you and so many others."

"Captain, I'm willing to wager all that I own (precious little, but all of a little is everything) that you can bear far worse than this. I conclude you can bear the worst the world has to offer and that, in truth, you are fearful of nothing."

"Father, I fear the fires of hell."

The priest pauses in mid-stride. Touches Barfoot's forehead, almost by thoughtless habit, as if he intends to bless and absolve him then and there.

"And so you should. So should we all. Well then, I shall pray for you."

"Thank you," Barfoot says quietly. Then: "An exchange of prayers would not be a fair transaction. What can I do for you?"

There is always something. And there is.

Seems that this priest has committed a most serious offense. Which, if known, could quickly bring him pains he fears he cannot bear and next perhaps the crown of martyrdom he is unworthy of and is not seeking. What can that be? He has earlier delivered a copy of a pamphlet, one printed in the Low Country and concerning a subject forbidden in this kingdom, to a printer here in the City.

Was it, then, someone trusted and tested?

Not so. Rather someone who professed to be willing to risk the publishing of the pamphlet for the sake of profit. For gain, pure and simple.

"Not so pure and simple," Barfoot says with a sigh. "True, gain may be the most reliable motive in these matters. But you have to remember there is gain, also, in betraying you. I believe I shall have to go and talk to the man."

The priest laughed.

"'Tis a woman, Captain. A printer's widow who manages her late husband's affairs."

"Your case grows worse with every word," Barfoot says. "These women in business are as inconstant as weather vanes in April. Who knows? She might read the thing and find herself in disagreement with the argument. I will do what I can for you."

"What can you do?"

"I will pay a call on this woman and see what needs to be done."

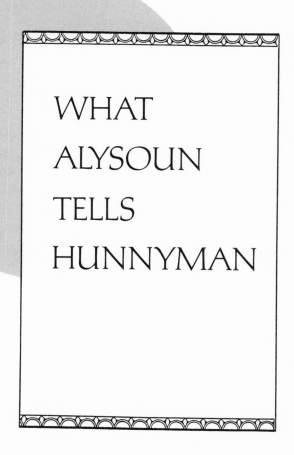

WHAT ALYSOUN TELLS HUNNYMAN

There was much on my mind this morning. We are, as ever, far behind in all of our printing and too slovenly with our work. How can I even turn my back on them for a minute when the apprentices are lazy and ignorant and the journeymen are already thinking ahead to dinnertime before their breakfast bread and beer has settled enough to produce a satisfactory belch?

They eat too much and too well.

It is much too warm in the printing shop. If I have to leave the chamber for a moment or two to attend to other duties (which are endless), why, they will heap up the fireplace with wood and the stoves with charcoal until it becomes like a sweat-dripping summer afternoon in there. And then they begin napping and nodding on their feet.

My printers have some modest skill at their craft and they often exercise good judgment. They are hardworking men. But they can never do any better than the compositors and proofreaders will allow them to. There are far too many errors to be tolerable. We are extravagant and wasteful with precious ink and paper.

How can I manage to turn even a little profit when I must feed and clothe and house such a crew of idle, careless fellows and pay the outrageous prices people are asking these days for paper and ink and lead and found type?

And, as if to add insulting weight to the cross I have to bear, there was a gentleman poet on my hands here for an hour or so this morning. A fellow who thinks that, because the words (such as they are) are more or less his very own and because he is paying out a very modest price for the printing and publishing of them, he has some inherent and inalienable right thereby to oversee the printing thereof and to insist upon endless corrections and revisions.

I tell you I am sick to death of their verses! Especially of sonnets which can turn pure and simple lust into all kinds of fancy phrases. They talk of love as if it were either the Plague or a Coronation Procession. Let men begin to say what they mean! Let us have a keyhole glimpse of the truth!

Well, no matter. We finally pleased the fellow with a proof of pages where his poems looked better than they scan and I found a perfect woodcut for his title page. And we sent him on his way, happily mumbling his own phrases and so pleased with his creation that he looked likely to walk in front of a carriage or a cart before he found his way home. Which will be no great loss to the poetry of England, but would be a loss to me and one more than I care to contemplate.

Where was I? Ah yes. Our other visitor.

Came, not long after our poet went mincing on his way to some tavern or other, the ugliest man I have seen in a long time if not my whole lifetime. A strutting, swaggering soldier I took him to be. So carved and stitched with scars and wounds (what could be seen of him, anyway) that it was not difficult to believe that most of his insides must have long since leaked out of one place or another and the fellow's skin been stuffed with straw like a rag doll.

As soon as he was admitted to the house, as soon as I saw him, I remembered your own account of the man at the playhouse and, again, at the churchyard bookstall. I can understand your concern. And I can see how and why he disturbed you. He is a formidable and dangerous man. Without so much as a moment's notice he would cut off your nose and ears and probably feel no better for doing it. He would most likely feel nothing at all.

So here he was in the house, as neat and clean as can be, soft-spoken and polite. Which raised the goose bumps all over me, I'll tell you; it would have been better and easier if he had shouted or, maybe, growled like a dog.

Spent not much time on amenities. Looked me directly in the eye and said he had come to take back a manuscript which had been left with me for printing.

What manuscript would that be? I asked him.

Why, says he, it is a treasonous and subversive Papist pamphlet which, among other things, does touch upon the forbidden subject of the Succession.

I protested I had never even heard of such a thing, let alone considered risking life and limb to print it, not for love or money.

"Stop your babbling, woman," he told me. "I know that it was given to you, together with some money in advance for the cost of printing. No question. I will now be content to have the manuscript and you may keep the money. You deserve some recompense for the enormous and incredible folly of keeping such a thing under your roof when the very least you were risking was a turn or two on the rack, time enough to pull your pretty arms and legs out of their sockets and leave you a cripple for the rest of your life. Do you have any picture of the pain of the rack?"

"Please, sir."

"Then give me the manuscript here and now. And we can forget each other forever."

"Oh, how I wish that I could do that! And I would if I could."

And then (what else could I do?) I told him how, realizing my own ignorant foolishness and acting upon the good advice of a good and true friend—and, no, I did not tell your name or give even a hint as to who you might be—I cast the manuscript into the fire and turned it into ashes and smoke. Adding that I planned then and was prepared now to give back the advance.

I wish I could describe the weary contempt of the fellow's expression. He looked at me, head to toe, as if I were a large, fresh, steaming horse turd in his path.

"Well then," he said, after considering a moment, "that does make a change in the scheme of things. You have just now introduced faith and trust into what should have been the briefest kind of business between strangers."

He continued, explaining very slowly and patiently that he sincerely hoped I was telling him the truth, that the manuscript had indeed gone up the chimney in smoke. But that neither he nor anyone else could be content to take my word for it. That if I had not truly (yet) burned the manuscript, I should be well advised to do so at once, as soon as he left this house. But that whether I had the said manuscript or not anymore was a matter of no interest to him or much concern.

What had happened (he said) was that we, who were strangers until here and now will not ever be strangers again. I must be watched, and so I would be. I should therefore come and go very carefully. I should be exceedingly careful in all things. And if I had lied to him or if I ever took it upon myself to speak of any of this to anyone (presumably including yourself, Joseph Hunnyman), I should prepare myself for the worst I can imagine, the best being a quick death.

And did I fully understand him?

To which I replied with eager affirmation.

"Good," he said and then, strangely, he smiled at me. "Keep me a hostage in the back of your mind and I am sure all will be well. And you can be sure, also, that you will be on my mind. We could not be closer or more concerned if we were lovers."

Touched the brim of his hat, tipped me the least bow, and walked out the door into the noisy street. Leaving me covered with a cold sweat.

And what do you think I did next?

I went and found myself a nice supple birch rod. And I took it into the printing shop and beat my lazy apprentices across their fat little arses until they squealed like pigs in the barnyard.

HER LITTLE DECEPTION

I t is one of our oldest stories . . . perhaps it is the oldest story if you take Adam's first lame efforts at deception to be an apt example. An old story, anyway, how one lie leads quickly and surely to another and another. What was merely feigned becomes, child into fullgrown man, utterly false. What was light and unimportant, thoughtless, becomes, in its full maturity, a matter of premeditation and, sometimes, inevitably, life and death.

Alysoun lied to Hunnyman not so much in the account of her encounter with Barfoot—for in retailing that meeting she simply subtracted her own feelings from it; thus her distortion of the truth, though large and emphatic, was not based upon a litany of falsehoods, but on an absence of full detail; a different sort of untruth, then, a failure to be forthcoming—as in her slight and amusing version of the visit of a foppish poet that came first. Her little story was not true. First, the poet came more to see her than to see how his publication was progressing. She knew this very well. Poet had other business with her and she knew it. Moreover, the poet, more than somewhat smitten, was troubled by an overwhelming desire for her. This poet was a creature of desire. Say it: of lust. And his hunger for her at that time was, it seemed to him, unquenchable. She knew this and did nothing to discourage him. Indeed, she might be said to have encouraged the poor fool with some dangerous (for there is precious little privacy in her house, excepting for her bedchamber, from which he was, for the time being though not, perhaps, he could hope, forever, barred) and sweetly offered kisses. Promising nothing more for certain, yet not firmly denying or forbidding him anything either. You could call it teasing. And you would call it that if you were that poet.

But there is more. Another kind of teasing. For the Widow Alysoun professed to admire the poet's art. Proposed to publish his poems, his only good, last chance to find and snare a patron, without any charge. Saying it would be pleasure and privilege to publish his excellent verses. And that the costs could, justly, be hidden among the charges to other, less impecunious clients. Perhaps he would remember her when, as it seemed evident and certain to her, he earned the fame among poets that he deserved.

What could he do in return? Why, perhaps one day he might be moved to write a poem for her. Something whereby she might be well remembered, too, albeit by strangers.

You can see what a perfect fool that poet was. He was prepared to believe anything she said or might say—even flattery. Perhaps flattery most of all. For though flattery is deadly poison, however sweet, to kings and other great men of the world, it is meat and drink to poets. Though they may die from it (like kings), they cannot live without it.

And so Alysoun told a little lie to Hunnyman. Made up a wholly imaginary poet, more clown than poet, to divert him, yes, from suspicion of the real poet. Made no mention of a limp and a red beard. Simple enough. And why not? It was none of Hunnyman's affair or concern even though he would surely try to make it so. Why let Hunnyman make an unpleasant fool of himself? Lie to him a little and let him be ignorant and happy. It gave her no pleasure to quarrel with Hunnyman, at least not on his own terms. And it was Barfoot who troubled her mind and her being. The poet had, for the time being, disappeared, would not return to her memory until she invited him to do so. And so one poet, real or imaginary, true or false, was as good as another as a prologue to her scene with Captain Barfoot.

Besides which, Hunnyman happened to know this poet, not well, but by name and face; and she knew it. No use (not yet) in making Hunnyman suspicious or discontent. No need for him to know anything that he did not need to know.

An unimportant, insignificant lie and no harm done. The whole point of the lie was to spare harm. For everyone.

And how well did that work? I'll tell you. It caused trouble for one and all. Most of all for the poet. In the end her simple little deception almost cost him his life. Not her fault that it did not. Even though, considering all things, there was never any good reason for her to care if the poet lived or died. And you can be sure that she cared not at all. If, indeed, she ever heard or troubled to ask whatever became of the poet.

How do I know these things? You ask. How can I be so sure?

Because—you must have guessed it from my tone, my irrepressible self-pity—I was, of course, the poet who called on Alysoun that morning.

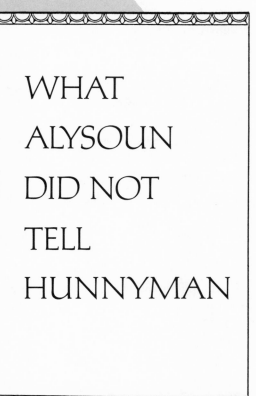

WHAT ALYSOUN DID NOT TELL HUNNYMAN

Her beauty is her weakness. Has always been. For as long as she has any memory of herself. As a child, with golden hair and fair, smooth, completely unblemished skin, and with blue-bright eyes, she was spoiled and protected. Pleased with herself even as others took a deep and curious pleasure simply from her appearance, her presence. Pleased with herself, as her mother and father were most certainly more tenderly concerned with her health and well-being (a form of constant solicitous tender concern that she confused with love) than with the mundane welfare, the aches and pains, of her brothers and sisters. Who were, as she early observed and not without a wincing of envy, far more free than she was, free at least to live, to suffer and rejoice, to die, as some of them surely did in infancy and childhood, not without arousing a measure of grief and sorrow, true, but also a grief that was not without the common sense of resignation, even, in passing of time, of cheerful acceptance. She knew that they would not resign themselves to her death so gracefully. Knew also, sensed strongly, anyway, long before she had learned any words for it, that her brothers and sisters shared some things with her father and mother, kinfolk, and others of the village—which was to her the world, and all of it, then. And one of these shared things was a clarity of expectation. Best and the wisest among them were never wholly hopeless, not by any means; but they learned early in their lives to hope for the simplest things. And learned to be well pleased, indeed content, by the slightest and the least. They were not safe from pain and disappointment, not ever, but neither were they at the mercy of bright and bitter expectations, especially the demanding expectations of others.

And she might have come to share this common strength and heritage, by birthright, if she had not been, from infancy, exceptionally beautiful. And, thus, at the mercy of the hopes and envy, the love and hatred of others. Others who mysteriously were empowered to invest her life with cast-off expectations of their own, with all of the selfish hopes and fancies which they had suppressed in and for themselves, but which they now felt free to set free (like, oh!, those winged and terrible creatures from Pandora's box) in her name. For her name's sake. They might well believe her to be worthy of their admiration or envy or even of a form of bitter contempt. Yet they could never imagine her as she conceived herself to be—sacrificial, a perfect and living sacrifice to alien beings who were like shadows of themselves. An offering up of self to strange gods and spirits who filled her dreams with their murmuring voices and who riddled the frightening darkness with their invisible wings.

So you can see how it was that to all the natural woes of childhood was added an additional burden of fears, at times reduced to the pure, chilled, cold-sweat terrors of awareness, as in the heart and center of an evil dream, that she was not so much blessed by being spared from so many commonplace, quotidian bruises and breakings, itches and winces, fevers and chills, these things which make up such a large part of the lives of less lucky others, not so much blessed as she was being raised up like some fat goose, prize pig, spring lamb, kept and preserved for something yet to come, perhaps for some enormous and surprising agony. An agony of flesh or spirit or, most likely, of both. An agony which, whenever and wherever it might come and seize her, she surmised, would serve as a blessing for all the others, those whose indifferent lives and losses ran gently away like water dribbling from cupped hands.

This was the playhouse of her childhood.

Earlier in the age, in the old days of the Old Faith, she might very well have studied and dreamed the lives of the saints and perhaps found her own vocation in a nunnery. But here and now in this new/old world, all of it aflame with an indescribable changing, she found no sanctuary for herself except whatever imaginary edifice she could build and inhabit by the power of her mind and by the strength of her indomitable, aspiring will.

Call it paradoxical, if you choose to, and the purest form of irony, but nevertheless what the world took to be her greatest blessing, gift, and asset, an extraordinary beauty of face and form which, no matter how or how often threatened, has never yet failed her, she took and takes to be a weakness and a curse. And so her secret, thus her strength, was to be found elsewhere, at home not in the commodity of wonderful flesh but in both mind and spirit, unsexed, being neither the common attributes of man or woman, and also ageless. And yet so long as she was, or seemed to be, both young and beautiful, she remained desperately vulnerable. Many times she found herself longing for some deformity, for a siege of any one of the much dreaded diseases of the flesh which would, at least, set her mind and spirit truly free from the tyranny of skin and bones. Times when, staring into her looking glass, she could picture herself clawing her perfect face to bloody ribbons and raw meat. Times when, looking into a candle flame or a fire on the hearth, she felt a sudden and powerful need to plunge herself into it as (for so she heard long ago) great ladies from time to time do place their pampered bodies into warm and scented baths.

Scent was how he came to her first, an odor of sweet distilled perfume. And she thought, as she followed her servant into the chamber where he was waiting for her, facing away toward the fire, that there must be a lady here to see her.

Entered the chamber and saw instead his broad thick back, square, close-clipped hair, flecked with stains and spots of gray, he turning,

light on the balls of his feet, like a dancer or a swordsman, at the first
sound of her shoes in the room, not smiling, but still somehow affable
enough, polite, a formal greeting not without a certain warmth. Hat
in hand, sword at hip, a gentleman clearly, yet clad in plain and sturdy
clothes; a military gentleman then, every inch of him, turning and
taking a step or two, no more, his eyes brightening and then (it
seemed) withdrawing into shaded, hooded caves in his scarred face.
Seeing Captain Barfoot, firelight behind him, candlelight revealing his
face and figure, she surveyed, unflinching, the brute handiwork of his
visible scars and then looked away into his shadowed eyes, eyes which
had seemed bitter cold to her before they first brightened, stared into
his shadowy eyes and was possessed of a vision of herself, stepping out
of all her clothing then and there, naked and shining in candlelight
and firelight, swimming in those dark cold eyes and finally shedding
her skin as well. In a moment exchanging, as it were, one body for
another. Wrapping his strangely bruised and battered flesh around
herself, the bones of her, like a warm cloak or a clean blanket, now at
last somehow truly invulnerable; because now at last she would be the
owner, in a wink of time, of all of the pains and grief and woe she had
been hidden from and which had been so hidden from her. Because
now at last, and all in a wink of time like putting on a cloak, just so
simply, no worse pains or grief or woe could come to pass.

What she felt, then, was a raw surge of desire, almost irresistible,
an overwhelming need not merely to offer up herself, the best parts of
herself, to him and his pleasure (whatever that pleasure might prove to
be), but, much more, to offer herself, such as she was, to him so
completely that she would be consumed by the act of giving and
would, in truth, become him, to live after that in the habitation of his
large bones, his hard muscles, his ugly scars, looking out upon a world
restored and more, transformed and transfigured, seeing it through his
dark cold brutal eyes.

At first she heard next to nothing of what he was saying. She
looked into his eyes and felt a tremble of weakness, as if she were about
to faint, and a sudden wetness of the crotch. As if they had been toying
and teasing with each other for half an hour.

Whatever it was he wanted from her, she would not have lied to
him to save her own life.

As it was, he did not ask anything much of her. He stood there politely, fastidiously clean, scented with that expensive womanly perfume, and proceeded to ask her about and for that foolish Papist pamphlet that she had never seriously considered publishing.

He warned her, in his soft, hoarse voice. Tipped her a slight bow of farewell, put on his hat, and turned and walked outside to vanish into the busy street. Walked away to leave her standing there with a weak-kneed feeling close to the pangs of hunger and thirst. Until, after a moment, hearing herself breathing like a sleeper, coming to herself, like waking with a fury at the weakness she had allowed to invade herself, she went back into the printing shop. Where, finding them all loafing and idling the time away, she fell into a great rage.

Later she could not, would not tell Hunnyman much of this. And nothing at all about her deepest feelings lest some way or other it might serve him to free himself from the sense of need (*his* hunger and thirst) for her and the enchanted spell of his own false and foolish hopes.

NEWS AND SMALL SURPRISES

Whatever they learn, coming to view the same events differently, by different paths—Barfoot by papers and the words of shepherding clerks; Hunnyman by talking and listening to other players as if he were cast in a minor part, a role designed mostly to cue and to prod others into recollection, all part of a strange play that will end, bloody and mysterious, with the death of its hero—both of them able, by inclination and experience, to read through the text, the outward sense of what they are learning, to the kernel of meaning, which may well be, as they well know, something much more or far less than they hope for.

Must, first of all, go back to the year of '93. Only a little time, as years are measured, but, Lord, it might as well be a world and a lifetime away from them both.

Terrible year of the sickness in London. Bodies in the street or in the houses *(Bring out your dead!)*. Creak and groan of the cart that hauled these to their common graves. Doors of houses of the afflicted painted with a cross and "Lord have mercy on us!" Thousands dying and many thousands more fleeing elsewhere.

Hunnyman elsewhere, traveling with his company. For there was no playing in the playhouses of the City during the sickness. No playing and no living; so they packed their cart with costumes and properties and prompt books, bade farewell to wives and children, kith and kin, and went off seeking places to ply their trade.

Barfoot was plying his soldier's trade, too, that year. Having endured and survived the Plague himself, he felt briefly (and foolishly) immortal. Until, in a skirmish of no consequence at all, he earned the wounds which sent him home in a basket, thinking (what else could he think?) that he would never stand and walk again. Thinking, as he moaned in spite of himself, that with the blessing of good luck he might die of his wounds this time.

For Hunnyman the time for groans came later.

Now in their separate searching they must force themselves to be present where they were absent.

What can they learn of the time and the place?

That by late springtime, with no easing of the sickness or the numbers of the dead, and with summer, always the worst season for Plague, promising to work its worst, the people, humbled now and terrified, looked for any cure they might find for their misery.

That someone or other began to plant and to sow the thought that all the sickness and trouble must have come about on account of the presence of so many Flemish strangers living in the City.

And that this very same issue, presence and place of many strangers among them, had been for some time a matter of debate and argument, of faction, in the Court and Council. But that before the sickness reawakened the matter, it had been considered settled for good.

That it was the policy of the Queen and Council to permit, even to encourage, the strangers to live here in peace and quiet.

So that when, on night of the fifth of May of '93, in darkness and by stealth, person or persons unknown did place libelous and threatening placards on the walls of the church of the strangers at Austin Friars, warning them to leave the City, this was taken to be a grave provocation. Not the righteous outburst of popular anger it professed to be. But as a provocation against peace and good order at a time of trouble and danger.

That, for the sake of peace and quiet and good order (with the whole sorrowful, fearful City like a barrel of gunpowder waiting only for a match flame), it was necessary at once to determine the origin of the libels against the strangers.

That nevertheless, by night, the placing of these placards against the strangers continued.

That, therefore, a group of the Council, from among those still remaining at Westminster, including Archbishop Whitgift and Burghley, Lord Treasurer, wrote to Richard Martin, goldsmith and Lord Mayor of London, and to others among the aldermen, informing them that "her Majesty's pleasure is that some extraordinary pains and care be taken . . . for the examining of such persons as may in this case be any way suspected. This shall be therefore to require and authorize you to make search and to apprehend every person so suspected. And for that purpose to enter into all houses and places where any such may be remaining. And to make like search in any of the chambers, studies, chests, or other places for all manner of writings or papers that may give you light for the discovery of the libellers."

And more: "That after you shall have examined the persons, if you shall find them duly to be suspected and if they shall refuse to confess the truth, you shall, by the authority hereof, put them to the Torture in Bridewell. And by the extremity thereof, to be used at such times and as often as you shall think fit, draw them to discover all their knowledge concerning said libels."

That, on the following day, May 12, during a search of the chambers of one Thomas Kyd, poet and playmaker, sufficient evidence was discovered to cause him to be arrested and taken to Bridewell.

. . . Well, a player tells Hunnyman, for all the blood and thunder of his plays, Kyd was a timid man. Shy, if the truth be known. It is often the case, I find, with poets, that those who write most of blood will faint to see the head cut off a chicken. And for all his hard heart, Thomas Kyd was a very soft man, fearful of pain in all of its forms. When they showed him the rack and put him on it, he was prepared to tell them anything they might want to hear. Fellow was prepared to betray his mother and father and all of his friends to ease his pains.

. . . I do not know what papers they may have found in his chambers. But whatever they may have been, it was serious enough. And I heard, on good authority, that he tried to place all the blame on Marlowe. Saying the papers belonged to him. For, you know, they had shared lodgings for a time a year or so before . . .

• • •

Clerk will have some papers to show Barfoot. He will read how the arrest and the strict questioning of the said Thomas Kyd came not from the libels against strangers but from other papers, written in his own hand and found in his chambers: "vile and heretical conceits denying the Deity of Jesus Christ, our Savior."

That Kyd then blames Christopher Marlowe and further affirms that the said Marlowe is an atheist. No news there, for Greene had written the same thing in his *Groatsworth*, asking: "Why should thy excellent wit, His gift, be so blinded, that thou should give no glory to the Giver?"

Clerk will show to Barfoot, from his files and rolls, some correspondence from Kyd, writing from Bridewell in his beautiful scrivener's hand (which the racking had not yet ruined) to the Lord Keeper of the Great Seal, Sir John Puckering. Adding some fuel to the fire. Telling his lordship as much as can remember concerning Marlowe: "Pleaseth it your honorable lordship, touching Marlowe's monstrous opinions, as I cannot but with an aggrieved conscience think on him or them, so I can particularize but few in respect of them that kept him greater company . . .

"That it was his custom when I knew him first, and as I hear say he continued it in Table Talk or otherwise, to jest at divine scriptures, gibe at prayers, and strive to frustrate and confute what has been spoken or written by prophets and holy men."

All this is followed by a formidable list of Marlowe's habitual blasphemies and ending with the suggestion of treason as well:

"He would persuade with men of quality to go unto the King of Scots . . ."

Clerk will also show to Barfoot more papers concerning Marlowe's suspected atheism, most especially the document by one Richard Baines—"A Note Containing the Opinion of One Christopher Marlowe, Concerning His Damnable Judgment of Religion and Scorn of God's Word." Much the same, perhaps suspiciously so, as Kyd's complaints. With two new items to catch the eyes of Barfoot: *That if there be any God or any Good Religion, then it is in the Papists. Because the service of God is performed with more Ceremonies, such as the elevation of the mass, organs, singing men, shaven crowns etc. That all Protestants are hypocritical asses.*

"This Baines," the young clerk tells Barfoot, "was himself once a priest of the true Old Faith. And later became a spy against the faithful. One of those living day by day by his wits and trusted by no one. But you need to know, Captain, that the Council was collecting information against Marlowe."

"To what purpose?"

A shrug and a slight smile.

"If I knew that, or even held an opinion, I would tell you. See here."

Points a long, slender finger at one more item in the Baines notes:

That (Marlowe says) he had as good a right to coin as the Queen of England. And that he was acquainted with one Poole, a prisoner in Newgate, who has a great skill in the mixture of metals. And having learned some things of Poole, he meant, by means of a cunning stamp to coin French crowns, pistolets and English shillings . . .

Barfoot breathes lightly between clenched teeth.

"There is more than sufficient in that charge alone to have hanged him."

• • •

. . . God alone knows what Kyd may have said against Marlowe, the player tells Hunnyman. And they are both dead now. So it is a moot matter. But it was only a short time after they took Kyd to Bridewell that, as we heard, they had also arrested Marlowe.

And was he put to the torture? Hunnyman asks.

. . . No, the player says. He was put to death.

• • •

Clerk produces for the inspection of Captain Barfoot the warrant of the eighteenth of May issued by the Privy Council to one Henry Maunder, messenger of Her Majesty's Chamber: *To repair to the house of Mr. Thomas Walsingham in Kent, or to any other place where he shall understand Christopher Marlowe to be remaining, and to apprehend and to bring him to the Court.*

And another item with the date of May 20:

This day Christopher Marlowe of London, gentleman, being sent for by warrant from their Lordships, has entered his appearance accordingly for his indemnity therein. And is commanded to give his daily attendance on their Lordships until he shall be licensed to the contrary.

Barfoot allows: "Here is a man of whom the Council has heard news and charges that he is an atheist and likewise involved in overt acts of treason on two separate counts. Fellow is arrested and brought before Council. Is he packed off to prison and put to the question? Not at all. All that is required of him is that he make daily appearance before the Clerk of the Council. Otherwise he is free and untroubled, so long as he remains nearby. I find that very strange."

"So might I," the clerk says, "if I had never spent a day as a clerk here. Now I believe that nothing will ever surprise me again."

WHAT INGRAM FRIZER HAD TO SAY TO HUNNYMAN

"Before we begin things badly, my man, let me spare you from the temptation and embarrassment of lying to me. You come here in disguise, under a false name and on a false errand. Before you open your mouth to talk—and to trip over your own falsehoods and false pretenses—let me talk a little while you listen. It will save time that way. And though I believe that you have plenty of time on your hands, time to go and do as you please, I am still employed. And my master, though he is fair and just and pays me well for my services, does not lightly shrug off the idleness of his servants. Especially the most trusted of them. And I think I may safely say to you, without any kind of false pride, that no other servant of Sir Thomas Walsingham is more trusted than I am. And none, either, I assure you, will strive harder to be and to remain worthy of his trust.

"I wish I had some idle time on my hands now. For if I did, then I should have the pleasure of sitting back to enjoy you as you play whatever part you have rehearsed for my benefit and your own. I have no time, either, to waste upon stage plays and the like. I sometimes wish it were otherwise. For I hear tell from my friends that there are many delightful plays being performed these days, plays with true style and bravado. Oh, I've seen *The Spanish Tragedy* once or twice and some others of that kind. But nothing new.

"And, yes, to be sure, I have seen performances of all of Kit Marlowe's plays. Wonderful things! Though, for myself and my money, he was at his finest in the first of them, the Tamburlaine plays. A bit bookish for my taste, I suppose, whiff of the candle and the lamp, smell of the college library. But nonetheless powerfully exciting. And the man could write down words and lines like an angel. What matter if all the characters sound alike? They sound like him. Like poor Kit. And, God's holy name, the man could talk. And was a joy to listen to. Not to talk to. You couldn't get more than a word or two said before he stepped on yours and kicked them aside and went merrily along with his soliloquy.

"Just like this fellow Frizer, you are thinking. And you are not far off the mark. For though I will live and die without being able to utter one sentence as bright and shining as most of Marlowe's, still I learned much from him, a master. And I can more than hold my own with the likes of you, Joseph Hunnyman.

"That's who you are, no matter who you are prepared to claim and assert yourself to be. Nothing more or less than one Joseph Hunnyman, a common player without present employment in his craft. I know you. Because it's my business to know these things. And none of yours.

"Some woman, a rich widow as I hear, is your master . . . *mistress* I suppose is the better word for it, these days. And I say more good fortune to you, my good fellow. We each and all do what we can and have to and we make our living where we can.

"I will not make or pass judgment on you or your ways. I might, though, say this much. You would be better off, better advised to live off your widow or, worse comes to worst, off your amazing good luck with cards and dice (you see, I do know a thing or two about you) than to be digging around in someone else's garden on behalf of strangers. Let them do their own digging lest the garden turn out to be a graveyard. If you get my meaning. It could well prove to be a graveyard for someone. Why should that be you?

"But never mind. Who am I to advise you? You have come thus far in life's pilgrimage without my guidance. No doubt you can continue to the end of yours days without me, too. I hope and pray so. For both our sakes.

"Now then.

"At least you are more presentable and better to look at than the other one. No nonsense from him. Not from Captain Barfoot. Straight to the point he was. Wanted me to know, he did, that he was looking into the matter of Christopher Marlowe's death. And what did I think about that?

"And I chose to be as blunt and direct as he was. Told him what I thought and in clear and certain terms.

"And it soon turned into a serious conversation between a couple of gentlemen. Men of the world. A conversation not without some interest to me. Fellow told me a few small things which I never knew before and I, in turn, felt free to tell him a thing or two about Kit that he might not have learned from anyone else. If you would like to know the little things I told him, why, I suggest you go and seek him out and ask him. If you will come here, never mind under what pretense you planned, to ask me face to face, surely you are not too shy to go to him. Though—here I begin again, offering advice when it isn't asked for—I would leave that man alone, if I were you. He looks cruel enough to gouge out your eyeballs with his thumbs if the spirit moved him to do so.

"Although, to be sure, looks are not everything. Many a man with the look of a lion has the heart and stomach of a mouse. And vice versa.

"Mainly, Joseph Hunnyman, I told him the same thing I am now going to say to you.

"You have seen the findings of the Coroner's jury. You know I killed Marlowe with my own knife—*this knife here,* sir; have a look at it; here's what did the deed; it was returned to me when I was pardoned and set free. I killed the man with this very same blade. And it is the same knife I use at table to cut bread and meat.

"I killed the man, my good friend, and both of us, mind you, servants and, yes, according to our stations and our skills, good friends and true to Sir Thomas. I killed poor Kit. And it was exactly, no more, no less, as the jury found it to be. An accident and an act of self-defense. Kit was drunk and in a drunken rage. Would have killed me if I had not defended myself.

"I had no wish or intention to kill him. No. Purely and simply to save my life, which was in peril. And which, to kill for the defense of your own life, provided, of course, there is no way to flee to safety and no other alternative, the laws of England and nature and God do allow a man. For anyone else except for a saint or a martyr (and I was not born to be either one of those) to do less than whatever can and must be done to save his life is a deadly sin against the Holy Ghost. Or so, anyway, the ministers and preachers say.

"And that, Joseph Hunnyman, is all that there is to it and all that I will tell you. And all you need to know.

"No. I should say one or two things more. More than I have to, perhaps more than I ought to. But I do not wish to send you on your way with clouds of doubt troubling the clarity of your thoughts.

"First, my man, keep in mind that Kit Marlowe was a poet and was a friend and companion to my master. Who, likewise, honors his memory. If you have been near any bookstalls—as I know you have—you will know that Kit's poem of *Hero and Leander* has just now been published. Handsomely published. And Sir Thomas is the patron of that publication. Paid, and paid well (your widow would have been more than happy to have been paid for this book) for the publishing. And paid the poet Mr. Chapman to touch it up and to write the finish for it.

"Kit was writing the poem during that spring in '93 when I had to kill him. Now it has been close to five years since then and, nevertheless, Sir Thomas, still sensible of the loss, still grieving over Marlowe's death, has seen to it that the poem is well published.

"Now then, Hunnyman, ask yourself a simple question. If my master loved Christopher Marlowe and loves and honors his memory to this very day, would he have kept me on as his chief servant, and a trusted agent, if there were any question at all concerning what happened and the propriety of my actions and motives?

"I wish Marlowe were still alive, believe me. But nothing, not prayer, not fasting and weeping (and I have spent more than my share of tears on the man; and I have no more tears to show you; if you came for that, you are bound to be disappointed), nothing will bring him back.

"So be it. My conscience is clear.

"I suggest that you go back to whoever hired you to meddle in this and tell whoever it is that there is nothing more to be found out.

"And I urge you, Joseph Hunnyman, not to trouble the other two of us, if you can find them. They may not be so gentle with you as I have been or take you as lightly as I do. Especially Poley. He might lose his temper and cut off your ears or your private parts.

"Marry your widow. Find yourself some gainful and lawful employment if you can. And let this matter die quietly. Let Marlowe rest in peace.

"And now I have business to attend to.

"Goodbye to you. And I hope that if we meet again, it will be about something else.

"If you ever need to borrow money, you will find I can offer you better rates than any goldsmith in London."

Finally her majesty is particularly in-formed of some intentions of sundry per-sons, of ability to keep hospitality in their countries, to leave their said hospitality and to come to the City of London and other cities and towns corporate, thereby leaving the relief of their poor neighbors as well as for food as for good rule, and with covetous minds to live in London and about the city privately and so also in other towns corporate without charge of company. For withstanding whereby her majesty chargeth all manner of persons that shall have any such intention during the time of dearth not to break up their households nor to come to said city or other towns corporate; and all others that have of late time broken up their house-holds to return to their houses again without delay.

—*Royal Proclamation, Richmond,*
November 2, 1596

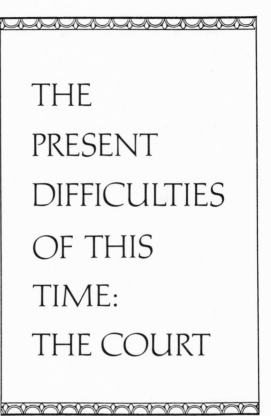

THE PRESENT DIFFICULTIES OF THIS TIME: THE COURT

With an old song made by an old aged pate of an old gentleman that had an old wealthy estate,
Who kept an old house, at an old bountiful rate,
With an old porter to relieve poor people at his gate;
Like an old Courtier of the Queen's,
And the Queen's old Courtier.

—*"The Old Courtier of the Queen's"*

Notwithstanding, when the pride of flesh, and power of favour shall close in these by death or disgrace, what then hath Time to register or Fame to publish, in these great men's names, that will not be offensive and infectious to others? What pen without blotting can write the story of their deeds? Or what herald blaze *their arms without blemish? And as for their counsels and projects, when they come once to light, shall they not live as noisome and loathsomely above ground as their authors' carcasses lie in the grave? So that the return of such greatness to the world and themselves can be but a private reproach, public ill example, and a fatal scorn to the Gov-ernment they live in. Sir Philip Sidney is none of their number. For the greatness he affected was built upon true worth, esteeming fame more than riches and noble actions far above nobility itself.*

—*Fulke Greville, Lord Brooke,*
The Life of the Renowned
Sir Philip Sidney

He knows no man that is not generally known. His wit, like the marigold, openeth with the sun, and therefore, he riseth not before ten of the clock. He puts more confidence in his words than meaning and more in his pronunciation than his words. Occasion is his Cupid and he hath but one receipt of making love. He follows nothing but inconstancy, admires nothing but beauty, knows nothing but fortune, loves nothing . . .

—Sir Thomas Overbury, *Characters*

There hence ariseth the insatiable desire of honor, stirring them up day and night, not to content themselves with base and casual things, but to seek by virtuous deeds to recompense the shortness of this life by the memory of all posterity. There hence proceeds the wonderful desire of making themselves known, of leaving a good opinion of them, of getting an immortal renown.

—*Louis Le Roy*, Of the Interchangeable Course or Variety of Things in the Whole World

Falstaff: . . . *Well, 'tis no matter, honor pricks me on. Yea, but how if honor prick me off when I come on? How then? Can honor set to a leg? No. Or an arm? No. Or take away the grief of a wound? No. Honor hath no skill in surgery then? No. What is honor? A word. What is in that word honor? What is that honor? Air. A trim reckoning. Who hath it? He that died a' Wednesday. Doth he feel it? No. Doth he hear it? No. 'Tis sensible then? Yea, to the dead. But will not live with the living? Why? Detraction will not suffer*

it. Therefore I'll none of it, honor is a mere scutcheon. And so ends my catechism.

—**William Shakespeare,**
The First Part of Henry the Fourth

Say to the Court it glows
*   and shines like rotten wood.*
Say to the Church it shows
*   what's good and doth no good.*
If Church and Court reply
*   then give them both the lie.*

—*Sir Walter Ralegh, "The Lie"*

Though man for a while seem never so honorable and mighty, never so rich and wealthy, never so young and lusty, never so beautiful and comely, never so fortunate and happy, yet he shall die, and the finger of God shall suddenly write . . . Thy days are numbered and cometh to an end: and thy pomp and thy pride shall be laid into the grave; worms shall lie under thee and worms shall be thy covering.

—"A Very Profitable Sermon
Preached at the Court"

The gloss of gorgeous courts, by thee did please
*   mine eye,*
A stately sight methought it was to see the brave
*   go by;*
To see their feathers flaunt, to mark their strange
*   device,*
To lie along in ladies' laps, to lisp and make it
*   nice;*
To fawn and flatter both, I liked sometimes well,
But since I see how vain it is, Fancy (quoth he)
*   farewell.*

—*George Gascoigne, "The Green Knight's*
Farewell to Fancy"

INTERLUDE:
ACCESSION
DAY

L et me tell you about the Queen's
Day.

Once upon a time, as the story they tell the children goes, the
young woman was walking with some of her ladies in the park near an
old palace. Sunlight played hide-and-seek among blowing clouds and
the bare limbs of oaks. Fallen leaves scurried, were lifted to turn and
dance a little by gusts and shifts of a light breeze. It was warm and
pleasant for November in this kingdom.

After a while of walking together, someone came and spread out a
cloth on the ground and placed some cushions where she and her
companions could sit and enjoy the good weather beneath a tree. From

where they sat there was a long view of the park and of the road to London.

Her companions were all elegantly dressed, but the young woman was dressed as simply, as soberly, and as plainly as a Princess can be. She might have been their servant. Except that her cushion, next to the trunk of the tree, was like a little throne around which theirs were scattered as though to honor and to protect her. They were busy with their sewing and embroidery. She held a Testament, following the tip of her finger as she pondered and savored each word of the Greek.

And it was thus that the Lords of the Council found her when, booted and spurred, dusty from the ride to Hatfield from Westminster, they came in a clutch and knot together, like a bouquet of spring flowers in their courtiers' clothing, walking through the crackle and scuttle of the fallen leaves, hats in their hands, moving as if to a stately, solemn, unheard music across the sun-dappled grass of the park. Ahead of them they saw the ladies rise all at once, smoothly, as if to some command no one has heard or has seen given. For the young woman, so plainly dressed, was still bent close to her little book.

Suddenly she closed it. And in one easy and graceful motion was up on her feet and striding toward them. Surprised, they stumbled to a halt.

Before they could fall down on their knees, before they could speak a word, still at a distance from them, she went to her knees and clasped her hands together in the attitude of prayer.

Her voice, high and clear and utterly calm as she spoke from the Psalms:

"It is the Lord's doing and it is marvelous in our eyes."

The great men of this kingdom, Lords of the Council, knelt down where they stood. And for a moment there was something close to silence. Except for the soft whispering of the wind. Except for the sound of someone (one of her servants perhaps) weeping.

• • •

Now on this holiday, better part of a lifetime later, we celebrate that moment with marvels of our own. Portraits step out of their frames. And from fading tapestries the brilliant ways and means of chivalry are to be once more restored and reborn at the Tiltyard.

By night the darkness of the City will be driven back to huddle in smallest corners by the blazing of many bonfires. By torches and lanterns and by bouquets of fireworks opening strange and glittering flowers in the echoing and astonished night sky. Bells will be ringing as if to shatter the last remnants of silence to broken bits and pieces now and forever. There will be music playing everywhere and singing and dancing; wine from the spigots of the public conduits and good food cooking for such feasting that you cannot believe there is any kind of shortage in England. Or that there is famine in far places. Tonight there will be such abundant pleasure that you can pretend, if you wish to, there will be no tomorrow.

But before all that and while daylight lasts, this day belongs to the Queen and her Court.

And long before first light, all over London and Westminster and the suburbs around them, gentlemen and ladies (false and true) are busy preparing to dress themselves for the pageants and shows at the Tiltyard. Truth is, they must *be dressed,* clothed with the aid and comfort of others. For other hands are needed to take care of the buttoning and snapping and lacing into tight, hidden places of the many parts that are the fashion these days. Clothing calling by its intricate artiface and design for others to help. And unlucky is that man or woman who has the benefit of the services of nobody else but an ancient, weak-eyed, stiff-jointed servant who has forgotten where all the parts come together and how. If she ever knew. Or perhaps only a loutish, heavy-handed, turnip-fingered apprentice lad, grinning and well-meaning and hopelessly inept. Or maybe a sour-faced scullery maid, as dirty as she is ignorant. Will take more than these to dress and send master and mistress forth into this day's daylight world. Unlucky the ladies and gents who will go forth, in spite of the riches of the materials (the silks and satins, taffeta and damask and velvet, finest leather, and lace so fern-fine and delicate that it must certainly have blinded the strangers who bent and squinted to make it), in spite of all fans and furs, jewels from slippers to top of curled and frizzed hair, in spite of all these things, even the least costly of costumes being worth the price, perhaps, of a fair-size farm, with farmhouse and barns and outhouses, with pasture and pond and woodlands; and the most expensive and elegant, being worn by the truly great and by those wishing to be mistaken for the like and the same, costing as much as some lord's estate with its mansion and park, village and parish, tenants and sheep—unlucky the lady and gent sent forth, dressed carelessly by careless hands, without each and every thing precisely in its perfect, casual place. Why, no matter how grand your clothing, how cut to the latest fashion, you might as well be a scarecrow or a country clown, the survivor of a shipwreck or a siege.

And so it is that an hour or so before the first hints of the day, by the light of candles and fireplaces, it is high time to begin business that begins (or has begun already, days ago) with unpacking and unfolding, with brushing and sponging and ironing, with scouring and polishing, with barbering and combing and curling. All this to be accompanied by no little bit of cursing and cajoling, tongue-lashing and fresh tears.

The truly great, fortunate few, may still be soundly sleeping, slugabed if that's what they choose to be. They will be in residence at Court in Whitehall or nearby in Westminster and will have many skilled and experienced hands to assist them whenever they desire it. But there are a few, heart and soul and future of the Court (and, thus, this kingdom), the young of whom this day will demand a public trial and performance. A showing off of timeless skills for the sake of present ambition. Preparation for this day for most of them began half or more of a brief lifetime ago, with hobbyhorse and wooden sword. Learning and growing into full body armor made and fitted in Greenwich, lance and broadsword and shield, all the old signs and symbols of chivalry. And this day began for them, as in days of old in the legends and chronicles (the truth of which is now beyond the memory of anyone alive, though there are old fellows, who will bear witness to this day's tournament, who can recall seeing Great Henry VIII at the tilt, and it is in Harry's Tiltyard where they will win or lose favor and honor this day), many hours ago. Began even at the strokes of midnight on the Whitehall clocks as, already bathed and barbered, already having prayed and been prayed over, they, like the young knights of ancient days, commenced all the elaborate and noisy business of preparing their weapons and the final fitting of scoured and shining, richly jeweled and decorated parade armor. Began, too, to oversee the chore of grooming and dressing their horses, in this case the huge English war-horses, larger than any other on the island. Which, for this occasion, are as carefully attended to as the finest

Court ladies. For these young men, as always upon Accession Day, there will be an old-fashioned chivalric tournament. Part of the lavish entertainments and several kinds of shows to be presented for the Queen and in her honor at the Tiltyard.

For them, after the music and ceremonial processional, there will be the Joust of Peace, a warlike exercise, called running at tilt, fighting each other in single combat from horseback with spears. Then the tourney fought with swords and shields. Finally running at barriers, settled with swords and pikes on foot. All of it sufficiently dangerous to make even the young and the strong sweat in their armor, hearts fisting and pounding. There will be some bloodshed; some broken bones, though not so much of the one and not so many of the other as there might well be, probably ought to be, except that the old Queen enjoys the ceremonies more than the combat. For her sake and special pleasure there are always more pageants and disguises than tournaments. Music (all her own half a hundred musicians are there in their new livery), singing, dramatic speeches written by the best poets. Strange devices—smoking dragons; canvas castles; moving trees and fountains; dwarfs in chariots; giants, fore and aft, as horses; Blackamoors (painted or real) and Indians, Jews and Gypsies. Her Champion, George Clifford, Earl of Cumberland, will stand by, dressed out in tilting armor, half of it silver and gold, worth a nobleman's estate, the Queen's favor (one of her long, slender gloves) pinned to his hat, ready to enforce all the rules of chivalry and likewise to defend his Queen if and when, as always happens, some stranger knight gallops suddenly and unannounced into the Tiltyard from King Street.

All of this, her special feast day, will be, as it must be, a rich surprise and delight for the frugal Queen. Who will not, as all the world knows, pay out one thin penny for any of it. Who stands to gain more than a little, not only from the expensive gifts and offerings presented by her knights, but also, and more directly to the point, from the extravagant charges, twelve pennies and more, which must be paid out by all but the holders of the highest offices of Court and government for the undeniable privilege of entering in at the gate of the Tiltyard to witness the shows there.

And to witness the Queen herself, when, in the company of her maids of honor and her guests and guards, she takes her place at an open window of the gallery overlooking the yard. From which she will, when and as the spirit moves her to, shout down encouragement or rebukes in a clear voice that can be heard the length of the yard.

This year there is much gossip and rumor concerning who, among the lords and factions, will be present. With the Earl of Essex still sulking in anger after the Islands Voyage, with Ralegh said to be sick in Sherbourne, the question is whether either of them will come (or come in disguise) to surprise the Queen and Court with some kind of show. It could happen. Has happened just so in the past.

Will they come, then, one or both of them? And if not, then which of their followers and faction, if any, will come?

No one will watch these things more eagerly and attentively than Joseph Hunnyman. Who would cut a purse and risk hanging, if he had to, rather than miss the tilts. He has sometimes played a part (never a true speaking part) in the shows. Once as an ape in a band of apes who were the retinue of a courtier who came as the Savage Knight of Africa. Once as a squire, bearing the plumed helmet of a great man who, for reasons of his own, most likely that he had fallen out of favor with the Queen, came in rusty, dented armor on an old, swaybacked nag, billed as the Knight of Melancholy. But Hunnyman would much prefer to pay his twelve pence and idly stroll about the yard, looking every inch a courtier himself in his rented clothing, to see and to be seen, and to be all ears for the latest gossip. He has been there often enough (always) over the past few years to have earned a vague familiarity, a face you have seen somewhere, maybe here, and maybe ought to know. Last year he earned a nod of recognition and greeting from a judge, slightly drunken to be sure, of the Court of Queen's Bench. And on that same day an officious usher raised his eyebrows as if in contempt for him, then suddenly seemed to know him and take him for a gentleman. Smiled and bowed. Who knows what this year, or the next, may bring to Hunnyman?

Barfoot, on the other hand, dearly loves all the pageant and ceremony, all the ancient military sports and rites, the ancient rules and customs of heraldry. Not that he is a pedant in these matters. Not at all. Which is just as well. Because the Queen's Court takes every kind of liberty. They leave more rigid observance to the likes of the French (ever punctilious) and the Spanish.

More to the point is how someone like Barfoot, who has seen and endured the worst that war can do, should take any pleasure in bloodless and antique military exercises. Which have no kinship to the horrid truths of then or now or ever.

"Ah, it does no man any harm," he would say. "What's the harm of it? Except that sometimes a young fellow will fall and break his neck. Well, the same oaf might have done the same thing tripping over a chamber pot.

"Say this. I like the shine and color of it all. Love the plumes and pennants, flags and banners and shields. My heart beats to the music of fife and drum, trumpet and bagpipe. I rejoice in the sight of sunlight on rich parade armor. Times like these and I can relish and delight in the sight of horseflesh as much as womanflesh.

"It has nothing whatever to do with war . . . No! By God, it does have to do with war. It is what war ought to be. What war wants to be. And if it ever came to pass, no sane and reasonable man would want to be anything else but a soldier!"

• • •

Wherever Barfoot's lodgings may be found, he is not there now, but instead in the high chamber of that old house near Lambeth Marsh. Where he has a pair of fastidious Dutch whores to help him dress himself. Court ladies they may not be. Now or ever. But they are wonderfully light- and deft-fingered (and experienced) at the taking off and putting on of clothes.

"It may very well be true, as the proverb tells it, that it takes nine tailors to make one gentleman. But, on my oath, the two of you are sufficient to dress a King for his Coronation."

They would prefer to be dressing up in their own best things to come along with Barfoot, arm and arm, turning heads at the sight of their coming and going, perhaps to see and be seen by the Queen. And once or twice he has taken them with him to the tilts. But today he has other business in mind. And they, too, had better mind their business on a holiday.

Anyway, he has not neglected them. End of October, for instance, he took them over the River to stand outside Westminster Hall, among some of the most important and honorable folk of the City, to see the new Lord Mayor of London, one Richard Saltonstall, skinner by trade, come by his barge in all of his robes and finery, to swear his oath of office. And you can easily imagine how the good City wives, wives of merchants and guildsmen and officers of the City, might take much offense at the close presence of a couple of very well-dressed whores. Court ladies, more sure of themselves, in the scheme of things, tend to be amused, to enjoy the irony, fully aware, if unlikely to broadcast that knowledge, that the difference between themselves and a couple of whores in this man's world (though, always be reminded, the men, themselves, are ruled by a Queen) is likely to be too subtle for comfort and more a matter of nuance and circumstance than any badge of virtue. Court lady, in her secret heart anyway, will say what no City wife will ever admit: that allowing for some of the more obvious differences of appearance—and remember that you can breed horses to be swift and strong, pigs to be fat, dogs to be large or small, fierce or gentle—the whore and the lady may otherwise be as near as blood kin in many ways. Earning their keep in much the same fashion. There are many among the ladies of the Court who have been tempted, at least by the idea of it, wondering how they might fare in the large world as common whores. And, if rumor can be trusted, there are said to be some, especially among the younger generation, who have done just that, tested themselves in disguise and for the oddly perverse pleasure of it.

• • •

At the house of the Widow Alysoun on Knightrider Street a busy little knot is hard at the task of preparing the widow to go with him, this for the first time in her life, to the Tiltyard. Hunnyman has found and collected some elegant clothing for her and for himself, renting this and that from the players' companies, from the Office of Revels. For the wonderful, nearly new farthingale skirt that Alysoun will wear, he has *(mirabilis!)* struck a fair bargain with Mr. Francis Langley of Paris Garden, whose playhouse, the Swan, is for now without a company to play there. And Hunnyman himself will proudly wear doublet and hose once worn (but only briefly; it's almost as if new) by some nobleman or other. Died of the sickness, perhaps. Or lives yet, but lacks the means to pay what he owes. Common enough. There are City merchants these days with ten times the ready money of the oldest noble names of England. Or, just as likely, this man wore it once or twice before he decided that it pleased him not; so he sold it to the players. And now, from time to time, can at least enjoy the pleasure of seeing someone, a player, suffer and rejoice on his behalf; can bear witness to this surrogate tearing strange passions to tatters in his own clothing. Anyway, a good tailor has made it fit Hunnyman well, like a buttoned glove, and has altered things somewhat to follow close behind the latest fashions.

She has surprises in store for Hunnyman. At this moment she has just unveiled one of these: a red wig, perfectly curled and cut and resting on a wooden wig stand. Her woman, Mary, is even now touching up the curls of it, here and there, with a brush and a heated comb. When she has done with all that, she will dust all with a glitter of diamond sparks, then fit and pin into place one perfect jewel, which Alysoun found by diligently searching the shops of Cheapside, the Bridge, and the Royal Exchange. It is a little sailing ship of fine gold, with brightly enameled sails and flags, to wear in her wig. Hunnyman stands near her, holding a large looking glass for her to make up her face. She is making her face an even milky white with a fucus made of (among other things, the apothecary told her) oil of white poppies and a fine powder made from the burnt jawbone of a fat and healthy hog. Rouge for her cheeks and a waxy paint to brighten her lips. Hunnyman is startled by the wig. More by the expense of it (for it is real hair shorn from some poor woman and most precisely coifed by the wigmaker, who is, as it happens, Mistress Dorothy Spekarde, the silkwoman and wigmaker for the Queen herself; truly it's fit for the Queen) than anything else. But chooses another line of argument, namely that with her own natural hair so beautiful, so richly golden—other women torment themselves with all kinds of expensive dyes and soaps and herbal bleaches, hoping to look even half so golden-haired as Alysoun—why on earth should she choose to hide her glory with a wig?

She looks closely at her face in the glass before she answers.

"Think, Hunnyman. Exercise your lazy mind. The Queen is an old woman now. It will give her no kind of pleasure that I can imagine to see and admire my golden hair. Nor will it be any pleasure to other Court ladies, young or old indifferently, who have struggled to turn their hair to gold for this occasion. A wig can offend no one or arouse any envy—except for the cost of it. Which they will know, within a halfpenny, at first sight. They will be left to imagine that I have spent a very large sum for this wig to cover some serious defect. That without my magical wig, I should be of no more interest than a brown house sparrow perched among his fellows on a roof. 'What an elegant wig!' they will say, smiling, without either envy or malice.

"Now, you see also how, against your objections, I am daubing my face white, painting my lips red, touching my eyebrows with a tawny orange to go with the wig. You say I have an unblemished face, so soft and smooth as to need not one touch of daubing. You say I will not look nearly as well as I do in my own natural state, untouched by any of these commonplace disguises.

"To which I answer that a woman with a painted face clearly has some blemishes to hide. They will think that without my painted face I would be nothing to envy or remember. My painted face—and tell me, Hunnyman, say that I am not beautiful, paint or no paint?—and my red wig will make my costume. Which will surely be among the most elegant and fashionable you shall see today at the Tiltyard.

"I understand these women, Hunnyman. And it is better, by far, that they should be more condescending than envious. Do you see how it is?"

"What I fail to see is the part I am supposed to play in this cruel parliament of women."

"Don't let it trouble you. You will merely be the handsome young man at my side. But, believe me, you will be noticed and maybe even remembered."

She has already risen up without warning from her three-legged stool, having finished (for now) with her face, and left him bent and standing there holding the empty looking glass.

"How do you happen to know so much?" he says. "You have never been near the Queen's Court in all your life."

She laughs lightly. "You are much mistaken, Joseph Hunnyman," she says. "I have been there and nowhere else for as long as I can remember."

He sits himself on the low stool, the looking glass dangling idly in his hand.

On the back of her looking glass, chipped and faded gilt and enamel, smoothing like an old coin that has passed from sweaty palm to palm (this, too, having belonged in its time to someone of high station), he can still make out the theme of it. A man and a woman, both of them naked, both richly endowed with abundant physical beauty, she no doubt, by dint of breasts and thigh and laughing belly, Venus; he, all large and clearcut muscles, power from tip to toe, must be Mars; and they, together, are locked in the wrestle and shudder of love. Not therefore seeing the third figure, hunched and crippled and furious, Vulcan the artificer; who crouches here like a fisherman, about to cast the fine unbreakable net which will, in a moment, entangle these sweaty perfect bodies and render them ridiculous, fit only for the amusement of the laughing white gods.

"Strange," he says. "When I was a small child, what I wanted most to become, more than anything else I could imagine in the whole world, was the village blacksmith. Fire and iron, the dull bell of hammer ringing on the anvil. That was as far as I could dream for myself, as high and mighty as I dared to aspire. And, God knows, to this day I often find myself wishing that it could have been so."

He raises the looking glass and stares sadly, eyes of a newly weaned calf, into it. She leans over his shoulder, filling the glass with herself, and breathes a fog that covers everything. When it clears, he can laugh again and make clownish faces at himself.

"Come now, Joseph," she says. "Be quick. Put on your magical coat of many colors and let's be off to Whitehall Palace."

• • •

Alysoun has not wasted her time and effort. For, though she will not now, nor ever know it, the Queen herself will look down and take some notice of her. Will poke with the point of her jeweled fan to gain the wandering attention of one of her young maids of honor.

"Do you see there yonder woman, the one with one of Mistress Spekarde's red wigs, leaning on the arm of that overdressed actor? I'll wager we could snatch off her wig and scrub that white fucus off her face and the paint off her lips and still she would be more handsome to behold than any of you."

"I do not doubt it, Your Majesty."

"And what do you think about that?"

"Why, nothing much, ma'am. Only that it seems a fair and just exchange. She is more beautiful than I, true. But I am here and she is there. And, too, I thank God, in sincere and humble gratitude, that I have been given something far more valuable and imperishable than beauty of face and form."

Queen will snort like an old man. "And what would that be, child?"

"Why, ma'am, it is the most precious gift of all. More so than gold or jewels or land or any worldly goods," the young woman will say. "I mean, of course, the love and favor and goodwill of my Queen."

"Go to, go to!" the Queen will exclaim as those in the gallery jump at her loud laughter. "I asked for that, child. And you gave me no more than I deserve. But, nevertheless, that's a beautiful woman yonder. And if she were only a lady, why, I could marry her off and make her a countess by tomorrow night."

But during this, Alysoun's attention will be altogether elsewhere. Spotting Barfoot in the crowd, she will contrive to have Hunnyman walk with her where she will have to pass close by to Barfoot. It will be necessary for her to divert Hunnyman's attention for a moment so that he may not see Barfoot at all and certainly will not see any sign of recognition between herself and Barfoot. All that is even easier done than said. Leans against Hunnyman. Points at something in the yard. His eyes follow her hand. Not even looking, she drops one glove at the boots of Captain Barfoot.

Who stoops, crouches, and picks up the glove. So that when, a little later, she feels free to and does look back over her shoulder to see him, Captain Barfoot's scarred, brutal face will wear its familiar, fixed, and expressionless public mask. But her glove will be pinned to the crown of his hat as a favor.

• • •

For the Dutch whores it has been an entertaining game, like dressing up a doll, preparing Barfoot for his annual excursion to the Tiltyard. Part of the pleasure of it is that Barfoot does not, as so many, even courtiers, do, rent his clothing. He keeps it year by year, folded carefully in a chest, to be worn one day a year. (Unless and until he is called for an audience with her Majesty or some such. A calling he doesn't count on.) Changes a little with accessories and odds and ends and through the services and suggestions of a good tailor from London Bridge.

So he's now become an elegant creature of excellent bits and pieces and patches, half in fashion and half out of another age.

And what is he wearing today?

Why, doublet and hose like any other well-dressed gentleman in England. Barfoot's doublet is of Genoa velvet, slashed and paned and pinked to show its lining of brilliant satin; faced with silk buttons, each with a little jewel at its center. Hooks and eyes are of silver. He favors the trunk hose which come halfway down his thigh and are also paned to show off flashes of bright silk; and are smoothly, tautly laced to his silk nether stocks. Wears high boots of a beautiful and shiny Spanish cordovan leather, but, at his request, cut not in the loose Spanish fashion but in the tight-fitting Italian style. Separate sleeves of silk, laced and tied to his richly embroidered shirt beneath the military wings at the shoulder. Never mind this latest affectation of allowing the laces and joints to be unconcealed. And no wide starched ruff for a collar either, fashion or no. For a ruff makes his head look like John the Baptist's on a platter. Instead he wears a delicate falling band of Flanders lace. And little lace hand ruffs at the wrists.

His whores have persuaded him this once to put aside his favorite Spanish half cloak with its hood, in favor of a Dutch cloak they bought him as a present—waist-length, full and short, with wide taffeta sleeves. Cloak is peppered with seed pearls.

Barfoot's soft leather gloves have gold buttons and are cut open at the fingers to show off his rings. Wears other jeweled rings on a gold cord round his neck. Likewise a pomander with sweet herbal scents on a stronger chain. His belt has a purse of silk and leather and a hanger of goldsmith's work for the fashionable rapier he wears in place of a heavy sword. His jeweled dagger is hanging on his right hip by a short gold chain.

Pearl earrings. High-crowned, wide-brimmed taffeta hat, brightened with ostrich feathers.

He takes a turn around the room, flashing color like a peacock's tail, jangling like a man in glittering chains.

"If I die and you are the first to find me, why, strip me naked and sell all my clothes and jewels. And you shall be the richest couple of whores in Lambeth."

Then he's off down the stairs in a clatter. And they watch from the window as the ugliest well-dressed man in England starts off, shoulders back and head high, down the lane. Not looking back at them once until, as he reaches the Anchor tavern at the end of the lane, pausing in mid-stride as if considering the need to go in there and have a glass of sack to carry himself across the River. Then turns around on the balls of his feet like a dancer and bows and tips his hat to them.

They applaud. And then he is gone around the corner and out of sight.

• • •

It is Blood Month in England, time for the slaughtering of beasts before winter.

And not far from here (and everyone here knows it and it gives an edge of dangerous sweetness to these leisurely and measured moments) animals are dying amid much groaning and squealing. Throats are cut and then the bleeding beast is hung up, hoisted by the heels to be gutted and cleaned. Oh, all that red and blue! All the slime and shit of it!

Never mind. Come this Christmas and that boar's head will be brought in to music on a huge platter. Smiling.

HUNNYMAN SEES THE FUTURE

To be just, it needs to be said that the Widow Alysoun is not without her own kind of generosity. True, as a matter of policy she would as lief be Hunnyman's wife as to be solemnly married to the man in the moon. Hunnyman, as her husband and, at least by Law and custom, her lord and master, is not a notion she cares seriously to entertain. Not even briefly.

Oh, she takes much pleasure in his company. Truth is, he is more pleasure to her than any husband she can imagine. Especially in old Adam's dance of the shaking sheets . . . and, no doubt and no denying, he is a lusty and, indeed, an indefatigable performer, an art that calls for more than simply natural skill and form which, being

young and spirited and not without art and skill herself, she finds to
be a comfort and a solace. And she is grateful—how could she be
otherwise?—to Hunnyman, who, in a sense, has been her schoolmaster, her tutor, in many of these things, as well as some others which
are more a matter of mind and spirit; who has taught her how to be,
as it were, sometimes the player and sometimes the plucked and played
lute and at some shining times to be both at once.

But beyond all of that . . .

Which, while a very great and deep pleasure (sometimes) is
likewise something to be offered up, something she will gladly offer up
at any time for the sake of her greater and deeper hungers for more
valuable and (her view) permanent things.

Ah, circumlocution!

Costuming truth with cap and bells of words. Fig leaves did well
for Adam and Eve. But we have since lost our simplicity along with
our innocence.

Let me put it another way and then be done with the subject. We
cannot begin to imagine Hunnyman and Alysoun without considering
the full commerce between them. Like nations exchanging goods with
each other. The white fever of their bodies joined together is common
enough and easy to understand; though it is somewhat more uncommon that, over time, the fever of it has not somewhat abated. Perhaps
that can be explained, at least for Alysoun and in her more thoughtful
view, as coming from the extraordinary good looks, the youth and
physical beauty they both possess. So that for Alysoun it is less like
giving herself, opening herself to another creature, than it is like
sharing herself with herself. If she were a man, she would probably be
very much like Hunnyman. Less of a clown, she hopes, and maybe
wiser and harder. There are times, when their bodies are locked and
rocking together, when she thinks they have somehow or other, by
some spell or witchcraft, come to inhabit the wrong bodies. That his
body rightly belongs to her. And she must, bounden duty, find some
means to reclaim it. He, meanwhile, must often feel the same
contradiction. For many times it seems to her that he is possessed with
a consuming hunger to be and to become her, to vanish like a soap
bubble in light and air. Becoming a spirit to enter and inhabit herself.

And that she cannot and will not tolerate, except the image of it:
Hunnyman's lean hard body turned to smoke and gone in a puff of

wind and then the soft and childish spirit of him, curling up inside her, covering himself with her flesh and beauty like a warm blanket and all accomplished at a brief dreaming peak of excitement and surrender.

She has other things in mind. And she will deny herself much, any pleasures that she knows of, and embrace any pains she can imagine (even, yes, the pain of childbirth) to gain her heart's desire. Whatever that may be.

Hunnyman is then (and to that extent he guesses right and is rightly concerned) an expendable pleasure in her life. But she does enjoy his company and for more than the shaking of sheets together. And she is grateful to him and would like, within reason, to be generous to him in return.

Which is how, simply enough, she has offered more than one time to assist him, by whatever means possible, to buy a share in an acting company or a playhouse. Or both.

It has become a sore point of disputation between them.

Begins almost always with a kind of elaborate game. She being plainly explicit. As if she were talking of buying cabbages or a fardel of firewood. He with pride and (slightly) injured feelings. He will, to be sure, as he always has thus far, make his own sweet way in the world. Need not, and no, *will not,* depend upon the kindness and generosity of others, or, for that matter, the *absence* of either or both, to make his way for him.

She, then, partly teasing and partly not. Would he, she asks, bite his thumb or thumb his nose if some worthy gentleman or even, why not, some person of honor, a nobleman, should for some reason, and never mind the reason, let us not argue about that, choose to become his patron?

Here, it must be said, there is a sharp edge to her teasing. For once upon a time, at a time of most intense intimacy, he weakened enough to tell her a secret. How when he was no more than a young boy with choirboy's voice who played the parts of girls and women in the traveling company of players who were all his family in those days, how he, not understanding any of this at first, caught the eyes and fed the lust—for what? for youth, for beauty, for another chance and a new life, for a shudder as the soul briefly departed its house of flesh like a sneeze—of certain men of worship and, yes, of honor, too. Young or old no matter; for at that age all men with hair on their faces and a curly pelt at the crotch are equally old. How the principal sharer of the little company—that was before this fellow died of a fit while playing the part of King Herod of the Jews, and the company fell into the hands and keeping of kindly and gentle old Henry, may his bones rest in peace!—this other stout, stone-hearted, trumpet-voiced player would sell him, his body, to give comfort and satisfaction to some gentleman or other. How he had no good choice in the matter except a bloody and bruising beating from his master and most likely, too, to be required to find new ways to comfort and satisfy him. Better the bodies and hungers of these strangers. Who might well be softer and kinder and were often generous, though his master would seldom let him keep any gifts or presents he earned by his ministry to these men. How he learned that ministry well enough. Thinking, in innocence and ignorance, that this is what all young boys must do to earn their way ahead in the world. Receiving no pleasure from it; yet, yes, taking some when he saw how easily he could master his masters by means of the power to deal out the pleasure they, sooner or later, humbled themselves to earn. Thinking, even at that age and time, that the pleasure of these men was never so simple as it had at first seemed; that humiliation and a kind of idolatry or worship were inextricably wedded to the physical pleasure. How, instead of what might have so easily turned to contempt and hatred, he came to pity these men. Came to pity them enough so that he sought ways and means to please them more.

She even at the time he whispered these things, and more, to her in the darkness, his warm breath on her pillow, lightly bathing her face, not wholly crediting his confession. He being first of all, boy or man, and never forget it, a player and as able and likely to step into the shoes of any one role as another. Might have been, most likely was, only something he had heard from other players. But in those days, when they were still shy and new enough with each other to make confessions, even as she doubted the truth of his, she was flattered, even, she's now ashamed to remember, somewhat aroused by the picture of it, that a hand of cards, shuffle and deal, in her mind; flattered that he, in the same terms he had described these others, real or imaginary, these lovers of boys who would pay for the pleasures of his flesh and humble themselves, he, too, was here and now—albeit in darkness and with nothing touching her but his surprising sweet breath and his whispered words—humbling himself to her. By this means. Flattered, touched, beginning to be aroused.

Thinking: *Yes, because you know what it is to be a woman and not only that but also a woman who is beautiful to behold, desirable at great price and risk, because you have known the inward and spiritual marriage and holy communion of humble subjection and servitude—not worthy so much as to gather the crumbs under thy table—with drenched and exalted power and strength—Take, eat, this is my body which is given for you.*

But even if flattered and aroused, feeling an undesirable contempt for him; not for this humbling of himself and shaming of himself, in fact or fancy—and in these matters of the wrestle of flesh and spirit, fancy has far more weight than any fact—but for using this means against her; yes, against her, for the purpose was, yes, in this and every other way, to capture and possess her, to hold her hostage and prisoner, to impose his fancy, his imagination, on her like fetters and chains, to force her to ransom herself from the power of his spirit by the abject surrender and expense of her own.

This much she knew, has known as long as she can remember knowing or surmising anything more than hot or cold, sweet or sour, smooth and rough, that since Adam and Eve were briefly content and innocent, there has been a state of warfare between men and women. And though it may be for a time, long time or short, fought out on the battlefields of flesh, with sieges and ambushes, frustration and satisfaction, pride and humiliation, still it is deeply and truly a matter of the spirit, of wounded spirits urgently seeking to be, somehow, healed and whole again.

She does not know, cannot imagine if the same paradigm and similitude holds true for the lusts of men for each other, except insofar as one or the other may become, like a player, *yes,* the woman of the pair. She doubts it is the same. Or, at other times, she allows herself to think that this warfare of body and soul will be found in every creature's love of and desire for anything.

Thus, and because she has felt these things, not as clear thoughts, but as muddy tides ebbing and flowing within her being, she felt contempt for him. Knowing that he must have felt the same for his masters and suitors. And that, out of an irreducible contempt for her, he feared to tell her the whole truth.

All this, then, beneath and behind the sharp point of her teasing. Do you see?

They might as well have been married and for a very long time.

He has said he will make his own way, thank you. And she has argued that he is deceiving himself. That if he could be the servant of some generous patron, he would surely do so. And if so, why will he not accept her generosity in the spirit intended?

At this point, and she knows it well before they arrive there, he will begin to parley and negotiate. Allowing that together they could accomplish many great things in the world. That, with his good advice and counsel, he could help her to become richer than she has ever imagined.

"I would find your suggestion much more convincing," she tells him, "if you had shown, before now, the wit to earn any wealth yourself on your own behalf."

Crestfallen: "Well now. Not all of us can be so fortunate as to marry our way into prosperity."

"I suppose I should be wounded to the quick. And I might be, too, if I were not struggling to keep myself from laughing out loud."

"Meaning what, madame? What do you mean?"

She says, "Oh, Hunnyman, you clown! Here you are, in the midst of our old argument, the sense of which is that, for my own good as well as yours, I should marry you. That I should marry you and make you as prosperous as you are hopeful. To which I have to say: *If wishes were thrushes, beggars would eat birds.*"

"Surely you can remember something better and more apt than that."

"It will do well enough."

"You take me as a beggar, then."

"How else could I take you?" Then: "Have I hurt your feelings? You are too tender. Ask yourself. Have I said that I disapprove of your begging? Who am I to judge you for it?"

He with the old, sly, childish smile: "What could I possibly have that you could beg from me?"

"We shall see."

Propped on elbow, stretched beside her, the smile the same.

"Let me rehearse this. You will not consider marrying me, at least at this time and for the time being."

"Not now. Not ever."

Brushes at her words as he might brush aside a shimmering cloud of gnats or a buzzing horsefly.

"You will not consider the prospect of marriage. Nor will you consider investing in any venture or enterprise I may have in mind, the purpose of which will be to make us both rich enough to be content."

"If you were a king, you would not be content."

"If I were a king, I would not spend precious time arguing with you."

"What would you do?"

"Why, madame, kings command and subjects must obey."

"What would you command?"

"All in due time, madame. We must settle this first."

"Let me be brief and to the point, then, Hunnyman. You are a player and a man of the playhouse. It is surely the vocation you know and understand best. You do well as a player. And, with a little luck, one good turn of Fortune's wheel, I am sure you could do better. I hear from you, and I see for myself, how others, these days, are making themselves fat and rich. Many of these less gifted than I take you to be. None with much more knowledge and experience.

"And I consider these things and think to myself: Here is where Hunnyman can succeed. Not as some kind of projector or adventurer. He means well enough, but would be a shorn lamb among the old wolves, among the merchants and moneylenders of this City. So it would be altogether ungenerous to assist him in that fashion. I think: All of his other schemes and plans—and there are new ones almost daily—are as unlawful as they are improbable. It is not only that I might as well pour money into Fleet Ditch for all that will be gained or accomplished. It is also that I would prefer not having on my conscience (which is busy enough as it is) the hanging of sweet Joseph Hunnyman for felonies I may have somehow encouraged."

"Your fastidious conscience be damned. I have no intention of being hanged. It would give too many folks too much unearned pleasure."

"But, Hunnyman, I have said before and say so now again, that I will do everything I can, everything within my means and power, more if need be, to give you a new beginning in your own profession.

And you cast aside this most generous proposal of mine as if I were a fool, a foolish, featherheaded woman, to make it at all.

"You are free to choose as you please. But I think, in justice, I deserve to know why."

"Very well. Because, woman, it is my considered opinion that the best days for players and playhouses, in England, anyway, are all behind us. And if, as I take the wrinkles on your brow and the purse of your lips to mean, you are doubtful or wonder how I have come to my judgment, I'll be pleased to tell you why."

A nod. And he tells her something about the state of things for players and plays and playhouses in England.

First, allows how the past few years, Plague and all, have been fine years for players, all in all. Never better for the sharers. Even the hired men making decent wages. Poets being adequately paid for their plays. Things look so well that there's no good incentive to take a closer, more skeptical look. And for many fools that is more than enough.

Claims he could probably raise the money to form an acting company in an hour's time in Paul's or outside in the Yard. And claims, too, he would regret it ever after.

Begins with the present state of the companies of players. That there are still a goodly number of strolling players in the country. But there are none of them yet rich or likely to be so. They are as uncertain as a flock of birds what they shall feed on tomorrow, he tells her. And they are none of them so well regarded as the players from London. Who, when they tour, take all the profits for themselves. There will always be a place in the country for some of our trade, though more so for jugglers and rope dancers and musicians and fencing masters than for common players. But there is no money to be earned in any of that nowadays. And if you happen to follow the drift of things, you can safely guess that, little by little, the preachers and citizens and lawyers and the like will sooner or later have their way. Soon our plays and players will be, everywhere except in London, no more than a memory, some old man's story like the great mystery plays of old.

"If it had not been for old Henry in our company," he tells her, "I doubt I would ever have heard a word about such things. Look at the ruins on our land. I've seen them often in my travels. There are huge piles of stone and no man knows who made them or for what use they were intended. It takes no time at all to forget the past."

"Well," she says, "there is always London."

Indeed, he tells her. And in London now, and in all of the suburbs, there are only two companies left performing plays—the Chamberlain's Men and the Lord Admiral's. There are more playhouses than companies, if you choose to count the Curtain and and that old hulk out at Newington Butts. Mr. Langely's Swan is closed now. And if it ever opens for playing again, it will be by default. Because the old Rose is rotting and one of these days will fall down. If it does not burn down first.

Now (he continues) over here, on this side of the river, in Shoreditch there are the old Curtain and the Theatre. Curtain is, properly, no more than a game house. Can do for a play, but not very well. As for the Theatre, well, James Burbage is dead and the lease on the land has expired. And they say the landlord will not renew it for any price. He had other plans for that place. So there goes home for the Chamberlain's Men. They might go over to the Swan, but working for Langley is worse than working for Henslowe. And he will contrive to take most of the profits, if any. And not to forget that with the Rose and the Swan so close to each other, it will clip and cut the profits of both of them. As was proved plainly enough a few short years ago.

Well, you might think there are other possibilities. If you do, tell me. For I can see none at all. The innyards, where everyone played before there were playhouses, are still there and busier than ever. But the City is now firm and strong against plays and players. We will not see players in the innyards of London again.

"Suppose," she ventures, "someone were to put up a new playhouse in some good place?"

"Why on earth would anyone do something like that?"

Before he died James Burbage saw the writing on the wall, Hunnyman continues. Went and bought the old Frater in Blackfriars and spent a fortune to refurbish it and make it the finest playhouse in this country. And one where plays can be performed year round and in any kind of weather. But divers of worship and of honor in that liberty came down against it and protested to Privy Council. No playhouse there and nothing but debts to show for it.

What I can see, and very soon, is only one company left. Perhaps the best of the Chamberlain's and the best of the Lord Admiral's joined and melted together under one head. There will not be places enough for all in either company. So half the players will be cast away to join their fellows, fellows like poor Hunnyman himself, without proper employment—clipping coins or cutting purses, holding horses outside the playhouse or, perish the thought, going back home to where they came from to take whatever labor or employment can be found.

"Or finding a widow who is always willing to listen to a tale of woe."

That there is more.

That if there will be, as it seems there must be, only one company of players remaining, the head of that company is most likely to be Mr. Henslowe. A hard-hearted, tight-fisted, cold-blooded, money-making man if ever there was one.

"He married a rich widow to get his start, did he not?" she says, with a polite, yawning cat's grin.

"Well, yes, I believe he did do that," he admits.

Then continues to tell her that Henslowe, with many irons in the fire and with his money engaged in more various adventures than anyone but himself can know, will be a manager (no patron he) for the players and the playhouse for just as long as it earns a satisfactory profit for him. And not one day more than that.

Which means that he and all those who serve him are bound to be the servants of the tried and true. They will do the old plays, sometimes much revised and disguised, but truly the same old creaking anatomy, over and over and over again. Which is all well and good. Except that the people who come to the plays—you can easily prove this with numbers and receipts and such—take most delight in what is new. Many, perhaps most, of the new plays fail to bring in crowds for long. But those new plays which do succeed will make a good profit, sometimes a small fortune, for everyone involved. Except, perhaps, for the poets who wrote them. And who cares about that?

But, and no denying it, it's more than a little like a game at cards or dice.

And you know the proverb, for it applies to publishers of books as much as or more than to makers of plays and to players: *Tailors and writers must ever mind the fashion.*

Well then.

Burbage is dead. Langley is a brute, an ape disguised as a goldsmith. Henslowe does well and is the best we have. But he hates throwing dice for a living. He would prefer to put new and extravagant costumes on the players for yet another performance of *The Spanish Tragedy* than to play the modest price for even an excellent new play.

Part of Henslowe's luck has nothing to do with new or old, but with his son-in-law and partner, Edward Alleyn. Thinks, and he is not alone thinking it, Alleyn is the greatest player of this age. He could play Mak among the shepherds and keep two or three thousand people perfectly silent or else exploding in laughter. And give the man a good part in a good play and he can make you laugh and cry just for the joy of being there and seeing and hearing him.

But he has heard, from an unimpeachable source, that Alleyn will retire this year or the next. When that happens—who knows?—it may be the end for the Admiral's men.

"Well then," she interrupts.

She has now moved off the high bed to stand and toast herself before the fireplace, standing there in her delicate shift with her clean limbs and the fine curves of her body lightly outlined and shadowed by the flames.

"Well then," she says. "It seems to me simple enough—though I do not, for a moment, profess to know very much about these matters, not nearly as much as you do. But, even in my ignorance, it seems to me you need two things. First some good players. And in your complaint you have made me a good case that there are or will be plenty of players here in London who would rejoice at the occasion to strut on the stage again. And, a player yourself and a good one, you can pick and choose wisely and well."

"Finding the players would be no great task."

"And next there is the matter of new plays."

And there is the bad news, he tells her. There is no one alive writing good new plays.

How can that be?

Well now. Look. Marlowe, best of the lot, is dead and mourned. But so are so many others. Kyd's gone. And Greene, who was dependable, if not inspired. And George Peele and Thomas Watson. Mr. Thomas Nashe, once burned, will write no more plays, if he can choose not to, after what happened to *The Isle of Dogs*. Satire may be all the fashion with poets and publishers, but once it walks the boards of the playhouse, it catches the eye and attention of powerful men. Who are not so easily amused by the exploration of their follies and foibles.

"What about young Benjamin Johnson?"

"Well now. After the performance of *The Isle of Dogs*, he was taken into custody and cooled his heels in prison for months. At least Nashe fled the City. Johnson was locked up in the Marshalsea and had a hard time of it, too, he says. He was even questioned by the famous Topcliffe. And that's enough to discourage any man from practicing his craft."

He goes on to tell her that he has spoken to Ben Johnson about the Marlowe matter. Even though Johnson was not in the City at the time, he is the kind of man who hears things.

Johnson knew nothing more than the common rumors about Marlowe's murder. Or if he knew more, he was not telling. He is trying to write a new play, some new sort of comedy, I gather. But it sounds to me most unlikely to be performed. If he fails with the new play, then I imagine (Hunnyman continues) he will be finished with plays and playhouses. He wanted to be an actor, but has no gift for it. Perhaps he will find a patron. For he is a poet of some promise and interest. And if worse comes to worst, he can go back to his trade of bricklaying. As long as there's building in London and the suburbs, he can find honest work. Not that he wants honest work.

"Are there no others?"

Oh, there are always others. There is a whole mews of them working together—for severality, a knot of poets together, is the fashion now—for Mr. Henslowe and the Admiral's.

And the very best of them have some skill. Anthony Munday may be the best plotter alive. And that's enough to create an afternoon's diversion. And not much more.

"You have not even so much as mentioned Mr. William Shakespeare. You have spoken of him often enough. Why not now?"

Well, perhaps, he says, because he always thinks of Mr. Shakespeare as more of a player, more like himself, than as a poet. Which, he admits, is a strange thing to say, all in all. For truth is no poet has done so much good work in so little time. No one, not even Marlowe, has written so many plays so quickly and so well. Close to a dozen, give or take and counting everything. Plays of all kinds.

"I would go again and again to see *Love's Labors Won*," she says.

And he laughs and tells her that he would, too, if only for the entirely improbable happy ending.

Then continues.

Not greatly original, to be sure, this Shakespeare. Borrowing wherever he needs and cares to. But borrowing wisely and well.

Looking at the record only, you might conclude that he is only just beginning and that there are no limits on his ending. For, you see, with all these others dead and gone, he stands almost alone. Playhouses crying out for plays and only a few left to write them. And he is among the very best.

"Yet I think he has shot his bolt and knows it too," Hunnyman says.

Tells her he has been to see the man—at his new lodgings over in the liberty of the Clink—to talk to him about Marlowe's death. Found that he knows nothing surprising about that business. ("Though," with a light laugh, "he knows as much as I do.") Knew Marlowe somewhat and honored his work with all his heart. Indeed, being a player and a quick study, he has whole speeches and swatches of Marlowe's words by heart.

"And, sir, it would be a wonder to play some of those parts on the stage," he told me. "But I fear I am not the man to do it. Best I could hope for would be Bajazeth in his horrid cage. A footstool for Tamburlaine."

Well, they were having a cup of wine together, Hunnyman and Shakespeare, and it seemed laughable at the time.

He seemed sorrowful to think again of Marlowe's death. But not at all surprised. Saddened by things (his only son, I hear, dead and buried in Stratford last summer), more serious than Hunnyman remembered from a few years ago, and then only a brief loud time in a tavern crowded with poets and players. He was solemn, but not sour or melancholy. Someone, like so many of us, who has seen the light fading on so much of the world. Yet not without a light heart and a good wit.

"And why not?" Hunnyman says. "Five years ago he had a wife and some children living in Stratford (as he does to this day), while he was here in London, not a pot to piss in of his own, trying to find and make his way. And now he is a rich man. Truly. He has just acquired arms, in his father's name, at the College of Heralds. And this very year he has bought himself the second-largest house in Stratford, a mansion called New Place which once belonged, he told me, to a Lord Mayor of London. Place will need money, will burn up money like firewood, he told me. And I have ten fireplaces to keep busy, says he, and do I know what that means?

"And I have to confess I do not. I am duly impressed that he owns a house with ten fireplaces, but . . ."

"But the whole point of it is, Hunnyman, that there is a tax, a hearth tax, on every one of them. Remember to ask about that when you come to purchase your own house."

"I might have taken offense from most of the people I know for saying that to me. For I sensed that he could read my bitterness in spite of my smiling and nodding politely. But I felt something else beyond the irony of one player telling another how well all things have gone and are going for him. He was telling me, plainly, there is a price for these things. For everything. That I should always remember that even as, and I think sincerely, he wished me well."

So, Hunnyman tells her, as he took it to be, the sense of his conversation with Mr. Shakespeare, the talk of a man coming near to the end of something. Has earned his money, and with it the arms of a gentleman. Has bought his mansion house and is surely going home now, to be with his family at last. To walk with his head high in his hometown.

"Perhaps," she says. "He may even believe that himself, though I would tend to doubt it."

"Woman, you are the greatest doubter and skeptic alive. You can doubt what I tell you when I was there and you were not."

"I do not doubt what you tell me. I doubt your good judgment. Someone might take other inferences from exactly what you saw and heard. I take it that the man has acquired some wealth from his playing and his plays. While you have been wringing your hands or drawing up schemes, this fellow, in your very own trade, has made a good thing of it. And now he has spent a goodly portion of it. Wisely, it may be. For a good house in a good place is a good investment. But now he must pay for all that. I take him to be telling you, with his ten fireplaces, that he may have *thought* of retiring to the country. But that now he must work and sweat to make that possible. Later. I take it he hopes and plans to be here for a long time to come. Ten fireplaces' worth, as it were. And beyond that I can tell you something else. He may live simply and favorably here to maintain a life for all his family, and another life for himself, in his home place. But London has infected him. He's long since caught the fever of it the same as you and I have. He will not go home yet, so soon, still young as the world counts age in these days. And if he does, he will not last out a year there, not half a year, before he comes back to London like a runaway dog, barking and wagging his tail and begging to be let in the door."

"Good God in heaven!" Hunnyman tells her, laughing. "I wish I could see the world through your fearless blue eyes."

He stops open-mouthed.

Because she has turned her back to him, bent at the waist, and shucked off her shift. In an instant she folds it and tosses it on the fire. It catches fire, burns and smokes and stinks. And she has turned back to face him, he propped on a pillow on her bed. She, naked as an apple, kneeling down on a Turkey carpet. Letting her hair free. Smiling.

"See the world through your own eyes," she tells him.

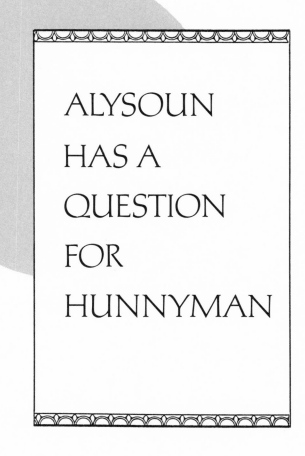

ALYSOUN HAS A QUESTION FOR HUNNYMAN

"Pray tell me something," she says.

"Now? While we are moving to-gether?"

"Some people are perfectly able to do more than one thing at a time."

"You are not among their number."

"Why then, I shall be as still and cold as a statue until you answer me."

"Ask. Ask anything."

"Very well," she says. "Did Christopher Marlowe have any sisters?"

"Yes, he did."

"How many?"

"Five."

"Five sisters? Living?"

"All alive and as well as can be to this day. Living still in Canterbury."

"Brothers?"

"Three. Two died as infants."

"Six women in his life, then, counting his mother."

"Meaning what?"

"Meaning that he could not help knowing something about women, could he?"

"What is there to know?"

"Nothing you could ever learn."

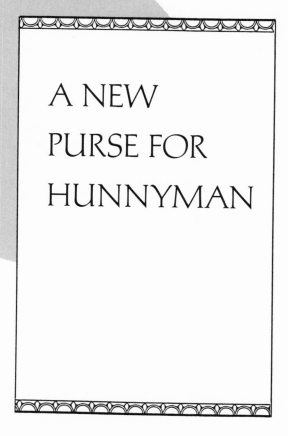

A NEW PURSE FOR HUNNYMAN

T his is the place where they will meet—the Royal Exchange, that huge, elegant building, made in the Flemish style, in the manner of the celebrated Bourse of Antwerp. Four streets of houses between Cornhill and Threadneedle Street were torn down to make way for this structure. Built in '66 by the great mercer and moneyman (the Queen's best moneyman) Sir Thomas Gresham, and declared to be Royal by the Queen, upon her visit to it, January 21, '71, it has a huge square, or piazza, surrounded by a colonnade. And on the floor above that colonnade, brightly lit, are one hundred of the finest shops in all of London. Everywhere there squat, as decoration and as weather vanes, golden grasshoppers, from the crest for Gresham. Largest of all of these is eleven feet long and perches at the top of a pillar as tall as a steeple.

An odd place for the two of them to have a private meeting.

Place he was told (nay, *commanded*) to come to and with other instructions given at the time by the smirking lout of a lad sent around to Alysoun's house—"My master also says that you are to appear there in your best and brightest finery, more in the manner of a gallant than your usual public role of country gent, more peacock than barnyard fowl, says he, allowing that you will understand him well enough." Surprised and troubled him. Might have angered him if he were not, at least in this still-unfinished matter of the dead Marlowe, more fearful now than anything else.

Fearful or no, he raises the question as he and the (still) nameless young gentleman he had met with only once before, and that late at night in a candlelit cellar, as the two of them stroll slowly around the square of the Exchange now filled with merchants and shopkeepers alike, all waiting for the summons of the bell. And so these two, Hunnyman and his elegant companion, moving counter the clock's direction, are walking slowly, arm in arm together amid these sober City people, all with some pressing purpose or other, and a few clearly from the country, here for the Parliament, still in session, and for the Michaelmas Term of the Law Courts, having slipped away from their affairs to visit the celebrated Exchange and, no doubt, to buy some things, needed or simply frivolous, to take home, toys or trinkets or tools, in the candlelit shops of the Pawn above the square.

"Well, it *is* somewhat of a strange place for us," the young man answers. "A gentleman of some kind (it seems) and a common player not presently enjoying employment, at least in the practice of his craft. And both of them the best-dressed men for acres around. At least according to their own tastes and the fashions they have elected to follow. And, sir, I defy any stranger, at least among this crowd here, to tell for sure which of us is truly the gentleman and which is no more than another masterless man in an age of suchlike creatures. Perhaps we could hazard a little money with a wager."

"Well, sir, I shall grant you this much. Neither of us is likely to be mistaken by anyone else to be an honest London merchant."

"Which is what I had in mind when I summoned you here to the late Mr. Gresham's grandiose monument to greed and himself. I want our meeting to be seen. And you can be sure that there is more to it than that."

"Pray continue," Hunnyman says. "I am only an apprentice at this craft of yours."

"And you should hope that you always will be. Never more than, and never more than briefly, an apprentice. Yet, for your own good (and for your good health), you may need to know a little more than you do now. *Item*. We are being watched over, witnessed at this very instant. And by more than Gresham's gilt grasshoppers. First, we are being observed by my own people."

"The bears?"

The young man laughs.

"This time I have spared you from them. To be sure, they would not be happy or do well here among decent folks in broad daylight."

"Decent, well-to-do folks, plump with their prosperity as any tame pigeon. With purses to cut and chains and jewels and such to snatch. With soft throats to cut if need be. But, more to the point, I venture their presence would tend to distract from our own."

"There! Do you see? You are learning a little."

"And if I were to double up my fist or (perish the thought of it) draw a blade against you, why, I doubt very much you would be in real danger."

"Not for long. Not long enough for your sake. But there is more than my safety involved here."

"No doubt."

"Do you care to make a guess?"

"Well now," Hunnyman says, "it might be that, for one reason or another, you need to identify me to some others in your crew, others who ought to be able to know me anywhere at sight."

"You are beginning to think, Hunnyman. Not deeply or very well. But let us always remember that even the longest journey begins with one bold step and must be taken one step at a time."

"So they say. And unless you happen to have the good fortune to ride in a coach or a cart."

"In your case, better be sure your journey is not taken stark naked at a cart's arse or upside down on a hurdle, dragged to some hanging place," the young man says. "But more to the point, my man, consider this. Consider that we now have some reasons to suspect—if not yet fully to credit—that we ourselves are being watched and studied, and have been carefully watched over for some time."

"By whom?"

"By others. Others who may or may not wish us ill. But who, anyway, and whatever they may wish on us, wish to know what it is we are doing and why.

"Now, Hunnyman, in a better and sweeter and simpler world than this one has lately become, we should be able to know such a thing easily enough, by reasoning alone. Should be able to learn who it is who has any good reason to be concerned about our various and sundry doings and undoings. Who may be concerned, for good or ill, about our welfare. But—and I hate to be the one to have to tell you this—this world has of late become sickly and corrupted—so sinful, sin-ridden you might well say if you were (as I am not and never will be, either) of a precisely religious state of mind—that all simplicity is dead and gone, even the ghost of it. What remains is all snarled and knotty. Full of dark puzzlement. A maze without any true entrance or an escape."

"Ah then!" says Hunnyman, abruptly. "You plan for someone, someone as yet unknown to you, someone you believe may be stalking you like a skilled hunter or a wild beast, you plan for the others to see me here, close and companionable with you, and then to begin to stalk me, too. I am to be the bait, the stale cheese, for some kind of snare or trap. Is that what it is?"

"Do not trouble yourself with it. It is beyond your experience and understanding. Let us talk about our affairs. Or, anyway, I shall talk and you will listen. But bear in mind that you and I are being watched. So, player, call on your true experience and understanding, your playhouse craft. Let your face and body and being show nothing more than an amiable, idle conversation between two fine young fellows who, in spite of matters of birth and vocation, might even be friends."

Then smiling and nodding all the while, himself the more polished player, Hunnyman bitterly thinks as he listens, the young man makes his case.

That, speaking on behalf of his masters, he is prepared, first of all, to compliment Hunnyman on a task well done. For though he has not dug deeply into matters, he has certainly discovered nothing new to cause any questioning of the Law's disposal of the matter of Christopher Marlowe. There are many loose points and laces, as there always will be in these things. And there are matters that can and will never be resolved. But—and no good reason to conceal this—his masters wanted to know, without evidencing interest or concern directly (and that for reasons Hunnyman need not trouble himself about, take it on faith), whether there might be any clear indication that the death of Marlowe came to pass more or less in accordance with the Coroner's finding.

"I have never said anything so certain as that," Hunnyman interrupts.

"Please let me finish. Then you can protest to your heart's content."

That his masters have been well pleased with Hunnyman's investigation of these things, indeed well satisfied. And that they would gladly and cheerfully give him due reward for his services and send him on his merry way, to marry his well-to-do young widow or to be done with her, set free from her, as the case may be. With enough money, gratefully given, in his purse, provided he does not waste it all on riotous living and so forth, to enable him, finally, to buy himself a share of one of these companies of players who are lately earning more profits than any high-seas pirate or privateer for themselves. Saying, no, asking, if that ambition—to be a player and a sharer in one of the better companies—were not the true burning coal in Hunnyman's breast.

And Hunnyman responding that he had long since outgrown all kinds of inward burning and desire, but that, yes, the thought of it has crossed his mind.

That, the young man continues, this new thing, however, this knowledge that there are some others who are also tracking the selfsame beast, changes their plans somewhat. And when their plans change, so must Hunnyman's. For now it will be necessary to determine, if it can be done, who these others may be. And what is the purpose of their interest in the matter of Marlowe. And what they may have learned, if anything, above and beyond what we know.

That he is therefore asking Hunnyman to continue in his employment for the time being. To continue to seek out all that he can find, if anything more, concerning Christopher Marlowe's death. And, from this time forward, to be much more open in his inquiry, discarding any strict discretion.

"You are to understand," the young man tells him, "that if you appear to throw all caution to the winds (as they say); if you, who have been, for the most part, moderately careful, should now seem to be not so much careless as utterly indifferent, we think this will trouble and confuse them. And they may tend to be careless, also. Careless enough to reveal more than they want to."

"I am afraid these stratagems are far beyond my understanding."

"Never mind. Believe me, fellow, in these matters it is always better to be ignorant than to know and understand too much."

That, therefore, Hunnyman should continue to concern himself with Marlowe's murder. And should be as openly busy about it as he possibly can be.

That he will, to be sure, need money in purse and purse in hand. That there is nothing that can so soon catch the attention of your true malefactor, be he cutpurse or greedy great lord, so much as a studied profligacy.

Suddenly then handing over to Hunnyman (who takes it like a hot dish) a fat, full purse.

"Go and spend it. As if you were newly rich and likely soon to be richer. Take pleasure in this. Though you should bear in mind, Hunnyman, that if you should try to cheat us in any way, we will know it. And you will soon be much poorer than you are now. And likely be lacking some prominent or favorite parts of your body, if not lacking a living body to inhabit and call home."

Continuing. That he should not permit his lust for the comely widow to allow him to spend too large part of it on her. Something to be sure, if only for the sake of good manners. But not too much. Lest (this with a tight insolent smile) it should all end up jangling in the purse of Dr. Forman of Lambeth Marsh, with whom (*does he know this?*) the widow is close and frequent company. To what purposes can only be imagined, none of them good.

Stung at last, Hunnyman cannot resist the impulse to stop in full stride, turning to face him as he stumbles slightly, looking eye to eye to tell him something more than he has to or ought to.

"Well, sir," Hunnyman tells him, "nothing you have told me thus far is entirely new and surprising. I know that for some time, indeed almost from the moment you chose to employ me in this matter, I have been watched and studied by others."

He tells the young man about the brief scenes with Captain Barfoot, first at the playhouse and then at the bookstall in Paul's Yard. And how in his inquiries he had too often found that Barfoot has also been there already before him, asking the same questions. And how this same fellow has lately come to the widow's house and, in a manner of speaking, threatened her life.

Now this news silences the handsome young man, for a moment at least, as they begin to walk again, walking side by side, though not touching as before, slowly around the square. Young man's smooth brow is now a net of wrinkles beneath the brim of his hat. His lips pout. Hunnyman, studying him with a player's interest at least the equal to his natural envy, would not be surprised if he began then and there to mutter a string of prayers. Or spit out imprecations and comminations.

And then, in an instant, that serious mood, whatever it may have been or meant, passes away like the shadow of a windblown cloud across grass. Color returns, and brightness of the eye. And the young man smiles at Hunnyman.

"Well, Hunnyman," he says, "you've told us some news we need to hear. It is for me to offer payment in kind. To share some news with you which, I think, you also need to hear, though you may not be much pleased with it."

He pauses, just as Hunnyman thinks he would, to wait for Hunnyman to ask, maybe to plead for whatever crumbs he can have. Well now. Hunnyman will not give him that satisfaction.

"Do not be troubled about what may please me or not," Hunnyman says. "Tell me what you want to and I shall be the judge of its value."

"By all means," the young man replies. "You make it easy for me where it might be difficult."

"Please go ahead."

"You should know, Hunnyman, that there is a poet who has been going to and from the house on Knightrider Street."

"There are always poets, all kinds and conditions of poets, coming and going from that place. It is, after all, a printing shop. The widow publishes the work of poets, among other things; though I could wish she did less of that. For there's no good profit there."

"Fellow with red hair and a red beard, and lame in one leg, who goes by the name of Peter or Paul Cartwright . . ."

"By God! I do know that man. Not by that name. But I know him. He has written some things, with others, for Mr. Henslowe. Why, I had all but forgotten the fellow!"

"A man who calls himself Cartwright and is not. Pretends to be a poet and, charitably, is no such thing. Think, Hunnyman, why would such a man seek out your friend, the widow, and enjoy the pleasure of her company? Always, of course, when you are safely elsewhere."

Too troubled for the moment to try to conceal his dismay: "I don't know."

"Nor do we, Hunnyman. Nor do we. But we have a notion and we intend to find out the truth."

"What's your notion?"

"That the fellow is an intelligencer, an agent for someone. That much as your widow seems to promise, and may well deliver, all the pleasures of Eve herself, still and all, nobody's spy can endure if he puts pleasure before his business."

"So?" He knows he looks as if he could cry. Bites his tongue to check any expression of sadness.

"So, Hunnyman. It looks as if he proposes to get to you by means of her. Possibly to enjoy himself in the process, but that pleasure is a gratuity for his trouble."

"What should I do?"

"We think if he is after you, then he will soon be after us, as well. He uses the widow to get to you, you to get to us, myself to get to my master . . . So goes the infected world."

"I ask again. What do you want from me?"

"Try to determine if our suspicions have any foundation. If we are right, then we shall have to stop his mouth, and soon."

"And will you have to stop my mouth, too, sooner or later?"

"I doubt it," he says cheerfully. "You see, Hunnyman, you are almost indispensable. Not quite. Because no man is. But, nevertheless . . ."

His lips move with words Hunnyman cannot hear and will never guess. For just then the bell of the Royal Exchange begins to toll noon.

And the crowd of merchants and shopkeepers and customers is moving all around them in all directions, all at once. The young man's words are lost and gone, taken by the noise of it. And then he is gone, too. Vanished, Hunnyman thinks, like a ghost down the trapdoor at the playhouse. He has managed, never mind his brightness and finery and feathers, to disappear. Might never have been there at all except that Hunnyman is holding tight to the heaviest purse he has ever had in his hands.

It should make Hunnyman happy, for once in his life to have enough money and the license to go and spend it freely. But at this moment he would gladly change places with Gresham's golden grasshopper, safely removed from all the schemes of mankind atop its high pillar, required only to turn and change direction with the wind, as the wind turns.

HUNNYMAN
IS PUZZLED

Close by the window in his own chamber (and small and plain and lightly furnished it is), in a stain of daylight, for he will not light a candle, Hunnyman is counting the money from the purse the young man gave to him. It is not enough. Not nearly so much as the weight and heft of the purse seemed to promise. Many coins, true, but not much gold and silver among them. Not nearly enough to justify all that elaborate game of meeting at the Exchange. In some way he has been deceived. Tricked. Or has played an innocent part in the deception of someone else.

Thinking, with reason, that he might be followed, Hunnyman took a long and roundabout way back to his chamber. Leisurely, wandering, doubling back, all in hope of finding out a guilty face. Could not. Then, all of a sudden, took the other track. Vaulted a fence. Ran down an alleyway. Vaulted another, muddying his shoes and hose. To crouch behind a tree in a garden and see if anyone might come along behind him. No one. Nothing. Except for a child, a boy at a window who made a face at him. What a clown he must have seemed—running as if pursued, jumping and splashing in mud! Hunnyman made an even more ugly face, fluttering his tongue, crossing his eyes for the boy. And then, with whatever dignity he could muster, walked away and out of sight as if he now had all time to be where he chose to be next.

Yet now alone in his chamber he fears to light one candle and to reveal his presence there to anyone who may be watching from the street.

He has no good answer to explain what has happened to him. There is something . . . no, there are too many things he does not know. Does not know enough, yet, to ask himself serious questions above and beyond the most obvious one. Which is (ever and always): *Why is this happening to me?*

And there is not any answer to that, either, except a ringing, pounding headache.

Maybe a strong drink will ease the pain of that. But, as luck will have it, he will have to go out to get that. Not a drop or dram of anything but some weak, sour ale (the thought of which turns his stomach) here in his chamber. And he is not yet prepared to leave and rejoin the world and the wicked human race. Better, for the time being, to be safely here with a pain in his head than outside in confusion, if not imminent danger.

Here, pain or no pain, he can tell himself he does not care, not a ripe fig, what the young man is doing or for whom he is doing it. His own part is small whatever it may be.

But he would prefer to think about that than to consider the meaning of what he has just learned about the Widow Alysoun. The poet is a problem, but his masters are prepared to help. It is thinking about her business (if any) with that odd man Dr. Forman that will pound and cudgel his aching brain to thin soup.

What can she want or need from Forman? What can it be that has sent her over there, across the River, more than one time, to seek out the nasty little fellow in his own neighborhood?

Could she be bewitched? No, he doubts that entirely. If there is any magic or witchery, it is the other way around. She bewitches and rules men with no other spell needed than her beauty, her animal being, the sway of her walking, the posture of her standing, the promise of her eyes, her lips. No, she draws men, any man, to sail after her. Like it or not, his compass needle pointing stiffly in whatever direction she may be. Look. Even here and now on his knees by the window, surrounded by a splash of coins, he can feel a stirring in the dark lair of his groin as the beast awakens and yawns.

No man, not even an old magician like Forman, possesses the power, not while he lives and breathes, to overcome hers.

No. He does not fear that she is under the baleful influence of that old fellow. Whatever she does, good or evil, by impulse or strategy, will be her own free-willed choice. And nothing much, *no, nothing at all,* tell the truth, he, or Forman either, or any other man he has ever known or known of, can do to inhibit her from her own purposes. Sometimes it is possible to *distract* her (if only briefly) from whatever it is she may desire, but then only by contriving to satisfy some other desire. She will do what she will do. Before he knew her, before he surrendered his five senses, unconditionally, he believed not a word about witches and goddesses. Loved women well enough, especially his wife (rest in peace), as creatures like himself, God's own good creatures, though perhaps a little unlucky not to have been born male. Loved women and often enjoyed their company, too. But never imagined he would worship one. Like a god in flesh.

She will do what she will do. And even if he sweats cold to think of it, she will do with old Forman or any other man, young or old, whatever she pleases and chooses. And any man, young or old, will offer his soul for a bargain to do whatever she wishes.

What he is thinking about (and trying busily not to think about), what is troubling him like a fever, is the question of what it can be, great or small, that she desires from Forman. He thinks it may be, simple enough, some kind of medicine. Very well. But what kind of medicine? Not salves and love potions and the like. Something more serious. Something she would prefer not to tell him, Hunnyman, anything about.

Which leads him to ponder on what things he has never yet confessed to her. There is no secret she could not tease and torture out of him, he supposes. But, so far at least, he has not been fully tested.

She believes, or so professes, that having lived as a wife for a few short years with her randy old stationer, whom she probably pushed into an early grave on the strength of his own insatiable hunger for her, she believes she has no fertility, cannot conceive children. She is convinced of this and indifferent to it. Otherwise she would surely be more fearful of the intimacy she allows Hunnyman.

Hunnyman thinks otherwise. Believes the old fellow, who had no offspring by his first wife, either, must have had seed too weak to make a child. Believes this young woman, a perfect being in every other way, can conceive and will one day. Likes to think he will father that child. That one day she will find herself swelling and will have no choice but to marry him.

Which is a happy ending, the only one he can imagine, to his tale of folly and woe. He has managed to convince himself—or, perhaps, she has helped him to arrive at this conclusion, never mind—that nothing will ever go right or well for him entirely on his own. That she alone possesses the capacity, like Dame Fortune herself, to bless him with a change of luck. Like a change in the wind.

She laughs when he talks of marriage. Does she have no shame or fear? A foolish question with a clear and obvious answer. Would swallow her laughter if she found herself swelling with his child.

Or would she?

Perhaps she would, fearless as she is, find some means to rid herself of the child before she swelled enough for anyone, even Hunnyman, who knows the inches of her body better than his own, could notice.

If you were a woman, with a child which you did not want in your womb, to whom would you turn? Oh, there are many, any number of old dames in London (more in Westminster, close by the Court), who, for a large price, will break the laws of God and Nature and man and can produce the potion which will flush a womb of every trace of the child. But the risk is far greater than the price. And he has seen what can happen—death or, perhaps worse, years of aging and ill health happening all at once.

Best and safest would be to go to someone like Forman. Who must have done the thing before. And done it well enough. For it must be a simple mystery for someone with true knowledge of it. And with a little encouragement *(cold sweat at the picture of that)* would be eager for her to live and be healthy. Would take good care of her. If only for the sake of his own insatiable appetite.

Well now.

He allows himself to think that is the most likely reason for her visits to Dr. Forman. And wonders if the young gentleman knows that, too. He seems to know everything else there is to know. Except, of course, why Marlowe was murdered. And maybe he knows that as well.

On hands and knees, among a pile of coins, in the dark now (for the last daylight has faded from the window), on hands and knees like a dog, Hunnyman, his head still hammering with pain, pictures a rush of blood and corruption as his unborn child is squeezed out of her womb. And hears himself, vomiting on the floor of his chamber, feeling, then tasting, the salt of his tears.

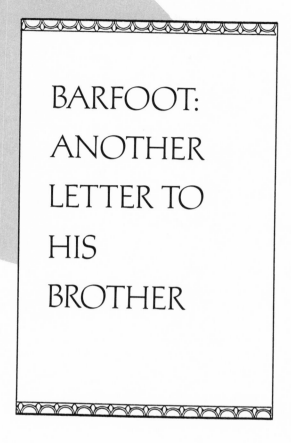

BARFOOT:
ANOTHER
LETTER TO
HIS
BROTHER

I encountered your old and trusted friend
. . . Richard at the Duck and Drake. And he
most kindly agreed to add the enclosed papers, concerning our
business with the London wool merchant and the suit at the Court of
Chancery, to his saddle bags.

. . . Among which I have included these notes and queries.

. . . I am aware that this is a serious imposition upon you. And
believe me, my brother, I would not choose to add to your troubles if
I did not conceive that, weighing all, it is better for you to know
something and somewhat of this matter, at least as much as is
contained herein, as it is to be able to claim ignorance. I mean to say
that your claim to ignorance most likely will not be believed or

honored. It will be assumed that I am your man in the City in all matters and that this matter of Marlowe is no exception.

. . . Moreover, I suspect—though without real cause or good reason—that whoever it is I am truly, if secretly, serving wants it to appear that I am acting as an agent for you. Wants a trail to lead to you. Perhaps.

. . . Strange as it may seem, in the event of any kind or form of investigation or interrogation, it is far better to be in possession of some information than none at all. World has grown older and wilder. No one allows for the possibility of innocence in anything nowadays. Only mad folk and fools are presumed to be innocent. Let one of their preachers make some sense and a public sermon out of that—that, in this sin-ridden, vice-haunted, cynical world, the only image of Adam, the prelapsarian Adam, himself created in the image of God Almighty, is to be found in the person of mad folk and fools. What does that say about the nature of God and of what we have done to His creation? You see why I could never have been priest or preacher. Either one, Papists or Protestants, would have been required, in good conscience, to burn me at the stake.

. . . Enough. Let me assure you that I have every intention now of determining, with certainty, who it is who has hired me to look into the murder of Marlowe. In large part this is because I have now come as far as I can on my own. Will have to know more to learn more. And there may not be much more to learn or to know.

. . . Meantime. Here, in some disorder, I admit—for I am writing this in haste by candlelight to have it in Richard's hands at dawn—are my views and questions concerning Marlowe's murder.

. . . As soon as I learned that Marlowe had acted as an agent for that old spymaster Sir Francis Walsingham a decade ago whilst Marlowe was still a scholar at St. Ben'et's in Cambridge, studying for his degree of master of arts, I was struck with the vague but persistent fear that some of our own Catholic hotheads might be involved in his murder. It would make some sense. For, as I learned without much difficulty, he left his college and his studies to cross over to France. Where, professing himself to be a Papist, he went and spied upon the English seminary at Rheims. His close friend, Watson, seems to have done the same thing. And, indeed, it may be Watson who first brought Marlowe to the attention of old Sir Francis and into his service.

. . . Anyway, Marlowe spent some time among the seminarians, evidently spying on them and sending reports back to England. And the Council, itself, seems to have been pleased by his services. When he passed all tests and disputations and petitioned for his master's degree, it was denied him by his college because he had not fulfilled the residency requirements. (It is somewhat difficult, even for a gifted poet, to be in Cambridge and Rheims at one and the same time.) I think, also, that his masters at St. Ben'et's may have believed that he had truly turned Papist, and so they wished to deny him the privileges of his degree. No matter what their motives—or the justice of their case—Council came down on them with force and alacrity, ordering the college to award him the degree and invoking the Queen's name and pleasure in the matter.

. . . Whatever Kit Marlowe had done for the sake of his country was known and well regarded by Queen and Council in '87. I assumed, from the first, that whatever he did had to involve injury to our people. But I can find no evidence of that, nothing save the surprising interest and intervention of Council in a collegiate matter. Moreover, as best I can determine, both alive and dead he seems not to have earned much ill fame among Catholics. When he was murdered, it was the more precise among the Protestant preachers who publicly rejoiced at his death and the manner of it and who preached against him, over his corpse as it were, as an exemplary sinner and an atheist who was providentially punished for his wicked ways.

. . . I believe it is safe to conclude that Marlowe was not murdered over any matters of religion. I could be wrong, but it surely seems doubtful to me.

. . . It would be a matter of interest, idle interest to be sure, to speculate that he was, in truth, converted to the Faith during the months he was among the faithful at Rheims. That he served them even as he served himself and seemed to be in the service of Walsingham. Who knows? All that can be said for sure about these spies, in this our age of spies, is that we can never know where their loyalty and allegiance may lie. I conclude that even the best among them must be assumed to have played on both sides in everything. Duplicity is the essence, the heart of their craft. I cannot imagine that they are able to believe in the value of anything much beyond the craft that they practice. True belief and perfect loyalty are weaknesses the crafty spy cannot allow himself to cultivate.

. . . Well then. Marlowe was a spy for a time and evidently a good one. Knowing this much has helped me not so much to understand the man as to understand and accept that there is much that neither I nor any other man can or will ever know. If I had him here on the rack, I am sure he would tell me a great deal and that most of it would be untrue. It would mostly be whatever I wanted to hear. Marry the gifts of an expert intelligencer to the gifts of a poet and the offspring will be a great and gifted liar. It may well be that his mocking ghost continues in the same fashion. Will reveal no sure truth to us now or ever.

. . . So be it.

. . . My truth is more simple. Although I have *found out* some things, *uncovered* this and that, I have in truth *discovered* nothing. All that I have found and determined or simply stumbled upon, all is surely known to others. Surely accessible to others.

. . . From what I have seen for myself, I have arrived at some tentative conclusions.

. . . First, judgment of the Coroner's jury and the Queen's pardon of Frizer are, in the Law, final. End of the matter. And must be said that, acting on all the evidence at hand and the sworn testimony of two eyewitnesses (never mind they are also two spies), as well as the testimony of Frizer (another spy, one time and another), this jury of sixteen good men and true could not come to any other conclusion than the one at which they arrived.

. . . We are left with a story which is somewhat implausible, but not at all impossible. A quarrelsome poet quarrels drunkenly over the reckoning for a day of debauchery. Attacks Frizer and is killed by him. More or less by accident.

. . . Even to my simple and not too suspicious mind, there does seem to have to be something more to this affair. But I must warn you that from this point onward I am indulging myself in free and easy speculation.

. . . I note that the three men in the room, including Frizer, suffered no known loss or pain on account of Marlowe's death. Frizer had to obey the Law and, thus, was held in prison for a short time—very short time as these things go—until he was granted his full pardon. The other two went directly about their business (whatever that may be) unimpeded, uninterrupted. And soon so did Frizer. Returned to his occupation as a trusted servant of Thomas Walsingham.

. . . Who is now *Sir* Thomas. For this summer past, the Queen and her Court in Progress went to Scadbury to visit; and there she honored him with more than her presence. Knighted the gentleman.

. . . Not clear for what service or sacrifice he may have received his knighthood. Until now she has been miserly with such honors and rewards. Maybe for some kinds of secret service.

. . . I make no connection between Marlowe's death and any of this. Only that the death of Marlowe, at the hand of his servant Frizer—who was, as he would have to be, visibly present during the visit of the Queen and Court—in no way seems to have tainted Walsingham's honor. Has not in any way served to dishonor Walsingham.

. . . Or Frizer either.

. . . Now consider this. Walsingham was certainly Marlowe's patron—and perhaps something more than that, who knows?—at the time Marlowe was killed. Marlowe was living at Scadbury and was arrested for the Council there. Arrested, but lightly, even gently, treated. Not held, but free to come and go as he pleased. Provided he honored his pledge to make daily appearance. Assumption is that he was not in any serious difficulty in this matter of atheism. Certainly not in the trouble that his friend Kyd was—held in prison and racked to encourage his free speech. Plague was at its worst in London that year, at that time. Playhouses were shut down. Perhaps (no man could know) never to be opened again.

. . . Then upon the thirtieth of May, Frizer kills Marlowe in the quarrel at Eleanor Bull's house in Deptford. We can never know what Walsingham may have said to his man Frizer. Or to the other two.

. . . Well, we know that Walsingham was Marlowe's patron. That he honored him as a poet. That he was, likewise, a friend. Perhaps even a good and close friend. And there's reason to imagine that Sir Thomas was grieved by the poet's death and, indeed, mourns him still. I offer in evidence the fact that a publisher, one Edward Blount, is to publish Marlowe's *Hero and Leander*.

. . . And Sir Thomas is the patron of this publication.

. . . That Ingram Frizer was in no way punished by his master, then or later, leads me to believe that, grieved as he may be and have been, Walsingham was at least not disappointed at the outcome. These three fellows meet with Marlowe in the morning, an hour or so before dinnertime. Spend the day, and part of the night, eating and drinking and talking. Quietly enough until the sudden quarrel at the end of it. At the very least, and in the simplest version of the affair, they know how to arouse Marlowe's temper to the point that will allow him to be killed in an act that can be taken as self-defense. But if that happened and if that were all, then Frizer and the other two might easily escape the rigor of the Law. As indeed they did. But they could hardly have escaped the outrage of Sir Thomas. Who could not easily forgive their behavior. They should have known better than to cause a quarrel with their master's friend and poet and then have killed him.

. . . Unless their master wanted him dead. Or unless the master believed he had no choice.

. . . There was a rumor, and Kyd on the rack confirmed it, that Marlowe was intending to flee from England to the Court of the King of Scots. Who, if I may say so, is reported to be a patron of poets and somewhat inclined to be tolerant of . . . what you, brother, call "the abominable crime of buggery."

. . . I must be brief. I believe that the three men—Frizer, Poley, and Skeres—spent most of that day trying to persuade Marlowe to do something . . . or not to do something. To flee to Scotland or *not* to break his arrest and flee. I can see it either way.

. . . Consider this. Possibility only. That Walsingham was in serious fear that if Marlowe fled to Scotland, the Council would inevitably turn to him, the patron. And that any investigation of himself would then lead to all kinds of other serious troubles. If Marlowe will not be persuaded to remain here in England, then he must die.

. . . But just as strong and firm an argument can be made for the opposite opinion. Marlowe *must* flee to Scotland. Bear in mind that to break the terms of his arrest and to flee to a foreign country is treason under the Law.

. . . So then. Marlowe must be persuaded to commit an act of treason to divert the attention of Council away from Walsingham and his various and sundry shady enterprises and adventures. Which, with a fellow like Frizer at the helm of things, are very likely to be, at the least, unlawful.

. . . Marlowe is not persuaded to flee and therefore must be killed.

. . . The other side of the coin, the argument that Marlowe proposed to flee the country and could not be dissuaded from his plan, seems to me more cogent. Though I have no more evidence than logic to support it.

. . . My thinking is that he, Marlowe, would have most to fear and to lose under strict scrutiny of Council. That he might be a useful Judas goat to be offered up in settlement of all the charges and countercharges concerning atheism in high places. At least he would see it that way, it being his hide and hair. He might also find the loose reins of Council to be suspicious. Were they trying to encourage him into a false sense of safety? Fleeing the country might offer true safety—provided, of course, he was not caught in the act of flight.

. . . Where? I would think that France would be a more likely place than Scotland. For many reasons. But he could not let it be known that he was planning to remove himself to Catholic France, could he? The evidently careless rumor that he planned to go to Scotland might well have been intended to mislead even his friends from his true purpose.

. . . In that case, it could be that they killed Marlowe when, after a long day of it, they got the truth of his destination from him.

. . . Must be allowed that what Marlowe knew, may have known, could be of value to a foreign kingdom. Could as well be an injury to Walsingham and others.

. . . The answer, if any, lies in who may have gained most by Marlowe's death. Frizer came through well enough, unscathed, with only a little loss of time for all his troubles. Walsingham seems to have risen up in the world. Indeed, as far as I can tell, no one has suffered any loss except the playhouses. And it could be argued, *has* been, that Marlowe's death has given his old plays a new life.

. . . There remains the question of who it is (and why) who is concerned enough, after all this time, to have set me, and others that I know of, to look into the murder once more. The answer to that may lead to other answers. We shall see.

. . . Frizer perhaps could tell us a thing or two if we had his feet in fire. But I am not even certain about that. We met and talked. I studied him out as best I could. Came to two conclusions. First, that he's a hard-hearted, vicious fellow who hides both qualities well behind an affable manner. Second, and more important, he is an obedient servant to his master. He will do what he is told to without asking why. It could very well be that he was told to kill Marlowe and did so. And has never known or even cared why.

. . . I have some sympathy for his cultivated ignorance.

. . . Still, if I can do anything to remedy my own ignorance, you will be the first to know.

. . . Be sure to burn this immediately.

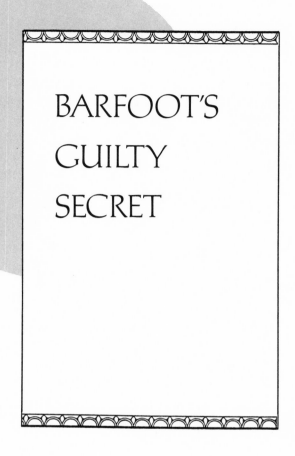

BARFOOT'S GUILTY SECRET

If Holy Scripture is truly believed; if, as
well, all of the best earned wisdom of
the ancients is to be trusted (insofar as it proves to conform to the
established truth), then it is the quest of a man to know himself, which
may well turn out to be the most difficult, the most subtle and
mysterious labor which any of us assigns himself to undertake. A wise
man knows that he must know himself before he can act either wisely
or well. Yet he also knows that he can never come to know himself well
enough. Time and tribulation are his schoolmasters. And sooner or
later he will learn how, even in the most naked and secret of all
confessions, the confession of the soul to itself alone, there is always
(yet) much concealment. Are not those fig leaves fearfully donned by

Adam and Eve the very emblems of the undeniable and irremediable truth of that—how, on account of our corrupt, fallen, and sinful (some insist it is *depraved* also) nature, we can, none of us, never ever be or become wholly and purely and simply naked and truthful again? Not to each other. Not to ourselves.

Do I sound too much like one of these public preachers? If so, please forgive me for it. He who preaches is a kind of spy, God's spy, and a kind of player also. His deepest and most hidden hope must be somehow or other to speak more wisely than he knows.

Well, we may not come to that. Now or ever.

None of us are preachers or prophets here.

All of us—Hunnyman, that sometime player and conny catcher; Barfoot, sometime soldier and sometimes a spy; Alysoun, widow and stationer and woman touched with the magic of beauty and the mystery of a restless soul; even myself, a common scribbler and hired pamphleteer who once upon a time in his lost youth so much aspired (O sadly foolish!) to become an uncommon and honored poet; for that matter, even the murdered man, Marlowe, whose plays are charged with more explosive ambition and aspiration than I allowed myself to imagine, than I could ever admit to myself, and yet who was himself, it truly seems, not much outwardly and visibly moved by either appetite; whose true hungers were and are (to me, anyway) a mystery, darkly enigmatic, deeply dangerous, violent, perhaps cruel; yet withal a man who was, for certain, if nothing else is, a gifted and uncommon and honored poet—we are all of us craftsmen, artisans, crafty men of the world, this old world, knowing ourselves well enough to name and enumerate most of our strengths and weaknesses, although, with the possible exception of the much wounded Barfoot, we have managed to preserve in ourselves something of the child's absurd faith that these selfsame things and, indeed, we ourselves, our bodies and souls, may yet be changed and changed for the better, if only we can some way discover or recover the spell, remember the magic words, the perfect ritual gesture; knowing, then, the world and the flesh well enough not to believe in or trust any others very much or very seriously, knowing the ways of the world and the flesh and ourselves at least well enough to doubt the powers of our own good judgment more often than not.

Skeptics, then.

We have followed too much the devices and desires of our own hearts.

We are skeptics. And we only half believe whatever we see and hear.

Now then.

As for the Devil.

We do not know him, but we do not doubt, either, that he is here and there and everywhere, always as next and near as a shadow. His language of whispers is forever rich with promises and the solace of false comfort.

Marlowe may at times have seen him face to face. Most likely did so. Most likely listened to him, too. Otherwise (I ask you!) how could he ever have achieved the undeniable glory and shining of his words?

Ah. God knows that for half a share, even less, of that glory I would gladly have knelt down and listened to the soft voice of the serpent. And would have done so at the risk and hazard of my immortal soul, my chance for everlasting life. That is how weak I became. Weak from hunger for even some measure of honor, some kind of fame.

Well . . . May be that God spared me from myself and my own ravenous hungers. Or more likely it seems, I was no more challenge to the wiles of the Devil than some dim-witted country woman who is all too easily seduced. Marlowe sold his soul more dearly. More dearly by far than his celebrated Doctor Faustus. God forgive me, but I swear to you that I would gladly have changed lives and places with him, Marlowe, I mean, even knowing *in advance* that Ingram Frizer would thrust his knife blade hilt-deep into my brain, in payment for having enjoyed a modest portion of Marlowe's gifts and good fortune and reputation.

Well then.

You can see for yourself at once how the alloy made from both my weakness and my ambition could render me a somewhat less than reliable and trustworthy witness. To which I could assert, if that kind of arrogance were my style, that in an age of false witnesses (yours as well as mine) who is to notice the difference or care if they do so?

Never mind. Barfoot, not I or anyone else, is the true subject here. Something he has withheld from us. Something he would like to withhold from himself.

This man of so many scars.

Man who, in his tavern talk, has sometimes not been too proud or too shy to answer even the most difficult questions.

"Tell me something, Captain Barfoot, an' it please you to."

"I will if I can."

"How did it truly feel? I mean, sir, when you truly believed that the Plague had killed you and you were thrown into that cart and looked to be as dead and gone as any cold corpse there?"

"How did I feel when I thought I was dying and would very soon be dead?"

"Exactly."

"Well, sir, I'll tell you I felt as if my skin had first been flayed—the pain of my skin was terrible!—and then it had been pulled and stretched to make the skin of a drum. And then that drum had been given over to a lunatic who was being allowed, indeed, *encouraged,* to pound upon it without ceasing or mercy."

"God save us from that fate!"

"Amen to that, my friend. All I can report to you with any certainty is this: that, by and large, living seems to be better than dying of the Plague. Try your best not to catch the Plague when it comes round again. And if you happen to be taken ill, try not to die of it."

Earned wounds may well be the one true source of worldly wisdom. But consider that the wounds you have inflicted on others, by chance or on purpose, can teach useful lessons, too. They can even bring joy, sometimes an unspeakable, ecstatic joy, not only at the time, but also in the halls and galleries of memory forever after. Is not the hope of just revenge perhaps one of the strongest appetites we experience? How else explain (Barfoot wonders) the almost universal appeal of Kyd's *Ieronimo* or Mr. Shakespeare's *Titus Andronicus*? And behind both of them the gigantic shadow of Marlowe's *Tamburlaine*?

But there are other inflicted wounds which, if summoned up for recall, bring with them a crippling sense of shame and a bitter self-contempt. Barfoot is not free from this kind of haunting. In and around the edges of the wars he has been witness to more than one man's share of blood and cruelty. And he has added his own contribution to the sum of the world's woe.

And there are some things he has seen and done, more than

commonplace crimes of wartime, that he would like to bury forever in forgetfulness, that he has told no one except once upon a time a priest at confession. Who was so startled and astonished by the account of it that he had nothing to offer Barfoot but pity.

How, in the prime of hot-blooded youth he and his companions, and once or twice later all alone, more than one time sought and found a grunting, teeth-grinding, joyous, joyless satisfaction of themselves upon the helpless terrified bodies of women. A few shuddering moments, wordless in any known language, except the brute language of barnyards, taken in a shadowy hovel, against a tree, or in the muck and wet or dry dust of a ditch. Cannot now remember any one face. Only tangled hair, stink of fear, his, hers, theirs, mingle of sweat and tears, choking sounds. Which will be swallowed to the rhythm of fists. Which will likely be finally silenced by the keen edge of a bloody knife.

In the beginning, in his youth, his shame made him desperately cruel. Made him also strangely eager to increase his weight of guilt and at ever greater risk to himself. But now, most of that rage and cruelty spent and beyond recovery, he is kind to strangers and gentle to the weak and helpless. Not for the sake of conscience or out of an attempt to ease the knotty cramps of his self-contempt. But because, as he views it, it is a final kind of ironic jig and jest, a laughable thought, that a monster, himself in truth as well as appearance, can be so misapprehended by his own kind. Their folly may be the beginning of his wisdom.

So be it. And so it will always be for him in this all-hating world.

DR. FORMAN, THE DREAM DOCTOR, PROPOSES A CURE FOR THE WIDOW

Whoever this dream ghost may have been, this much is sure. He was a woman, had the soul of a woman, trapped in the body of a man. Came to a violent ending, perhaps because of that selfsame contradiction of body and soul.

Was taken by surprise and with no preparation for death. Perhaps—it is often the case with a spirit seeking a home in a new body—in the act of a grave sin of the flesh. I would guess he was engaged in lewd practices at the very instant of his death.

It is not given to us, the living, to know why a soul has been given the liberty to remain for a time in our sphere and to seek out and inhabit another body. Some wise men believe that, in the case of this kind of murder, where the victim was killed while in the act of commission of sin, the victim's guilty soul, and especially if that soul is not otherwise burdened with a weight and multitude of other sins, if, then, there was some hope for the salvation of the soul had it not been untimely snatched away from life and the body, unrepentant and unabsolved, the soul is given another chance. Provided that soul can find a new living body to act as its host. And provided that the body, together with its own soul, proves to be a worthy host.

For you see, my dear, that by entering into another body the vagrant soul must assume all the guilt acquired by that other body and soul.

These things are complex and mysterious. And it will make your head ache to try to think about them.

Permit me to do that for you. To help you as best I can.

Clearly enough, some angry and lost soul, sinful but full of a great promise that was suddenly cut off, has been trying by means of dreams to enter and possess your body. Perhaps—who can say for sure?— because he judges your soul to be more or less blameless. And perhaps because he wisely judges your beautiful body to be a good home. A man who had always wanted to be a woman would want to live in the finest body he could find.

So far, by virtue and strength alone, you have been able to deny the fellow what he wants. But sooner or later a ghost can overpower almost any living being.

You must drive him away if you want to save yourself.

Here I do believe I can help you. There are some ways to drive a predatory ghost out of your dreams and your life.

I can show you how. If you will permit me to. If you will simply trust me . . .

ALYSOUN'S WONDERFUL SECRET

A nd so it was no surprise when Barfoot came back to her. Not at all surprising that he would come to the house on Knightrider Street to return her glove (carefully dropped at the Tiltyard on Accession Day) and to lay claim to whatever else he wished to. In a true sense she had planned for it all to happen. Had imagined it happening even before, swept by an impulse when she saw him there at the Tiltyard, she met his eyes directly for a moment only, saying or, anyway, hoping that her eyes said at least something of what she felt even as the calm painted mask of her face said nothing at all but itself. What she imagined, half dreamed, was brisk and brutal and somehow eminently satisfactory. Yet it took place, as she imagined it, entirely in darkness.

And so Alysoun was taken somewhat unprepared when, in the middle of a busy morning, Mary came into the printing shop to tell her that a man, the ugly one who had been here once before, the scarred soldier who wore women's perfume, had asked to see her about some private matter.

She went directly to him where he was warming himself by a fireplace. He stared at her, silent, hard-faced, expressionless, as she greeted him calmly and dismissed Mary.

"How may I serve you?" she asked.

"I have something you lost at the Tiltyard."

He produced the glove and moved toward her, so suddenly that she cringed a little as if she expected and perhaps deserved to receive a punishing blow.

Tapped her cheek lightly with the loose fingers of the glove as he stepped so close to her that she was abruptly bathed in the sweetness of his perfume, even as she could see now that his face had many more little scars on it than she had noticed before.

"I was born ugly," he said in a whisper. "The scars are no real damage. Some say they are an improvement."

She took the glove from his hand. At that moment she could have kissed him full on the mouth but chose not to.

"Well then," she said, moving herself, toward the fire, leaving him standing where he was. "I have something to return to you also."

She tossed the glove into the fire. Watched it begin to smoke. Then turned, lifted her head, shaking her bright hair, and walked out of the room, speaking over her shoulder.

"Follow me," she said, "and I'll return your seditious pamphlet."

He trailed behind her up the flights of stairs to her bedchamber. When they entered, she turned back, pulled the large door to, and shut and bolted it behind them. She went directly to a chest, unlocked it, opened it, and knelt, rummaging among books and papers. He came up behind her, looking down, over her shoulder. She stopped playing with the books and papers. He gave her a short, sharp painful kick with his pointed boot.

"Stand up."

She rose slowly—her knees weak. Turned slowly around to look at him. He had a fierce fixed smile.

She tried to speak but her mouth was too dry and her tongue was too heavy. She shook her head back and forth and tried to smile herself.

His expression did not change—the smile as if painted in place, eyes unblinking. But the meaning of it changed and drenched her body with a sweat as his arm moved and then next his right hand held the thick, shining, razor-keen knife. Sunlight from the window glinted off the polished edges and the point of the blade.

She could not have cried out for help if she had wanted to. She was breathless.

Locked his left arm roughly around her neck and pulled her to him. Kissing her fully on her mouth and with his lips opening hers to admit his tongue. She closed her eyes then, as he held and kissed her, face mashed to face, so that she could savor the odor of his perfume and the surprising meaty sweetness of his mouth.

Even as she did this, as they kissed and he held her head tightly, she could feel the knife at work, as he first, and more swiftly than she imagined it could be done, with a sweep cut away the long row of buttons of her dress, the buttons all at once cut loose and free and falling, like a broken string of beads or pearls, to roll on and across the floor. Then, still holding her, still kissing her, as she snorted for breath, he cut her clothing to ribbons. She could hear the sound of the cutting of cloth and feel the chill air of the fireless room playing upon patches of bare skin, but could feel no pain. He was not cutting her. And the groan she heard from herself as he placed the blade flat and cold between her bare breasts, the point beneath her chin, was as much made up of pleasure as of fear.

As if her groan had been a command or, better, a humble request, he twisted her around, facing away from him. Somehow slammed the chest closed and forced her over it, face to the floor in a tangle of her hair. And took her from behind. Like a dog, with short hard strokes. Now speaking to her. Talking quickly in that hoarse whisper of his. Speaking in a language she did not know, had never heard before.

Irish.

He must be speaking to me in the Irish tongue.

Bitter that she did not know the language. Because, above all things, she wanted to hear and remember these words (curses or blessings, no matter) for as long as she lived. Tears in her eyes because now she would never know what her devilish lover said to her while he took her, dog and bitch, to the edge, and over the edge, falling like a feather in air, of something more than the most ecstatic shuddering she had yet experienced or imagined.

Then he shuddered, too. Ceased and let go. She lay limp there on the chest, sweat-soaked, her hair a gold tangle over her face, seeing nothing but her own hair, smelling the sweetness of her hair, and even then, as she was almost certain the next thing she was to feel would be the edge of his knife as he cut her throat (knowing that he wanted to kill her then and there, but sensing and hoping that he might not do so, but herself, for that moment, indifferent to his choice, *let him please himself as he will),* smelling the sweetness of her own hair and hoping that she had been sweet enough for him, perfect for him, as he, like a brutal god, had taken her as he pleased and in extravagant return had lifted her to such a pitch of joy as to seem to be beyond the laws of flesh and bones.

His sobbing broke her thoughts. And she rose, stood, turned, faced him.

As he wiped his face with his sleeve and sheathed his knife, she stepped close to him, easy now, proud even, and she kissed him. Then he turned to leave her.

He unbolted the door. Leaned against it a moment, his face pressed against the door. Turned back again.

"There is no pamphlet, is there?" he said. "And there never was."

She laughed aloud and shook her head to answer no, no, no, as she listened to the sound of his heavy boots running downstairs.

And it was at that moment that she felt, no, she knew for sure he had given her a child to carry and to bear. Later a fortuneteller would confirm the truth of this for her. And later still a midwife. But for now she was as fully certain as if this child had already formed and was moving, kicking her belly. She felt proud and strong, content.

"There now," she said out loud, looking at her room, speaking to empty air. "It was what you wanted, wasn't it? It was what you were waiting for. It was why you were troubling me and my dreams.

"Was it," she continued, "what you hoped and expected? Pain of thrust and then the dance and swoon of it?

"Never mind. Like it or not, I will bear his child. Like it or not, it will be, strangely, but then the world is so much stranger than any of us knows, your child, too. Without you it would not have happened.

"What do you say about that? Speak now. Say something! Nothing? So be it. Rest in peace . . ."

It was not a sadness she felt, only an absence. She knew for sure that Marlowe's ghost was gone for good.

She lifted her looking glass and looked into her own eyes and smiled at herself and her wonderful secret.

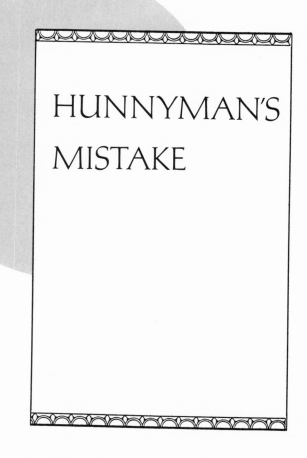

HUNNYMAN'S
MISTAKE

Coming along Knightrider Street, Hunnyman sees Captain Barfoot, looking somewhat distracted and disheveled, leaving the Widow Alysoun's house. Ducks quickly aside. Hides himself among others; skulks until Barfoot has passed and is gone. Stares at Barfoot's broad back until it disappears round a corner.

Surmises something terrible has happened or is about to.

And here, at this moment, even before he continues on his way to her house, Hunnyman makes a free choice that will change his life. Not that he intends to make any such significant choice. But ignorance and innocence have spared no one since Adam and Eve from the unexpected consequences of even sometimes idle and thoughtless choices.

His choice is this. That he will not mention seeing Barfoot to Alysoun. Will not say to her that he saw the fellow leaving her door and looking as guilty and unkempt as any country oaf who has just tupped a milkmaid in the far dark corner of the barn. And who had Barfoot played the two-backed beast with only moments before? Not Mary, that's for sure.

What Hunnyman does, thinking that he is being clever, is decide not to mention Barfoot at all. Let's see if she will find a way to confess and explain it, he thinks. Let it be a test of her character and trustworthiness.

Besides which, he had best be careful. If Barfoot, too, has fallen under her spell (and why not?), then does that not give him, Hunnyman, a certain kind of advantage over Barfoot? Witting or unwitting, as it suits him, Hunnyman, Alysoun can now become his private spy. Can find out anything and everything concerning Barfoot.

If he is prudent and patient, does not fall into a rage with her, does not give way to anger and shame—it's like being cuckolded! awarded horns by the ugliest man in England!—he will maintain his advantage over her. He is not a player for nothing. Can swallow his anger whole. Would swallow a toad with a smile if he had to.

So. Shock is replaced by shrewd planning. What he will do is not mention or refer to Barfoot. Which, since he will enter the house brief moments after Barfoot left, she will be anticipating. Instead he will astonish her by falling into a great rage about the red-bearded, stiff-legged poet. Fellow who is calling himself Cartwright. Forcing her either to deny everything or else to confess and ask forgiveness. And either way, equally, will leave him with an edge of advantage over her.

All of which might have been true yesterday and may be true tomorrow or the day after. Who knows?

But for today it is an utterly fallacious strategy.

What Hunnyman does not, cannot, know is that what is on Alysoun's mind, or what *will be* on her mind in a minute or two, when he enters her house and confronts her, is finding a father for Barfoot's child. She must marry again. Sooner the better.

What Hunnyman will not know, because he cannot, is that it is he who is being tested. That in a few minutes he could satisfy his most improbable hopes and aspirations. Live happily ever after as in the fairy tale he wishes were his life's history.

But Hunnyman is Hunnyman. As we all know.

He will berate her about the red-bearded poet.

And she, more cool and calculating than he can be or imagine, will decide on the spot that such a fool as this will never be her husband.

(Unless, of course, she can find nobody else in the short time she has.)

Leave Hunnyman smiling, pleased with himself, as he approaches her house. It will not be necessary for us to enter at his elbow and suffer through the painful scene that follows.

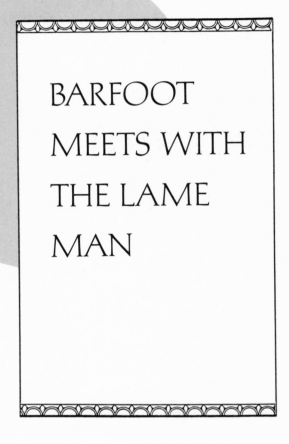

BARFOOT MEETS WITH THE LAME MAN

Cold and rainy day. They met first in the muddied, crowded nave of Paul's Church (where else), then moved to the warmth and light of a nearby tavern.

The red-bearded lame man came all alone, as far as Barfoot could determine. And the fellow seemed anxious, looking all around, over one shoulder and then the other. Furtively, as if he did not want Barfoot to notice his anxiety.

Well, Barfoot thought, maybe his greyhound, or whoever was supposed to accompany him and to keep watch over him, had failed to keep the appointment.

"From all that I have learned and now know," Barfoot told him, over strong mulled cider, "your interest in this matter is well founded. There is something more to it than I had guessed or even imagined. It goes somewhat deeper than you might think, deeper than I thought it would. But there are still many questions. If you want answers, then I shall need some means to dig deeper. And there is no promise that there are any satisfactory answers to be found."

"I see," the fellow said, still distracted, looking about the room as if for someone or something. "You are asking for more money. For this and for that."

"Not now. Now yet," Barfoot said quietly, his hands folded together on the table, trying to catch and hold the lame man's gaze. "Though, if I proceed, it will come to that soon enough."

"There may be some difficulty."

"Spare me your difficulties," Barfoot said curtly, suddenly taking the man's hand in his own, then staring into his eyes, looking for whatever might be registered and revealed there. "I did not call for this meeting to ask you for more money. When the time comes, you'll find I am not too timorous or shy to ask for money or anything else."

A tight little smile could have been intended to divert Barfoot from the eyes. Which were, if not fearful, then at least troubled, uneasy, doubtful.

"Then why, sir—besides good cider and pleasant company—are we meeting here?"

"Understand me. I intend to continue with this business. Because I agreed to do so. Agreed, anyway, that I would look into and consider the matter seriously. And also because, to tell the truth, the whole affair has begun to be of some interest to me. But before I continue, before I go much deeper, it is going to be necessary for me to talk directly to your masters."

"Ah"—the eyes widening now, even as Barfoot let go of his grip on the man's hand—"that is not possible."

Barfoot said nothing in reply.

Showed nothing, either, with his face, in his eyes. Sipped his cider and looked at the lame man.

"You can understand, I am sure, that if my masters had wished to be known, had wished to know you, if they had wanted to talk with you, Captain Barfoot, they would not have sent me to act in their behalf. I am sorry to disappoint you, but there is not a chance that you will see and talk to anyone else, concerning this matter, except for me."

"Too bad," Barfoot said. "A pity if that is true."

He signaled the tapster for more cider.

"It is all very simple," he continued. "All you have to do is do your duty. Go tell your people what I have said. You may also tell them that I am absolute. That you and I have, for the time being, finished our business. And that I have finished altogether with the business unless and until I can talk with them."

Cartwright (does he still call himself that? Who cares?) cleared his throat. Eyes lightly glazed now. Trying his best to suppress his new confusion and continuing anxiety.

"Very well," he said. "I will report what you told me. Because, as you say, I have to do so. But I do wish you would reconsider. Not for my sake, but your own. I mean to say, frankly as I can, these things are dangerous. Or can be."

"I am grateful to you for your candor. But I have made up my mind. I will talk with your masters or not at all."

"I wish I could persuade you otherwise."

"Believe me, I should prefer it otherwise, myself. But it is a matter of need, man, not idle curiosity. I have reached the point where I need to know what they know already and what they might want to know before we go any deeper or farther. That is as much as I can tell you. Except this. You may add, if you choose to, that I have uncovered some well-hidden things, small but not wholly insignificant, things that I feel sure your masters, whoever they may be, do not know and would like to know."

"Barfoot, you may be putting your life in hazard."

"I doubt it."

They stared a moment into each other's eyes until the lame man looked away. It is a trick of Barfoot's. You cannot look at his eyes alone, but only in their habitation, in his scarred, ugly face. Which, even if it is not always frightening, is always unpleasant.

"Let us have some dinner and not trouble ourselves more about this."

The lame man made a face and belched cider.

"You have spoiled my appetite."

Barfoot laughed.

"Nothing, sir, not even the prospect of hanging on the rack, should be allowed to spoil a man's appetite for dinner.

"Come"—rising from table now, tossing a coin to the tapster—"I know a place, an excellent place where the food is so well cooked you will forget your rebellious stomach and all your other troubles, too."

The lame man hesitated for a moment.

"Barfoot," he said softly, "I believe I have been followed. All morning."

"By whom."

A tip of his head and a lowering of his voice to a whisper.

"Those two. Close by the door."

Barfoot quite deliberately dropped a couple of coins. Knelt to retrieve them and, kneeling, half-hidden by the lame man, looked and saw the two very large, wild-haired, wild-bearded, rough and raggedy men, more like a couple of beasts than men.

"Well," he said, standing up, "if that pair were on your trail you would know it soon enough. You would smell them coming behind you long before you saw them. Come, let's see if they try to follow us to dinner. I know just the place. Place where they can be served chunks of raw meat."

Barfoot laughed at his own jest and steered the lame man by the elbow past the two. (Who had everyone near them as anxious as hens when a hawk flies over the barnyard.) Gave them a hard glance, eye to eye, and saw not enough light, between the two of them together, to give a dog an intelligent look.

"A pair of fierce fellows," he said out loud, once they were walking in the street. "Try not to let them catch you in the dark."

Barfoot was laughing. Probably because the lame man could not keep himself from looking back over his shoulder.

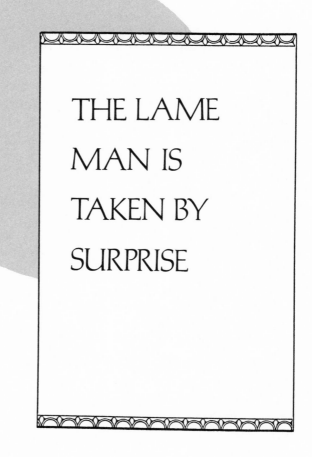

THE LAME MAN IS TAKEN BY SURPRISE

I t might have gone differently for me, I
suppose, if I had been more careful. If I
had not gone over to Lambeth Marsh alone. But it was broad daylight
and a fine day, too. And, to the best of my knowledge and judgment,
I had not been followed by the two ugly giants or by anyone else.

What was there to fear?

I went in search of Captain Barfoot, hoping to see him, face to face,
to deliver a message. Namely, that my employers, my masters, were
now prepared to meet with him and to discuss the matter of Marlowe.
Which matter, as I took it from my own people (who never troubled
to tell me much), was drawing to a close.

If I could not find Barfoot, then, as he had told me to, I could leave any message with one or both of his Dutch whores. Who were, he insisted, entirely reliable and trustworthy. If only because they knew nothing, and cared even less than that, about his business.

"They are wonderful women," he had told me. "They are scrupulously indifferent to everything except what directly and only concerns them. If they weren't whores, they would make some fellows a pair of perfect wives."

I went to the tavern he had told me of—at the sign of the Anchor. Pleasured myself with a quart of double-brewed beer and engaged the tapster in idle, usual talk until I judged him as easy and open to me as he ever would be.

"Do you happen to know a Captain William Barfoot?" I asked.

"Indeed I do."

"Do you happen to know where I might find the man?"

"I do not, sir. He doesn't live around here. He lives across the River, I hear, though where I do not know."

"He told me to look for him here at the Anchor."

Tapster laughed.

"Well, sir," he said, "if you stand where you are standing or else take a seat and relax, chances are Captain Barfoot will be along sooner or later. Might take a day or two, mind you, or a little longer. But I can safely wager he will be here once or twice a week at the very least. Unless, of course, he's left London behind him or fallen into some kind of trouble."

"The captain also told me that he had some friends I could talk to if I couldn't find him here, a couple of Dutchwomen . . ."

"The whores," said the tapster. "They live nearby."

"May I ask where?"

"Why, certainly you can. It's not a secret. You can ask and I may answer."

This fellow is calling for a coin, I thought to myself. And so I gave him one.

"Tall, old house at the end of the street, just at the edge of the Marsh," he said. "Dutch whores live on the uppermost floor."

"Thank you kindly," I said, finishing the last drops of the beer.

He nodded and I started toward the door.

"I could tell you something else," he said.

"Oh, you could, could you?" Not yet turning back to look at him.

"Something which might be important to you, for all that I know. Then again, it might mean nothing at all. That will be for you to judge."

And now I had come back to him and presented him with a second coin, for better or for worse.

"It may be of interest to you," he said, "that you are not all alone today."

"How is that? What's your meaning?"

"I mean that there was someone here before you—and not so long ago—asking for Captain Barfoot and then asking directions to find the Dutch whores."

"Well then," I said, "this has been a profitable day for you."

"Might have been," he said, "if they had elected to reward me for being so forthcoming. But they didn't offer me anything at all. And I can promise you it never occurred to me to ask."

"They. You said *they*. How many were there? And who are they?"

"Only two of them, sir, though they might as well have been half a dozen cutthroats or more. Couple of truly fearsome-looking fellows, as large and hairy as black bears. And as for who they are or may be, if they have names as other people do, I do not have any notion at all. Maybe you do, sir."

"I think I know who they are," I said. "And I thank you for telling me."

Outside, I followed the muddy lane, set between tall and somewhat delapidated houses, packed close to each other, cheek by jowl, to the tallest of these tenements, the one at the end of the street.

Oddly, not a sign of anyone alive. The whole lane and its houses seemed to be abandoned. No children playing, no people going about any kind of business, honest or dishonest, no dogs barking. Nothing moving that I could see except for a few gulls circling overhead looking for food. One of them cried out suddenly like a hurt child. And I nearly jumped over and out of my shadow.

Those two were somewhat near around, though I could see not so much as a sign of them anywhere. I was not sure what I should be looking for.

I walked down the lane toward the tall house, hand on the hilt of my knife and knife already eased an inch or so out of the sheath. Ready to strike and kill at sight if need be. Because I cannot run away.

Saw nothing. Heard nothing at all. In a moment, however, I smelled something, a foul animal stink like a little invisible cloud behind me.

Whirled, then, drawing my knife. But saw nothing except for blackness and fireworks, painful catherine wheels of light as I was struck a hard blunt blow on the head. Felt all my breath go out of me in a rush and my legs turn to loose rope and then my face in the mud. And then a sense of being dragged along the lane.

And that, my friends, is the last that you will see of me in this story. Now unconscious, half-dead from a savage blow to my skull and soon to be even closer to death's door—if that is possible. Spilling my blood in the marshy weeds.

That is the last you will see me. But not the last you will hear of me. Certainly not the last you will hear my voice. Which continues speaking in my absence like the immutable voice of a ghost in the playhouse after the ghost has disappeared.

What madness is it to tell night's pranks by day,
And hidden secrets openly to bewray?
—Marlowe, "Ovid's Elegies"

And I will make thee beds of roses,
And a thousand fragrant posies,
A cap of flowers, and a kyrtle,
Embroidered all with leaves of myrtle.
—Marlowe, "The Passionate Shepherd to His Love"

I'll make me bracelets of his golden hair;
His glistening eyes shall be my looking glass,
His lips an altar where I'll offer up
As many kisses as the sea hath sands.
—Marlowe, *Dido, Queen of Carthage*

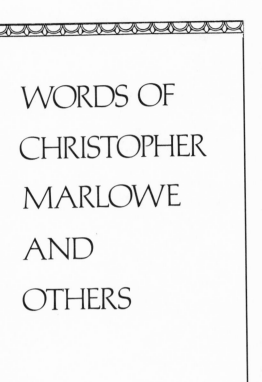

WORDS OF
CHRISTOPHER
MARLOWE
AND
OTHERS

The flowers do fade and wanton fields
To wayward winter reckoning yields;
A honey tongue, a heart of gall
Is fancy's spring, but sorrow's fall.
—Sir Walter Ralegh, "The Nymph's Reply"

I could not make my verses jet upon the stage in tragical buskins, every word filling the mouth like a fa-burden of Bow-bells, daring God out of heaven with that atheist Tamburlaine.
—Robert Greene, Preface to Perymedes

We'll lead you to the
stately tent of war,
Where you shall hear the
Scythian Tamburlaine
Threatening the world
with high astounding
terms,
And scourging kingdoms
with his conquering
sword.
View but his picture in
this tragic glass,
And then applaud his
fortune as you please.
—Marlowe, Prologue to
*Tamburlaine the
Great, Part the First*

. . . But the party, perceiving his villainy,
prevented him with catching his hand and
turning his own dagger into his brains. And so
blaspheming and cursing, he yielded up his
stinking breath. Mark this, ye players, that live
by making fools laugh at sin and wickedness.
—*Edmund Rudierde,* The Thunderbolt of
God's
Wrath Against Hard-Hearted and Stiff-
Necked Sinners

As the poet Lycophron was shot to
death by a certain rival of his: so Christopher Marlowe was stabbed to death
by a bawdy serving man, a rival of his in
his lewd love.
—*Francis Meres,* Palladis Tamia

*Whereas it was reported that Christopher Mar-
lowe was determined to have gone beyond the
seas to Rheims and there to remain, their
Lordships thought good to certify that he had no
such intent, but that in all his actions he had
behaved himself orderly and discreetly whereby
he had done her Majesty good service and
deserved to be rewarded for his faithful dealing:
Their Lordships request that the rumor thereof
should be allayed by all possible means, and
that he should be furthered in the degree he was
to take this next Commencement: Because it was
not her Majesty's pleasure that anyone employed as he had been in matters touching the
benefit of his country should be defamed by
those that are ignorant in the affairs he went
about.*
—Privy Council, June 29, 1587

*Why should thy excellent wit, His gift, be so
blinded, that thou should give no glory to the
Giver? Is it pestilent Machiavellian policy thou
hast studied? O punish folly! What are his
rules but mere confused mockeries, able to
extirpate in small time, the generation of
mankind . . . And if it be lawful to do
anything that is beneficial, only tyrants should
possess the earth. And they striving to exceed in
tyranny should each to the other be a slaughter
man.*

—Robert Greene,
Greene's Groats-worth of Wit

Albeit the world think Ma-
chiavel is dead,
Yet was his soul but flown
beyond the Alps,
And, now the Guise is
dead, is come from France
To view this land and
frolic with his friends.
—Marlowe, Prologue to
The Jew of Malta

Within this circle is
Jehovah's name
Forward and backward
anagrammatiz'd.
　　　　—Marlowe, *Dr. Faustus*

. . . *And so it befall that the said Christopher
Marlowe on a sudden and of his malice towards
the said Ingram aforethought, then and there
maliciously drew the dagger of the said Ingram,
which was at his back, and with the same
dagger the said Christopher Marlowe then and
there maliciously gave the aforesaid Ingram two
wounds on his head of the length of two inches
and of the depth of a quarter of an inch.
Whereupon the said Ingram, in fear of being
slain, and sitting in the manner aforesaid
between the said Nicholas Skeres and Robert
Poley, so that he could not in any wise get
away, in his own defense and for the saving of
his life, then and there struggled with the said
Christopher Marlowe to get back from him his
dagger aforesaid; in which affray that the said
Ingram, in defense of his life, with the dagger
aforesaid of the value of 12 pence, gave the said
Christopher then and there a wound over his
right eye to the depth of two inches and of the
width of one inch; of which mortal wound the
aforesaid Christopher Marlowe then and there
instantly died.*
　　　　　　　　—*from "Inquisition
　　　　　　　　taken at Deptford
Strand in the aforesaid County of Kent within
the verge on the first day of June in the year of
the reign of Elizabeth, by the grace of God of
England, France, and Ireland Queen, Defender
of the Faith etc. 35th, in the presence of William
Danby, gentleman, Coroner of the Household of
our said lady the Queen, upon view of the body
of Christopher Marlowe, there lying dead and
slain . . ."*

*Of Sir Walter Ralegh's school of atheism by the
way, and of the conjurer that is Master thereof,
and of the diligence used to get young gentlemen
to this school, wherein both Moses and our
Savior, the Old and New Testament are jested
at, and the scholars taught among other things
to spell God backward.*
　　　　　　　　—Robert Parsons,
　　　　　　　　An Advertisement

That Christ was a bastard and his
mother dishonest.

That Christ deserved better to die than
Barabbas and that the Jews made a good
choice, though Barabbas were both a
thief and a murderer.

That all Protestants are hypocritical
asses.

That St. John the Evangelist was bedfellow to Christ and leaned always in his
bosom. That he used him as the sinners
of Sodom.

That all they who love not tobacco and
boys were fools.
　　　　　—from "A Note Concerning
　　　　　　　the opinion of one
　　　　　　Christopher Marlowe,"
　　　　　　　by Richard Barnes

Let mean consaits and baser
men fear death.
Tut, they are peasants; I am
Duke of Guise;
And princes with their looks
engender fear.
　　　　　　　　—Marlowe,
　　　　　　The Massacre at Paris

Base Fortune, now I see that
in thy wheel
There is a point to which when
men aspire,
They tumble headlong down.
That point I touched,
And, seeing there was no place
to mount up higher,
Why should I grieve at my
declining fall?

—Marlowe, *Edward
the Second*

*Sir: we think not ourselves discharged of the
duty we owe to our friend when we have
brought the breathless body to the earth; for
albeit the eye there taketh his ever farewell of
that beloved object, yet the impression of the man
that hath been dear unto us, living on after life,
in our memory, there putteth us in mind of
further obsequies due unto the deceased . . .
I suppose myself executor of the unhappily
deceased author of this poem, upon whom
knowing that in his lifetime you bestowed many
kind favors, entertaining the parts of reckoning
and worth which you found in him, with good
countenance and liberal affection, I cannot but
see so far into the will of him dead, that
whatsoever issue of his brain should chance to
come abroad, that the first breath it should take
might be the gentle air of your liking . . .*

—Edward Blount (publisher),
"To The Right
Worshipful, Sir Thomas Walsingham,
Knight"; dedication of Hero and Leander
by Christopher Marlowe

*When I was first suspected for that libel that
concerned the state, amongst those waste and idle
papers (which I cared not for) and which,
unasked, I did deliver up, were found some
fragments of a disputation, touching that opinion, affirmed by Marlowe to be his, and shuffled
with some of mine (unknown to me) by some
occasion of our writing in one chamber two
years since.*

*. . . Besides he was intemperate and of a
cruel heart, the very contraries to which, my
greatest enemies will say by me.*

*. . . It is not to be numbered among the
best conditions of men to tax or upbraid the
dead . . .*

—Thomas Kyd, letter to Sir John Puckering,
Lord Keeper of the Great Seal

*. . . The manner of his death being so
terrible (for he even cursed and blasphemed to his
last gasp, and together with his breath an oath
flew out of his mouth) that it was not only a
manifest sign of God's judgment, but also an
horrible and fearful terror to all that beheld him.
But herein did the justice of God most notably
appear, in that he compelled his own hand,
which had written those blasphemies, to be the
instrument to punish him, and that in his brain,
which had devised the same.*

—Thomas Beard, Theatre of God's Judgments

*To Watson, worthy many epitaphs
For his sweet poesy, for Amyntas' tears
And joys so well set down. And after thee
Why hie they not, unhappy in thine end,
Marlowe, the Muses' darling, for thy verse
Fit to write passions for the souls below.*

—George Peele,
The Honor of the Garter

It lies not in our power to love
or hate,
For will in us is overruled by
Fate.
When two are stripped, long ere
the course begin
We wish that one should luse,
the other win;
And one especially do we affect
Of two gold ingots like in each
respect.
The reason no man knows; let it
suffice
What we behold is censured by
our eyes.
Where both deliberate, the love
is slight;
Who ever loved, that loved not
at first sight?

　　　—Marlowe, *Hero and Leander*

Next Marlowe, bathed in the Thespian Springs,
Had in him those brave translunar things
That your first poets had; his raptures were
All air and fire, which made his verses clear,
For that fine madness still he did retain,
Which rightly should possess a poet's brain.

　　　　　—Michael Drayton,
　　　　　Of Poets and Poetry

Let me see. Hath anybody in Yarmouth heard of
Leander and Hero, of whom divine Musaeus
sung, and a diviner Muse than him—Kit
Marlowe?

　　　—Thomas Nashe, Nashe's Lenten Stuff

Marlowe was happy in his buskin Muse,
Alas, unhappy in his life and end.
Pity it is that wit so ill should dwell,
Wit sent from heaven, but vices sent from hell.

　　　　　—The Return from Parnassus

It so happened at Deptford, a little village about
three miles distant from London, as he meant to
stab with his ponyard one named Ingram, that
had invited him thither to a feast, and was then
playing at tables, he quickly perceiving it, so
avoided the thrust, that withal drawing out his
dagger for his defense, he stabbed Marlowe into
the eye, in such sort that his brains coming out
at the dagger's point, he shortly after died.

　　　　　—William Vaughan,
　　　　　Golden Grove

　　Destiny never defames herself but when she lets
an excellent poet die; if there be any spark of Adam's
paradised perfection yet embered up in the breasts of
mortal men, certainly God has bestowed that, his
perfectest image, on poets. None come so near to God
in wit, none more contemn the world . . . Seldom
have you seen any poet possessed with avarice. Only
verses he loves, nothing else he delights in. And as they
contemn the world, so contrarily of the mechanical
world are none more contemned. Despised they are of
the world because they are not of the world . . .
　　It was one of the wittiest knaves that ever God
made. His pen was sharp pointed like a poniard. No
leaf he wrote on but was like a burning glass to set on
fire all his readers . . .

　　　　　—Thomas Nashe,
　　　　　The Unfortunate Traveller

Weak elegies, delightful Muse, farewell;
A work that after my death here shall
dwell.

　　　—Marlowe, "Ovid's Elegies"

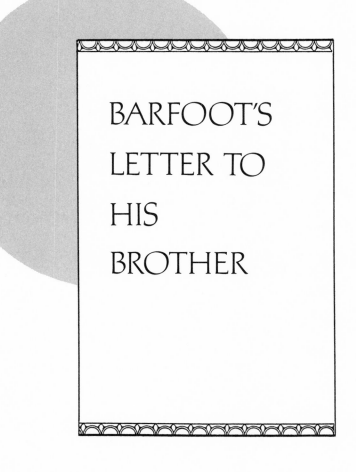

BARFOOT'S LETTER TO HIS BROTHER

I commend myself to you most heartily. This letter will come into your hands from the hands of an honorable gentleman with whom I have sometimes served in the wars.

Among other things, he will have in his possession, to establish his identity, that jewel which once belonged to our father which you gave to me. Only you and he can know which jewel it is.

You can trust him with your life and mine, if need be. Please offer him, in my name and for my namesake, your most liberal hospitality.

If you are wondering why I am here making use of the services of a stranger to you to carry this news to you, instead of using one of our own people, let me hasten to reassure you. Truth is, I do not, at least at this time, perceive any serious threat to myself, to my life, or, in a larger sense, to our various interests. But, on the other hand, I have every reason to believe that I am still being closely watched. And so I would prefer not to involve you or our family and friends, or any of our faithful servants, any more than may already be so. I act then, more on a strong sense of suspicion than anything else. But, nevertheless, I suspect that these people might not hesitate to kill any servant of ours who was found with this letter in his possession. My friend and courier is both experienced and careful. He will not be easily surprised or taken by a trick. Indeed, it is unlikely that he will be taken alive by any enemy. Still, I continue to take all precautions.

All the news from your letters to me and, lately, from any number of others whom we both know, including some who have come here to the City for the Parliament and for the Law Courts, is most troubling to me. The worst news is that the harvests have been meager again this year. Many will go hungry (again) over this long winter. I heard a preacher at Paul's Cross not long ago say: "Our summers are no summers. Our harvests are no harvests. Our seed-times are no seed-times." Those of the Puritan persuasion seem inclined to blame all this dearth, like the Plague, on the general sinfulness of the age. If they are correct, then there's no cure for it. For neither Plague nor Dearth nor Famine, here in England or anywhere else I know of, seem to encourage more true piety and virtue. Quite the contrary. Others blame it on these last years of bad weather, on the enclosures, and on merchants hoarding and forestalling grain.

Some gentlemen from the northernmost counties have told me that there is worse than storage there. There is already famine. And in some places, they allow, there are already as many deaths from famine as ever there were in the worst times of the Plague. God alone knows what will follow if the Plague should return to these parts.

None of this is widely or openly talked about in the Court and the City. But those who seek to make profit from these things are said, on good authority, to be guilty of hoarding grain in large quantities.

My informants in the Parliament tell me that Mr. Secretary Robert Cecil was of the opinion that too much of our good grain is wasted in brewing beer and ale. He even spoke in favor of closing down alehouses and taverns for one day out of a week in order to ease the shortage. Thanks be to God, he was hooted down by the members.

I hope and trust that you fare well and that you have been able to make ample and appropriate provisions for our people. No doubt prayer will always be efficacious, but meantime, never doubting God's grace and goodwill toward us, it is also prudent to lay in stores against the hardships of these lean years.

The Parliament will pass a treble subsidy. Which will be an aid and comfort to the Queen and altogether more just and proper than the forced loans we have had to depend on to continue the active prosecution of the war against Spain and the League.

By the way, my news of the secret proceedings of the House of Commons has chiefly come to me from a servant of the Earl of Essex, one Henry Bourchier, member of the House, a sly fellow, a true creature of this sly and incautious age, whose price of betrayal is not at all exorbitant. This same fellow created considerable excitement in the House in November by speaking out with great force and passion against all those who were guilty of revealing the proceedings of the House to outsiders; and he has been named to a committee to investigate the matter.

His master, the young Earl, has attended neither the sessions of Lords nor any meetings of the Privy Council. At least not yet. On account of the failures of the Islands Voyage (could any military failure have been more complete?) this year and the blame attached to himself by everyone except the ignorant rabble of the street for these failures, he has claimed to be suffering from a grave illness—more likely a touch of the French pox—and sulks like a spoiled child in his house in Wansted. Still, I must be grateful to Essex, if only by indirection. For some of his people, Bourchier, for example, have most generously supplied me with helpful intelligence on this and that. And, indeed, I have had some trivial dealings with his principal spymaster, Anthony Bacon, who is living at Essex House these days. Just to know the man and to be sure he knows me. But I must walk with great care, on tiptoes, in these matters. The Earl's people are too many and too various to be properly controlled or trusted. Bacon has his hands full. They are often working at cross-purposes and, ever and always, to their own advantage.

Our own business fares as well as can be expected. Our little suit at Chancery, I am told, moves imperceptibly forward. Perhaps some of us, your children or grandchildren, will live to see it resolved. I have paid attorneys and judges on all sides. So we can at least be allowed to hope that the case will be settled on its merits.

Bargaining with the wool merchant continues at the pace of a lazy snail in a summer garden. No matter. I will write you separately concerning this matter and some others when there is more to report. For now I can only offer my best opinion and judgment that in the end I shall make the most favorable arrangements possible with that old man. Having made his fortune, a large part of it by a clever marriage, to be sure, in his youth, he has grown content and confident enough to believe that he owes his worldly prosperity, not to the whims of Fortune, but to his own shrewd dealings and the brightness of his mind. I will not disabuse him of his illusions. Lucky for him that I am acting, purely and simply, as your agent in this matter of greasy wool and in nothing else. If I were completely serious, like so many new men of this City, in matters of money, I don't doubt that I could steal him blind and leave him a beggar. It is my fervent hope that we can conclude our business before some fox or other discovers he is there to be taken.

Speaking of foxes, I have a story, the chief occasion of this letter, to tell you. But that must wait its time and turn.

Parliament, which is now adjourned until January 11 for Christ-mastime, will surely pass the tax bill, the treble subsidy. There are also, as ever when you gather together people from all over the kingdom and so many of them new Parliament men, many other matters. The certainties are acts for relief of the poor; for the punishment of rogues, vagabonds, and sturdy beggars; and for the building of hospitals and working houses for the poor. There has been a good deal of talk in the House against the enclosures, the decline in tillage, and the depopulation of towns, with all the attendant evils of vagrancy and general poverty. Much quarreling between those who represent the wool growers and those who wish Godspeed to the plow and the plowman. Another of Essex's men (yet he is also kin to the Cecils), the attorney Francis Bacon, spoke out strongly against enclosures. And is thought by many to have been, in this matter, speaking for the government. Something, a bill of some sort, will probably come out of it. But the great landowners and wool men are very strong. So the bill will likely be a weak one.

You will not be surprised that the matter of monopolies and the

Queen's letters patent, royal grants and favors, became a topic of serious discussion in spite of many firm warnings against dealing with matters of royal prerogative. The Queen herself, ever alert and as shrewd as the best men who serve her, chose to put an end to it by allowing that there have, indeed, been abuses of the monopolies lately by some, particularly among the younger courtiers, and by permitting those who have real grievances to seek redress under the Common Law. This will settle nothing, of course, but at least defers the problem until some undefined later date.

All the fears of our fellow Roman Catholics, that this Parliament would use the wars and the conversion of Henry IV to the True Faith as excuse and occasion to add more chains of statute law to our many burdens, have proved false and unfounded. There will be no easing of intolerable burdens, either. And I have no doubt at all that given opportunity, our enemies will rise up again and seek to destroy us. But they need the unity, the goodwill, and the loyalty of all Englishmen now. I see this sense clearly enough in the speech of the Speaker of the House, old "silver-tongued" Christopher Yelverton, when Parliament assembled. Addressing his words to Her Majesty, he said (amongst other things): "As all great alterations in commonweals are dangerous, so is there no alteration so perilous as that of religion. But although all the world did abandon your Majesty and become your enemies, laboring to rear up accursed Jericho and to restore confused Babel, yet because no worldly danger hath daunted your Majesty's earnest profession, the Lord hath thrust their own swords into their own sides. You behold other kingdoms distracted into factions, distressed with wars, swarming with rebellions, and imbued with blood. Yours— almost only yours—remains calm, without tempest, quiet without dissension, notwithstanding all the desperate and devilish devices of the Romish crew and Jesuits, whose unnatural affections, bloody hands, and most cruel hearts do too, too evidently betray their religions . . ." Etc., etc., etc.

Well, I have heard worse by far and many times. I judge that they need us so long as the wars and dangers continue.

Our Catholic people are torn apart, split into many different factions. Some look to Spain for leadership and some to Rome. Some are strong for war; some are hopeful of a peace. The Succession is much on their minds, if seldom on their tongues. We, all of us, have enemies who do not wish us anything but evil. And our divisions offer our enemies aid and comfort and, I fear, much encouragement.

Yet none of this, I venture, is news to you. All that I can add to old news is that there is now sprung up in the City a new generation of young Catholic hotheads and swordsmen, impatient, conniving, and with all the dangerous bravery of the deeply inexperienced. More seasoning may cure them of their false hopes and rash stratagems. But meanwhile we must hope and pray they do not do anything so foolish and ill-timed as to bring down troubles on the heads of all of us.

All that can be said for certain about spies, in this our age of spies, is that we can never truly know where their loyalty and allegiance may lie. I conclude that the best of them must be assumed always to have played on both sides in everything. Duplicity is the essence of their craft. And I cannot imagine that they ever believe in much more than the craft they practice. True belief and sure and certain loyalty are weaknesses these spies cannot allow themselves to cultivate.

Knowing that Christopher Marlowe was a spy has helped me, not so much to understand him as to understand that there is much about him that neither I nor any man will ever know. If I had him here stretched on a rack, I am certain he would tell me much, and most of it would be untrue. Would prove to be only what I wanted to hear. Perhaps even his ghost continues this craft and will reveal no certain truth, now or ever.

So be it. I have, I believe, arrived at some kind of ending in this matter of Marlowe. Which is the reason for this letter to you.

On a night not long ago I ate my supper at the Swan on Fish Street, aiming to return to my own lodgings early, for it was a wet and windy night and too cold for comfort. I ate well and perhaps drank too much (they serve a good canary wine at the Swan) and lingered somewhat longer than I had intended. When I went outside into the dark, well wrapped and covered against the chill rain, I was at once approached by a small group of men with torches who asked me, politely enough, to come with them if I pleased. In their clothes of leather and canvas and their soft caps they looked to be seamen or some such. The weather meant nothing at all to them.

I do not know what might have happened if I had then and there elected to resist their invitation. Which, as I say, was made politely and without any explicit form of threat except the number of them standing there in the windy dark, their torches dancing to the whims of the wind. Must have been a dozen men at the least. More than enough to take me wherever they pleased to before I could do much harm to more than a few.

I think I took them a little by surprise when, without more than the briefest pause and not once moving as if to reach for the hilt of my sword or my dagger, but calm as if the invitation had been for a pint of ale, and asking no questions of any kind, I told them to lead on.

Down to the River we went, where there was a small barge with several oarsmen waiting. Rain was coming down harder and flashed brightly as it passed through the flickering light of the torches. Several men, not all, boarded the barge with me. Some took places as oarsmen. I was appointed a place beneath a canvas covering, not much more dry than the open air, but offering the intent of some comfort at least. A fellow, dressed like a gentleman and wearing a sword, joined me under the cover and greeted me by my name.

In a moment we were out on the River, rowing westward with the tide running in behind us. These men were skilled oarsmen, used to working together, and I was now certain they were deepwater seamen and not Southwark watermen. For handling that barge in the wind and rain and rough water required not a word of direction or conversation from any of them. Watermen would have wanted more pay for the danger of it and you would never have heard the end of their complaints. It might as well have been a bright April morning as far as these men were concerned.

For myself, I fixed my concentration on the hope that I could stand relaxed by the gent beneath the loose and flapping canvas and not lose my supper or the canary wine I had so pleasantly drunk within the half hour. Talking might help.

"I reckon your lame man, the red-haired fellow, arranged for this," I said.

"Well, sir, you asked him to, I believe."

"True. But pardon me if I am a little confused. I would have expected him to be here, if only to introduce me to you and the others."

He looked at me for a moment, studying me, it seemed.

"Did you really expect to see him here?"

"I expected nothing. But I find it strange that he is not among us."

"It would require a miracle for him to be here with us tonight."

"What are you telling me?"

"Nothing. Except that it seems to be a good time for you to meet and talk with my master."

"And who, may I ask, is your master?"

"You'll see for yourself soon enough."

Soon, with tide pushing and smooth oaring, we were passing the great houses of great men. That row of palaces and mansions facing the River off the Strand, lights burning in many windows. Came to land at the water gate of old Durham House. Which, I must confess, was something of a surprise to me. Because I had not imagined, not until that instant, that Sir Walter Ralegh was any way involved or interested in these things.

Until the instant I stepped off the barge at the water gate of Durham House I had not even known that Sir Walter Ralegh had returned to Westminster. When he came home from the unfortunate Islands Voyage, and as soon as the threat of the new Armada was diminished, he was said to be ill. Took the waters at Bath (how I envy him that!) for a while and then retired to the country. Now, as I surmised and would shortly confirm, he had come to Court to resume his duties and also to serve in the Parliament.

From the water gate we crossed the gardens to the house and then climbed a winding stair to the topmost chamber of the tower overlooking the River. Many times, passing on the River, I had looked at that one round tower of old Durham House with curiosity. Never imagining I would find myself there.

I mentioned this, for something to say, to the gentleman who had accompanied me here. My guard, I suppose.

"Well," said he, "you should see it by daylight and in good weather. It's a wide, long view of the River and a fine place to be."

We entered the high chamber by a low door, ducking our heads. Room was well lit by candles and there were a pair of charcoal stoves to take the edge off the chill if you came near enough to them. A large table with shiny instruments of navigation and science, might have been magic, for all I knew, and books and maps and papers. Chests and joint stools. A sturdy chair with an embroidered cushion and a footstool. Outside, the weather was worsening. Cold rain now lashed and spattered the windows, making the warmth and light of this chamber all the more pleasant.

"Irish weather," I said to the men in the room, none of whom I knew, though I knew that none of them was Ralegh.

Someone laughed.

My guide and guard pointed to a stool and I sat down. A servant brought me a cup of wine.

"Do you take tobacco?"

"Sometimes," I said. "But not tonight."

All of them were sitting in a kind of ring facing me. Only the fine chair with the cushion remained empty.

They were all, by the look of them, seafaring men, sunburned and weather-stained. For merry company I think these fellows are the best in the world, better even than soldiers. And God knows, I should have been content to sail with them, or the likes of them, to the edges of the world and back, if it were not for my affliction of seasickness.

"Well then, Captain Barfoot," the eldest of them, a dark man with some splashes of white in his beard, said. "Let us talk a little about the murder of Christopher Marlowe."

I swallowed some wine and cleared my throat. Then I began to tell them almost everything I knew, all that I passed on to you in my most recent letter. Withholding nothing, really, except for small matters that seemed, truly, beside the point. They looked and listened. Except for my voice and the splatter of the rain in the wind, it was quiet in the chamber.

Then, all of a sudden, they were not looking at me any more, but beyond me, over my head toward the door. Next they were all up on their feet, and so was I, hats off. The servant moved to open the door, and the great man himself entered, bent awkwardly at the doorway because he is so tall, a very tall and broad-shouldered man. Curly beard, small bright eyes, and a stiffness in his left leg. He carried a cane to favor that leg. But did not seem to need it much.

"Please be seated," he said in a soft voice as he settled on the cushion of the chair.

We all sat down.

He gripped his cane and looked at me.

"I regret to bring you out in this kind of weather," he said.

"Irish weather, he calls it," someone said.

"Well, Captain Barfoot, we both know something about Irish weather, don't we?" Ralegh said. "And we both know something more as well. That the weather in Ireland is bound to be worse before it turns better. Do you agree?"

"With a difference," I told him, looking straight into his bright greenish eyes. "I believe and fear that Ireland will never take a turn for the better, not in my lifetime at least."

"Well, we are allowed to hope otherwise."

"Oh, sir, I am always willing to hope. But I would never make a wager on it."

"Well then," he said. "Let's see if the wine will help you tell the truth concerning something else."

"Try me."

"One of my servants, a sort of poet, a redheaded man with a limp somewhat worse than my own . . ."

"Calls himself Cartwright, Peter or Paul."

"Does he? Well, tonight, if he is still among the living, he can call himself lucky, fortunate almost beyond belief."

"What has happened to him?"

"We thought you might know better than we do. We thought you might care to enlighten us."

"I'm sorry to say you are altogether wrong about that," I said.

There was some stirring among the men in the circle. As if they were prepared or preparing to seize me then and there. Poised, as it were. But I saw they were looking at him, at his eyes. Not going to move at or against me until he told them to.

"I know nothing of this," I continued. "You are correct, though, to imagine that I would enlighten you if I could. As it were, shoe's on the other foot."

He looked at me for a while before he spoke again. Neither of us blinked our eyelids.

"Someone has broken his crown with a cudgel and cut his throat with a knife," he said, still not raising his voice. "The man was out looking for you to tell you to meet with us here tonight. They found him in the weeds of Lambeth Marsh."

"You say he is still alive. That's a wonder."

"It is that. How he lived to be found alive I do not know, cannot imagine. We have him in the care of an excellent surgeon. He may live and he may not. You know how that goes."

"I do," I said. Then: "And I am sorry to learn it. For I had nothing against the fellow. I did not wish him any harm. And I did not do this deed."

"We know that," he said with a sigh. "We had someone else watching over you at the time."

"Do you know who did it?"

"No, Captain. Do you?"

"I do not, sir. But I will know. Sooner or later."

"Then what?"

"What is your pleasure?"

"That, one way or the other, the malefactors should be punished for it. And that the master or masters shall be deterred from future acts of this nature."

"Consider it accomplished, sir. I owe that much to you and even more to a man who was nearly killed while seeking to bring me a message."

Ralegh motioned to the servant who brought him a cup of wine. Then gave him his pipe. Which he lit, not with the smoldering match the servant offered, but with the raw flame of a candle. He pulled deeply on the pipe and drank and puffed a little cloud of sweet pale smoke.

"Tell me, Captain Barfoot, in all of this digging and uncovering, did you find anything touching directly on us?"

"On yourself, sir?"

"On myself and my people."

I told him that, until this instant, I had not known I was looking for anything to connect him, or his people, to Marlowe's murder. That it is possible I might have found such a thing if I had been looking for it. But I was not and did not. I told him there was this much and none of it news to him: that Marlowe was reputed to be among his inner circle of friends. That their friendship, such as it may have been, was said to be less a matter of patron and dependant than of one poet to another.

"Well," he said, somewhat stiffly, "I was his patron for a brief time. But when he had his troubles and came to his sad end, I was under a cloud—disgrace is the plain word for it—on account of my secret marriage. And I was absent from Court. Indeed, I was forbidden to come to Court."

He then asked me if I knew that at that time he had been accused of having atheistical opinions.

I replied that rumor reached me, as no doubt it did, and was intended to, half the people of England and all the citizens of London. But that, I had to confess, it passed through my mind like a bird in and out of an open window. For I had no reason to care if the rumor were true or no. But that, anyway, I would have given such a rumor small credence. Because it was a charge laid upon so many people.

"Christopher Marlowe also."

"That's true, sir. And, perhaps, more reasonable."

"You are a Papist, are you not, Barfoot?"

"I believe you are asking only because you already know the answer, sir."

"It was your people," he interrupted, "who first charged me, in some damned book or pamphlet, with having atheistical opinions."

"Not my people, sir," I answered as evenly as I was able. "None of mine. I have none . . . except my blood kin. And there are some Papists who have called me heretic for my own opinions. Others who have called me a traitor to the Faith for serving and fighting for the Queen."

"No one here questions your loyalty or your honor, Captain Barfoot. If we had doubts, we would never have called on your services."

"If I had known who my masters were, I might have served you better."

"Perhaps," he said. "But it was entirely inappropriate for you to know until now."

He continued with the subject of atheism. Marlowe had been named, by Kyd and others, to be of an atheistical persuasion. And indeed arrested by Council. But he was neither charged nor strictly held. Marlowe was named and known to be part of his circle. When Marlowe was arrested, Ralegh, at home in Sherborne at the time, took it to be pointed at him. A kind of warning. One which proved to be justified; for soon enough there was a commission investigating his own actions and opinions.

"All that much may be true," I said. "But I very much doubt that his death, his murder, was intended to be a warning to you or to anyone else. I have thought of that. And I doubt it."

"I am wondering something else."

"What would that be?"

"Did you ever hear, have you found anyone who has said or might be likely to say that *we* killed him, that *I* had him murdered to stop his mouth on my account?"

"Oh, sir," I told him, "I have come to believe he was most likely killed to stop his mouth. But not on your account."

"Please be so kind as to explain yourself."

"I will, sir. But, first, if I may ask a favor. Your man there offered me a pipe when I arrived. I have been sitting here, enjoying the odor of yours. And I think some tobacco would lighten my heart and ease my fears."

He laughed at that, motioning the servant to bring me a pipe.

"By God, Captain, you are a player—a comedian. I think I have never seen a man less burdened by fear than yourself. I doubt we could frighten you with rope and rack."

"I would much prefer not to test that proposition."

Taking my time, I told him as much as I knew and the gist of my opinion (opinion only, after all, though based on more than idle conjecture). The same opinion, more or less, that I gave to you. That Marlowe was planning to flee the country and they wanted to stop him. Or that they wanted him to flee the country and he would not do so.

One or the other.

"Well, there is yet another possibility, still on your own terms," Ralegh said.

He signaled for his pipe again and kept us waiting while he lit it and puffed.

"The third version is that he was a dead man from the moment of his arrest. That Walsingham, true to the ways and means of his blood kin, planned on the precaution of stopping Marlowe's mouth before he ever had the chance or the temptation to utter anything against his patron . . . or his patron's patron. So the three merry fellows spent a day with Marlowe in pleasant and idle pastime until the time came and occasion arose to kill him."

"I concede it is possible, sir," I said. "But I would prefer not to believe it."

At that the great man laughed aloud.

"It's a cruel world, Barfoot. Surely your wounds and scars have taught you something of it."

"I would not have earned so many scars if I had been a better pupil. It always seems to be somewhat worse than I imagined."

"And so it is. Worse by far than any of us can imagine. Except in our dreams."

Then, all of a sudden, he stood up. Full height, nearly half a foot above six feet, leaning slightly on his walking cane. This is the man, I was thinking to myself, who led his company of soldiers in the killing by hand of something more than two hundred prisoners at Smerwick years ago in Ireland. And I could believe he would cut my throat here and now in the high tower chamber of Durham House. If it pleased or suited him to do so. If it seemed necessary. For a moment, hat in hand, looking into his eyes and tight-lipped smile, I felt a gust, ghost of something I had not felt in a long time. A breath, a touch of unalloyed fear along my spine.

But there was nothing threatening in his outward manner or his words.

"Well done, Barfoot," he was saying. "Whether you know it or not, you have told us, told me all that I wanted and needed to know. Thomas Walsingham killed him, as sure as if he had wielded Frizer's knife, for his own reasons. We shall never know whether they were good reasons or not. A pity, though. For Marlowe was a wonderfully bright mind and a poet of the greatest gifts—'the Muses' darling,' George Peele called him. And so he was. But Muses are no kind of aid and comfort against murderers.

"If Christopher Marlowe had not been such a rogue, I would sententiously say he was too good for the world we have made.

"You can be sure," he continued, "that no one will consider saying that about either you or myself, Barfoot. And we can be grateful for that much, after all."

Turned to the others.

"Give this man a full purse and send him on his way. He has done well for us and now we are almost done with him."

He was moving toward the low doorway.

"Sir?" I said.

He stopped and turned back to face me.

"Who are these others who are digging into Marlowe's grave and, evidently, watching over me?"

"None of ours," he said. As if that were to be his last word on the subject. But then continuing, as if in reconsideration: "You mean, I reckon, this ne'er-do-well player."

"Hunnyman," someone behind me added. "Joseph Hunnyman."

"Yes, sir."

"Well now," Ralegh said. "It could, of course, be anyone alive. Maybe, don't discount it, even Walsingham himself, testing to see if the trail to him has vanished. But never mind. Whoever it is must sooner or later belong to one of two factions—that of the Earl of Essex or that of Mr. Secretary Cecil. Either of whom would like to link me to the matter if they could. But they cannot. So it is not a matter of my concern.

"Nor is it yours anymore, Captain, now that you are discharged. I am convinced that you know all that can be known about the matter (by anyone except Frizer and the others and Walsingham). That if you, or they, were to spend another year or a hundred, no one will arrive any closer to the answer to it.

"However," he added, "this may not make them, the others, happy. If I were you, I would watch my back, at least for a while to come. Or else"—he laughed—"offer your services to one or the other. Essex can use you and he is more generous than Pigmy Cecil."

Ducked down to pass through the doorway and was gone.

I had another cup of wine with the others. Then I was given a most generous purse for all my troubles and led down the winding stair and across the windswept garden to the water gate. Where two mariners waited for me with a wherry. The barge was secured and empty.

"Carry Captain Barfoot across to Lambeth Stairs."

I had to laugh that they chose my destination for me, since, at that moment, I had no idea where to take myself next. They chose wisely for me. And soon enough I was warm and dry in the large bed between my warm Dutch friends and snoring and dreaming like an old man by the hearth.

I hope that it will be possible, all in due time, for me to come home for a visit. First I shall need a good purging and the restorative of the waters at Bath or perhaps at Buxton. But soon, as I tell myself, I shall be as new and fresh as any bridegroom.

I look forward to seeing you again when that miracle has happened.

Meantime I hope and trust that the Christmas season is a happy time for one and all.

Remember me always in your prayers.

ENDINGS

And now I must confess that even though I knew some of them at and by sight, at one time and another, and, as you have seen, knew something of their doings, their comings and goings and—in our world of equal importance and value to all things done and left undone—knew something of their reputations as well, I can claim no knowledge or clear notion of what finally became of them.

And where they went and what became of them God alone knows. They vanished.

Not into history, or you would most likely have encountered them or, anyway, heard of them, before now.

Went first, then, into silence and common obscurity. Later found their comfortable lodgings in Oblivion.

May we all be so fortunate, after all is said and done, as to be well forgotten.

Yet, even so and nevertheless, unperturbed by ignorance, the restless imagination, which is the life and death of us all, goes round and round, windmill and waterwheel, turning and churning. Imagination, like old Adam in his breeches made of fig leaves, cannot cease its endless hard labor of delving and digging.

I like to pretend I know what became of each and every one of them. You are free to invent your own versions. Here are mine:

• • •

There is a space of time during which Barfoot, having talked to the little group in the tower of Durham House, is preoccupied with business matters for his brother. Some modest buying and selling. Some arrangements to be made. It is a fortnight, then, at least before he feels free to go back across to Lambeth Marsh again and visit with his old friends there.

What does he find?

One of the Dutch whores is dead. Drowned in the River. Somehow. Fell or jumped to her death. No one witnessed this. Anyway, found dead and floating and swelled with water and rot, all dressed in her finest clothes. Found after high tide in the Marsh halfway down toward Paris Garden.

Not a mark on her body, they say. Except for the swelling and rot, looking as if she were sleeping, her face a mask of calm.

"Well," says Barfoot bitterly, "at least she lived out her days without a whipping."

He goes to see the other woman in their high chamber. In broad day she keeps it dark. Blinds tight. She curtained in the bed. Her voice broken and hoarse. Perhaps from grief. Stink of the room. A full chamber pot.

She groans and will not leave her bed.

He carries the pot downstairs and empties it in the cesspool behind the house. Returns with a lighted candle. She cringes away, hides face and head beneath a pillow.

Speaks harshly to her. Tones of command. Candle in one hand, he gently lifts the pillow away from her face. She winces and groans. Reveals in the candlelight a badly bruised and swollen face. Yellow and black bruises, scabs. Nose broken and swollen. Lips puffed and cracked.

Still touching lightly, gently, speaking as if to a soldier, he eases her out of her shift. Her naked body is battered and bruised also. A long thin scabby line just below her large breast. Someone cut there, not deeply, as if (in threat perhaps) to flay off the skin or to cut off the breast.

She is shaking with soundless sobs.

Putting the candle on a chest (noticing, as he does so, that the chest has been broken and rifled), he helps her into her shift and back to bed. Pours her a cup of wine. Holds it to her lips, ever so gently, as she tries to sip. Sees then that her tongue is swollen and bitten.

"Who has done this to you?" he asks now, very quietly.

• • •

When the bodies of the bears were found, as they were, by first light . . .

Pause to consider, if you will, and I say this without any pride or judgment. Our City, London, was not, in the years we are remembering, a place where murder was common. I will not here venture into the maze of argument concerning such matters as comparing the mundane violence of daily life then and in your time. Except to say this much which I would surely argue against you, if disputation and debate between us were possible: I would say the violence of deeds is to be measured and to be understood by intention and by custom. We paid each other a considerable sum of bodily pain. Yet even when, under the law of treason, for example, a living body was killed by hanging, drawing, and quartering, or when, under the laws of heresy, a body was burnt to black and howling ash at the stake, we never allowed ourselves to imagine we had any power over the spirit, the immortal soul of another being. Only God Almighty possesses the infinite power to judge, to punish or to forgive, His will be done, a soul. The body might belong to Caesar's world, but the soul of every human being belonged, simply and irrevocably, to God. If debate and disputation, ghost and flesh, were here miraculously to be allowed, you can be sure I would argue not merely that the staggering record of your violence to each other (rivers and oceans of blood, tides of the blood of innocents ebbing and flowing throughout all your time) not merely far outweighs all your passionate concerns for human comforts and for the rights of human beings, but also that you have learned, in your brutal and boundless pride, to inflict great injury, deep wounds, without so much as breaking skin or bones. And, in your brutal innocence and boundless pride, you have come to believe that it is within your power to shape and even to break the souls of others as you please. I leave you to wonder which is worse.

Well now.

Enough.

You say I sound like a preacher (meaning no compliment). I say perhaps you are right. That may indeed have been my calling, though, for one reason and another, I never answered it.

Pardon me. All I meant by untoward interruption was to come on this stage, chorus-like, to tell you that bloody murder was so uncommon, so rare in our City, that any murder was always the subject of a wildfire of rumor and speculation.

So when the bodies of the two bears were found, as they were, in the first light, there was great excitement in the City. Constables and Coroner were called and soon the stately process of the Law began. And it was not a matter of much difficulty. In the absence of any witnesses, Coroner and jury were compelled to look strictly to the evidence at hand. Two men of the worst kind of repute, widely believed to be cutthroats and cutpurses, two felonious types, born to be hanged, somehow escaping their foreordained fate by killing each other with knives in a dark narrow alleyway, shaded and shadowy even in broad daylight. And there they lay, stiffened into death, bloody knives rigorously gripped in bloody fists, both of them covered with a wealth of many wounds. One of them, sprawled flat on his wide back and open-mouthed (though with a newer and smaller mouth carved in his throat) as if drunk and asleep. Even dead he looked as if, any moment, he might begin to snore deeply through a bloody, clotted nose. The other one lay a few yards away, face down, looking as if he had collapsed in the act of trying to crawl away from the body of the man he had killed. Crawling on hands and knees, seeking to escape from the scene. Perhaps to find help. Maybe in his last folly believing that he would still somehow save himself and live another day.

There were a couple of oddities about this simple double murder. One was that no one living and sleeping nearby admitted to having heard anything. Not one sound of what surely must have been a noisy struggle between two large, powerful, armed men. Not a cry. Not a groan at the end.

Well.

Perhaps they fought and killed each other silently.

Then there was the matter of the blood. With so many large and small stab wounds and ragged slices, shouldn't there have been much more blood soaked into the earth than the skinny little pools, like no more than touches of rust nearby? Plenty of gore stained on knives and fists, but no signs of any deep bleeding from their wounds. Yet each of them was as well drained and as bloodless as a cleaned rabbit ready for the cooking pot. Where was all their blood?

Well. Perhaps wild dogs had, silently to be sure, come in a pack and licked them clean. No doubt there was some explanation. All that was certain to one and all, and to the majestic Law, was that this world was better off, a better place, without them.

Joseph Hunnyman was not so certain that this world, bad as it may be, and has been ever since Adam, was now to be taken as a safer place on account of these two violent deaths. Not without his own reasons, he assumed it was most unlikely that these two men, who had never yet been known to quarrel or to fight with each other, beyond the most usual kinds of scuffling and blows, half in jest, would have had a falling out that ended in bloody murder. And so crudely. So many wounds inflicted as if each one were in a frenzy like feeding fish.

"Cutthroats tend to cut throats," he said, unsmiling, to the handsome young man when they met and talked of these things in whispers in a wherry they hired to carry them, slowly, against the full flow of the incoming tide, eastward on the River from the public stairs at Westminster to that landing just beyond busy Three Cranes in the City.

The young man found it difficult to believe also.

"They were a pair of brute beasts, true enough," he said. "And so it is conceivable they might have done this thing—or anything else—to each other. But I doubt it. I have to think they were murdered. But by whom and for whatever reasons I have no idea. Do you?"

Hunnyman shrugged, hugging his cape a little tighter round his shoulders and squaring the brim of his hat as the day's rain began to fall in large drops, speckling the gray surface of the river.

"I think they must have been killed somewhere else in the City, or even across the River, in Southwark or perhaps Lambeth Marsh. And then brought to that alleyway in the darkest hours."

"Surely someone, if only a boatman, would have witnessed this."

"It wouldn't take a fortune to stop a boatman's mouth."

"Two dead bodies, cut to pieces, would plead an eloquent case for silence."

"Do you see? We are both thinking much the same thing. Collusion. It would take a good number of men, working together and working well together, to accomplish it all."

"They would have to ambush or trap Quigley and Duggan."

"Who?"

"They had names."

"Even dogs have names."

"Well. These dogs, my dogs, had names."

"Whelps, too?"

"God knows," the young man said, then laughed out loud.

Through the light rain the two hard-faced oarsmen looked at him, expressionless but surprised at inexplicable laughter coming from someone so conspirational, so serious. Hunnyman could feel wrinkles form on his own face, too.

"God knows," the young man repeated. "But I would like to believe there are bastards out there somewhere. I would like to think the beastly breed will continue."

Then looking directly into Hunnyman's eyes. The little burst of laughter spent now. His own eyes bright and hard, his mouth a grin of small white teeth.

"If you have any hope for the name of Hunnyman, if you plan to breed any more of your own," he said, "I think you would be wise to leave this City behind you. And the sooner the better."

"Surely," Hunnyman said, without much conviction, "there's no good reason for anyone to want to kill me."

"Why not? And it can be easier done than the business with those two."

"Duggan and Quigley. But where can I go? What can I do?"

The young man fished beneath the folds of his own expensive Spanish cape (on which the rain beaded in large drops like pearls) and produced a small wool purse. Gave it to Hunnyman.

"Not much, but more than you deserve, really, for what little you have done for us," the young man said. "And as for the answer to your question. I would prefer not to carry the burden of that knowledge with me. I would prefer not to know where you go or what becomes of you."

"Are you afraid also?" Hunnyman asked.

Again that odd loud laughter, catching the attention of the boatmen. Ending in a cough, fist at lips. And then a fine bright smile with neither arrogance nor malice in it.

"God in heaven, no," the young man said now, speaking in his full voice, whispering no more. "I have never yet, at least in all of my memory, felt any fear of anything. Who knows why? Not I. Perhaps it would have been better, would be better for me if I could feel fear. Like you. Like other men. I've even seen Quigley and Duggan afraid. And I'll wager they tasted some fear before they finally tasted death. But, Hunnyman, I have never yet been able to muster fear against anything. Perhaps it will come to me at the right time and I shall be all heels like any other coward."

They had eased past Three Cranes, where some good-size barges were being offloaded. Shouting voices and the rock of hulls in the tide and the light breeze which had begun to chase the raindrops across the River. Had eased past Three Cranes, and the oarsmen were skillfully nosing the wherry up to the landing.

"No matter," the young man continued. "I would never leave London even to save my life."

Took two bold steps in the tipsy boat and leaped past the boatmen, over a space of water, to land, lightly as a dancer, on the landing. Rain falling harder now. Cupped his hands to call out and be heard.

"Goodbye, Hunnyman. You pay for the boat hire."

• • •

When Barfoot left her, Alysoun, spent, yet fulfilled beyond anything she had imagined or dared to hope for, would surely have known two things. First, that he would never come back to her again. That when he went down the stairs and into the street he would neither look back nor feel any need, then or later, to return. For this she was grateful.

The other knowledge she had was that she would have his child. There was a deep feeling, loins and womb, she had never before known. Except in some old wives' tales. And she, half witch, as she liked to think, knew it at once. Believed without doubt our question.

If it had by chance been Hunnyman's baby, she would not have hesitated. She would have taken a strong potion and voided herself of it. No one the wiser. But this child she wanted as much as she had ever wanted anything. Therefore this child would have to have a father. She would have to take a husband.

Not another old man, though that might add to her estate. Still, it would take too long to woo and win some rich elder. No use or thought at all in selling her sweet goods to a *poor* old man. If young it must be, as it must, then why not someone young enough to be taught and directed, to be ruled?

Young Richard, her special favorite among the apprentices, is a pretty fellow. Hungers for her, pleasures of her body, like a dog at a bowl. Drools. And, an inward and spiritual drooling, he is even more hungry with ambition. Like herself, and in spite of all the world's preachers and as much of the world's history as he knows, he allows himself, much of the time, to believe he is a character in a child's tale of transformation. Believes, secretly, he must be the bastard child of some great lord who is only pretending to be an apprentice boy come to London from a Warwickshire village. When the transformation comes, as he never doubts it will, he will accept it gracefully, yet not with any unseemly surprise. He will be thankful, but not overwhelmed with emotions of gratitude. He has watched and even practiced the style of the world's great men as and when they accept the service and deferential honor of their inferiors. Good manners forbid making too much out of what is the bounden duty of others.

Richard will be perfect, then. Careless enough in his triumph, marrying a rich widow, he will never quite know enough to defend himself from her guile. Though he is only a very few years younger than she is, they are an age apart. He will never be a match for her in matters of worldly wisdom. Which is the only wisdom he will ever learn and have. She, on the other hand, has at least peered into the keyholes of other, deeper knowledge. Knows there is more wisdom than the world's, though she may never live to learn it.

So she will begin by holding both hands against her belly just below the navel as if she could feel the child already. Meanwhile knowing what Richard's young hands would feel and how, at least at first and long enough, he would be half in a swoon of pleasure to be permitted to touch something so soft and smooth and cool with his eager hands, wooing and winning the lad this very day. And soon enough they will be lawfully married man and wife. And soon enough after that he will be the father for, if not of, her child.

• • •

While all this was taking place, indeed, on the same morning that the murdered bodies of that pair of vicious cutthroats were found, lying together in the dirt *(and thank you kindly for it, sir)*, Captain Barfoot chose to honor a pledge he had made somewhat earlier. Brushed and scrubbed and barbered (and, yes, well perfumed), he hired a two-oared wherry for the whole day long. And early in the morning was carried three miles downriver to Deptford. Pleased Barfoot's sense of irony to come in and tie up, for a fee, at the very dock and water gate of the Hall of the Guild of St. Clement, dedicated to pilots and seafarers and home for ten Elder Brethren of the seafaring trade. From which he went directly to the house of the widow Eleanor Bull.

He did not have to ask her if she remembered him. One of he qualities of being truly ugly and more than a little frightening, he would be the first to admit, is that most people do not easily forget you. May not remember your name or your business. But they will ever after know your face at sight.

What he asked her was something else.

"Mistress Bull," he said, "do you remember a promise I made you last fall? A promise you made sport of at the time. Because you said you didn't believe I would keep it.

"I told you then—and I'm sure it flew into one of your pretty ears and out the other—that I would come back here and take you to the playhouse. And here I am, ma'am, for that purpose. And I will accept no excuses and listen to no explanations of why you can't come with me. Look me in the eyes, Eleanor Bull, and see if you dare to tell me no.

"Good, then. I take your silence for what it is—acceptance and assent. Go now and get yourself as dressed and beautified as you please.

"And when you are ready, soon, I hope, you and I will walk out of here and down to the River to take a boat, which I have waiting for us even now, upriver to the City. Where you are to be my guest for an excellent dinner at a pleasant and merry place I know out beyond Bishopsgate and close by Finsbury Fields.

"High time, and don't you agree?, you sat down and ate a dinner that someone else had to prepare and worry over.

"And after our meal, assuming the weather of this sunny morning continues, why, we can take an easy, leisurely walk over to the playhouse called the Theatre. Where I am told there is a new play by Mr. Shakespeare to be performed. Perhaps a bit too much of bawdry and of blood and thunder for your taste—who knows? I do not know your pleasure in plays, Mistress Bull. But no matter. It's the best and the newest of the plays we can see today.

"And today must be the day. For the Lenten season is now hard upon us. We shall soon enough be fasting and eating smoked fish. And there'll be no plays again until after Easter. And I shall be gone home for Eastertide. It might be summer or even the autumn before I can be free again to keep my promise.

"So today is the day. And today's play is what we will see. It might be better, more apt, to be sure, if one of Marlowe's plays were to be performed this afternoon. But no such luck. The Shakespeare will have to do.

"Let's make the most of the day we have before us and let tomorrow care for itself."

Then, with a light crisp slap across her wide, soft bottom, brisk, but with an intimate touch, brief as it was, that brought a blush to the widow's cheeks: "Now, hurry off to your chamber and make yourself ready for a full day in the City in the company of a friend and admirer who keeps all his promises when he can. And in the meantime I'll take a pint of your best beer."

• • •

You are wondering more about the stage play that they witnessed than you are about Barfoot and the Widow Bull. And I can understand that and wish I could assuage your natural curiosity and tell you more about it and in more detail. But I am not the one to do it. Was not there with them. Never, as it happens, happened to see that particular play. Though, and how could I help it, being alive then and there?, I witnessed the playing of a good many other plays by Mr. Shakespeare. Even in my worst and darkest days, I would still, if I could, cadge a penny somehow or other and, drunk or sober, sick or well, find my way to the Globe (to be put up on the South Bank in a year or so) or the Fortune and stand there in the sweaty, garlic-breathed, groundling crowd hoping to be lifted out of my battered, world-weary body, as if on wings of words, and carried away to strange places, old and new, far and near, to live among familiar strangers for a little time. To laugh at their follies. To weep over their sufferings. As if I were, indeed, for that span of time at least, truly a winged angel, freed of my mortal flesh with all of its fires and hungers; free, too, from the fevers and festering sickness of mind and soul. Free, in that waking dream, to be fully compassionate, sensitive to the woes and misery of others, without envy or contempt. And able, also, to laugh out loud at all their manifold misfortunes, even while wishing them well.

The Puritans were right to fear the powers of the stage.

Never mind. Neither Barfoot nor the Widow Bull troubled themselves with thoughts of Puritans or angels on that sunny afternoon. Full of good food and a little hazy from sweet wine, they sat on soft cushions on a gallery bench to see the play. And the play they saw performed was *The Second Part of Henry the Fourth*. Which, surely, has something to please everyone.

Did I say I have never seen the play? I did say so. But, like the best half of London, I also read it as soon as it was printed. Read it and rejoiced in it.

And it pleases me to think of the two of them there on that

afternoon. Pleases me to try to imagine what it was that pleased and surprised them. What it may have been that they prized.

A motley story, particolored, half and half. New silk and old sack. Half solemn history (and ancient and honorable moral instruction) and half pure foolery, the greater part of that being bawdy talk and double-duty, double-meaning jests. Half set in the grand and pomp-ous (likewise duplicitous) conferences and speeches of great and public men of the world. The other half partly in the inimitable language of irredeemable rascals whose same wild words you could have heard, even as this play was being performed by the Chamberlain's Men, in certain well-known streets and lanes, alehouses and brothels, all over this City and its suburbs. Likewise—for we visit the country in this play as well, you could listen to English country gents and yokels whose accents are as fresh off the farmyard as if they had arrived on the back of a cart at Smithfield market on this very day.

Everyone knows that, on account of Mr. Burbage, the Chamber-lain's Men are sworn to a naturalness of acting and to what they call *personification* whereby the player uses all art and craft to inhabit the skin and bones of an imaginary person.

And what persons Barfoot and the Widow Bull would meet that day in this old story of how the handsome and dissolute Hal, Prince of Wales, did shrewdly put down a northern rebellion ("base and bloody insurrection") and then at the death of his father become both a man and a king himself, great Harry Fifth he would be, putting on wisdom with his Coronation robes and crown, putting his wild youth and wilder, riotous companions ("I know thee not, old man: fall to thy prayers; / How ill white hairs become a fool and jester!") behind him.

But it's not that story, is it?—for how much can Mr. Shakespeare, or anyone for that matter, twist and tamper with the chronicle of our own English history; I ask you; except, to be sure, what happened then and there must always be smoothed and sanded to be joined smoothly with what is taken to be true for here and now. No, the pleasure of this play, and what most pleased Barfoot and the Widow Bull, separately and differently for sure, lies in the people of it.

For the widow there are some great ladies, briefly on stage, though long enough to let her nod wise approval and stifle a yawn and a belch. But she will be wide awake and soon ready to hoot, clap her hands, even chime in with comments of her own, when the two clever boys playing Hostess Quickly (and *that* comes close to home, in a fashion, does it not?) and foul-mouthed, sharp-tongued, undefeated (easy to board but wellnigh unsinkable) Doll Tearsheet. Who cares not a gooseberry for all these books and homilies which tell a woman how her place and station is to be quiet and modest and obedient. Doll's too featherheaded and English—*unruly,* Barfoot would say, but will not today, to the Widow Bull—for anything like that. What does she say to Ancient Pistol's courtly suit? "I scorn you, scurvy companion. What, you poor, base, rascally, cheating, lack-linen mate! Away, you mouldy rogue, away!" And what does she say, not without affection, to fat Sir Jack Falstaff, her true love? "Hang yourself, you muddy conger, hang yourself!"

And what is her gentlest, most poetic declaration of love to the naughty old knight? "Come on, you whoreson chops. Ah, rogue, in faith, I love thee. Thou art as valorous as Hector of Troy, worth five of Agamemnon, and ten times better than the Nine Worthies. Ah, villain!"

Enough. You can see why Eleanor Bull would be delighted by Doll. And so am I. And with a little wince for her when she and the Hostess are dragged away by the Beadle and his officers at the end of things to enjoy "whipping cheer." All the more sympathy from the audience, though many may laugh and it is as funny as it is just, after all, because she shows not one ounce or inch of pity for herself: "I'll tell you what, you thin man in a censer, I'll have you soundly thrashed for this—you blue-bottle rogue, you filthy, famished correctioner, if you be not thrashed, I'll forswear half-kirtles!"

For Barfoot there is that great character, that great lecher, glutton, thief, and conniver and devoted coward and liar, old tub of guts himself, often defeated but never, sir, daunted, oh no, Jack Falstaff. Whose appearance on the stage, before he utters one word, now that he's as widely known as any knight in England, past or present, raises up a full concert of shouts and laughter from everyone standing in the audience and most of those comfortable on their cushions, too. "I am not only witty in myself, but the cause that wit is in other men." For Barfoot there are moments to choke him and shake him to tears of laughter. As when Jack Falstaff and Justice Shallow ("I was once of Clement's Inn where I think they will talk of mad Shallow yet . . . Jesu, Jesu, the mad days I have spent!") call up a muster of almost "half a dozen sufficient men"—Rafe Mouldy, Simon Shadow, Thomas Wart, Francis Feeble, and Peter Bullcalf—and take the most unlikely for the army. "Feeble!" says Falstaff. "Thou wilt be as valiant as the wrathful dove or most magnanimous mouse."

Sir Jack in praise of the medicinal properties of his favorite nourishment—sugar and strong sack: "It ascends me into the brain, dries me there all the foolish and dull and crudy vapors which environ it, makes it apprehensive, quick, forgetive, full of nimble, fiery and delectable shapes, which, delivered over to the voice, the tongue, which is the birth, becomes excellent wit."

None of which wit will serve and spare the old fellow, and his companions, from a time in Fleet prison, when the Lord Chief Justice orders him sent there. But will earn him the applause of the audience as he's marched away, and chances are they will send a few apple cores and nutshells sailing through the air to bless the Chief Justice's exit.

All of which will be followed by an Epilogue, as the author, Mr. Shakespeare himself, comes out on the stage for a few final remarks. He began the play, as well, in Prologue as Rumor, in person, clad in a gown of tongues. Played in it, too, no doubt, as he usually did in those days, some of the lesser, briefer parts. But here he comes, for once, as himself and in no costume but his own clothes. The usual witty appeal for goodwill. Mending and amending some matters of no meaning to you. Promising something more—"If you be not too much cloy'd with fat meat, our humble author will continue the story, with Sir John in it, and make you merry with fair Katharine of France: where, for anything I know, Falstaff shall die of a sweat, unless already a' be killed with your hard opinions . . ."

Picture the hooting that greeted the very idea of wishing Jack Falstaff anything but long life.

At the end Mr. Shakespeare bowed to a burst of applause, then turned and left the stage for the tiring rooms as the musicians began to play the audience out of the playhouse.

And in the waning light, some lamps and lanterns already lit here and there, and a chill of evening in the air, Barfoot and the widow walked back to the River to the boat. Talking about the play and the players and the meaning of it all.

Let us leave the two of them, feeling good and easy in the crowd coming from the Theatre and the Curtain in the fading daylight.

Does Captain Barfoot spend this one night in the large, soft, curtained bed of Eleanor Bull? Perhaps . . . Why not? She had been lonely for a good while. And he has things he would as soon not be alone to think about. At least until tomorrow.

What about the rest of us, myself and my friends and ememies, the university wits, living and dead? What about Kit Marlowe and Robert Greene and the others? Did Mr. Shakespeare have them, in part ironically, in mind when he had Prince Hal say: "Well, thus we play the fools with time, and the spirits of the wise sit in the clouds and mock us"? There is an audience sitting in the clouds, to be sure; but it is not composed only of the spirits of the wise.

From us the new plays, like the suddenly new age, demanded not something more but something other than simply envy and malice and regret. These things called for our applause and earned it. How could we offer any less?

This play, this *Second Part of Henry,* was not anything that any of us, the young and gifted, doomed and despairing fellows from the universities, would ever have written. Called for another kind of gift, another sort of grip and touch and tuning of the immemorial lute strings.

Mr. Shakespeare has, as was his habit, a little salute to the days (already?) gone by, greetings for a ghost. Early on he has one character make a somewhat garbled allusion to some words of a celebrated scene in Kit Marlowe's *Tamburlaine.* And in whose head, in whose money, does this scene reside? Why, nobody else but the notorious Ancient Pistol! Who hasn't the slightest idea where any of these words and thoughts, or any others that crowd his brain like a flock of crows in a tree, may come from.

• • •

Upon the twenty-seventh of March, a bright and blustery day, Alysoun, her young husband, and her fat and healthy infant boy, christened Richard after her husband, joined in the throngs, the crowds lining both sides of wide Cheapside to watch the procession of the Earl of Essex and his army as they departed for Ireland. He bareheaded on horseback, graciously acknowledging the cheers and shouts of the crowd, bowing this way and that, a pleased smile on his long, soft, handsome face. Dressed with the elegant negligence that was his style.

Behind him, as the procession moved through the high streets of the City, the largest army sent forth out of England in the Queen's reign, more than twenty thousand foot and horse, going to the aid of the hard-pressed, battle-weary troops in Ireland and the settlers who had been driven from their ruined plantations into the Pale.

Young Essex, like a young king, hero of Cadiz in '96, victim of the envy and folly of others in the '97 Islands Voyage, going off now to root out the rebellion in bloody Ireland.

It seemed, for a little while, the most joyous occasion the City had ever seen or could remember. And so many thousands from London and all the suburbs, and indeed, from towns and villages far and near, came out to cheer the army. And many to follow in the fields as they left the City.

Music playing, bells ringing, cannon salutes booming from the Tower and the ships on the River.

Sooner than she expected, and easier, too, amid the crowds and noise and confusion, Alysoun saw what she was looking for. Among a cluster of captains on horseback. Barfoot squat and hunched on his thin saddle. Standing out clearly among and against the others in part because of his clothing. For they were all wearing their best and their bravest, their shiniest furniture. Painted toy soldiers. Barfoot (or so it seemed to her as she stared) like an uninvited guest. Or like a dog whose duty is to guard this bright flock. Or, she thought, like a ghost, a stage ghost, silent and frightening amidst a scene of courtly revelry. Like old Death, himself. In his plain and sad-colored wool and leather and canvas. Oil and stains on the pieces of light armor he wore and on the dark, dented, open-faced helmet. Looked ready to ride directly into battle just as soon as they passed through the Wall.

Unsmiling, heavy-lidded, his face in half shadow like a playing-card knave, he might have been half-asleep or many miles elsewhere in his thoughts. But at a moment, as if moved by some intuition, he looked up, turned his head slowly, lazy look of a coiled serpent, and must have seen her there. His face said nothing. His eyes were cold as springwater and empty. Yet (she believed then and ever after) their eyes met as she snatched and held up the infant high for him to see.

And then he was gone. Forever, she knew. Knew he would die, and best that he should. No sadness in her, body or soul. She was as near to contentment as she would ever be as she held her child in her arms and walked slowly with her young husband back to the house on Knightrider Street.

They were safely inside when, an hour later, the weather turned suddenly and violently around. Sky black with heavy clouds. Lightning and thunder and a driving rain that soaked everyone, soldiers and citizens, before the procession had even reached the village of Islington.

A bad omen, that storm. Everyone said so.

And Alysoun had an odd thought that made her smile. Barfoot, old Captain Death, her father and lover, her true husband and the father of her child, Barfoot had been riding, when she saw him, like a man in the rain. That was the meaning of his hunch and bend in the saddle while the others rode so tall and proud in the light. Not a cloud in the sky at that moment. And he was riding exactly like a man in a rainstorm. She could see that, too. Part of the cause of her smiling. The others, even proud Essex, limp and wilted. Barfoot went forward. Rain pelting his oily helmet, beading on the greasy wool of his cloak.

She wondered how he would die, wishing him well.

As for Alysoun and her new young husband, both so handsome, so fortunate, so full of hope and with every good reason for hoping, I have heard that they both died in the terrible sickness, the Plague time during the last days of the Queen's life and the first summer of the reign of the new King come down from Scotland.

Died and were buried in great common graves with many thousands more, beyond naming or counting.

I do not know what may have become of the child.

• • •

This will be during July or August of '99. Summer of musters and alarms at home when (once again) the coming of the Spanish fleet will be greatly feared.

This will be in July or August in Ireland, in Munster. By early September the Earl of Essex will finally and reluctantly obey his instructions and go into Ulster to wage war. By then it will be too late, with his forces dwindled away through death and disease and desertion to a few thousand, three or four thousand at the most, and these not dependable. Which is how, you know the story, he, Essex, will come to a little hill near Lough Mill where he will have no other choice but to disobey the direct orders of Queen and Council and to parley with the Earl of Tyrone. And that will be the beginning of the end for Essex, as all the world knows. But that is all another story.

Here it will still be late July, or early August at the latest, in Munster. High green summer. Summer of skirmishes, ambushes, defeats.

High green Irish summer, and over the top of a hill and down to the edge of a brook, bubbling over rocks beneath the slight shade of an old and somewhat stunted oak tree, here come three hot, dusty horsemen riding. They pull up and dismount to rest their horses and to let them drink. These three have been scouting the countryside all morning looking for the rebles. Who will have been sighted in large numbers all week long. Who vanished completely yesterday. Perhaps they have run away from the column which is slowly, bag and baggage, marching and rattling its way across the county. Seeing they have no chance in a battle, the Irish may have fled. Planning to fight on another day in another peace.

Barfoot will doubt that. He will believe they are near here somewhere. Patiently waiting. He will believe that many men will die today or tomorrow. And that many of those dead will be Englishmen unless he and his two companions are lucky enough to find the wild Irish kerns first.

He waters his horse, then lets her browse and graze a little, holding the horses for the other two and watching carefully all around them while his companions kneel to scoop up and drink the clear cool water of the stream. Water over rock is the loudest noise in the world, together with a soft, easy breeze, rising and falling, teasing the tall Irish grass, lightly troubling the oak leaves. He could stretch out in the shade of that tree and in a moment be asleep. He could sleep there forever.

When they finish drinking and stand up, he removes his helmet and takes his turn at the stream, kneeling down on a large flat rock at the edge of a quiet pool around which water sparkles and flows over the rocks in boisterous braids of white. Plunging his hands and arms into the pool up to his elbows, then holding them still there in the little pool while the scattered sky reassembles itself and his face greets him as if he were looking in a steel glass. There are new flecks and patches of white in his beard.

And as he bends to drink, his face grows suddenly wild and strange, murderous and sunburned. And, too slowly to suit himself, he rolls away, splashing in the water as an ax blow falls loud on the flat rock where he had been. Rolling, then half standing, he steps forward and guts the fellow with his knife before he can strike with the ax again. And now his sword is drawn, too, in his right hand. Frog picks a man who stands between himself and the trunk of the oak. Leaps over crumpled body and whirls round, back pressed against the tree trunk.

Holy Mary, Mother of God, pray for us sinners, now and at the hour of our death.

Now he will be able to see it all. Close by (he could step and kick the nearest) his two companions lie flat on their backs bubbling blood. Throats cut ear to ear from behind. As he will have feared all along, neither of them had the skill or the quickness to draw and fight even to save their own lives. Good lads but no soldiers when the time for killing came. Died without a word or a sound.

O my good Angel, stand by me in this hour.

Far off across the field he will see the horses running away. Being chased by bare-legged Irishmen.

All around him, staring like cattle in a field, creatures made of Irish earth and grass, a band of kerns, motionless, their weapons old but keen at blade edge.

And, wet as he is, Barfoot will be almost wild with thirst. For he never drank a drop at the stream. Mouth puckered and dry. A soldier's mouth. From somewhere within his chest he will find a dusty gob and spit it on the ground.

They will react, dancing back, as if they expected it to explode or maybe suddenly change into an armed creature.

I renounce Satan and all his suggestions: O ye blessed Spirits of God, drive this wicked enemy far from me.

He will laugh and rub his itchy back against the tree. Will speak to them in their own language.

"Come now, you Irish devils! No need to be shy. The music is ready to play . . ."

Here he will leap forward into the midst of them, striking down hard on a rock with the flat of his sword, and the loud twang and clang will make them start and jump with surprise once more before they begin to move toward him.

"And the time has come for us to have our dance."

• • •

Picture the great hall of a very old house. Many torches and smoky candles toss brightness and make huge shadows. Large fireplace at far end and where half a tree could burn and, indeed, huge logs are now aflame sputtering and sparking. Once there was only a smoke hole at the center of the hall. You can see where it has been patched and covered over on the high roof. And on the stone floor of the hall you can also see darker stones where fires were laid and burned in times beyond the remembering of anyone alive now.

It is night and, outside, the wind blows in hard gusts rattling the windows. Where once there was nothing but air; then dull sheets of horn; now leaded glass. Snowflakes in the air, in the wind, sticking to the windows.

Now picture it, as it often is, crowded with people, with guests and servants, with tenants and villagers, with men and women and children. With large dogs running loose, barking and begging for food. Or maybe curled up snoring, as close as can be to the fire. Picture how it looks on feast days, any of the many feast days of the wonderful Christian year, old ones and new ones, and all of them kept with hospitality in this house. The long trestle tables burdened, yes, groaning with the weight of food, fresh things, in their seasons, and in the long winter the best that has been smoked and spiced and candied and dried. But always fresh-baked bread and fresh-brewed ale. And wine and distilled spirits, too, poured and served with full cups from the side tables. Much belly cheer for all in the great hall and likewise all in the kitchen and for those in need, begging for orts at the gatehouse, never turned away empty-handed or -bellied. Music and singing always and often some quick-footed, sweaty country dancing after the meal. And sometimes, more often here than in many prouder and grander and newer places, there will be a little traveling company of players to perform. With their juggling and jigs; with their fencing and dancing; and with some play, old and remembered or newly come from the playhouses of the City so far away.

All of this for the sake of the old master who, gossip will have it, was once upon a time no more than a common player in such a company himself. Story is how he came to this house and place after performing at the Guildhall of a town some miles from here. Widow who owned this house and the village and many good acres of park and timber and pasture for sheep and cattle and farmland for crops and grain, the widow took a sudden fancy to this fellow, this London player, and hired the company to come out here and put on a play on the evening of Candlemas. How it snowed that night as never before or since and buried the roads and piled high round the house. And next thing you know the handsome player and the widow lady, plain in the face as a cow in a field, but a good woman withal, and of a merry spirit, found themselves arm in arm and knee to knee in a snowdrift of clean sheets. And soon after there was a new master of the place. For better and worse, though, all in all, mostly for better.

And the widow woman has long since gone to her glory, no doubt with the slight gap-toothed smile on her face, that very same face you will find on the portrait painting of her in her best clothes in the gallery. Looking solemn, but pleased with herself, for the itinerant limner who painted her on board. Pleased, and why not. For her handsome young husband could tell her news and old stories of all the places, especially London, she had never been to. He was like a peddler with a huge sack of stories, endless it seemed; a magical sack, then, of magical stories of all the great names he had known so well, poets and soldiers, great lords and ladies, merchants and cutthroats, sailors and whores, in his time. They would sit close together and close by a fire, while she busied her long fingers with some sewing or knitting. And he busied himself with the spinning of tales, out of memory or thin air. The difference and distinction being of no importance for her. She could believe anything, all of it, at least for the time that it took him to tell it. Which was all that she needed, more than enough. And he had such a good clear voice for telling stories and for playing the various parts in them. Music to listen to. And he could play any part with all of his heart and body. So that (difference and distinction being nothing to her), true or false, he also played her attentive husband, well and faithfully, until the night she died and he gently closed her eyes for good.

Which is not to say (nothing to her) he did not sometimes teach a milkmaid some new London manners behind a haystack or in a dark corner of the barn.

She died a lady, then, and left him a gentleman.

Or so the story goes.

For all that was a long time ago in the time of the old Queen, they say. New master is old master now. Bent and stooped a little, his fine handsome face somewhat wrinkled above his white beard. But his eyes as blue-bright as ever they were. And they brighten most when, as tonight, traveling players have come and are acting out an old play that he knows by heart. See him there on his chair—the only chair and place to sit except for the benches and some few joint stools, rest of us all standing—see how his lips move with the lips of the players. And sometimes he will surprise himself and them, too, by speaking aloud.

When the playing has finished he will lead the applause, call for his cup, and then dance the first dance, stiffly, but graceful, when the hall is cleared. Wearing a smile like a twin to the slight smile of his dead wife, the widow, the one thing of hers, not counting the house and the lands and everything else, he earned without thinking or intention, as happily married couples will sometimes do. Wearing her slight smile, gap-toothed himself now, the gentle and ironic smile of someone (himself or herself, the same and quite different) who has come through time and by chance to be given all that he had ever hoped for and never truly expected, though, as ever and always, in a different shape and form than he could ever have imagined and at a price which, though modest, was probably more than he would have been willing to pay if he had any choice in the matter.

• • •

Touchstone: When a man's verses cannot be understood, nor a man's good wit seconded with the forward child, understanding, it strikes a man more dead than a great reckoning in a little room. Truly, I would the gods had made thee more poetical.

—William Shakespeare, *As You Like It*

AUTHOR'S FAREWELL

Well now.
Here we are at the end
of it.

I have been happy for a time, living among Elizabethans. Happier,
I do believe, than I could have been living only in our own century.
Our bitter shiny century. I like to think that since I was no more than
a visitor to theirs (though I visited, off and on, for many years, a
persistent kind of tourist you might say), I am even entitled to prefer
their time to ours. If I care to. Entitled to imagine, if I feel like it,
that, by and large and in many ways, they were more interesting than
we are.

Of course—and it is an enormous fact—I never had to live there all the time. That might have changed my tune. I am not, never have been, and never will be a proper scholar of those times. Nevertheless, how greatly I admire them, one and all, the scholars, living and dead, who have so carefully performed their duty and service of hard labor, against huge and discouraging odds, often in the face of no little indifference and even less reward from and respect of others, to preserve our past, to keep that lost past time available for us, accessible to us.

We are, each and all, debtors and creditors of each other. Like it or not.

I hope that I shall always be able, for as long as I may live, to go back to the Elizabethans for delight and instruction. I hope that I will not cease to visit that age and my old friends and enemies who live there. It seems that I could not even if I wanted to. I can't promise anything. Oh, I could make myself a solemn promise, I know. But what on earth would that mean? I can tell you what Elizabethans thought. I have quoted them on the subject in several books: "Promises are like piecrusts—they are made to be broken."

Well then.

There were priceless moments, unearned and unanticipated, even if always hoped for, during the making of these stories. Moments of ineffable joy when (it seemed) the whispering of ghostly voices became a kind of song in air. It was as if I had knelt by a spring and cupped my hands to drink something clean and cold, something like pure energy. And then the sky turned round and around overhead, leaves danced, light and dark; and voices sang and said extravagant things.

Christopher Marlowe's death may have been sudden and brutal and sordid and, finally, mysterious. But the greater and deeper and very joyful mystery is how, beyond all the known facts of his life and death, beyond the boundaries of the age he found himself living in, his living words, as best we can still recollect and resurrect them, thrive and flourish even here and now—*shining!*

Shining in and out of darkness.

It was that quality of shining I had in my mind so many years ago when I set out to describe the vanishing ghost of a courtier in *Death of the Fox.* May I now be allowed to reverse it, to turn that brief paragraph inside out and claim and use it here again as the farewell of the author to his book?

"This ghost, an ageless young man, ever idle and restless,

courteous and cruel, unchanging child of chance, this man will say no more. He touches one finger to his lips to call for silence. He smiles and then, miming the act of blowing out a candle, he takes a thief's farewell, first color fading, then the sad cold light of his eyes gone, and then one last blinking of something—a jewel, a ring, a gold coin cupped in his palm, and the darkness comes between us and is final."

Book Mark

The text of this book was set in
the typeface Granjon by Books,
Inc., Deatsville, Alabama

The display was set in
Michelangelo by Artintype/
Metro, New York City,
New York

It was printed
and bound by R.R. Donnelley,
Crawfordsville, Indiana

Designed by Anne Ling